LONDON RULES

Books by Mick Herron

The Oxford Series
Down Cemetery Road
The Last Voice You Hear
Why We Die
Smoke & Whispers

The Slough House Series
Slow Horses
Dead Lions
The List (a novella)
Real Tigers
Spook Street
London Rules

Other Novels
Reconstruction
Nobody Walks
This Is What Happened

LONDON
RULES

Mick Herron

Published by Soho Press, Inc.
853 Broadway
New York, NY 10003

Library of Congress Cataloging-in-Publication Data

Herron, Mick, author.
London rules / Mick Herron.

ISBN 978-1-61695-961-6
eISBN 978-1-61695-962-3

1. Intelligence service—Great Britain—Fiction. I. Title
PR6108.E77 L66 2018 823'.92—dc23 2017055378

Interior design by Janine Agro, Soho Press, Inc.

Printed in the United States of America

10 9 8 7 6 5 4 3 2 1

To Sarah Hilary

LONDON RULES

The killers arrived in a sand-coloured jeep, and made short work of the village.

There were five of them and they wore mismatched military gear, two opting for black and the others for piebald variations. Neckerchiefs covered the lower half of their faces, sunglasses the upper, and their feet were encased in heavy boots, as if they'd crossed the surrounding hills the hard way. From their belts hung sundry items of battleground kit. As the first emerged from the vehicle he tossed a water bottle onto the seat behind him, an action replicated in miniature in his aviator lenses.

It was approaching noon, and the sun was as white as the locals had known it. Somewhere nearby, water tumbled over stones. The last time trouble had called here, it had come bearing swords.

Out of the car, by the side of the road, the men stretched and spat. They didn't talk. They seemed in no hurry, but at the same time were focused on what they were doing. This was part of the operation: arrive, limber up, regain flexibility. They had driven a long way in the heat. No sense starting before they were in tune with their limbs and could trust their reflexes. It didn't matter that they were attracting attention, because nobody watching could alter what was to happen. Forewarned would not mean forearmed. All the villagers had were sticks.

One of these—an ancient thing bearing many of the characteristics of its parent tree, being knobbled and imprecise, sturdy

and reliable—was leaned on by an elderly man whose weathered
looks declared him farming stock. But somewhere in his history,
perhaps, lurked a memory of war, for of all those watching the
visitors perform their callisthenics he alone seemed to understand
their intent, and into his eyes, already a little tearful from the
sunshine, came both fear and a kind of resignation, as if he had
always known that this, or something like it, would rear up and
swallow him. Not far away, two women broke off from conversation. One held a cloth bag. The other's hands moved slowly
towards her mouth. A barefoot boy wandered through a doorway
into sunlight, his features crumpling in the glare.

In the near distance a chain rattled as a dog tested its limits.
Inside a makeshift coop, its mesh and wooden struts a patchwork
of recycled materials, a chicken squatted to lay an egg no one
would ever collect.

From the back of their jeep the men fetched weapons, sleek
and black and awful.

The last ordinary noise was the one the old man made when
he dropped his stick. As he did so his lips moved, but no sound
emerged.

And then it began.

From afar, it might have been fireworks. In the surrounding hills
birds took to the air in a frightened rattle, while in the village itself
cats and dogs leaped for cover. Some bullets went wild, sprayed
in indiscriminate loops and skirls, as if in imitation of a local
dance; the chicken coop was blasted to splinters, and scars were
chipped into stones that had stood unblemished for centuries. But
others found their mark. The old man followed his stick to the
ground, and the two women were hurled in opposite directions,
thrown apart by nodules of lead that weighed less than their fingers. The barefoot boy tried to run. In the hillsides were tunnels
carved into rock, and given time he might have found his way
there, waited in the darkness until the killers had gone, but this
possibility was blasted out of existence by a bullet that caught him

in the neck, sending him cartwheeling down the short slope to the river, which was little more than a trickle today. The villagers caught in the open were scattering now, running into the fields, seeking shelter behind walls and in ditches; even those who hadn't seen what was happening had caught the fear, for catastrophe is its own herald, trumpeting its arrival to early birds and stragglers alike. It has a certain smell, a certain pitch. It sends mothers shrieking for their young, the old looking for God.

And two minutes later it was over, and the killers left. The jeep, which had idled throughout the brief carnage, spat stones as it accelerated away, and for a short while there was stillness. The sound of the departing engine folded into the landscape and was lost. A buzzard mewed overhead. Closer to home a gurgle sounded in a ruined throat, as someone struggled with a new language, whose first words were their last. And behind that, and then above it, and soon all around it, grew the screams of the survivors, for whom all familiar life was over, just as it was for the dead.

Within hours trucks would come bearing more men with guns, this time trained outwards, on the surrounding hillsides. Helicopters would land, disgorging doctors and military personnel, and others would fly overhead, crisscrossing the sky in orchestrated rage, while TV cameras pointed and blamed. On the streets shrouds would cover the fallen, and newly loosed chickens would wander by the river, pecking in the dirt. A bell would ring, or at least, people would remember it ringing. It might have been in their minds. But what was certain was that there would still be, above the buzzing helicopters, a sky whose blue remained somehow unbroken, and a distant buzzard mewing, and long shadows cast by the stunned Derbyshire hills.

PART ONE

COOL CATS

In some parts of the world dawn arrives with rosy fingers, to smoothe away the creases left by night. But on Aldersgate Street, in the London borough of Finsbury, it comes wearing safecracker's gloves, so as not to leave prints on windowsills and doorknobs; it squints through keyholes, sizes up locks and generally cases the joint ahead of approaching day. Dawn specialises in unswept corners and undusted surfaces, in the nooks and chambers day rarely sees, because day is all business appointments and things being in the right place, while its younger sister's role is to creep about in the breaking gloom, never sure of what it might find there. It's one thing casting light on a subject. It's another expecting it to shine.

So when dawn reaches Slough House—a scruffy building whose ground floor is divided between an ailing Chinese restaurant and a desperate newsagent's, and whose front door, made filthy by time and weather, never opens—it enters by the burglar's route, via the rooftops opposite, and its first port of call is Jackson Lamb's office, this being on the uppermost storey. Here it finds its only working rival a standard lamp atop a pile of telephone directories, which have so long served this purpose they have moulded together, their damp covers bonding in involuntary alliance. The room is cramped and furtive, like a kennel, and its overpowering theme is neglect. Psychopaths are said to decorate their walls with crazy writing, the loops and whorls of their infinite equations an attempt at cracking the code their life is hostage to. Lamb prefers his walls to do their own talking, and they have cooperated to the extent that the cracks in their plasterwork, their mildew stains, have here and there conspired to produce something that might amount to an actual script—a scrawled observation, perhaps—but all too quickly any sense these marks contain blurs and fades, as if they were something a moving finger had writ before deciding, contrary to the wisdom of ages, to rub out again.

Lamb's is not a room to linger in, and dawn, anyway, never tarries long. In the office opposite, it finds less to disturb it. Here order has prevailed, and there is a quiet efficiency about the way in which folders have been stacked, their edges squared off in alignment with the desktop, and the ribbons binding them tied in bows of equal length; about the emptiness of the wastepaper basket, and the dust-free surfaces of the well-mannered shelves. There is a stillness here out of keeping with Slough House, and if one were to seesaw between these two rooms, the bossman's lair and Catherine Standish's bolt-hole, a balance might be found that could bring peace to the premises, though one would imagine it would be short-lived.

As is dawn's presence in Catherine's room, for time is hurrying on. On the next level down is a kitchen. Dawn's favourite meal is breakfast, which is sometimes mostly gin, but either way it would find little to sustain it here, the cupboards falling very much on Scrooge's end of the Dickensian curve, far removed from Pickwickian excess. The cupboards contain no tins of biscuits, no jars of preserves, no emergency chocolate and no bowls of fruit or packets of crispbread mar the counter's surface; just odds and ends of plastic cutlery, a few chipped mugs and a surprisingly new-looking kettle. True, there is a fridge, but all it holds are two cans of energy drink, both stickered "Roddy Ho," each of which rubric has had the words "is a twat" added, in different hands, and an uncontested tub of hummus, which is either mint-flavoured or has some other reason for being green. About the appliance hangs an odour best described as delayed decay. Luckily, dawn has no sense of smell.

Having briefly swept through the two offices on this floor—nondescript rooms whose colour schemes can only be found in ancient swatches, their pages so faded, everything has subsided into shades of yellow and grey—and taken care to skirt the dark patch beneath the radiator, where some manner of rusty leakage has occurred, it finds itself back on the staircase, which is old and rackety, dawn the only thing capable of using it without making a sound—apart, that is, from Jackson Lamb, who when he feels like it can wander Slough House as silently as a newly conjured wraith, if rather more corpulent. At other times Lamb prefers the direct approach, and attacks the stairs with the noise that a bear pushing a wheelbarrow might make, if the wheelbarrow was full of tin cans, and the bear drunk.

More watchful ghost than drunken bear, dawn arrives in the final two offices and finds little to distinguish them from those on the floor above, apart, perhaps, from the slightly stuccoed texture of the paintwork behind one desk, as if a fresh coat has been applied before the wall has been properly cleaned, and some lumpy matter has been left clinging to the plasterwork: best not to dwell on what this might be. For the rest, this office has the same air of frustrated ambition as its companions, and to one as sensitive as light-fingered dawn it contains, too, a memory of violence, and perhaps the promise of more to come. But dawn understands that promises are easily broken—dawn knows all about breaking—and the possibility delays it not one jot. On it goes, down the final set of stairs, and somehow passes through the back door without recourse to the shove this usually requires, the door being famously resistant to casual use. In the dank little yard behind Slough House dawn pauses, aware that its time is nearly up, and enjoys these last cool moments. Once upon a time it might have heard a horse making its way up the street; more recently, the happy hum of a milk float would have whiled away its final minute. But today there is only the scream of an ambulance, late for an appointment, and by the time its banshee howl has ceased bouncing off walls and buildings dawn has disappeared, and here in its place is the day itself, which, once within Slough House's grasp, turns out to be far from the embodiment of industry and occupation it threatened to be. Instead—like the day before it, and the one before that—it is just another slothful interlude to be clock watched out of existence, and knowing full well that none of the inhabitants can do anything to hasten its departure, it takes its own sweet time about setting up shop. Casually, smugly, unbothered by doubt or duty, it divides itself between Slough House's offices, and then, like a lazy cat, settles in the warmest corners to doze, while nothing much happens around it.

Roddy Ho, Roddy Ho, riding through the glen.
(Just another earworm.)
Roddy Ho, Roddy Ho, manliest of men.
There are those who regard Roderick Ho as a one-trick won-der; a king of the keyboard jungle, sure, but less adept in other areas of life, such as making friends, being reasonable, and ironing T-shirts. But they haven't seen him in action. They haven't seen him on the prowl.

Lunchtime, just off Aldersgate Street. The ugly concrete tow-ers of the Barbican to the right; a hardly more beautiful housing estate to the left. But it's a killing box, this uncelebrated patch of London; it's a blink-and-you're-eaten battlefield. You get one chance only to claim your scalp, and Roddy Ho's prey could be anywhere.

He knew damn well it was close.

So he moved, pantherlike, between parked cars; he hovered by a placard celebrating some municipal triumph or other. In his ear, driven like a fence post by the pounding of his iPod, an overexcited forty-something screeched tenderly of his plan to kill and eat his girlfriend. On Roddy's chin, the beard he'd grown last winter; rather more expertly sculpted now, because he'd learned the hard way not to use kitchen scissors. On Roddy's head—new development—a baseball cap. Image matters, Roddy knew that. *Brand* matters. You want Joe Public to recognise your avatar, your avatar had to make a statement. In his own personal opinion, he'd nailed that angle. Neat little goatee and a baseball cap: originality plus style. Roderick Ho was the complete package, the way Brad Pitt used to be, before the unpleasantness.

(Gap in the market there, come to think of it. He'd have to have a word with Kim, his girlfriend, about coining a *nom de celeb*.

Koddy.

Rim . . . ?

Nah. Needs work.)

But he'd deal with that later, because right now it was time to activate the lure module; get this creature into the open and bring that sucker *down*. This required force, timing and use of weapons: his core skills in a nutshell . . . Whoever came up with *Pokémon GO* must have had Roderick Ho on their muse's speed dial. The name even rhymed, man—it was like he was born to poke. Gimme that stardust, he thought. Gimme that lovely stardust, and watch the Rodster *shine*.

All reflex, sinew and concentration, Ho shimmered through the lunchtime air like the coolest of cats, the baddest of asses, the daddy of all dudes; hot on the trail of an enemy that didn't exist.

A little way down the road, an enemy that did turned the ignition, and pulled away from the kerb.

That morning, on her way to the Tube, Catherine Standish had dropped in at the newsagent's for a *Guardian*. Behind the counter a steel blind had been drawn to hide the array of cigarette packets, lest a stray glimpse prove a gateway to early death, while to her left, on the topmost row of the rack, the few pornographic magazines to survive into the digital age were sealed inside plastic covers, to nullify their impact on concupiscent minds. All this careful protection, she thought, shielding us from impulses deemed harmful, but right there by the door was a shelf of wine on special offer, any two bottles for £9, and up by the counter was a range of spirits all cheerfully marked two quid down, none of them a brand to delight the palate, but any of them enough to render the most uptight connoisseur pig-drunk and open to offers.

She bought her newspaper, nodded her thanks and returned to the street.

One journey later, she remembered it was her turn to pick up milk for the office—no huge feat of memory; it was always her turn to pick up milk—and dropped into the shop next to Slough House, where the milk was in the fridge alongside cans of beer and lager, and ready-mixed tins of G&T. That's twice without trying, she thought, that she could have bought a ticket to the underworld before her day was off the ground. Most occasions of sin required a little effort. But the recovering alcoholic could coast along in neutral, and the temptations would come to her.

There was nothing unusual about this. It was just the surface tension; the everyday gauntlet the dry drunk runs. Come lunch-time, the lure of the dark side behind her, Catherine was absorbed in the day's work: writing up the department's biannual accounts, which included justification for "irregular expenses." Slough House had had a lot of these this year: broken doors, carpet cleaning; all the making-good an armed incursion demands. Most of the repairs had been sloppily done, which neither surprised nor bothered Catherine much: she had long ago grown used to the second-class status the slow horses enjoyed. What worried her more was the long-term damage to the horses themselves. Shirley Dander was unnervingly calm; the kind of calm Catherine imagined icebergs were, just before they ploughed into ocean liners. River Cartwright was bottling things up too, more than usual. And as for J.K. Coe, Catherine recognised a hand grenade when she saw one. And she didn't think his pin was fitted too tight.

Roddy Ho was the same as ever, of course, but that was more of a burden than a comfort.

It was a good job Louisa Guy was relatively sane.

Stacks of paper in front of her, their edges neatly though not quite neurotically aligned, Catherine waded through the day's work, adjusting figures where Lamb's entries overshot the

inaccurate to become manifestly corrupt, and replacing his justi-
fications ("because I fucking say so") with her own more diplomatic
phrasing. When the time came to leave for home, all those temptations would parade in front of her again. But if daily exposure
to Jackson Lamb had taught her anything, it was not to fret about
life's peripheral challenges.

He had a way of providing more than enough to worry about,
up front and centre.

Shirley Dander had sixty-two days.

Sixty-two drug-free days.

Count 'em . . .

Somebody might: Shirley didn't. Sixty-two was just a number, same as sixty-one had been, and if she happened to be
keeping track that was only because the days had all happened
in the obvious order, very, very slowly. Mornings she ticked off
the minutes, and afternoons counted down seconds, and at least
once a day found herself staring at the walls, particularly the one
behind what had been Marcus's desk. Last time she'd seen Marcus, he'd been leaning against that wall, his chair tilted at a
ridiculous angle. It had been painted over since. A bad job had
been made of it.

And here was Shirley's solution to that: think about something
else.

It was lunchtime; bright and warm. Shirley was heading back
to Slough House for an afternoon of enforced inertia, after
which she'd schlep on over to Shoreditch for the last of her
AFMs . . . Eight months of anger fucking management sessions,
and this evening she'd officially be declared anger free. It had
been hinted she might even get a badge. That could be a problem—if anyone stuck a badge on her, they'd be carrying their
teeth home in a hankie—but luckily, what she had in her pocket
gave her something to focus on; to carry her through any dodgy
moments which might result in the court-ordered programme
being extended.

A neat little wrap of the best cocaine the postcode had to offer; her treat to herself for finishing the course.

Sixty-two might just be a number, but it was as high as Shirley had any intention of going.

Being straight had had the effect of turning her settings down a notch, and the world had been flatter lately, greyer, easier to get along with. Which helped with the whole AFM thing, but was starting to piss her off. Last week she'd had a cold-caller, some crap about mis-sold insurance, and Shirley hadn't even told him to fuck himself. This didn't feel like attitude adjustment so much as it did surrender. So here was the plan: get through this one last day, suffer being patted on the head by the coun- sellor—whom Shirley intended to follow home one night and kill—then hit the clubs, get properly wasted and learn to live again. Sixty-two days was long enough, and proved for a fact what she'd always maintained as a theory: that she could give it up any time she wanted.

Besides, Marcus was long gone. It wasn't like he'd be getting in her face about it.

But don't think about Marcus.

So there she was, heading past the estate towards Aldersgate Street, coke in her pocket, mind on the evening to come, when she saw two things five yards in front of her, both behaving strangely.

One was Roderick Ho, who was performing some kind of ballet, with a mobile phone for a partner.

The other was an approaching silver Honda, turning left where there was no left to turn.

Then mounting the pavement and heading straight for Ho.

So here's the thing, thought Louisa Guy. If I'd wanted to be a librarian, I'd have been a librarian. I'd have gone to library school, taken library exams and saved up enough library stamps to buy a library uniform. Whatever they do, I'd have done it: by the book. And of all the librarians in the near vicinity, I'd have been far and away the librarianest; the kind of librarian other librarians sing songs about, gathered around their library fires.

But what I wouldn't have done was join the intelligence service. Because that would have been fucking ridiculous.

Yet here I am.

Here she was.

Here being Slough House, where what she was doing was scrolling through library loan statistics, determining who had borrowed certain titles in the course of the last few years. Books like *Islam Expects* and *The Meaning of Jihad*. And if anyone had actually written *How to Wage War on a Civilian Population*, that would have made the list too.

"Is it really likely," she'd said, on being handed the project, "that compiling a list of people who've borrowed particular library books is going to help us find fledgling terrorists?"

"Put like that," Lamb had said, "the odds are probably a million to one." He shook his head. "I'll tell you this for nothing. I'm bloody glad I'm not you."

"Thanks. But why do they even stock these books, if they're so dangerous?"

"It's political correctness gone mad," agreed Lamb sadly. "I'm rabidly anticensorship, as you know. But some books just need burning."

So did some bosses. She'd been working on this list, which involved cross-checking Public Lending Right statistics against individual county library databases, for three months. It now stretched not quite halfway down a single sheet of A4, and she'd reached Buckinghamshire in her alphabetical list of counties. Thank Christ she didn't have to cover the whole of the UK, because that would have taken even an actual librarian years.

Not the whole of it, no. Just England, Wales and Northern Ireland.

"Fuck Scotland," Lamb had explained. "They want to go it alone, they can go it alone."

Her only ally in her never-ending task was the Government,

which was doing its bit by closing down as many libraries as possible.

In the War Against Terror, you take all the help you can get.

Louisa giggled to herself, because sometimes you had to, or else you'd go mad. Unless the giggling was proof you'd already gone mad. J.K. Coe might know, not so much because of his so-called expertise in Psychological Evaluation, but because he was a borderline nutter himself. All fun and games in Slough House.

She pushed away from her desk and stood to stretch. Lately she'd been spending more time at the gym, and the result was increasing restlessness when tethered to her computer. Through the window, Aldersgate Street was its usual unpromising medley of pissed-off traffic and people in a hurry. Nobody ever wandered through this bit of London; it was just a staging post on the way somewhere else. Unless you were a stalled spook, of course, in which case it was journey's end.

God, she was bored.

And then, as if to console her, the world threw a minor distraction her way: from not far off came a screech and a bump; the sound of a car making contact.

She wondered what that was about.

Hi Tina

Just a quick note to let you know how things are going here in Devon—not great, to be honest. I've been told I'm being laid off at the end of the month because the boss's sister's son needs a job, so someone has to make way for the little bastard. Thanks a bunch, right?

But it's not all bad because the gaffer knows he owes me one, and has set me up with one of his contacts for a six-month gig in—get this—Albania! But it's a cushy number, doing the wiring on three new hotel builds, and it'll be cheap living so I'll

Coe stopped midsentence and stared through the window at the Barbican opposite. It was an Orwellian nightmare of a complex, a concrete monstrosity, but credit where it was due: like Ronnie and Reggie Kray before it, the Barbican had overcome the drawback of being a brutal piece of shit to achieve iconic status. But that was London Rules for you: force others to take you on your own terms. And if they didn't like it, stay in their face until they did.

Jackson Lamb, for instance. Except, on second thoughts, no: Lamb didn't give a toss whose terms you took him on. He carried on regardless. He just *was*.

Tina, though, wasn't, or wouldn't be much longer. Tina wasn't her real name anyway. J.K. Coe just found it easier to compose these letters if they had an actual name attached; for the same reason, he always signed them Dan. Dan—whoever he was—was a deep cover spook, who'd moled into whichever group of activists was currently deemed too extreme for comfort (animal rights, eco-troublemakers, *The Archers'* fanbase); while Tina—whoever *she* was—was someone he'd befriended in the course of doing so. There was always a Tina. Back when Coe had been in Psych Eval, he'd made a study of Tinas of both genders; joes in the field were warned not to develop emotional attachments in the group under investigation, but they always did. You couldn't betray someone efficiently if you didn't love them first. So when the op was over, and Dan was coming back to the surface, there had to be letters; a long goodbye played out over months. First Dan moved out of the area, a fair distance off but not unvisitable. He'd keep in touch sporadically, then get a better offer and move abroad. The letters or emails would falter, then stop. And soon Dan would be forgotten, by everyone but Tina, who'd keep his letters in a shoebox under her bed, and Google-Earth Albania after her third glass of Chardonnay. Rather than, for example, dragging him into court for screwing her under false pretences. Nobody wanted to go through that again.

But of course, joes don't write the letters themselves. That was a job for spooks like J.K. Coe, whiling away the days in Slough House. And lucky to be doing so, to be honest. Most people who'd shot to death a handcuffed man might have expected retribution. Luckily, Coe had done so at the fag-end of a series of events so painfully compromising to the intelligence services as a whole that—as Lamb had observed—it had put the "us" in "clusterfuck," leaving Regent's Park with little choice but to lay a huge carpet over everything and sweep Slough House under it. The slow horses were used to that, of course. In fact, if they weren't already slow horses, they'd be dust bunnies instead.

Coe cracked his knuckles, and added the words *be able to save a bit* to his letter. Yeah, right; Dan would save a bit, then meet an Albanian girl, and—long story short—never come home. Meanwhile, the actual Dan would be undercover again, on a different op, and the ball would be rolling in a new direction. On Spook Street, things never stayed still. Unless you were in Slough House, that is. But there was a major difference between J.K. Coe and the other slow horses, and it was this: he had no desire to be where the action was. If he could sit here typing all day and never have to say a word to anyone, that would suit him fine. Because his life was approaching an even keel. The dreams were ebbing away at last, and the panic attacks had tapered off. He no longer found himself obsessively fingering an imaginary keyboard, echoing Keith Jarrett's improvised piano solos. Things were bearable, and might just stay that way provided nothing happened.

He hoped like hell nothing would happen.

The car smeared Roderick Ho like ketchup across the concrete apron; broke him like a plastic doll across its bonnet, so all that was holding him together was his clothes. This happened so fast Shirley saw it before it took place. Which was as well for Ho, because she had time to prevent it.

She covered five yards with the speed of a greased pig, yelling Ho's name, though he didn't turn round—he had his back to the car and his iPod jammed into his ears; was squinting through his smartphone, and looked, basically, like a dumb tourist who'd been ripped off twice already: once by someone selling hats, and a second time by someone giving away beards. When Shirley hit him waist-high, he was apparently taking a photo of bugger-all. But he never got the chance. Shirley's weight sent him crashing to the ground half a moment before the car ploughed past: went careering across the pedestrianised area, bounced off a low brick wall bordering a garden display then screeched to a halt. Burnt rubber reached Shirley's nose. Ho was squawking; his phone was in pieces. The car moved again, but instead of heading back for them it circled the brick enclosure, turned left onto the road, swerved round the barrier and went east.

Shirley watched it disappear, too late to catch its plate, or even clock the number of occupants. Soon she'd feel the impact of her leap in most of her bones, but for the moment she just replayed it in her head from a third-party viewpoint: a graceful, gazelle-like swoop; lifesaving moment and poetry in motion at once. Marcus would have been proud, she thought.

Dead proud.

Beneath her, Roddy yelled, "You stupid cow!"

The internet was full of whispers.

No, River Cartwright thought. Scratch that.

The internet was screaming its head off, as usual.

He was on a Marylebone-bound train, returning to London after having taken the morning off: care leave, he'd claimed it, though Lamb preferred "bloody liberty."

"We're not the social services."

"We're not Sports Direct either," Catherine Standish had pointed out. "If River needs the morning off, he needs it."

"And who's gunna pick up his workload in the meantime?"

River hadn't done a stroke of work in three weeks, but didn't think this a viable line of defence. "It'll get done," he promised.

And Lamb had grunted, and that was that.

So he'd taken off in the pre-breakfast rush, battling against the commuter tide; heading for Skylarks, the care home where the O.B.

now resided; not precisely a Service-run facility—the Service had long since outsourced any such frivolities—but one which placed a higher priority on security than most places of its type.

The Old Bastard, River's grandfather, had wandered off down the twilit corridors of his own mind, only occasionally emerging into the here and now, whereupon he'd sniff the air like an elderly badger and look pained, though whether this was due to a brief awareness that his grasp on reality had crumbled, or to that grasp's momentary return, River couldn't guess. After a lifetime hoarding secrets the old spook had lost himself among them, and no longer knew which truths he was concealing, which lies he was casting abroad. He and his late wife, Rose, had raised River, their only grandchild. Sitting with him in Skylarks' garden, a blanket covering the old man's knees, an iron curtain shrouding half his history, River felt adrift. He had followed the O.B.'s footsteps into the Secret Service, and if his own path had been forcibly rerouted, there'd been comfort in the knowledge that the old man had at least mapped the same territory. But now he was orphaned. The footsteps he'd followed were wandering in circles, and when they faltered at last, they'd be nowhere specific. Every spook's dream was to throw off all pursuers, and know himself unwatched. The O.B. was fast approaching that space: somewhere unknowable, unvisited, untagged by hostile eyes.

It had been a warm morning, bright sunshine casting shadows on the lawn. The house was at the end of a valley, and River could see hills rising in the distance, and tame clouds puffing across a paint box sky. A train was briefly visible between two stretches of woodland, but its engines were no more than a polite murmur, barely bothering the air. River could smell mown grass, and something else he couldn't put a name to. If forced to guess, he'd say it was the absence of traffic.

He sat on one of three white plastic chairs arranged around a white plastic table, from the centre of which a parasol jutted upwards. The third chair was vacant. There were two other similar sets of furniture, one unused, and the other occupied by an elderly couple. A younger woman was there, addressing them in what River imagined was an efficient tone. He couldn't actually hear her. His grandfather was talking loudly, blocking out all other conversation.

"That would have been August '52," he was saying. "The fifteenth, if I'm not mistaken. A Tuesday. Round about four o'clock in the afternoon."

The O.B.'s memory was self-sharpening these days. It prided itself on providing minute detail, even if that detail bore only coincidental resemblance to reality.

"And when the call came in, it was Joe himself on the line."

". . . Joe?"

"Stalin, my boy. You're not dropping off on me, are you?"

River wasn't dropping off on him.

He thought: this is where life on Spook Street leads. Not long ago the old man's past had come barking from the shadows and taken large bites out of the present. If this were common knowledge, there would be many howling for retribution. River should be among them, really. But if his own murky beginnings had turned out to be the result of the O.B.'s tampering with the lives of others, they remained his own beginnings. You couldn't argue yourself out of existence. Besides, there was no way of taking his grandfather to task for past sins now those sins had melted into fictions. The previous week, River had heard a story the old man had never told before, involving more gunfire than usual, and an elaborate series of code names in notebooks. Ten minutes on Google later revealed that the O.B. had been relaying the plot of *Where Eagles Dare*.

When the old man's tale wound itself into silence, River said, "Do you have everything you need, grandad?"

"Why should I need anything? Eh?"

"No reason. I just thought you might like something from . . ."

He tailed off. Something from home. But home was dangerous territory, a subject best avoided. The old man had never been a joe; always a desk man. It had been his job to send agents into the unknown, and run them from what others might think a safe distance. But here he was now, alone in joe country, his cover blown, his home untenable. There was no safe ground. Only this mansion house in a quiet landscape, where the nurses had enough discretion to know that some tales were best ignored.

On the train heading back into London, River shifted in his seat and scrolled down the page of search results. Nice to know that a spook career granted him this privilege: if he wanted to know what was going on, he could surf the web, like any other bastard. And the internet was screaming. The hunt for the Abbotsfield killers continued with no concrete results, though the attack had been claimed by so-called Islamic State. At a late-night session in Parliament the previous evening, Dennis Gimball had lambasted the Security Services, proclaiming Claude Whelan, Regent's Park's First Desk, unfit for purpose; had sailed this close to suggesting that he was, in fact, an IS sympathiser. That this was barking mad was a side issue: recent years had seen a recalibration of political lunacy, and even the mainstream media had to pretend to take Gimball seriously, just in case. Meanwhile, there were twelve dead in Abbotsfield, and a tiny village had become a geopolitical byword. There'd be a lot more debate, a lot more hand-wringing, before this slipped away from the front pages. Unless something else happened soon, of course.

Nearly there. River closed his laptop. The O.B. would be dozing again by now; enjoying a cat's afternoon in the sun. Time had rolled round on him, that was all. River was his grandfather's handler now.

Sooner or later, all the sins of the past fell into the keeping of the present.

"You stupid cow!"

He'd been thrown sideways and the noise in his head had exploded: manic guitars cut off midwail; locomotive drums killed midbeat. The sudden silence was deafening. It was like he'd been unplugged.

And his prey was nowhere to be seen, obviously. His smartphone was in pieces, its casing a hop-skip-jump away.

It was Shirley Dander who'd leaped on him, evidently unable to control her passion.

She crawled off and pretended to be watching a car disappear along the road. Roddy sat up and brushed at the sleeves of his still-new leather jacket. He'd had to deal with workplace harassment before: first Louisa Guy, now this. But at least Louisa remained the right side of her last shaggable day, while Shirley Dander, far as the Rodster was concerned, hadn't seen her first yet.

"What the hell was that for?"

"That was me saving your arse," she said, without looking round.

His arse. One-track mind.

"I nearly had it, you know!" Pointless explaining the intricacies of a quest to her: the nearest she'd come to appreciating the complexities of gaming was being mistaken for a troll. Still, though, she ought to be made to realise just what a prize she'd cost him, all for the sake of a quick grope. "A bulbasaur! You know how rare that is?"

It was plain she didn't.

"The fuck," she asked, "are you talking about?"

He scrambled to his feet.

"Okay," he said. "Let's pretend you just wanted to sabotage my hunt. That's all Kim needs to know, anyway."

"... Huh?"

"My girlfriend," he explained, so she'd know where she stood.

"Did you get a plate for that car?"

"What car?"

"The one that just tried to run you over."

"That's a good story too," Roddy said. "But let's stick with mine. It's less complicated. Fewer follow-up questions."

And having delivered this lesson in tradecraft, he collected the pieces of his phone and headed back to Slough House.

Where the day is well established now, and dawn a forgotten intruder. When River returns to take up post at his desk—his current task being so mind-crushingly dull, so balls-achingly unlikely to result in useful data, that he can barely remember what it is even while doing it—all the slow horses are back in the stable, and the hum of collective ennui is almost audible. Up in his attic room, Jackson Lamb scrapes the last sporkful of chicken fried rice from a foil dish, then tosses the container into a corner dark enough that it need never trouble his conscience again, should such a creature come calling, while two floors below Shirley Dander's face is scrunched into a thoughtful scowl as she replays in her mind the sequence of events that led to her flattening Roderick Ho: always a happy outcome, of course, but had she really prevented a car doing the same? Or had it just been another of London's penis-propelled drivers, whose every excursion onto the capital's roads morphs into a demolition derby? Maybe she should share the question with someone. Catherine Standish, she decides. Louisa Guy too, perhaps. Louisa might be an ironclad bitch at times, but at least she doesn't think with a dick. Some days, you take what you can.

Later, Lamb will host one of his occasional departmental meetings, its main purpose to ensure the ongoing discontent of all involved, but for now Slough House is what passes for peaceful, the grousing and grumbling of its denizens remaining mainly internal. The clocks that each of the crew separately watches dawdle through their paces on Slough House time, this being slower by some fifty percent than in most other places, while, like the O.B. in distant Berkshire, the day catnaps the afternoon away.

Elsewhere, mind, it's scurrying around like a demented gremlin.

There was a story doing the rounds that the list of questions traditionally asked of head injury victims, to check for concussion—what's the date, where do you live, who's the Prime Minister?—had had to be amended in light of the current incumbent's tenure, as the widespread disbelief that he was still in office was producing a rash of false positives. Which might explain, thought Claude Whelan, why he insisted on being addressed as PM.

But like all his ilk the man was dangerous when cornered, and one thing politics was never short of was corners.

"You know the biggest threat Parliament faces?" he asked Whelan now.

"A cyber—"

"No, that's the biggest threat the country faces. The biggest threat Parliament faces is democracy. It's been a necessary evil for centuries, and for the most part we've been able to use it to our advantage. But one fucking referendum later and it's like someone gave a loaded gun to a drunk toddler." He was holding a newspaper, folded open to Dodie Gimball's column. "Read this yet?"

Whelan had.

The PM quoted from it anyway: "'Who are we to turn to for protection? Yes, we have our Security Services, but they are 'services' only in the sense that a bull 'services' a cow. In other words, dear readers, a cock-up of the first magnitude.'"

Whelan said, "I'm not entirely sure that works. She goes from plural to—"

"Yes yes yes, we'll get the grammar police onto her first thing. Do they have actual powers of arrest, do you think? Or will they just hang her from the nearest participle?"

Whelan nodded his appreciation. He was a short man with a high forehead and a pleasant manner, the latter a surprise given his years among the intelligence service's backroom boys, a fraternity not known for its social skills. His ascent to the top rank had been unexpected, and largely due to his not having been involved in the crimes and misdemeanours which had resulted in the desk being vacant in the first place. Having clean hands was an unusual criterion for the role, but his predecessor's shenanigans had ensured that, on this occasion at least, it was politic.

It did mean, though, that his experience of actual politics was on the thin side. His required learning curve, as Second Desk Diana Taverner had pointed out, was steeper than a West End bar bill.

Now he said, "Twelve people died. However indelicately she phrases it, it comes under the heading fair comment."

"Fair comment would be laying the blame with the homicidal cretins who committed the murders. No, Gimball has her own agenda. You're aware of who she is?"

"I know who her husband is."

"Well then," said the PM. "Well then," and slapped the newspaper against his thigh, or tried to. There wasn't really room for the manoeuvre.

They were in what was best described as a cubbyhole, though was informally known as an incubator. Number Ten was a warren, as if an architect had been collecting corridors and decided to use them all up at once. Offices of state aside, every room in the building seemed an excuse to include a bit of extra space between itself and the next one along, in most of which, at any given time, a plot was being hatched. Hence "incubator." They were ideal for the purpose, as they were only really big enough for two people at a time and thus reduced the amount of political fear that could be generated, political fear being the fear that the blame for something bad might fall on those present.

The meeting they'd just come from, discussing the events in Derbyshire, had triggered an awful lot of this.

"And the bastard wants my job," the PM continued.

"He certainly gives every indication that he'd enjoy running the country," Whelan agreed. "But, Prime Minister, with all due respect, he's his party's sole MP. What possible threat could he represent?"

"He's indicated that he might be willing to rejoin *the* party."

". . . Ah."

"Yes, bloody *ah*. And not indicated to me, you understand. To various . . . sympathetic ears. Which includes half of those in my own damn cabinet."

It didn't much matter whether this meant the entire cabinet had offered one sympathetic ear apiece, or half the cabinet both. Either way, the PM was beleaguered: the referendum voting the UK out of the European Union meant he had to steer a course he'd openly campaigned against, whatever his private views on the subject, and only the lack of a strong contender within the party— the most obvious candidates having been brought low by a frenzy of backstabbing, treachery and double-dealing on a scale not seen since the Spice Girls' reunion—had allowed him to hang onto power this long. But if Dennis Gimball had indicated that he might be tempted back into a fold he'd left "with supreme reluctance" some years previously, in order to join a one-issue party spearheading the Brexit campaign, a whole new ball game was in the offing. And few believed the PM's balls would see him through the current game, let alone a new one. Apart from anything else, he had a terrorist atrocity to deal with.

But all Whelan found himself able to say was, "Rejoining? That's not terribly likely, surely."

"Not likely? Have you been paying attention? Not likely is the new normal. He's got a wife writing a twice-weekly column that amounts to a press release for the Sack-the-PM brigade, and when he's ready to make the jump he'll expect to be warming his arse on my seat within two months. And this newfound taste for democracy—which he made sound like a synonym for paedophilia—means he'll have fifty-two per cent of the population scattering rose petals at his feet while he does. And it's not just me they've got in their sights, either. The main reason he's appointed himself scourge of the Secret Service, ably abetted by his tabloid totty, is that I've given you my full backing. One hundred per cent confidence, remember? An actual hundred, rather than a hundred and ten, or even, God forbid, a hundred and twenty, which I like to think speaks to the absolute fucking sincerity of the gamble I'm taking here. What I'm saying, Claude, is, we stand and fall together. So I'm going to ask you again, without my oh-so-honourable chums taking notes on your answer, how close are you to rounding up these trigger-happy bastards? Because if we don't see closure on this soon, the second highest-profile casualty is going to be you. Maybe they'll stick our heads on adjacent spikes. Won't that be cosy?"

It occurred to Whelan that if the PM showed half as much fervour when addressing the nation as he did when contemplating his job security, he wouldn't be regarded as such a lightweight.

Whelan said, "I held nothing back from the report I just delivered. Arrests aren't imminent, but they will take place. As for guarantees that another attack of the kind can't happen, I'm not able to give that. Whoever these people are—"

"ISIS," the PM spat.

"Well, they've claimed credit, yes. But whoever the individuals are, they're currently under the radar. They could be anywhere, and they could be planning anything. We're not in a position to deliver certainties. But I'd repeat that I don't think door-to-door searches in areas with a high Muslim population would be useful at this stage."

"Well, that's where we differ. Because anything to show that we're actually doing something would, I feel, be useful at this stage."

"I understand that, Prime Minister, but I'd urge caution. Provoking resistance from the radicalised segments of the community would be playing into their hands."

It was an argument Whelan had made three times already that morning, and he was prepared to make it again but was distracted by an alteration in the offstage atmosphere. The background noise from the nearest corridor, the hum people make when they want everyone else to know they're busy, had subsided over the last ten seconds, to be replaced by the lesser but far more ominous sound of the same people reading news alerts on their phones.

"What's that?" he said.

"I don't hear anything," the PM said.

"Nor I," said Whelan. "That's what worries me."

They emerged as someone was turning up the volume on a rolling news channel, which was screening amateur footage of a violent aftermath.

There was blood, there was panic, there was debris.

Closure, it appeared, wasn't happening any time soon.

"It's been brought to my attention that you arsewipes are not happy bunnies."

This was Jackson Lamb. The arsewipes were his team.

"So I've convened this meeting so you can air your grievances."

"Well," River began, "—"

"Sorry, did I say 'you'? I meant me."

They were in Lamb's office, which had the advantage, for Lamb, that he didn't have to move anywhere, and the disadvantage, for everyone else, that it was Lamb's office. Lamb smoked in his office, and drank, and ate, and there were those who suspected that if he kept a bucket there, he'd never leave. Not that its attractions were obvious. On the other hand, bears' caves weren't famously well appointed either, and bears seemed to like them fine.

"Did one of you jokers put a whoopee cushion on my chair, by the way? No? Well in that case I've just farted." Lamb leaned back and beamed proudly. "Okay, you're all uptight because there's a national emergency, and somewhere at the back of your tiny little minds you're remembering you joined the Security Services. That rings bells, yes? The bright shiny building at Regent's Park?"

"Jackson," Catherine said.

"It gives me no pleasure to have to say this, but keep your fucking mouth shut while I'm talking, Standish. It's only polite."

"Always happy to have you mind my manners, but do we really need to hear the lecture?"

"Oh, I think it'll be good for morale, don't you? Besides, the new boy can't have heard it more than once. I'd hate him to feel he was missing out. What was your name again?"

"Coe," said J.K. Coe, who'd been there a year.

"Coe. You're the one gets panic attacks, right? BEHIND YOU! Just kidding."

Catherine put her head in her hands.

Lamb lit a cigarette and said, "Where was I? Oh yeah. Now, I'm a stickler for political correctness, as you know, but whoever decided we're all equal needs punching. If we were, you wouldn't be in Slough House touching your toes when I tell you, while the cool kids over at Regent's Park are saving the world. Except for parts of Derbyshire, obviously." He inhaled, and let smoke drift from his mouth, his nostrils, possibly his ears, while he continued: "And if we let you help them out, you'd doubtless end up doing the only thing you've ever proved yourself good at, which is making a bad situation worse. Any comments so far?"

"Well," River began, "—"

"That was rhetorical, Cartwright. If I really thought you were going to speak, I'd leave the room first."

"Every manhunt needs backup," Louisa said. "CCTV checks, vehicle backgrounds, all the stuff we're used to. You don't think the Park would appreciate our help?"

"Make an educated guess."

". . . Yes?"

"I said educated," said Lamb. "That guess left school at fifteen for a job at Asda."

"I just thought—"

"Yeah, well, you don't get paid to think. Which is just as fucking well in your case." Lamb shifted in his chair, and shoved his free hand down his trousers. Scratching commenced. "Now. As I was saying before everyone decided this was an open forum, there's a lot going on, and you're not part of it. So let's fuck off back to our desks, shall we? Devil finds work for idle wankers, and all that."

"Hands."

"Yeah, hands, sorry. Word association."

They trooped out, or half of them did. Lamb leaned back, eyes closed, his hand still down his trousers, and pretended not to notice that Shirley, Louisa and Catherine remained in the room. Chances are he'd have kept this up all day, but Catherine was having none of it.

"Are you done? Or have you not started yet?"

He opened an eye. "Why, are you running a meter?"

"Shirley has something to tell you."

"Oh, fuck."

"I think you mean, 'What is it, Dander?'"

"Yeah, that's probably what I meant," said Lamb. "But my autocorrect kicked in." He withdrew his hand and opened his other eye. "What is it, Dander?"

"Someone tried to run Ho over."

"Just now?"

"At lunchtime. In the street." Shirley paused then added, for clarity's sake, "With a car."

"Maybe they mistook him for a squirrel. I've talked to him about that beard."

"It was deliberate."

"Well, I'd hate to think of Ho being run over accidentally. It would be robbing the rest of us of a moment's pleasure. Where did this happen?"

"Fann Street."

"And the three of you witnessed it?"

"Just me," said Shirley.

"So what are you two, her backing singers?"

Catherine said, "If someone targets one of us, it means we're all at risk. Potentially."

"And Slough House has been under attack before," said Louisa.

"You don't have to remind me," said Lamb. "It's muggins here had to delegate the paperwork last time. What sort of car?"

"A Honda. Silver."

"Any identifying characteristics? Like, oh, I don't know, a number plate?"

"I was too busy rescuing Ho to get it."

"If it happens again, you might want to reprioritise. What did it do, swerve at him?"

"It mounted the kerb."

"Huh."

Catherine said, "There's no cameras there. Hit or miss, they got clean away."

"Leaving the scene of an accident doesn't make whoever it was an assassin. Your average citizen would sooner pay tax than make a statement to the cops. Anyone lean out of the window, shouting 'I'll get you next time'?"

Shirley shook her head.

"Well then, let's assume it was a tourist. An unexpected sighting of Roderick Ho would alarm almost anyone, and you know what foreigners are like. Excitable. And rubbish drivers. Why didn't Ho bring this up himself, anyway? Not usually a shrinking violet, is he? More like poison ivy."

"He didn't notice," Shirley said.

Lamb stared at her for a moment or two, then nodded. "Yeah, okay. I can see that happening."

Louisa said, "Silver Honda. It headed east. We can find it."

"And offer it another go? I like your thinking. But me, I'd be more inclined to stick than twist. Ho survives a second attempt on his life, he'll start to think he's special. In which case I might have to kill him myself."

"Are you going to take this seriously?" said Catherine.

"I'm glad you ask. No, I'm not. Dander, you're not the best eyewitness in the world, what with being a coked-up idiot with anger management issues, so I don't think I'm going to be allocating our puny resources on your say-so. Of course, if any of you think I'm making a managerial misstep here, you're more than welcome to piss off. I don't want to close down your options or anything."

"So we just forget it happened?" said Catherine.

He sighed. "I'm not playing devil's avocado here. It was almost certainly nothing. Our Roderick, as I'm sure you know, spends half his time fucking up the credit ratings of people who nick his seat on the Tube. Sooner or later he'll try that on with someone who works out what happened. So yes, he might well end up u smear on a pavement one day, and it'll be a huge loss to the Kleenex corporation, but meantime let's not get our knickers in a twist about a badly executed three-point turn." He bared his awful teeth in a widemouthed grin "Now, I'm an ardent feminist, as you know. But haven't you girls got better things to worry your little heads about?"

They filed out. Before leaving, Catherine turned. "Advocate," she said. "By the way."

"Up your bum," said Lamb. "As it happens."

"Fourteen dead," Diana Taverner said. "And more to follow."

"Any CCTV?"

"Nothing of immediate use. Too chaotic. We'll pass it to the sight and sound crew, see what they come up with. And there'll be citizen journalist stuff, we'll gather that in too. Christ on a bike, though. Who'd do something like this?"

Whelan raised an eyebrow.

"Yes, okay, we know who'd do this," she said. "But why? Random carnage is one thing. But this is like something from *Batman*."

Whelan had returned from Number Ten with Prime Ministerial outrage echoing in his ears. On the journey back the car had halted momentarily outside a TV showroom, and exactly the way it happened in movies—God, he hated it when that happened—every screen on display was showing the same footage he was watching now: blood and debris and—thankfully muted by distance—the awful screams of the dying. His phone had rung while he'd been stranded there: Claire. His wife. Was he watching this? Yes, he was watching this. She hoped he'd do something, hoped he'd bring this to an end. So much violence, so much horror.

There'd been violence and horror at Abbotsfield too, but she hadn't called him in the middle of the day to say so. Her shock and disgust had awaited his return, in the small hours. But this— no. This couldn't wait. She had to tell him now.

He had assured her that all that could be done would be done. That those responsible would swing, though of course not really. But this was the acceptable language of vengeance. You visited your angry fantasies upon the guilty, but in the end settled for whatever the courts handed down.

Now he said, "You think it's the same crew?"

"Different approach," said Lady Di. "Different target. Different kind of attack altogether."

"I can see that. Everyone can see that. But still. Do you think it's the same crew?"

She said, "If it is, we're in trouble. Because there's no way of knowing what they might do next. Random, erratic acts of slaughter don't make for an M.O., which leaves a hole in any profile we build up. Whoever did this used a single pipe bomb. It could as easily be a lone wolf, a disgruntled teenager. But yes, it could be part of a larger campaign, with the differences deliberately built

in, to throw up a smokescreen. We'll know more when the forensics come through."

Or when someone claims responsibility, Whelan thought.

The footage ended, and he folded the laptop shut. Di Taverner
walked back round the front of the desk. She didn't sit. Prowling
was more her style: one-to-ones often meant watching her pace
a room like a cat mapping out its territory. Which all of this would
be, if she had her way. Claude Whelan's role as First Desk often
seemed like a balancing act, and Lady Di—one of a number of
so-called equals, all termed Second Desk—was waiting for his
fall, not to be ready to catch him, but to be sure that when he hit
the ground he never got back on his feet.

Which was why she was his usual sounding board when shit
hit the fan. At least when she was there in front of him, he could
be sure she wasn't behind his back.

Besides, she had a wealth of experience of shit hitting fans. In
her time, she'd lobbed more of the stuff around than a teenage
chimpanzee.

He watched her pace for a while, then said, "What do we know
about Dennis Gimball?"

He meant, of course, what did Di Taverner know about Gimball that wasn't already in the public sphere, which itself was a fair
amount. While a party backbencher, Gimball's few forays into the
wider public consciousness had revolved around incidents in pubs
and speeding offences, but he'd blossomed into celebrity once he
found his USP: cheerleading the campaign to get the country out
of the European Union and back into the 1950s. Spearheading
this crusade had involved leaving the party, a departure he under-
took with an oft-mentioned "great reluctance" but few inhibitions
about making bitter personal attacks on former colleagues, whose
responses in kind he cited as evidence of their unworthiness for
public office. With his tendency towards maroon blazers, slip-on
shoes and petulant on-camera outbursts he made for an unlikely
media star, and having him step centre stage had been, one
sketchwriter commented, like watching a Disney cartoon in which

Goofy took the leading role: at once both unexpected and disappointing. What should have been a cameo became a career, and the whole thing went on for what felt like decades, and when it was over there was more than one bewildered voter who wondered if the referendum hadn't swung Gimball's way in the hope that victory would guarantee his silence on all future topics. So far, this wasn't working out.

"Well," said Lady Di, "I think we can safely say he's found the new flag he was looking for."

"Critic-in-chief of the Security Services, you mean."

"I doubt it's a matter of keenly held principle so much as a convenient handle on the public attention," she said. "If that's any comfort."

"Anything we know that he'd rather we didn't?"

She gave him an approving look. "You're coming on, Claude. Six months ago, you'd have been shocked at the very thought."

Whelan adjusted the photo of his wife on his desk, then adjusted it back to the way it had been. "Adapt and survive," he said.

"I'll check his file. See if there's any peccadilloes worth airing. Hard to believe he'd have managed to keep anything under wraps, though. His wife makes Amy Schumer look like a model of discretion." She paused. "That was a cultural reference, Claude. I'll make sure you get a memo."

He smiled faintly. "Didn't she once write a column describing refugees as earwigs?"

"Which is exactly what she was fed on a reality TV show soon afterwards. Not often you see karma actually landing a punch."

"Did she say what they taste like?"

"Somalians," said Lady Di. "You have to hand it to her. She doesn't go out of her way to make friends."

But as was often the case with columnists, the more contempt they expressed for those unlike themselves, the more popular they became. Or more talked about, anyway, which they deemed the same thing. A kill list of people actually harmful to the national well-being, thought Whelan, would vastly differ from the official one used in the bunkers where they steered the drones.

Lady Di said, "But we're just the stick she's beating the PM with. Once he expressed his absolute confidence in us, in you, we became the enemy. It's a zero-sum game, remember. If the PM gave a speech in praise of lollipop ladies, Gimball would declare them enemies of the state. And Dodie would devote her next three columns to recounting how many traffic accidents they've caused."

Most things Claude Whelan knew about the treacherous nature of those who sought power he'd learned from Diana Taverner, but rarely because she spelled it out like this. Mostly, he just observed her behaviour.

He said, "So what does that make Zafar Jaffrey? Our enemy's enemy?"

"You're asking because we're interested? Or because the PM wants to know?"

It was because the PM wanted to know. Earlier, before the meeting at which Whelan had been invited to address the cabinet, the PM had taken him aside. *Jaffrey. He's squeaky clean, yes? Because I'm hearing rumours.*

"She's been putting the boot into him too," said Whelan. "His picture appears on her page any time she's referring to Islamist extremism. You don't need a psychology degree to join the dots."

"Well, he's black," said Lady Di. "They don't actually use the words 'send 'em back,' but I think it's safe to say the Gimballs aren't about to endorse a rainbow coalition." She paused. "Jaffrey's been poked at by everyone from us to the transport police, and I expect the Girl Guides have had a go too. Nobody's caught him making suicide belts in his basement yet."

"Any dubious connections?"

"He's a politician. They all share platforms with dodgy customers one time or other, because dodgy customers make it their business to share platforms with pols. But if he was into anything seriously muddy, it would have shown up by now. Let's face it, he's in his forties, he's got a dick. If he was the type to fall for a honeytrap, he'd have done so already."

"No buts?"

"There are always buts," said Lady Di. "We've been fooled before."

"Then let's take another look," Whelan said. "Just in case he's trodden somewhere he shouldn't since last time we checked."

She regarded him with a face so innocent of calculation, it was clear her brain was in overdrive. "Any particular reason? I mean, it's a busy time for us to be re-marking our own homework."

But Westminster, Whelan reflected, wasn't the only zero-sum game in town. He had no intention of letting Diana Taverner know all the angles. At any given moment she had enough of her own in play to make a polyhedron.

"Call it housekeeping," he said. "Use the Dogs, if you want. They're not tied up with Abbotsfield, or this latest thing. I'm sure they'll welcome the distraction."

Lady Di nodded. "As you wish, Claude."

"Oh, another thing. There's a service at the Abbey, day after tomorrow. For civilian casualties of war? In the light of recent events, it'll act as a memorial. There'll be high profile attendance, so we'll need to run the usual checks."

"And meanwhile we'll keep seeing if we can track down the Abbotsfield killers, yes?"

Sometimes it was worth letting Lady Di have the last word, if only to guarantee that the conversation was over. He nodded curtly and watched her leave the room; then, alone, reached out and let his fingers dally a moment on Claire's photograph, accessing her calm fortitude, her moral certainty. *Bring this to an end*, he thought. It would be nice if things were that simple.

In the kitchen Louisa stopped to make a cup of tea, because any time spent not looking at lists of library users was a small victory in life's long battle. Shirley was on her heels, a little close for comfort. Shirley, thought Louisa, was not quite as manic these past few weeks as formerly. Which some people might take as a good sign, but which Louisa thought more a distant early warning.

Without preamble, Shirley said: "Whose side are you on?"

"I'm going to have to say Daenerys Targaryen," Louisa said, without looking round. "It's not so much the dragons, more the whole freeing the slaves bit. Though the dragons do get your attention, don't they?"

"Because I know what I saw," Shirley went on. "And that was definitely an attempted hit."

It didn't look like there'd be an early exit from this encounter. Suppressing a sigh, Louisa filled the kettle. "Want a cup?" This was, she thought, the first time she'd asked Shirley if she wanted tea in however long it was they'd worked together, and was oddly relieved when Shirley ignored the offer.

"I just wish I'd got the plate."

"Might have helped clarify the situation," Louisa agreed.

"Hey, you weren't there. It happened pretty fast."

"It wasn't a criticism," Louisa said, though it had been. Shirley was pretty swift when it came to a lot of things: taking offence, changing her mood, eating a doughnut. Gathering data, it turned out, not so much.

"Anyway, it was a hit. Whoever it was would have stolen the car. All we'd find would be a burnt-out wreck in the middle of nowhere. Plate wouldn't help."

"If you say so."

"Lot of fucking use, talking to you."

And that was the old Shirley right there, but what was different was she didn't storm out of the kitchen after saying it, and start a lot of door banging and equipment abuse. Louisa knew she'd been attending anger management classes, but this was her first clue that they were actually working. Which she'd have thought required whatever the female equivalent of chemical castration was, but there you go. The miracles of counselling.

"Thing is," she said, since Shirley was still hovering, "I can't get too excited either way."

"Why not?"

"Well, on the one hand Lamb's probably right. What are the chances Ho's on a kill list? I mean, a professional one. Obviously anyone who knows him wants him dead." She fished a teabag from a battered tin. "And on the other hand, if he's wrong and Ho gets whacked, well. I'm not sure there's a downside."

"Unless Ho's been targeted because of what he is," said Shirley. "One of us."

"Ho's a lot of things," Louisa said. "But 'one of us' is not the first that springs to mind."

"You know what I mean. It's funny, sure, because it's happening to Ho, and he's such a tit he doesn't even know it. But what if whoever's after him thinks it'd be simpler to plant a bomb in the building? Or storm in with a shotgun? Have you forgotten what happened last time?"

Louisa said nothing. Last time Slough House ended up in the crosshairs, it was Marcus who'd paid the price. And if she and Shirley had anything in common apart from pariah status, it was that they'd both cared for Marcus.

The kettle boiled, pluming steam into the small room. She brushed a lock of hair behind her ear, and poured hot water into her mug. Shirley still wasn't going anywhere, and Louisa was starting to feel a tug of compassion for her. When Min Harper had died, Louisa had had nobody to talk to. Marcus and Shirley hadn't been lovers, but they'd been the closest thing to partners Slough House had to offer. The grief Louisa had felt, Shirley was going through now. Not the same—no two feelings were ever the same—but close enough that Louisa could almost reach out, almost touch it.

But once you started breaking down those walls, there was no telling what might come crawling through.

She looked in the fridge, found the milk. Added maybe half a teaspoon of it to her cup. Funny how you always stuck by your own rules of tea making, even when the bag you were using was full of flavoured dust, and the water tasted tinny.

Shirley said, "So what I was wondering," then stopped.

Louisa waited. "What?"

". . . Nah. Forget it."

"Shirley. What?"

"Maybe I'll keep an eye on him a bit. Ho."

"You're gunna watch Ho's back?"

"Well. Yeah."

"Seriously?"

"Just in case. Case it happens again, you know?"

Jesus.

"And that's what you were wondering?" Louisa said. "Whether I think that's a good idea?"

"I was wondering if you wanted to help," Shirley mumbled.

"Spend my free time watching Roderick Ho," said Louisa. Just releasing that thought tainted the air, like a fart in a crowded lift.

"Just for a day or two. Not long."

Louisa sipped her tea and decided it would have tasted a whole lot better if, instead of adding half a teaspoon of milk, she'd gone and hidden in her office until Shirley had left the building.

"You're basically going behind Lamb's back, you know that, right?"

"You have an objection?"

"Well, not a moral one," said Louisa. "I just wouldn't want to be you when he finds out."

"What makes you think he'll find out?"

"Experience." She remembered the shunt and crash she'd heard earlier. It wasn't that she didn't think something had happened, involving a car. She just didn't think what happened had been what Shirley thought had happened. "Look, Shirley." And she didn't feel great about saying this, but said it anyway: "I get it that you're worried. I just don't think you need be. What happened last time, Marcus and everything, that was bad, sure. But that was just us getting caught up in bigger events. Nobody's targeting us. Why would they?"

"You think I'm a flake," said Shirley. "A cokehead flake."

Well, yeah, basically.

"No," said Louisa. "It's not that."

"Yes it is. So fuck you anyway."

But she said it quietly, and didn't look close to grabbing the teaspoon and attempting to gouge Louisa's eye out. So again, Louisa thought: this anger management course seems to be working. Who knew?

"Yeah, okay," she agreed. "Fuck me."

She carried her rubbish tea out into the hallway, but before she could enter her office, River called from his.

"Louisa? Come see this."

He was watching something on YouTube, it looked like; some amateur video, anyway. J.K. Coe was at the other desk, and didn't look up when Louisa entered. That was par for the course. He spent most of his time on Planet Coe: must be lonely up there, but at least the air was breathable, or he'd have choked to death by now. But what was River looking at?

"Holy Christ," she said.

"It was posted about forty minutes ago."

The video showed a blurry mass of people running from what must have been an explosion of some sort. Whatever it had been, it had happened on the other side of a glass pane, which was now spattered and mottled with blood and what looked like fur or maybe feathers.

"Who . . . what was it? What died there?"

"Penguins," said River. "Some bastard lobbed a pipe bomb into the penguin enclosure at Dobsey Park. That's near Chester. Fourteen of the little buggers died. Most of the rest will too, probably."

The bomb had landed in the pool, and half the colony had dived in after it. Curious little beasts, penguins, and now half of them were dead.

"Do they know who . . ."

"Not yet." River switched browsers. The BBC front page was scant on facts, but had a screenshot from someone's iPhone of the carnage, which looked like a butcher's back room. Bits of penguin here and there. What looked like an intact flipper. Penguins were funny on land, ballet dancers underwater, but mostly mince once you applied brute physics.

Shirley had joined them. Her face squashed in horror. "God. That's fucking horrible."

"'The Watering Hole,'" River read. "That's what they called the penguin enclosure. Sounds more like somewhere for elephants and gazelles and things, doesn't it?" he asked, displaying more zoological knowledge than Louisa was aware he possessed.

J.K. Coe looked up from his desk and stared at them for a moment. Then his gaze clouded over, and he looked out of the window instead.

Louisa felt bad. Twelve dead in Abbotsfield, and now this. She looked at Shirley, whose expression had set into one of sorrowful disgust. It was spooky really, inasmuch as the Shirley she was used to would have been punching holes in the wall by now. Not that she was especially fond of penguins, as far as Louisa was aware, but any opportunity to kick off was usually seized upon.

Before she could stop herself, she said, "Shirley reckons we should keep an eye on Ho."

"What, watch his back?"

"That kind of thing."

"After hours?"

"The only harm he'll come to here is from us."

"You know he goes clubbing, don't you?"

"I figured."

"With, I can only assume, like-minded people. People like Ho." He paused. "We'll want hazmat suits."

Shirley said, "That means you're game?"

"Nothing better to do," River said. He looked at Louisa. "You too, yeah?"

Louisa shrugged. "Okay, why not? Count me in."

When the question arose, which it often did in interviews, Dodie Gimball had her answer down pat: "Oh, make no mistake. It's Dennis wears the trousers in our house." And this was mostly true, but what she never added was that he also, on occasion, wore a rather over-engineered red cocktail dress he'd bought her for her fortieth, along with various items of her lingerie that he was scrupulous about replacing when accidents happened. It was a harmless peccadillo—in her dating years Dodie had exclusively enjoyed beaux from public school, so hadn't batted an eye when Dennis's little foible came to light. At least he had no interest in putting on a wetsuit and having her walk on him in stilettos, which not one but two old Harrovians had suggested as an after-hours treat. (They'd been in the same year.) And say what you like about the system, it did grace its pupils with a smattering of the classics, a bulging address book and a knowledge of which fork to use. State education was for chemists and the grubbier sort of poet. Though she was still a trifle miffed that Dennis had chosen her fortieth birthday gift with his own pleasure in mind.

Anyway, that little item had been ticked off the Gimball agenda last week, so wouldn't arise again for a while. What they were discussing now, in the sitting room of their Chelsea apartment, fell into the realm of their joint professional interests rather than their more-or-less shared leisure pursuits.

"And you're sure the information is accurate. That this man . . ."

"Barrett."

"That this man Barrett knows what he's talking about."

These weren't questions, and even if they had been, Dodie had answered them twice already. But that was Dennis's way: when he was processing information, he liked to have it run past him a number of times. And when he got on his hind legs and spouted it for the benefit of the public, there'd be no glancing at notes or scrambling for the right word. There'd be confidence and the ring of truth. Even—especially—when the material was fabricated.

She said, "He's done work for the paper in the past, and we've never had to retract anything. He used to be a policeman, I think. Or gives that impression. Either way, he's our go-to chap for the backdoor stuff. You know, following people around. *Listening*. All in the public interest, of course."

"Of course."

"And he's been keeping an eye on Zafar Jaffrey's bagman."

Zafar Jaffrey: the PM's favourite Muslim, in the running for Mayor of the West Midlands, and exactly the spokesman his community needed, being decent, reasonable, moderate and humane; the first to condemn extremism, and the first to defend his fellow Muslims from Islamaphobic abuse. That was the official line, and even Dodie admitted he looked good on TV, but surely there was a point beyond which you needn't go when opening doors to those of other faiths—was it so wrong to add "races" there?—and that point had been reached when you were handing over the keys to the house. Besides, there was the issue of his brother. Not one he'd ever tried to conceal, true—that would have been a non-starter—but even public acknowledgement didn't lance the boil: the fact was, Jaffrey's younger brother had gone marching off to Syria, where he'd died waging jihad. A terrorist, in fact. On a par with those who'd gunned down innocents right here in moderate Britain.

Dennis closed his eyes and recited: "The bagman. A thirty-something ex-con called Tyson Bowman, whose CV includes two stretches for assault. Nasty piece of work. Claims to have found

Allah inside and now adheres to the straight and narrow, but has one of those face tattoos, like a tribal marking?"

"Best not say 'tribal,' darling."

"Suppose not. Anyway, most of Jaffrey's staff have records. That's his thing. Rehabilitation." He sniffed: lefty nonsense. "Jaffrey's not going to deny he has criminal connections."

"Jaffrey's not going to be there to confirm or deny anything, so don't mention the policy and simply highlight the fact that Bowman's done time. Anyway. Our man Barrett has film of Bowman visiting a frightfully seedy little place near St Paul's, a stationer's shop apparently, though that's just—do they call it a 'front'? The proprietor is one Reginald Blaine, though he goes by 'Dancer.' And this Dancer creature has underworld connections, Barrett says. He's rumoured to supply guns, and he specialises in creating false IDs."

"So how come he's at large?"

"Because, my darling, the world is mostly grey areas. If the man is a source of useful information to the authorities, then no doubt he's given a certain amount of latitude. But none of that is our concern. What matters is, one, that he deals in guns and fake paperwork, and two, that Jaffrey's man had dealings with him."

"But not Jaffrey himself."

"Of course not Jaffrey himself. That's precisely why—"

"—he has a bagman," Dennis finished.

They were a team. This was how they did things.

His wife's glass was empty, so he refilled it: a rather amusing claret from one of those wine warehouses on the outskirts of town. Never did harm to be seen shopping where ordinary people did, provided they were the right kind of ordinary.

"And we're sure a public meeting is the place to air this information? The House might be safer."

"Yes, but we're not hiding behind the Mother of Parliaments' skirts," said Dodie. "We're taking our sword of truth and getting out there and defending the people."

He raised his glass to her, in appreciation of her pronouns.

"Besides," she continued, "it's verifiable fact. The story will appear in my column the following morning, with accompanying photographic evidence. Jaffrey's not going to sue. Because if he does, we'll bury him."

Dennis switched roles; no longer testing the content of his forthcoming speech but rehearsing it, feeling its weight. "There are no innocent explanations for wanting fake identities. And the fact that Jaffrey—"

"Or his bagman."

"—or his *underling* has been making contact with a known supplier of fake identities within forty-eight hours of the Abbotsfield outrage surely speaks for itself."

"'Demands explanation' might be better."

"Surely demands explanation," Dennis amended. "Is it expecting too much of the Prime Minister that he require such explanation from his associate forthwith?"

"Unnecessary," Dodie said. "Everybody else will join those dots, trust me. And even if they don't, I'll do it for them in my column. Meanwhile, the PM will be reeling from your announcement that, after full and careful consideration as to where and how you might best serve your country—"

"In these difficult times," Dennis said.

"—in these difficult times, you have decided to rejoin the party whose aspirations and ideals have always been closest to your heart, and on whose backbenches you will gladly toil alongside those whom you have always counted your closest friends."

"Actually, dreadful little tykes, this current intake," he said.

"Though not as bad as our own shower."

This was true. The party that Gimball had joined might only have had a single issue at its core, but a single issue was enough to sow division among the uncomplicated minds of its activists, for whom a punch-up in a car park passed for debate. There would doubtless be hysteria at his defection—or redefection—but it would be a three-day whirlwind.

He raised his glass to her again. They were awfully jolly, these strategy sessions. A model of cooperative planning. "I wonder how the PM'll react," he said.

"Oh, he'll mime slaughtering a fatted calf and try not to show he's soiling himself. He's just got through announcing that Jaffrey has his full support, and after my article the other day—"

"Servicing a cow, ha ha! Very good!"

"—he had no choice but to wave the flag for the MI5 chief, what's his name? That common little man."

"Claude Whelan."

"So the PM's tame Muslim celebrity turns out to be what we're not allowed to say is usually found lurking in a woodpile, and the man responsible for establishing said Muslim's credentials has fallen down on the job. The PM does rather seem to be lacking in judgment, doesn't he?"

"Almost as if a replacement were called for."

"And who better than the hero of the referendum? Darling, happy endings are so rare in politics. This one will be celebrated for years."

Like other newspaper columnists, like other politicians, they genuinely thought themselves beloved.

Dennis Gimball finished his wine and stood and stretched. "Well," he said. "That's all marvelous. And now perhaps I'll just . . . take a stroll. Fetch a newspaper."

"Darling, if you're seen smoking, it'll be headline news. You very publicly gave up, remember?"

"It wasn't front page of the manifesto, though."

"That was funny the first time, dear, but don't ever say it again. If you're going to smoke, do it in the garden. And make sure nobody's watching."

Sometimes, she thought, it was like having a child.

While he was in the garden she scrolled through her calendar, checking the details of the following evening's public meeting, back in the constituency. Keeping it local was deliberate. Dennis's strength lay in the way he tolerated ordinary people, pretending he was no more important than they were, and this stage of his career would rely on that more than ever. When he made his announcement, he would do it to his home crowd, in front of home cameras. His supporters would feel they were part of the moment, and the ensuing wave of good feeling would carry him through the next few months. Meanwhile, that same wave would send the PM onto the rocks. An amiable idiot whose amiability was wearing thin, the PM's idiocy was growing more apparent by the day; he'd surrounded himself with his familiars to the point where a cabinet meeting resembled his sixth form common room, and he had no idea of the resentment this was generating. The tide was turning, though, and he'd soon be high and dry.

This was jolly good stuff, by the way. She should jot down notes—wave of feeling, onto the rocks, turning of the tide . . .

Dodie finished her drink and turned to the next item on her agenda: what to wear for the event. Something sober, something serious, something not too flashy but oozing class. Which, truth to tell, that red cocktail dress never had. It wouldn't do to let Dennis know that, though. Even the best-matched couples need their secrets.

After five, the stairs in Slough House only went in one direction. That was the general rule, anyway. Shirley's final AFM was at six, and it wouldn't take her half an hour on foot to get there, which was just one of the many annoying things about having her anger managed: if she had to spend time kicking something, her heels wouldn't be her first choice. Besides, she wanted to get on with the evening's main business: tailing Roddy Ho, and seeing what reptiles crawled in his wake. Was so intent on that, in fact, that the wrap of coke in her pocket kept slipping her mind.

And then, as is the way with such things, slipping back into it again.

Maybe she should take it now? Start the evening with a buzz: give herself an edge. She'd never taken coke before an AFM, except for once or twice, and what the hell: she'd survived the

course, right? Had only had it extended once, or maybe twice . . .
Actually, maybe coking up wasn't the best idea.

Kicking her heels in her office, then. Extending the stupid day's
work another thirty stupid minutes, knowing all the while that
River Cartwright and Louisa Guy were already on the job: *her*
job. Just her luck if she missed the action altogether. Worst case
scenario: Ho got whacked in an interesting way, and she wasn't
there to see. She'd never hear the end of it. And here she still was,
another twenty-eight minutes to go, and all alone in Slough
House, except for . . .

Lamb and Catherine.

There was something else on her mind—had been for a
while—and the right moment for dealing with it had never come
up, largely because such a moment quite likely didn't exist. But
now would be a good time to establish that, one way or the other.
Because it was either that or sit here counting minutes, to add to
her tally of days . . .

Fuck it.

Shirley got up, left the office, took the stairs in the wrong
direction.

"**How come** Ho lives in a house?" River said

"What were you were expecting? An upturned pizza box?"

"You know what I mean."

She knew what he meant.

He meant Ho lived in a house. A *house*. Not a flat, not a bedsit;
an actual London property, with a front door and a roof and
everything in between. River himself lived in a one-bedroomed
flat in the East End, with a view of a row of lock-ups, fistfighting
drunks a regular lullaby, and rent getting steeper by the quarter.
Louisa owned her own place—also a flat—but it was miles out
of town; was part of London the same way its airports were. But
Ho, apparently, lived in a house: not in the cleanest area of the
capital, nor its brightest, but still. A fucking house.

"Bank of Mum and Dad," said Louisa.

"Has to be. And with a weird . . . what would you call that?"

"A feature."

Which looked like an upstairs conservatory: a room whose outer wall was mostly glass, and through the gaps in whose curtains the pair could see stacks of electronica, which they guessed were either for playing music with or wandering the web on. It was currently lit, and Ho—or someone—was pacing the floor within.

"I think I remember him telling me about that," she said.

"Ho talked to you about his house?"

"I think."

"You *listened*?"

She said, "I'm a spy, remember?"

They were in Louisa's car, and were, well, spying. To help with this, both were eating burgers out of polystyrene containers, and were sharing a portion of cheesy potato wedges, after a prolonged bout of negotiation ("You don't need to put salt on. They put salt on them already. They *do*.") the stress of which probably undid the good that forgoing half a portion of cheesy potato wedges did. Ho had been home an hour, and they had already agreed that if he stayed in all night and nothing happened, they were going to toss Shirley from a bridge first thing in the morning.

The car was swampy with food odours. Louisa wound the window down to let some of them escape.

"Speaking of houses."

This was River.

She said, "Yeah?"

"I went to the house the other day."

"Your grandad's?"

River nodded.

"Must be strange, him not being there."

"I think it's the first time I'd ever been alone in the place. That can't really be true. But it felt like it."

It had been like stepping into someone else's past. The books on the shelves, the coats on the rack, the Wellingtons by the back door. It had been a decade since River moved away, and there'd be remnants of his presence, sure; chips on the skirting board, boxes in the attic, the odd shelf of teenage reading. But the house was the O.B.'s now, and before then had been the O.B.'s and Rose's, River's grandmother. Walking through it, he had felt himself a stranger, as if someone had curated a museum of his grandparents, and forgotten to apply the labels. He had found himself touching objects, trying to place them in a chronology he had only ever known a small part of.

"What'll happen to it?"

"Happen to it?"

Louisa looked away, then looked back. "He's not going to live forever, River."

"No, I know. I know."

"So are you his sole heir?"

"My mother's his next of kin."

"But is he likely to leave it to her?"

"I don't know. No. Probably not."

"Well then."

"It's not like I'm just waiting for him—"

"I know."

"—to die, I'm not—"

"I know."

"—counting the days. Yeah, I'll probably inherit. And yes, it'll come in handy. God knows, London's pricey. But I'd rather have him around, if it's all the same to you. Even now. When he's away with the fairies half the time."

"I know," said Louisa.

Between his fingers, his styrofoam container screamed like a clubbed seal. Or like one of those murdered penguins: a mad target. Did it even count as terrorism when no mammals were killed?

"Here he comes," Louisa said.

Ho was leaving his house, stepping straight into an Uber.

"Game on," she murmured, and took off in its wake.

• • •

Lamb was coiled like a spring, if you meant one of those springs on a rusted old bedstead. He was semisprawled on his chair, eyes closed, one foot on his desk, a cigarette burning to death in his right hand. Through a gap in his unbuttoned shirt Shirley could see his stomach rise and fall. The smoke from his cigarette was a blue-grey spiral, but broke into rags when it hit the ceiling.

Still daylight outside, barely evening yet, but Lamb punched his own clock, and won on a technical knockout. In his room it was forever the dead zone; the same time it always was when you woke with a start, heart racing and all your problems waiting by the bed. Shirley was half minded to turn tail, and use the stairs the way they were intended: down and out. But she'd already missed that window.

"If you're after a raise," he said, still with his eyes closed, "just think of me as Santa Claus."

". . . You're giving me a raise?"

"I'm saying ho ho ho."

"I'm not after a raise."

"Holiday? Answer's the same."

"Marcus had a gun," Shirley told him.

This caused one eye to open. "Okay," he admitted. "That wasn't going to be my next guess."

"Can I have it?"

"Yeah, why not? It's on a shelf back there." Lamb indicated a corner with a blunt head movement. "Help yourself."

". . . You're kidding, aren't you?"

"Course I'm fucking kidding. I don't read all the management shit, but I'm pretty sure I'm not allowed to arm staff just 'cause they're bored. That's the main reason British Home Stores failed."

"I'm not bored."

"You're not? Sounds to me like a criticism of my leadership style."

"I'm bored," Shirley amended, "but that's not why I want Marcus's gun."

"If you need a paperweight, steal a stapler. Everyone else does."

"The Park has an armoury."

"The Park has a spa and a gym too. It even has a crèche, can you believe it? If you were keen on employee benefits, you should have borne that in mind before fucking your career up." He moved his foot from the desk, dislodging some probably unimportant papers in the process, and leaned forward to kill his cigarette in a teacup. "Telling you that counts as pastoral care, by the way. There's a feedback form somewhere, if you can be bothered."

"If the shit hits the fan again," Shirley said, "I don't want to be left hiding behind a door that's mostly cardboard. When that mad spook stormed the place, we were fighting him off with a kettle and a chair."

"Dander, I'd hate you to get the idea that I give even the smallest of fucks about this, but you're a junkie with a short fuse. Putting you in charge of a loaded gun would be like giving a three-year-old a box of matches. It might make for an entertaining ten minutes, but I'd have HR on my back before you can say fuck me, smells like bacon. Besides, I hate to harp on about the paperwork. But Standish has me signing fifteen forms a day as it is." He held his hand up in front of him, and grimaced sadly. "I think I'm developing repetitive strain injury."

"Nobody would know," she said. "Marcus shouldn't have had it in the first place. It's not even legal."

Lamb affected shock. "You mean, if he'd been caught with it, he could have been charged with a criminal offence?"

"Yep."

"Dodged a bullet there, didn't he? Shame he didn't make a habit of it."

For what might have been half a minute she stared at him, but he'd adopted his most benign expression—postcoital warthog, or thereabouts—and gave every indication of being prepared to hold it until his final trump. And given Lamb's capacity for farting, which was paradoxically bottomless, that could be a long time coming.

Anger fucking management. Her session should be a doddle after this little chat.

"What happens if we get attacked again?" she said by way of farewell.

"The kettle got replaced, didn't it?" Lamb said, closing his eyes once more. "Go quietly on the stairs please. Some of us are of a sensitive disposition."

Over at the Park, meanwhile, orders were filtering down the great chain of being.

Jaffrey's squeaky clean, yes?, the PM had asked Claude Whelan. *Because I'm hearing rumours.*

"First Desk wants to be sure that Zafar Jaffrey is . . . reliable," Lady Di now told Emma Flyte.

Nobody's reliable, Flyte thought. This is politics, not DIY.

But all she said was, "How soon does he want to know?"

"Ten minutes ago," said Lady Di. "Why are you still here?"

There was bad blood between them, if not as bad as there might have been. Both, for instance, were still standing. But Emma Flyte, being cursed with exceptional beauty, was used to hostility from both genders, though it was usually delivered in disguise. In some ways, Lady Di's frank dislike was refreshing. And besides, Flyte had Claude Whelan's support, so here she still was: Head Dog, which meant chief of the Service's internal police, a branch of Five which had historically morphed, now and again, into a private squad administering to the merciless whims of one First Desk or other, but under Flyte's leadership had become what it had originally been meant to be, or at least be seen to be; an impartial department dedicated to the purging of unacceptable in-house activity. Hunting out naughty spies, basically. Flyte's usual intractability on this point was the main bone of contention between herself and Taverner, but here and now, she was prepared to allow the margins to grow misty. Nothing to do with a quid pro quo for Whelan's backing, but a tacit acceptance that when the Park was under the hammer, everyone did what was needed. And since Abbotsfield, the Park was under the hammer.

Besides, Lady Di—ever the professional—never let her animosity show unless it was absolutely necessary, or she felt like it.

So Flyte simply said: "Just planning my next move, sir," and headed off to set things in motion, which first off involved getting Devon Welles to access the available background and bring her up to speed.

Devon, like herself, was former Job: real police, which meant he knew when to follow orders, when not to bother and where the nearest pub was. In this instance, it took him forty minutes to pull together the threads the Service had wrapped around Zafar Jaffrey to date. Two full-scale vettings, and a handful of once-overs.

"A lot for a middleweight pol," she observed.

"It would be a lot for a middleweight white-bread pol," Welles corrected. "But outside the London Mayor, Jaffrey's the highest profile Muslim player in the country. And each vetting preceded a public handshake with the PM. Who is not the type to be seen cuddling up to anyone dangerous."

"Are you allowed to say white-bread to me?"

"I'm pretty sure you just asked for a black coffee in my hearing."

They were in the canteen, which was where a lot of meetings took place that either weren't private at all, or were so private they wanted to appear not to be.

Welles said, "The scanners were run over the whole family three years back, when his brother went off to Syria, and again when he announced his candidacy for Mayor. He came through with, well, nobody ever has flying colours. But clean in every way you'd want him to be. Family's middle class but he's got the common touch, v. good on TV—did that interview, you probably saw it, where he cried on screen talking about how he and his family had failed his brother, how it was imperative that other Muslim families in the UK did not fail their sons. After that he sat on a few committees, made the right noises on *Question Time*, got himself appointed a special adviser to the PM. And here we are."

"Tell me about his brother."

"Karim. Quite a bit younger, twelve years, that area. He was radicalised without anyone noticing. Bad internet connections, mostly—that sounds like a techy problem, but you know what I mean. He got involved in a couple of forums that've since been shut down. First the family knew about it, he was posting a video from Syria. And the last thing they knew, a couple of months later, he was playing gooseberry in someone else's date with a drone. Syria's one place where you really don't want to go celebrity spotting, isn't it?"

"I'll scrub it from my bucket list. What about entourage?"

"Jaffrey does a lot of work with radicalised youngsters—recovering radicals, that is. Gets them speaking in schools, writing blogs, doing podcasts. And he recruits his staff from their number. So what we've got is a lot of vetting reports with more hedges than Hampton Court Maze. That's just a quick overview, obviously. But still..."

"Nobody's putting their career on the line to guarantee they're all spotless."

"That's about the size of it." Welles paused. "Plus, I just had a word with a former contact. A print reptile."

She said, "You spoke to a journo?"

"When the digital revolution's won, we'll all be speaking to them on a daily basis. 'Yes, I will have fries with that.' Meanwhile, they have their uses. And this one works on Dodie Gimball's paper. It seems Gimball's filed a piece claiming Jaffrey has links to an, ah, unsavoury individual dealing with guns and fake paperwork. Dodie's done the sums, and come up with terrorism. In fact, she's drawing a direct connection between Jaffrey and the group responsible for the Derbyshire killings."

Flyte said, "Oh—kay. Ten minutes after I'm handed a brief to make sure our man's a white hat, it turns out he's in the frame for a mass murder."

"More like an hour," Welles said. "And are you allowed to say white hat?"

"Even we haven't tagged those responsible for Derbyshire. How the hell would Gimball know?"

"Doesn't matter. She's got some dirt and is about to throw it, that's all. She's married to Dennis, the anti-Europe MP. Probably has an agenda we don't know about."

"Everybody does," grumbled Flyte. She finished her coffee and stood. "Thanks, Dev. But keep digging."

"Will do."

She left in search of Lady Di.

Catherine put the kettle on and, while waiting, scrubbed at a stain on the kitchen counter. There was always something. Not long ago, she'd imagined herself out of Slough House for good, and the life she'd led during those few months had been serviceable enough: evenings had followed afternoons had followed mornings, and during none of them had she drunk. But they weighed heavy. There are worse things an alcoholic can have on her hands than time, but not many. Her flat was a model of order; virtually a caricature. In order to spend time tidying, she had to mess things up first. Here in Slough House, mess came as standard. So yes, there was always something.

But not all stains scrubbed away. Some while back there'd been three deaths inside Slough House, which even Lamb allowed was pretty high for a mid-week afternoon. They'd lost a colleague, a former spook, and a captive had been shot dead too. Catherine was perhaps the only one to mourn this final death. It wasn't so much the loss of life as the manner of its taking: J.K. Coe had committed murder, and Catherine believed that such actions had consequences. This was nothing to do with religion or spiritual awareness, just her hard-won knowledge that bad things followed bad. Circles were traditionally vicious. Catherine suspected other shapes had teeth too, but better PR.

She finished scrubbing, made two cups of tea, and carried both, along with the dishcloth, up to Lamb's room.

He stirred. "Did I accidentally establish an open-door policy? Because if so, I didn't mean my door. I meant everyone else's."

Catherine put the two cups on his desk, removed a single sock, a comb missing so many teeth it needed dentures and an empty sandwich carton from the chair on the visitors' side, and wiped it with the dishcloth. Then she sat.

"It's like a royal visitation," he grumbled. "If your arse is so particular, why's it attached to you? What are you after, anyway? As if I didn't know."

"Someone tried to run Roddy over."

"Yeah. You might have missed the bit where we had a meeting earlier? That was covered under Any Other Business."

"And you said it never happened."

"I pointed out that Dander's a coked-up idiot," he said. "A subtle difference, I know. But subtlety's always been my strong point."

He farted, and reached for his tea.

"Can you actually do that at will?" Catherine asked, despite herself.

"Do what?"

"... Never mind. So you believe her. Despite her issues."

The slurping noise he made would not have disgraced a pig.

"And yet you let her think you didn't."

"Jesus, Standish." He opened his desk drawer. She knew what was coming, and here it was: a bottle of Talisker. He opened it and poured about a week's worth into his cup. "Complete the following, would you? Upon receiving information of a credible threat to an agent ..."

Light dawned.

"... Okay."

"Yeah, that's not the exact wording."

She could see no way out of this. "A report of same must immediately be made to local station head (Ops)."

"I could actually hear the brackets there," he said. "And what's our local station, remind me?"

"Regent's Park."

"Regent's Park. So Service Standing Rule number whatever it is—"

"Twenty-seven (three)."

"Thank you. Demands that a full report of this morning's events be made to Lady Di Taverner, who will doubtless copy Claude Whelan in. For a supposedly secret service, there's a lot of stuff happens in triplicate." Lamb took a healthy gulp of what had been tea. "Ah, that's better. Luckily, Service Standing Rule twenty-seven three is superseded by London Rules, rule one. Which is . . . ?"

He cupped a hand behind a monstrous ear.

London Rules were written down nowhere, but everyone knew rule one.

"Cover your arse."

"Precisely." He belched, proudly. "Because you may not have noticed, but Slough House isn't exactly in Regent's Park's wank bank. In fact, there are those who'd happily tie us in a sack and drop us in the Thames." He shook his head at the thought of being unpopular, produced a cigarette from somewhere, and lit it. "So any time they get an opportunity to start writing memos about us, it's in our interests to squash such opportunity before it comes to fruition. Do stop me if I'm going too fast."

"Your turn of speed is always impressive," she said. For someone your size, she meant. She waved away smoke. "Have you ever thought about quitting? You might live longer."

"Why would I want to do that?"

"Good point. So what you're saying is, whatever's put Roddy in someone's crosshairs has also put us in Regent's Park's firing line."

"But only if they find out about it."

"What do you think Roddy's done? Or seen?"

"Christ knows. Downloaded the Archbishop of Canterbury's kiddy porn? Whatever it is, I doubt he knows he's done it. There's something about him, what's the word I'm looking for?"

"... Otherworldly?"

"Fuckwitted. Too fuckwitted to know when he's stepped in someone else's shit. Then starts treading it everywhere."

"He's left for the evening," Catherine said.

"I know. I felt the average IQ rise."

"What happens if they take another pass at him?"

"If this morning's attempt is anything to go by, it'll end up on one of those video blooper programmes. It's a good job they're not on our side. If they were, they'd be assigned here."

"So we do nothing?"

"Well, I personally don't plan to do much. But if you think our little gang of Jason Stillborns'll pass up the chance to mount their own private op, you've forgotten what testosterone smells like. I've already had Dander in here wanting to know if she can have a gun."

"You didn't give her one!"

"I was tempted. She was on her way to an anger management class. Imagine her turning up armed." His eyes glazed over while the headlines wrote themselves. Then he leaned across and knocked ash from his cigarette into Catherine's cup. "Ta."

"I can't help feeling our lives would be much easier if we could trust the Park," she said.

"Well, I'm not on our Claude's Christmas list, on account of my knowing about him putting his dick where he shouldn't. That's the same Claude whose rock-solid marriage is the stuff of Service legend." He leered. "He regards his wife as a saint, I gather. Which means she only gets down on her knees when in church, if you catch my drift."

"It would be hard not to."

Something in her word choice triggered a response, but before Lamb could get it out a burst of coughing overtook him—a great heaving earthquake of a fit, heavy enough to rattle not only his own body, but some of those he'd buried. The desk trembled. Catherine watched, wordlessly, and it occurred to her to wonder what she'd do if he died, which didn't, at that moment, seem out of the question. He could die right there in front of her eyes. Well, a cold voice deep within her suggested—the same voice that kept her from dropping a bottle of wine into her basket during her weekly shop—well: she'd had a boss die on her before. She wasn't collecting the set or anything, but she supposed she'd get through it if this one died too.

But her natural instincts took over. She returned to her own office and came back with a clean glass, a bottle of water and a box of tissues. She poured him some water, handed him the tissues. He grabbed a handful and buried his face in them, and then, when the heaving started to subside, poured the water in one seamless dazzle down his throat.

Before he'd finished mopping himself, she said, "When was the last time you had a checkup?"

"There's an annual medical. You know that."

"Yes. And when was the last time you took it?"

"It was a coughing fit. It's passed."

"You smoke too much. You drink too much. I doubt you sleep at night so much as pass out. Do you ever exercise? Don't even answer that."

"My body is a temple," said Lamb.

"Interesting viewpoint," Catherine said. "So what does that make your lifestyle choices? The Taliban?"

He grunted.

She stood again. "So where are we? Something's going on, we don't know what, but at least one of us is bang in the middle of it. And meanwhile, the country's on red alert. Does any of this seem familiar to you?"

"My whole life feels like a repeat most days."

"It's going to feel like a series finale if you don't start taking some exercise." She left him there, and went to put her coat on.

Lamb sat in the dark and poured another drink.

And after a while, lit another cigarette.

The club couldn't have been Ho's choice, they decided, because instead of a soundtrack that was to the brain what the cider press was to an apple, it had a buck to school days vibe going on. They were in a mezzanine booth with a view of the dance floor; a view, too, of Roddy Ho, part of a group on the far side of the open space. He hadn't seen them, being busy with his companions, plus he was wearing sunglasses. This had nearly tipped the balance in favour of abandoning him to possible death, but River had argued that this wouldn't be fair on Shirley.

"Since when have you given a toss what Shirley thinks?"

He shrugged.

The club was in Stockwell. After being dropped at its door, Ho had marched up and down the pavement for forty-seven minutes, texting. Louisa had circled the block a few times, but he hadn't clocked her; she'd dropped River at a nearby junction, where he'd have been spotted easily if Roddy had shown even the mildest interest in his surroundings. If I wanted to kill you, River thought, you'd be dead already. But this probably wasn't true: there'd been many previous occasions on which River had wanted to kill Roderick Ho, and his innate sense of not wanting to go to prison had always held him back.

Eventually another taxi had arrived and disgorged about sixteen people, one of them a young, attractive, possibly Chinese woman, who suffered Roddy to kiss her on the cheek, and briefly held his hand while he paid first the taxi fare, then the entrance fee at the club. By the time River and Louisa had regrouped and made their own way inside, the gang had found a table and were waiting for Roddy to return from the bar, to which he had to make three trips. This kept him busy enough that he didn't see them coming in, though the shades couldn't have helped.

"You reckon that's the fabled girlfriend?" Louisa asked.

"Her name's Kim."

"Actually, yes, he may have mentioned that. You think he ordered her off the internet?"

"I'd guess he made her in his basement, except she looks too well put together."

Because they were on an op they were drinking mineral water, or would have been, but it cost so much they decided to have beer instead: if they were going to be scalped, they might as well feel some benefit. River had texted Shirley to say where they were. She hadn't replied, but that didn't surprise them: Shirley could be pissed off for days after an AFM.

"Though she's been less . . . disruptive lately," River said. "More muted."

"I think she's off the marching powder."

"She misses Marcus."

Louisa didn't want that conversation. She looked around. "Do this often?"

"Clubbing? Please."

She eyed him critically. "You brush up okay. Or might do. I've never actually seen it happen."

"We're supposed to be on surveillance."

"We're supposed to be in a nightclub. Chatting, drinking, whatever. There's a girl over there giving you the eye, by the way."

He turned to see.

"Gotcha."

"Thanks. You think somebody's gunna try and whack Ho?"

"Not in here, probably. Or not a professional. A punter might."

"He seems to have plenty of friends."

"He's buying plenty of drinks. There's a difference."

Kim, if that's who she was, was now dancing with one of the other boys in the group, and Ho was watching them, a tight smile on his face.

Louisa said, "Ah, that's sad, never mind."

"Why would anyone want to blow up a pool full of penguins?"

She'd been wondering that too. "The Watering Hole," she said. "That's what it was called."

"You think it was some madman?"

"Can't think of a sane motive."

"Maybe there's a link with Abbotsfield."

Louisa couldn't see how. "Unless something just infects the air. Some kind of blood lust, where you don't even care what it is that's bleeding."

Shirley was suddenly there. "Did you get me a beer?"

"No," Louisa explained. "Because we didn't know when you'd get here, and we didn't feel like buying you a drink."

Shirley squeezed onto the banquette, where she could share the view. She took in Ho—still oblivious to their presence—and the direction of his gaze. "Who's the cock candy?"

"That would be Kim."

"Ho is dicking *that*? Someone's being scammed."

"How was the AFM?" River asked.

"Over."

"Maybe you could celebrate by getting a round in," Louisa suggested.

"I'm a girl. Girls don't buy drinks in nightclubs."

They both looked at River.

"Oh, great."

"We won't let anyone kill him while you're gone."

"Don't do me any favours."

He went to fetch more beers, and by the time he got back Louisa was telling Shirley her idea for a TV show, which would open with a view of Tom Hiddleston walking down a long, long corridor, shot from behind.

River waited. "Then what?" he asked at last.

But the women had misted over, and didn't hear him.

Eventually Kim stopped dancing and sat next to Ho. The view became restricted, with the dance floor fully occupied, and the music grew louder, battling with the aggregated noise of mating rituals. River watched these with the air of a man trying to remember a long-discarded habit.

"Taking notes?" Louisa asked.

"When women touch their hair it's a sign of sexual attraction, right?"

"Can be. But some men just make women feel like they've got nits."

Shirley said, "He's leaving."

He'd played it cool. Chicks like Kim, his girlfriend, they kept you on your toes: knowing you were alpha, they felt compelled to grade the other males too. He'd seen a documentary on the subject. It was about turtles, but same difference. He'd had a laugh with the other guys anyway, and bought a few drinks, and now he was heading home in a taxi, Kim right next to him—going back to his place—and once she'd finished texting she'd probably snuggle up, get them both in the mood. Not that he needed help. Fact was, he was in the mood anytime Kim was near, though the stresses of her job—she worked in retail—meant she was usually too fatigued or headachey. But still. Here she was.

The Rodster getting into gear now. This was going to be oh so smooth.

"Who you texting, babes?"

". . . Huh?"

"Who you texting?"

A streetlight they were passing under caught her face in its glow.

". . . No one."

They were about ten minutes from home. The driver glanced in the rearview and his gaze met Roddy's: *Yeah*, thought Roddy. *You wish*. He put a hand on Kim's shoulder and felt her tense. Excitement. You and me both, babes. He started planning the order of events: bit of mood music, and a celebratory drink. He had a bottle of fizz in the fridge for exactly this situation. It wasn't vintage, or hadn't been when he bought it, but it would hit the spot.

Roddy Ho, Roddy Ho, riding through the glen . . .

Bring it on.

Louisa kept the taxi in view the whole journey. It wasn't the hardest tail job in the world, particularly as it was going back the way they'd come earlier. Getting their collective heads round what they'd seen, Roderick Ho heading home in a taxi with a woman, was a trickier business.

"What the hellfuck is going on?" Shirley asked.

"Roddy's taking a girl home," River said, in a stunned tone.

"I know. That's why I'm asking. He's a brand ambassador for twattery. How come he's pulled?"

"We knew he had a girlfriend," Louisa said. "He's mentioned it a couple of times."

"Yeah," objected Shirley. "But I didn't think she actually existed. Let alone looked like that."

A brief poll they'd taken had Kim an eight and a half, possibly a nine.

"Did you see her skin? It's fucking flawless."

"Are you switching sides again?" asked River. "You were mooning about Tom Hiddleston's bum an hour ago."

Shirley didn't dignify that with a response. It was up to Louisa to explain: "Tom Hiddleston's bum transcends gender preference."

River said, "Anyway, maybe we're missing the point. Maybe she's the one trying to kill Ho. In which case, going home with him is part of her plan."

"I so want that to be true," said Shirley.

"Why wait so long?" Louisa said. "They've been going out for months. If I was Roddy Ho's girlfriend, I'd have killed him long before now."

"Maybe she's been using him for something."

Shirley gave a low, unhappy moan.

"Christ," said River. "Not *that*. I meant using him for the only thing he's good at."

"Hacking," said Louisa.

"So it is a scam," Shirley said, brightening.

"Makes more sense than the alternative," said River. "Which is that Ho does, in actual fact, have a girlfriend who looks like that."

"Well if he does, I wish I hadn't saved his life."

"Nearly there," said Louisa. "Taxi's slowing down."

"Here we go, babes," said Ho, paying the fare.

"Actually, Roddy, could you bung an extra twenty on?"

"... I ... Twenty? A tip's a tip, but—"

"No, I need him to take me home, that's all." Kim smiled. "Tomorrow's a big day for me. Huge. I need a night's sleep. Twenty should cover it. But make it twenty five, yeah?"

"... I ... Yeah, babes. Sure. But I thought ..."

"What did you think, Roddy?"

"... Nothing, babes."

He fumbled for more notes while Kim told the driver where she needed to go. When she'd finished, she put a hand under Ho's chin and drew his face close to hers. "You were so damn ... *sexy* back there, Roddy. When you were watching me dance. I swear, I was *wet*."

"... Ngh ..."

She kissed him long and hard, then gave him a little push. "Go on. Meter's running."

He stepped out of the taxi like a man emerging from a train wreck, then looked back when she called his name:

"Roddy?"

"Yeah, babes?"

"Goodbye."

"... G'night, Kim."

The taxi stayed where it was while Roddy, after a brief struggle, removed his keys from his trouser pocket, and Kim waved at him until he was through his front door.

Then it pulled away.

"There is a God," said Shirley, watching this from Louisa's car, a little way up the street.

In the taxi, Kim tapped on the dividing glass and said to the driver, "Actually, I need to go somewhere else," and gave him a new address. Then she took her phone out again, and instead of texting made a call.

"He's home," she said. "Alone, yes."

She seemed about to end it there, but changed her mind.

"And listen . . . Make it quick? He's harmless."

She put her phone in her bag, and let the taxi carry her off.

"So now what?" said Louisa.

"He's home. Nobody tried to kill him. I vote we call it a night," said River, stifling a yawn.

"Lightweight," said Shirley.

"No, he's right," said Louisa. "What else do we do? Sit and watch Ho's front door?"

"Just because he's back doesn't mean he's safe," Shirley said, with a taut note in her voice that hadn't been there earlier.

"But nothing we've seen suggests he's in any danger, either."

"Someone tried to whack him this morning."

"We remember."

"If I hadn't been there, he'd be dead."

"That doesn't mean you're responsible for him from now on," River said. "That only happens in films."

"Besides," said Louisa, "he pretty clearly didn't notice it himself."

"It fucking happened."

"Yeah, okay, but—"

"No, not fucking *okay*. It happened. And until we know why—"

"Shirley—"

"—then it could still happen again. And if it happens to him, it could happen to any one of us."

"That's not strictly—"

"Fuck off, Cartwright."

"Okay."

Louisa said, "Shirley, you have a point. Sure. But three of us, in one car? Is that any way to run a surveillance?"

"You're trying to get me out of your car?"

"I'm saying we can't take shifts if we're all crammed in here. There's no chance of any of us getting any sleep. And I don't know about you, but I don't intend to be awake all night."

"So . . . So what are you suggesting?"

"That we need a plan," Louisa said. "And here it is. We take shifts. The best surveillance point's that bus stop on the corner. Bound to be night buses on this route, so waiting won't look suspicious. First relief's at two, then five. The others kip in the car. Okay?"

"Here in the road?"

"No. I'll park further down, past the shops. Won't be so conspicuous."

Shirley said, "We gunna draw straws or what?"

"I'm moving the car. No offence, but nobody else drives this baby. And River's had two beers, so he'll be useless until he's had some kip. So . . ."

"So I'm first up."

"Well, this whole thing was your idea."

Shirley scowled. "You'd better not be late."

Contrary to most approved covert surveillance techniques, she allowed the door to slam behind her when she got out.

Louisa said, "No, really. Happy to help," and waited until Shirley was halfway to the bus stop before starting the engine.

"You were trying to get her out of your car, weren't you?" River said.

"Yeah. Fuck her. I'm going to bed. Want a lift?"

"Please."

They left.

Roderick Ho let himself into his house, turned the hall lamp on, then leaned against the wall. "Yeah, course, babes," he murmured. Big day tomorrow. Need your beauty sleep. Best not come in, because you'd not get much of that in the Rodster's bed.

You rock my world. He'd said that to her a time or two. You rock my world. Chicks liked it when you quoted poetry; it made them feel special. And Kim deserved to feel special, but still, he wished she'd stay the night once in a while. Because he wasn't ashamed to admit this, but he actually, you know, *loved* the girl. His days of playing the field were over. But he wished she'd stay the night after another evening of letting him pay for taxis and clubs and drinks and taxis.

Still, though. Getting out there, being seen, everyone knowing Kim was with him: yeah.

Roddy Ho, Roddy Ho, manliest of men . . .

That was the tune on everybody's lips.

He dumped his jacket on a chair, headed into the kitchen and scored an energy drink from the fridge. Not the common choice for a nightcap, but that was how he rolled. He'd have energy sleep, dreaming energy dreams. Wake full of energy visions. He sent a quick text to Kim—*You don't need beauty sleep, babes*: she'd work out what that meant—put both his phones on to charge, and headed up the stairs. Some nights he sat for a while in what the estate agent had called his midstorey conservatory, an upper room with a mostly glass wall where the previous owner had grown flowers or herbs or shit, but which Roddy used as a den: computers, sound system, high-def screen. Maybe a few tunes before bed, he thought. Sit in his comfy chair and grab a few melodies: he liked big-ass guitar sounds this time of night. Above him a floorboard squeaked. He rose two more steps then stopped, listened. The floorboard squeaked again.

There was someone in his house.

• • •

No night bus used this stop, it turned out, so anyone standing here
was going to look pretty conspicuous pretty soon, Shirley thought.
And then: those fuckers have driven away, haven't they? To be
certain she'd have to walk all the way to the shops, and if it turned
out they were there after all it would look like she didn't trust
them, which would piss them off, so as soon as she walked back
here again, they would, in fact, drive away. It was what Shirley
would have done.

Fuck it.

In her pocket was the wrap of coke, and now would be the
perfect time. Keep her sharp, keep her vigilant. But though her
hand strayed there and fondled its comfortable shape, that was as
far as she went for the moment. Soon it would be midnight, one
day sliding into the next, and then she'd have sixty-three days. It
was still just a number, but a bigger number than the one she had
now. Did that matter? Not really. But just because something
didn't matter wasn't a reason for not taking notice of it. If it didn't
matter, then it wouldn't matter if it actually happened, either. The
number reaching sixty-three, that is.

She shivered, the day's warmth having dissipated. If Marcus
were here he'd be grumbling about how he could be in bed, though
they both knew he wouldn't be in bed; he'd be in front of an online
casino, in the neverending bid to recoup yesterday's losses. She
shook her head. Some losses stayed lost. Her mind drifted back
to the morning: the car mounting the pavement, and her own
instant reaction. She hadn't been wrong. Someone had tried to
kill Roderick Ho. That was why she was here: not because it was
imperative that Ho remained unkilled, but because this was real,
and it was happening, and it was something to do.

Her hand still in her pocket, she wandered down the road. Ho's
house was easy to keep an eye on: it had that big window, glass
wall almost, on the first floor. The kind of thing estate agents
creamed over, but anyone with sense just thought: what the fuck?

There was little point in adding features to London houses. If you wanted to increase the value of a property, you only had to wait five minutes. Meanwhile, Ho was home, but hadn't turned lights on. The others were probably right: nothing suggested he was in danger. But it was her own time she was wasting—well, and theirs—and she'd look an idiot if she cashed out now.

After eleven. Twenty-five minutes until the numbers rolled over. The wrap in her fingers was warm to the touch, but she'd leave it intact for now. Maybe later, if she started to fade. But right now, all was quiet.

His first thought was, *She's come back*. Had only been teasing: he'd go into his den and there she'd be, down to her underwear already. Surprise! It was for just such an eventuality that he'd given her a key . . . But that didn't work, or only for a moment. Kim was heading home in a taxi, fully clothed. There was no way for her to be upstairs. Whoever it was, it didn't seem likely that ramRodding was on their mind.

And then he thought: all that stuff that Dander was going on about this morning, when she'd ruined his Pokémon moment. The car she'd said tried to take him out. Had that been for *real*?

He was on the staircase, two steps from the landing, and frozen in the moment. On and up or back and down? If he turned and headed down, whoever was up there would know. And they'd be behind and above him, which wasn't where you wanted an enemy to be.

Where you wanted an enemy to be was a long way away.

Roderick Ho lived a rich, full life. Admired by all who knew him, envied by all the men; and if he weren't commited to Kim, he'd be up to his neck in hopeful women every night of the week. So a player, definitely, and one who could handle himself—his Pokémon agility underlined that—not to mention an active agent of the Security Services: he was basically born for situations like this. So how come his knees were turning to water, and he couldn't move from this stair?

Seconds passed. There was no more creaking from above, as if whoever it was had also frozen in place, and was waiting for Roddy to appear. If they were an enemy, they'd be armed. Nobody broke into a place intending harm without carrying the tools for the job. And if it were a friend—his reasoning broke down. The only person who had a key was Kim, and she'd never used it.

Stay or go?

Fight or flight?

His hands curled into fists.

Whoever was up there, they were hiding in the dark. That would be because they knew about Roddy, knew his reputation, knew they needed darkness and surprise. Well, they'd already lost one of those, and didn't even know it yet. Roddy knew they were there. He also knew his house the way a cat knows its whiskers. He could glide through its rooms like a phantom on a skateboard while an intruder would blunder haplessly into unexpected doors and furniture. It would be the work of a moment to assert his dominance. This guy, whoever he was, had better be prepared to rue the day. Roddy was coming for him. He took a step up, caught his foot on the riser and fell flat on his face.

Which wasn't great, but the momentum was there now, the decision taken. Roddy had to move, and move fast. Scrambling to his feet, he launched himself up the remaining stairs and burst into the darkened room like a lightning bolt, adrenalin flooding his system: his hands now chopping machines, ready to slam into an opponent's throat; his feet deadly weapons, aching to kick and bruise and kill. He snarled, a low deadly sound. His teeth were bared. Victory was his for the taking.

From the corner of the room Lamb said, "Not now, Cato."

Standish has been on at me to get more healthy, so I've had a little detox. Found some sparkling water in your fridge. Knew you wouldn't mind."

". . . That's champagne."

"Is it? Thought it tasted funny."

Lamb scowled at the treacherous beverage.

". . . Er . . . Why are you here?"

"Just checking to see if you're dead." Lamb belched, paused, then belched again, more loudly. "No need to thank me. But if you want to ring out for a pizza, it wouldn't go amiss."

"There might be some in the fridge."

"Yeah, there was, but I fancy a hot one."

He had dragged a chair into the corner and taken his shoes off, though he still had his coat on. Bits of leftover pizza were scattered on and around his frame, and the champagne bottle dangled loosely from his hand.

"So. Anyone try to kill you or anything?"

". . . No."

"Pity. Would have been nice to get this sorted, one way or the other." Lamb stood suddenly—he was capable of sudden movement when least expected—and peered through the big window. What he saw out there provoked what might have been a chuckle, if it wasn't another belch. He turned back to Ho. "And there was no one tailing you?"

"I'm pretty sure I'd have noticed," Ho said, allowing himself a quiet, professional smile.

"So either you're getting worse or your colleagues are getting better. Fuck me, that's a puzzler."

"Why do I need protecting?"

Lamb shrugged. "I'm not convinced myself. That you're worth protecting, I mean. But someone's clearly got it in for you. I mean, look at the facts. Dander saw someone try to run you over, and you seem to have a girlfriend. I'm not a conspiracy theorist, but *something*'s going on."

". . . I don't get it."

Lamb turned and clapped Ho on the shoulder. The younger man nearly buckled under the weight. "We should get that sewn onto a sampler for you. Save a lot of chat. Now, where's the bed? This champagne of yours has made me right sleepy."

". . . Bed?"

"Yeah, it's starting to look like you're too tight to stand your boss a pizza. And some of us have offices to run in the morning."

"I thought you were here to keep guard."

"Christ no. What gave you that idea? I'm here to make sure somebody else is." He nodded towards the window. "Give her a sword and a helmet, she'd look like a brave little hobbit. Now, I'll give you five minutes to change your sheets. And I'm busting for a piss. Where's the nearest basin?"

Ho pointed towards the landing, numbly.

"I'll have a fry-up in the morning," Lamb said, heading in that direction. "But no beans. They play havoc with my constitution." He farted on exit, to illustrate the problem.

Ho moved to the window, and looked out. A hobbit? He couldn't see anyone. He rubbed his eyes, but that didn't help. And Lamb, here, at this hour? For half a moment he constructed a world in which Lamb had got word to Kim, warning her to keep clear of the house tonight, and this made things a little happier, but unfortunately didn't make sense. Maybe it was true, though. Maybe he was on somebody's list. He stepped back from the window abruptly, in case there was a nightscope trained on him, and felt his foot crack the fragile neck of the discarded champagne bottle. It was starting to feel like things were not going entirely his way.

He wondered if he had clean sheets.

When two rolled round and rolled away again, and nobody came to relieve her, Shirley had a brief moment during which she rained imaginary hellfire down on Louisa and River, and then thought: sod it. Being here was her idea. She could either man the fuck up or head the hell home. And home had its own issues, being haunted this time of night by memories of her ex. Might as well be standing at a bus stop, cold and hungry, keeping a watch over a colleague she had no particular interest in keeping alive. It wasn't, anyway, the need to save Ho that was keeping her here. It was that she hadn't been able to save Marcus.

And again she felt the wrap of cocaine in her pocket, and the needle-sharp suggestion it was making to her fingers: *take me.*

Yes, okay.

But not quite yet.

Something moved.

It was a man, briefly caught by a streetlight, walking towards her on the opposite side of the road. Shirley was cloistered in shadow and didn't think herself visible. Even so she held her breath as the figure reached Ho's front door and let itself in using a key.

Ho has a housemate?

Not possible. It couldn't be possible to share a house with Roderick Ho.

She was already moving towards the door, though the figure had closed it behind him. The house remained in darkness, quiet as a nunnery, but damage required no noise; he might emerge in seconds, leaving silent carnage in his wake.

Lamb should have let me have the gun.

Though actually, it's not entirely clear how useful it would be right now.

She reached the front door and stood for a moment. She had a set of skeleton keys she'd inherited from Marcus, but not with her. Kick it in?

Yeah, right. And break a leg.

But there was a ground-floor window, and she had a fist. She shrugged her jacket off, rolled it round her right hand, and drew her arm back to punch through the glass.

Inside, somebody screamed.

There was someone in his house.

Hadn't he already had that thought? If so, he was having it again:

There was someone in his house.

Roderick Ho was lying on a makeshift bed of clothes and cushions and wondering why his ear was bleeding. Broken glass, it turned out. Maybe he should have swept that broken bottle up before settling down to sleep. But while reaching for a box of tissues, which for strategic reasons he kept handy at night, he felt the air shift, or a noise being stifled; something, anyway, to indicate a foreign presence on the stairs. Lamb. But why would Lamb be on the stairs when he was already in Ho's bedroom?

Ho was trying to remember what else he had in his fridge worth stealing when a dark figure entered the room, heading towards him in a crouch, the way Roddy himself moved in his ninja dreams.

He felt like a Pokémon character, about to be bagged and boxed.

"Kim?" he said hopefully.

A light went on. The room went white. The figure turned and faced the nightmare in the doorway: Jackson Lamb, teeth bared, naked belly pendulous over a grubby pair of boxers.

And a plastic blue bottle in his hands.

"Evening, sunshine," said Lamb, and squirted bleach in the stranger's face.

The man dropped whatever he was holding, and screamed.

Lamb swung a hammer-like fist into his chest.

The man staggered backwards, tripped over Roddy's still-recumbent form and fell through the big glass window onto the street below.

When Shirley punched the glass a figure crashed to the pavement, as if she'd won a prize at a fairground attraction. She tried to turn, but her rolled-up jacket snagged on the broken window, and before she could tug free a car pulled up. Glass was falling like slivers of frozen rain, and through the large jagged hole it had left the bull-like figure of Lamb appeared, apparently naked, unless she was having a mental episode.

Lamb?

At Ho's?

Naked?

. . . Whatever.

She wrenched loose, aware she was ruining her jacket, and turned in time to see a black shape being hauled into a silver car. At the same time someone leaned through the passenger window and pointed something at her. While she dropped behind the nearest car's wheelbase bits of wall flaked from Roddy Ho's house, and chips flew from his door. Shirley could feel the pavement against her cheek, smell the filth in the gutter. A car door slammed, and the vehicle moved. When she risked a look she saw something bounce off its roof—a blue plastic bottle?—but it was gone a moment later, a diminishing wraith amid the fuzzy glows that hang around lamp posts at two in the morning. She shook her head and rubbed her cheek, feeling the latter beginning to swell. Another chunk of glass fell loose, and shattered on the ground.

When she looked up, Lamb was scowling down at her, his bare chest and shoulders carpeted with greying curls.

"Ten out of ten for attendance," he said. "But *nul* fucking *points* for getting the job done."

Then he withdrew, leaving shards of the night still falling from the sky.

It began to rain that morning, about the time London was coming to life; a series of showers that rolled across the city, reminding its inhabitants that summer wasn't a promise, merely an occasional treat. The skies loomed grey and heavy, and buildings sulked beneath their weight. On the streets traffic played its wet-weather soundtrack, a symphony of hissing and slurring against a whispered backbeat of wipers, and in Slough House there was a muted atmosphere, because rain on office windows is a sad and lonely affair, and life in Slough House was hardly a barrel of laughs to begin with.

The car that pulled up on Aldersgate Street was black, as befitted the general mood, and sleekly rejoined the flow as soon as Diana Taverner alighted. She ignored its departure, as she had its driver throughout their shared journey; stared instead at Slough House's front door, which was also black, or had been—was now faded, and almost green around the edges—and shook her head. Any lesser reason than planting a bomb under Jackson Lamb's backside, she'd not come within a mile of the place. Up above, on a second storey window, the words WW HENDERSON, SOLICITOR AND COMMISSIONER FOR OATHS were etched in gold paint; a long-forgotten cover story or simply the relic of a previous tenant: she had no idea which. Only now, as she stood before the door, did she remember that this was itself a cover; a barricade masquerading as an entrance. She imagined its key tucked away in a drawer of Lamb's desk; imagined, too, that if the door were ever opened, the building would crumble like a betrayed network. Her collar was up, but she had no umbrella. How long was she supposed to stand here, waiting for Slough House to welcome her in? But that wouldn't happen, and there was, she now recalled, an alleyway to her right, a door set into a wall, a backyard. These she found with no difficulty. The building's backdoor, though, required effort, as if it preferred that she remain out in the rain. When it gave way at last, opening onto a staircase, it did so with a squeal like a distressed cat. The staircase smelled of mould and dashed hopes. One of its bulbs had died, and the other buzzed a bluebottle serenade.

Someone appeared on the next landing, a short broad figure that might have been of either sex. It seemed about to challenge her, but then, evidently realising who she was, retreated back into its room. Which displayed good sense, Lady Di conceded, but didn't inspire confidence as to the security of the premises.

Onwards and upwards. The staircase grew no cleaner or brighter, and all the office doors were closed.

On the top floor she paused. She knew, though the available doors offered no clues, which would lead to Jackson Lamb: its lower panels were punctuated by toe-cap impressions, the pedal signature of one whose preferred method of entry is the abrupt. She should knock, but wouldn't. But before her hand had reached the handle, a gravelly tone sounded from inside: "Well don't just stand there."

She opened the door, and went in.

It was a dark room, cramped, its only window veiled by a venetian blind. A lamp sat on a wobbly-looking pile of thick books, and the shadows it cast didn't reach the far corners, as if whatever lay back there was best left undisturbed. A print in a smeary-glassed frame was of a bridge somewhere in Europe, while a cork noticeboard, hung lopsidedly, was mostly buried beneath a collage of brittle yellow clippings. And in the air, beneath the taint of stale tobacco smoke, a tang of something older, something furious and unreconciled. Though that was probably just her imagination.

With no great hopes of it working, she flicked the lightswitch next to the door. All this triggered was a grunt from Jackson Lamb.

So she removed her coat and shook it. Droplets scattered, little rain dances picked up briefly by lamplight. There was a hook on the door, and she hung the coat there, then ran both hands through her shoulder-length curls. She turned to face Lamb. "I'm wet," she said.

"Nice to see you too," said Lamb. "But let's not get carried away." He eyed her critically. "You look like all your birthdays came at once."

"I look *happy* to you?"

"No, old. Am I the only one round here speaks English?"

She didn't smile. "Old, how kind. And busy too, what with the country being on high alert. Yet here I am, slogging across London to discover precisely what manner of shit you're pulling now. Roderick Ho? I thought you kept him in a cage, like a gerbil."

Lamb gave it some thought. "That's pitching it a little high. He's more like a verruca. You're never entirely sure how you ended up with one, but they're a bugger to get rid of."

"But we both know he can make a line of computer code sit up and beg. So what the fuck's he been up to, Jackson? There was a knife at the scene, bullet holes in his walls and broken glass all over his neighbourhood. And the Met were less than impressed with your witness statement. A domestic?"

"I thought it best not to air the dirty laundry in front of the help. Especially Ho's dirty laundry. Trust me, you don't want to know." He waved a hand at the visitor's chair. "It's fine, it was wiped down yesterday."

"What with?"

"Suit yourself."

Taverner remained standing, hands resting on the back of the chair. "Playing the national security card for the cops is one thing, Jackson, even though we both know your clearance is just marginally higher than Thomas the Tank Engine's. But acting dumb for the Park's another story."

"I'm not sure you're allowed to say dumb any more. It offends the vocally impaired. Or idiots. I can't remember which."

"I'm not in the mood."

"Yeah, I caught that vibe."

"You were there, at Ho's house, at whatever time in the morning it was. Which means you knew there was something going on. But didn't report it. Service Standing Order whatever the hell it is—"

"Twenty-seven three," Lamb said.

"If you say so."

"The three's in brackets."

"I don't care if it's in fucking Sanskrit, it's there for a reason. If you knew there was a hit on one of your team, the protocol's clear. You report it upwards. In this case, to me."

"Ordinarily, I would have. But there were special circumstances."

"Which were?"

"I couldn't be arsed."

She drummed her fingers against the chair briefly, then stopped. Not letting Lamb see your annoyance was a primary objective of any encounter with him. A bit like not letting a shark notice your blood in the water. "That's not a special circumstance, Jackson," she assured him. "That's your prevailing condition. And this time, it might just prove terminal."

"If you want to go to the mats, Diana, you let me know. Because I have so much dirt on you, I've started an allotment."

"I'm sure that'll be a distraction in your forced retirement, but it certainly won't save you. Not this time."

He leaned back heavily in his chair and swung both feet onto his desk. "If I'm gunna be threatened I'm getting comfortable. You mind if I loosen my trousers?"

"I'd prefer it if you changed them occasionally. Look. I'm aware there are . . . incidents in the past—"

Lamb ticked some of them off. "Attempted murder. Kidnapping. And I'm pretty sure treason's in there somewhere."

"—which might allow you a certain amount of leverage when it comes to negotiating your position. But we're way past that here. So before you start stroking yourself, there's a couple of details you might want to consider."

"Always like to get the details straight before I start."

"The Met reported a burnt-out car two miles from the scene. No body in it, so maybe whoever took a high dive through your boy's window survived the fall. Or maybe his pals just took his corpse somewhere else, in which case I'm sure he'll turn up in due course."

Lamb yawned, and put his hand back down his trousers. "So somebody's either dead or they're not. This is high class investigative work."

"And the bullets found at the scene have been subjected to forensic examination."

"Don't stop. Nearly there."

"The weapon they came from's a match for one used at Abbotsfield."

Lamb froze.

"Fuck," he said.

"Yes," said Taverner. "For once, I think we agree."

Zafar Jaffrey had to stop three times on his way to the Dewdrop Café: twice to accept good wishes from members of the community; once to buy a *Big Issue*, and to discuss with its seller the problems faced by the nearby homeless shelter, where younger clients were being targeted by drug dealers. Jaffrey took notes and did a lot of nodding. He was handsome, clean shaven, his hair just straggly enough to show independence of spirit and when off-camera favoured jeans and open-necked shirts; a light bomber jacket today, despite Ed Timms's warning.

"Really, Zaf, you can't be too careful."

"So I can't wear a bomber jacket. Are you *serious?*"

"It's a gift to the Dodie Gimballs of this world."

But whatever he wore, whatever he said, the Dodie Gimballs of this world would attack him for it; a series of hostile discourtesies for which the Dodie Gimballs of the next would answer. Besides, he liked the jacket. He thought it took a couple of years off; pushed him the right side of forty.

Now, to the *Big Issue* seller—"It's Macca, right?"—he delivered promises of action, of investigation and he'd already made one follow-up phone call before arriving at the Dewdrop; pushing through the door with a shoulder, hand raised in greeting to Tyson, who sat with a bucket-sized mug in front of him, his tattoo oddly out of synch with his formal wear: white shirt, grey suit, mathematically precise knot in a red tie. Face ink aside he looked more the politician than Juffrey himself, though that was, admittedly, a big aside.

His phone was back in his pocket. Tyson Bowman stood as he approached, and they hugged briefly, a one-armed embrace—"Tyson." "Boss."—then sat at opposite sides of the small table, its cloth the ubiquitous red-and-white-squares pattern; its ornament a cutlery holder into which sachets of ketchup and brown sauce had also been stuffed. He remembered bringing Karim here, back in the day; his younger brother not yet the aspiring martyr, but already, in Zafar's twenty-twenty hindsight, distancing himself from what had been, until then, the everyday: people drinking tea and sharing jokes, living ordinary, Godless lives. Zafar felt then what he still felt now. That there were better ways of achieving your goals than wrapping yourself in a semtex vest.

Be that as it may, Karim's story was not yet over. And the country he'd grown to despise remained in desperate need of betterment.

Zafar said, "No problems, then?"

Tyson shook his head.

"When will it all be ready?"

"Couple of days." He rubbed two fingers against his thumb. "On payment."

Close up, the aspiring pol disappeared. It wasn't that Tyson looked a thug—though he'd been anointed as such during his first two assault hearings—and it wasn't that he looked an aspiring terrorist, though having been radicalised during his second prison term, he'd served a third for possession of extremist literature. Nor was it the colour of his skin, the close-shaven head, or even, particularly, the face tattoo—a usually reliable hallmark of forthcoming violence. No, thought Zafar; it was the attitude bottled within that package; one suggesting that social interaction of any kind was unwelcome. Except with Zafar Jaffrey, who had reached out a helping hand when Tyson Bowman had been jobless, homeless and friendless. Zafar alone put a light in Bowman's eyes; one he should, he knew, feel guilt at exploiting.

The waitress was hovering, pad at the ready. "Morning, Mr. Jaffrey."

"Angela," he said. "Radiant as ever."

"You said that yesterday, Mr. Jaffrey. You want to watch that. People'll think you're not sincere."

He reached a hand out and touched hers. "People can think what they like, Angela. You'll always be radiant to me."

And now she smiled, and her sixty-something years fell away. "Will you still come here for breakfast when you're mayor?"

"While you're serving, yes. But just coffee this morning, thank you."

When she'd gone, he gave his full attention to Tyson. His bagman: a word not quite rinsed of its shadier connotations. But Tyson did, after all, carry bags on occasion.

His coffee arrived, and they talked of changes to the day's schedule: one meeting cancelled, another brought forward. A five-minute slot on local radio would now happen in a van, not the studio, saving everyone concerned, van driver apart, thirty minutes. Each day was busier than the previous, but then, the election was in three weeks. Jaffrey was an independent candidate, and though he had "disappointed" the Prime Minister by refusing to adopt the party's mantle—despite having been appointed to two select committees in recent years—the pair remained "close personal friends," the PM's oft-used tactic, when he couldn't get popular figures to endorse him, being to endorse them instead, and hope something rubbed off. Jaffrey accepted this unsought chumminess in the same way he did the Opposition leader's frequently mentioned "respect": in politics, ticking the no-publicity box was not an option. Besides, appearances to the contrary nothwithstanding, neither of those worthies were deluded enough to imagine their own candidate had a snowball's chance in hell: unless the polls were even more disastrously askew than last time, or the time before that, at the end of the month Zafar Jaffrey would assume the mayoralty of the West Midlands.

Of course, there were those—the Gimballs their standard bearers, but by no means their only champions—who believed that the election of another Muslim mayor would be one step nearer Sharia law. So far, their brickbats had bounced away: there remained, at least insofar as local politics was concerned, a resistance to dogwhistle racism, which was how most observers interpreted attempts to paint Jaffrey an Islamist sympathiser. Every time Dodie Gimball illustrated an article about him with a photo of a bombed-out bus, he enjoyed a bounce in the polls. But he had no illusions about the outcome should Tyson's recent activities become public knowledge. He'd go from persecuted minority to certified terrorist before you could say Operation Trojan Horse.

Tyson, too, would come under the hammer. Easy enough for Zaf himself to say: *Well. Won't be the first time.*

His mobile rang, rupturing the moment. Ed Timms, his press flack.

"Chief, I'm hearing rumblings."

He said, "You want to share them?"

"Word is, Dodie Gimball has some high explosives set to go off in tomorrow's column. After Dennis has his own firework display this evening."

"Could you maybe turn the colour down a notch? I find facts easier to process than images."

"Tonight, Dennis Gimball is giving a constituency speech in which he's going to claim you have terrorist connections. And this will be followed up by his missus in her column tomorrow. Accompanied by art, as they say. They have pictures, Zaf. I don't know what of, but you know what they say about pictures. They prove *something* happened, and once we're at that stage, it doesn't much matter what."

And this was how swiftly it happened; how quickly a situation burst from the realm of the potential into the here and now.

"Where's this speech happening?" he said.

"On Gimball's home turf. Slough."

"Okay, Ed. It's just more bluster. Let's not sweat it yet."

"Yes, but—"

"Later, Ed."

He disconnected.

Tyson raised an eyebrow, alert to Jaffrey's possible requirements. "Something need fixing, boss?"

"Possibly. One or two things."

Tyson said, "Whatever you want, boss. You know that. Doesn't make any difference to me."

Zafar reached out and they shared a handclasp. It was true, he thought; it genuinely didn't matter to Tyson what Zafar asked him to do: he was happy to do it. And the thought made him sad and glad at the same time; gave him hope for the future, but removed it altogether.

It was just like everybody said. Politics was the art of compromise.

Lamb had found a cigarette about his person and, in a rare bout of chivalry, had come up with a spare to go with it. He lit his own before lighting Taverner's. Manners were manners, but no point getting carried away.

"According to the BBC," he said, "which I accept means according to whatever's trending on Twitter, the Abbotsfield killings were ISIS."

"That's the assumption we're working on."

"Which would make the attempt on Ho ISIS too. And frankly, that buggers belief."

"Beggars."

"Sorry. Freudian slit." He inhaled deeply. "Apart from anything else, they don't do plots, do they? They do parking a bomb in a marketplace, or driving into a village and shooting everyone in sight. But they don't do *plots*."

"They hit specific targets. They've done that before."

"High profile, yeah. But they don't whack seventh-tier desk jockeys under cover of darkness." His eyes narrowed. "If this turns out to be one of your games, Diana, I can't begin to express how disappointed I'll be."

She looked around for somewhere to tap her ash, then gave in to the office ambience and knocked it onto the carpet. "Games?"

"It's not escaped my memory that someone tried to kill me in this very room not long ago. We've never discussed that properly, have we?"

Every so often, when you were gazing into the fetid swamp of Lamb's personality, a fin broke the surface.

Taverner said, "Let's stick with the evils of the day, shall we? What shape is Ho in?"

"He's got a cut on his ear."

"Bullet wound?"

"Poor housekeeping."

"Nobody else damaged?"

"Dander was there. She had to hit the deck sharpish. But one of the advantages of being built like a football is, you learn to take a kicking."

"Everyone on the premises now?"

"I don't take a fucking register, Diana."

"I thought you did."

"Well, yeah, okay, I do. But that's just to annoy them, not for official purposes."

"So ..."

"So everyone's here, yes."

"Good. Because as of now you're in lockdown."

Lamb rolled his eyes.

"I'm serious. No phones, no internet and nobody leaves. Ho's coming back to the Park. Whatever shit he's stepped in, we need to examine his shoes. Meanwhile, the rest of you are in detention. With debriefing to follow."

Lamb said, "Okay, why not? I'll keep 'em in order. We can play murder in the dark while we wait for you lot to clear your schedules."

Taverner laughed then stopped. "Oh, sorry, were you serious? When I want a fox to guard a hen house, you'll be top of my list. But meanwhile, I'll have Flyte babysit. You've met our Emma?"

"The thought of her has gladdened many a long night."

"Careful. Some of us are used to you. Others might bring charges. Get your crew organised, why don't you? I'm surprised Standish isn't already here."

"Do you know, I'm not sure she likes you all that much."

"I'm not sure she likes you, either. And yet you keep her on. Have you ever told her why?"

Lamb gave her a long hard look, but Diana Taverner sat on committees; Diana Taverner chaired meetings. If long hard looks could make her crumble, she'd have been dust long ago.

At last he said, "She knows her old boss was a traitor, if that's what you mean."

"And does she know he tried to implicate her in his treachery? That she was his cutout, all set for framing?"

"She's probably worked that out."

"And that you put the bullet in his brain? Or does she still think he did that himself?"

Lamb didn't reply.

She said, "Be fun to be a fly on the wall when she finds out."

"What makes you think she will?"

"Christ, Lamb. Of all the secrets you've ever kept, which one screams to be heard the loudest?"

There were noises off: bodies arriving downstairs. The Dogs, Lamb assumed. Come to take Ho to the Park, and nail the rest of them down. He heard Standish open her door and emerge onto the landing. "What's going on?" she called.

"There you go," said Lady Di. "Keen investigative mind at work."

Roderick Ho would have been pleased, though unsurprised, to learn that he was the reason Kim's heart was beating faster.

When she'd got home last night, the taxi having dropped her two streets away—in her line of work, it was best to keep her address quiet—she'd sat up late watching *The Walking Dead* and drinking vodka mixed, at first, with cranberry juice, and when that ran out, with more vodka. Sleep had come suddenly, without warning, and she'd woken with drool bonding her to her pillow and a thumping heart. Things had gone bad. Or were about to. Sometimes these feelings were misaddressed, emotional mail meant for someone else, but they were always worth acting on. The worst case scenario was the one you planned for.

So she showered and dressed in three minutes, and grabbed her emergency kit from the wardrobe: passport, both savings books and two grand in cash, plus a change of clothing and the bare minimum of warpaint, all bundled inside a getaway bag. Nothing else in her room mattered. The rent was by the month; her housemates temporary friends. She'd leave them a note—an invented emergency—and walk out of their lives forever. Or run. Her heart hadn't slowed yet, and if it wasn't the organ you placed the most trust in, it was certainly the one you wanted to keep doing its job.

Roderick Ho, she thought. The reason her heart was in warning mode was Roderick Ho.

Make it quick? He's harmless.

They were only going to work him over, they'd said, but she hadn't really believed it. Which meant, her beating heart whispered, that making herself scarce was the wise next move.

Slinging her bag over her shoulder, she left the room and was on the landing when the doorbell rang.

She froze.

But why worry? It was midmorning, in one of the world's biggest cities. There were postmen and people peddling religion; there were meter readers; there were pollsters who wanted to know what you thought about things you'd never thought about. The shape behind the mottled glass above the front door could have been any one of these. When she altered position, light slid across the blurred outline of a face, as if it were being scribbled upon.

The doorbell rang again.

There was a back way, through the tiny garden, over the fence; an escape route, except one that meant going down the stairs, making her briefly visible to whoever was at the door. Who was rattling the handle now, and meter readers didn't do that. They just pushed a card through the slot. Kim backed away from the landing and re-entered her bedroom. Its window gave onto the garden, a drop about twice her own height. There came a splintery whisper from downstairs, as if a metal lever had been inserted into a gap too small for it. The window was a sash and was locked; a screw device that only took seconds if you weren't panicked by intruders. Kim's fingers leaked fear, and kept slipping. The splintery sound became a crack. The window lock gave, and she pulled the rod free. There were footsteps on the stairs, and her heart battered her ribs as she pulled the window up and tossed her bag out. She would follow it. It would take a second. Less. But her top caught on something as she bent to lever herself through the gap: lives have hung on less. Threads, promises.

When she turned, he was in the room with her, his gun pointing directly at her face.

Emma Flyte didn't seem too enamoured of Slough House. She wasn't actually running her finger over surfaces and tutting, but that might have been because she was trying to avoid touching anything. "I'm familiar with the phrase 'office culture,'" she'd said, on looking round. "But yours appears to involve actual spores."

River wouldn't have minded, but he'd cleaned up just last week. Or thought about cleaning up, he now remembered. A plan he'd ultimately rejected in favour of doing sod all.

Flyte had chosen his office to assemble them because Lamb's room barely had space enough to roll your eyes. Lamb, pouting like an emperor in exile, had commandeered River's desk, and was currently rearranging its clutter with his feet. But at least he'd kept his shoes on. River was leaning against a filing cabinet, his instinct being to keep everyone in sight, while Coe was at his own desk, acting, as usual, as if he were alone. Catherine had pulled a chair against the wall and sat calmly, a folded newspaper in her lap, and Louisa and Shirley were either side of the window, like mismatched candlesticks. Ho, of course, had been hustled away by Dogs and Lady Di, so wasn't there. That's all of us, thought River.

Shirley had glowered at both him and Louisa that morning, but her heart hadn't been in it, mostly because she'd wanted to tell them that she'd been right and they'd been wrong. Somewhere around two in the morning, there'd been broken glass all over Ho's street. A body had come through a window, and been spirited away. It all sounded like the kind of thing slow horses daydreamed about while fiddling with spreadsheets—action, excitement, other people getting hurt. Though Shirley's vagueness with the details suggested she hadn't covered herself in glory.

"So Lamb was there all the time?" Louisa asked.

"Go out with Kim, go home to Jackson Lamb," said Shirley. "Ho's priorities are seriously fucked."

Afterwards there'd been police followed by, in short order, the Dogs. It had been, Shirley said, a travelling circus, and nobody had a clue what was going on.

Situation normal, then.

Flyte, who had positioned herself by the door, was casting an eye over the assembled company. River's previous encounter with her had involved his head coming into violent contact with hers, and the fact that this was accidental probably didn't console her as much as it did him. At the time she'd suffered bad bruising, but the damage had left no permanent trace. If Kim was an eight-and-a-half, possibly a nine, Emma Flyte was a ten, possibly an eleven.

What she was focusing on now was Coe, who was fixing buds in his ears.

"What's that?"

He didn't respond.

Lamb said, "He's a bit standoffish. Try punching him in the face."

"Coe," Louisa said. "Someone wants a word."

Coe looked at Flyte.

"What's that?" she repeated.

"iPod."

"Put it away."

"Why?"

Emma Flyte said, "Do I look like I'm here to answer questions? This is a lockdown. No comms."

"It's an iPod," Coe repeated.

"I don't care."

Catherine said, "You're familiar with Slough House's brief, I assume?"

"I've had that pleasure."

"Then you'll know that some of us have . . . issues."

"What's your point, Ms. Standish?"

"Just that listening to music has the effect of calming Mr. Coe down. He's subject to panic attacks, you see."

"And what happens if he doesn't listen to music?"

"I'm not sure," Catherine said. "We've never prevented him before."

"But he carries a knife," Shirley put in.

Flyte looked at Coe. He was thin, white and wearing a hoodie that had bunched around his shoulders: if you were looking for someone to play Bowie on an off-day, he'd not be a bad start. When he had first arrived in Slough House, River recalled, J.K. Coe had been tense as a fist. If he'd loosened up a bit since, he'd become no friendlier.

"Do you always talk about him as if he weren't here?" Flyte asked.

"Yes."

"And is he always like this?"

Shirley said, "It's part of his transitioning process. He's spending six months living as a prick."

Coe didn't bat an eye. He did, though, look as if he were about to say "It's an iPod" again.

Maybe it was this that triggered a sigh from Flyte. "Okay," she said. "Listen to the damn thing."

Coe's only response was to plug himself in.

River glanced at Shirley, who had been known to get angry when a tense situation resolved itself without violence, but she just shook her head as if disappointed but not surprised. She caught his glance, though, and stuck her tongue out. Then looked at Louisa. "I spy," she began.

Louisa said, "Continue with that, and I will kill you. I will kill you dead."

"Well we have to do something. Apart from anything else, I don't plan to quietly starve."

The idea that Shirley could quietly do anything was unnerving.

"We need provisions," she said.

"She has a point."

"I'll go get some treats, yeah?"

"Nobody leaves," said Flyte. "You do know what 'lockdown' means?"

"Nobody's leaving," Lamb explained. "Dander's just popping out for a few minutes."

River, Louisa and Catherine were excavating money from pockets and purses, and passing it to Shirley.

"Just make sure there's nutrition involved," said Catherine.

"And maybe sugar," said Louisa.

"You're not going anywhere," Flyte said.

"Yeah, right," said Shirley. "Back in five."

For a moment it looked as if Flyte might attempt to physically prevent Shirley from going through the door, which both River and Louisa, for different reasons, imagined might be a valuable use of the next five minutes, but it was not to be. Shirley simply ducked under Flyte's arm and was off down the stairs, her heels a receding rhythmic clatter.

Flyte looked at Lamb. "Ever considered instilling discipline into your staff?"

"All the time. I favour the carrot and stick approach."

"Carrot *or* stick."

"Nope. I use the stick to ram the carrot up their arses. That generally gets results." Lamb frowned. "I hope you don't think I'm using metaphor. This is not a fucking poetry reading."

It looked like a fucking poetry reading, though, inasmuch as there were few people there, and none of them stylishly dressed. Well, Flyte was an exception, though River suspected she'd make a plaid skirt and woollen tights look good. As it was, she wore a dark business suit over a white shirt. Her hair was tied back, her eyes were unamused, and he probably ought to stop contemplating how she looked: hot or not, she was Head Dog, and her predecessor had once kicked River in the balls. If she caught him eyeing her up she might follow suit. She probably wanted to anyway, for old times' sake.

Lamb seemed happy enough to engage with her, though. "So you're on Claude Whelan's list of things that make him happy."

"What makes you think that?"

"Well, Lady Di doesn't like you. Usually, that's the fast track to a UB-40. And yet you're still in place. Which means either First Desk fancies you or you've got dirt on him."

"I do my job," Flyte said. "I do it well. Whelan knows that."

"I don't trust him. He's got vicar's eyes."

". . . Vicar's eyes?"

"Too bright. Too shiny. Give him half a chance, he'll start a conversation with you." He turned to River. "I'm devoutly religious, as you know. But priests give me the creeps." Back to Flyte: "He's First Desk because he was in the right place when the music stopped, that's all. Taverner would sell her mother's kidneys for the job, and the thing is, she'd do it well. But Whelan's middle-management. Which is PC for mediocre."

"He's got the Prime Minister onside."

"I rest my case."

Catherine said, "What will happen to Roddy?"

Flyte's eyebrows twitched, which River interpreted as a shrug. "Debriefing."

"Will it be hostile?"

"I don't imagine it will be especially gentle."

River, Louisa and Catherine each contemplated that, two of them with light smiles playing on their lips. J.K. Coe was away with whatever fairies were whispering in his ear, but wasn't—River noticed—miming the piano parts with his fingers. And Lamb had assumed what the slow horses called his hippo-at-rest position: apparently docile, but you wouldn't want to get too close.

Nobody doing anything remotely useful. Just an ordinary day in the office, River thought.

Shirley returned lightly speckled with rain and clutching emergency provisions. Which turned out, on inspection, to comprise two bottles of red wine and a family bag of Haribo.

"Oh, for God's sake," said Louisa, at the same time as Lamb said, "Give me one of those."

Shirley offered him the Haribo.

"Very funny."

She passed him a bottle of wine.

"I can't work out which is going to be worse," Flyte said. "The alcohol intake or the sugar rush."

Catherine said, "You used my money to buy wine?"

Shirley said, "Yeah, see, what I thought was, there'd be that much more for the rest of us."

"Well, you can't fault her logic," Lamb said. He'd opened his bottle, and was drinking straight from it. "Okay," he said. "Brainstorm." He looked at Flyte. "I hope you don't find the term offensive."

She shrugged. "I'm not epileptic."

"No, but you're blonde. Some of you get touchy when brains are mentioned." He looked round the room. "Someone wants to kill Ho. Someone not one of you, I mean. Any ideas?"

"Kim," said Shirley. "His girlfriend," she added.

"Why? Apart from the obvious."

River said, "She's way out of his league. Way, way out."

"Doesn't always result in homicide." Lamb looked at Flyte. "You ever shag a two?"

". . . I'm not answering that."

"There you go."

Louisa said, "She's scamming him. Has to be."

"Okay. And while he has more money than the rest of you, on account of he had the sense to be the only child of a successful businessman, he's still not worth the long-term investment of a serious con artist. If it was just his money, she'd have cleaned him out and hit the bricks months ago. And probably not bothered hanging around to have him whacked, unless she was acting on a purely aesthetic basis." He looked at Flyte again. "I'm going to assume you don't have your pity-fucks executed."

"Not so far. But I'm thinking of introducing a shoot-to-kill policy for fat bastards."

"There. Ten minutes, and you're fitting right in."

Louisa said, "Information."

"That has to be it. Let's face it, Ho's a dick, but he knows his way around a password. If he didn't, I'd have squashed him into a plastic bag and dropped him in a river long ago. So this female—"

"Kim."

"His girlfriend."

"—whatever, she's a honeytrap. What do we know about her?"

"She's Chinese," Shirley said.

River said, "She *looked* Chinese."

"Yeah," said Lamb. "Let's not jump to racist conclusions. She might be normal, but just look Chinese. One other thing, though—"

J.K. Coe gave a start, and sat upright.

"Oh, did we wake him?"

Louisa, who was nearest, kicked Coe, and he reached up and pulled his earbuds loose.

Lamb said, "Excellent, I do like it when people at least pretend to pay attention. One other thing I forgot to mention. Whoever she's in cahoots with was responsible for Abbotsfield."

The silence that greeted this was marred only by the sound of Shirley masticating a Haribo.

Then J.K. Coe said, "I think we've got a problem."

During the winter the day tires early, and is out of the door by five: coat on, heading west, see you tomorrow. The night then takes the long shift, and though it sleeps through most of it, and pays scant attention to what's occurring in its quieter corners, one way or the other it muddles through until morning. But while summer's here the day hangs around to enjoy the sunshine, and allowing for a post-lunch lull, and the odd faltering step when its five o'clock shadows appear, generally powers on as long as it's able. And in those unexpectedly stretched-out hours, there's more opportunity for things to come to light; or, failing that, for light to fall on things.

The light that fell on Regent's Park that afternoon cast perfect shadows. As if designed by a professional, these were sliced laterally by venetian blinds to etch themselves onto desks and walls and floors, turning the upstairs offices into pages from a clothing catalogue, needing only model or mannequin to complete the effect. But as with swans, all the actual work at the Park went on out of sight; as picturesquely industrious as the upper storeys looked, it was down on the hub where the sweat and toil happened; where Lady Di Taverner and Claude Whelan gazed through glass walls at the boys and girls monitoring the world, and all the varied realities it had to offer. Here, the hunt for the Abbotsfield killers continued. It was slow progress. This surprised nobody. If you turn up out of nowhere and kill everything in sight, you don't leave much to be tracked by. The origins of the killers' odyssey were shrouded in static. Their jeep first appeared on CCTV eight miles north of Sheffield; backtracking took it to the outskirts of that city, where it disappeared in an electrical storm: the jerky whirr and buzz of too many cameras watching too much traffic, and skipping too quickly between too many points of view. Even a jeep could disappear in the stillness between digital breaths.

And when this happens, conspiracy theories blossom like mould. There must be a reason why the jeep had been able to evade surveillance so effectively; there must be an underlying cause. And there was a reason, and the reason was this: shit happens. When everything goes smoothly and the wind blows fair, the men in the jeep are arrested before they've finished oiling their weapons, and their victims continue their lives without ever knowing the fate that sidestepped them. But when shit happens the bad guys disappear, and their victims' names grace headlines, and the boys and girls of the hub work on through the everlasting day, in a doomed attempt to atone for failures that others have laid at their door.

Meanwhile, other hunts were afoot as the afternoon light continued to poke and pry into disused crannies. Files were opened—some of them actual cardboard folders, containing actual paper, the idea being that to steal these you'd have to be in the building, whereas digital theft required no presence—and perused for hot content, this being highlighted for First Desk's attention. Members of Parliament aren't spied on as a matter of course, though many believe themselves to be. But the awkward customers among them, and the notoriously indiscreet, the suspiciously innocent and the flamboyantly wayward, all pass across the Service's radar, often at the behest of their own leaders, for while the Service exists to preserve the security of the nation, the insecurities of the political elite need tending too. The current Prime Minister, like many of his predecessors, had an overtuned ear for possible treachery—he had, as a wag once noted, predicted seven of the last two backbench rebellions—and throughout his inexplicably prolonged residence at Number Ten had demanded in-depth reports on pretty much every MP in his party who had achieved more than two column inches or seven minutes' airtime on consecutive days. This had resulted in a lot of paperwork, and much of what it revealed was never in fact disclosed to the PM, it being determined that the information in question was politically irrelevant, or personally embarrassing, or too potentially useful to be squandered so lightly. And as a result, in Molly Doran's collection there existed a file on Dennis Gimball; a file tagged not with a black label, nor with a red or a green—any one of which would have pegged him as requiring close attention, up to and including discreet retirement from public service, as several former Home and Foreign Secretaries might attest—but with a white label to which a small cross had been added by hand, probably Molly's own, to indicate that between its covers might be found a quirk or a dropped stitch, an unexpected weave in the fabric of a life; a chink into which a makeshift key could be slotted, and made to turn.

Claude Whelan didn't get out much. He travelled from home to Regent's Park; from Regent's Park back home again; he shuttled between the Park and Whitehall; he mostly lunched at his desk. Occasionally, true, he would be called upon to attend gatherings further afield, but unlike his lamented/lamentable—according to choice—predecessor Ingrid Tearney, he spent as little time as possible on the Washington circuit, holding that if improved communications didn't result in fewer air miles, they weren't worth the fibre optics that produced them. And when the invitation was impossible to refuse, he spent the odd early evening nursing a G&T at one members-only watering hole or another, between whose antique furniture big beasts like Peter Judd could be glimpsed, plotting their comebacks. But for the most part Claude was an office-bod: papers arrived on his desk and were signed and spirited away again; messages pinged into his inbox, and were swallowed by electrical circuitry. There was no shame in being tethered to the furniture. No especial dignity either, or heroism: everything a joe might endure could happen to a drone, treachery not excepted. Whelan well remembered his first traitor, a man he'd shared projects with, sat in meetings with, discussed geopolitics with over a sandwich, back, as they said, in the day. The man had, it turned out, been prey to demons, the kind which had left him in need of money, and open to temptation. A shopping list of secrets had been found in his flat, and a roster of potential buyers. It had been Claude himself who had suggested that the opportunity for spreading misinformation was too good to miss; that his erstwhile friend, if no longer reliable, was at least a valuable conduit. It had been Claude who devised Operation Shopping List, a plan that misfired when the embryonic traitor committed suicide before its full implementation. All very messy, and none of it involving travel. No, Claude had never felt his horizons limited by his disinclination to abandon his safe places; he'd seen enough, good and bad, without having to pack. Not getting out much wasn't a weakness. It was Claude, playing to his strengths.

Today, though, was a day for leaving the office. The file on Dennis Gimball had landed on his desk, and a swift read through was enough to have Whelan rearranging his afternoon. Apart from anything else, Gimball had lately taken delight in stamping on Claude's reputation. Claude wasn't a vindictive man, but this was largely because the opportunity to be one had rarely presented itself. In this he resembled most other people, with the added advantage that he was Head of the Secret Service, with access to files like the one in front of him now.

But before leaving, he had another matter to deal with.

"This man Ho," he said.

"He's downstairs, sir."

Which had various meanings in Regent's Park. Claude was downstairs himself, inasmuch as he was on the hub. But further below lay rooms where you really didn't want to spend much time, if you were keen on leaving them under your own steam. As opposed to being stretchered out, or carted away in a bucket, by someone much like the man he was talking to now: one of Emma Flyte's Dogs.

"Who's talking to him?"

"Nobody, sir. We were told to leave him to sweat."

A good, if obvious, ploy. Sooner or later, if you were in one of the downstairs rooms, with its single plastic chair whose legs weren't quite of equal length, you would start to wonder why the floor was ever so slightly off-level, and what the tap in the corner was for, when there wasn't a basin there. Just an open drain, to allow for runoff.

After a few hours' contemplation, this could start to seem a pressing matter.

There was, as yet, no certainty that the attack on Roderick Ho was part and parcel of the Abbotsfield massacre. "Guns are currency," Whelan had said to Lady Di earlier. "It's possible the Abbotsfield killers ditched theirs as soon as they were able. And other bad actors picked them up. In which case what we have is a coincidence."

"I don't like those."

"No, well, neither do I. But if it's the same crew, it's a very different plan. Murdering random strangers is one thing. This was an attempted hit on Service personnel. Chalk and cheese, no?"

"Yes. Or . . ."

"Or what?"

"Or someone was tying up a loose end," said Lady Di. "Perhaps Ho was aiding them, intentionally or not. In which case . . ."

In which case they might want to sever the connection.

Diana had a point, and it needed testing. If there was a link between Ho and Abbotsfield they had to discover it, and the fastest way would be to squeeze Ho none too gently. But Roderick Ho was a slow horse, and though on one level this meant he could be screwed up and tossed away like so much waste paper, there was a complication in that he was one of Jackson Lamb's crew, and Lamb was inclined to play rough when you messed with his things. Which meant that any attempt to do so would have to involve snookering Lamb: not a step to take lightly, because if it failed, Whelan would be left standing on scorched earth. Lamb knew more about Whelan than Whelan was comfortable with. And Whelan had yet to think himself out of this corner, so for now had to tread carefully.

Lady Di might have delivered Ho. But it was up to Whelan what happened next.

So before he headed out to beard Dennis Gimball, he gave the instruction: "Keep sweating him for now. Another couple of hours' soft time. It'll pay off in the long run."

Because soft time or not, a few hours in below-stairs accommodation and Roderick Ho would turn to jelly; just a messed-up ball of anxious worry, dying to spill his guts.

Well for a start, thought Ho, the plumbing's fucked.

Single tap, jutting out of the wall at a height you'd have to be seriously below average to use comfortably: whose idea was that? But this was what you got when you used cowboys. You'd have thought the Service would rise to something a bit less cheap, a bit more reliable, but the austerity bug bit deep. Look at Slough House, and his own kit—years out of date, and while Roddy Ho could make a PC cable of any vintage come rising from a basket like a snake, that didn't make it right to foist him off with substandard gear. It had long been on his mind to raise the issue first chance he got, but he wondered whether now was, in fact, the right time. People here had problems of their own. Even the floor was wonky. And besides, there were other matters to discuss.

Someone had tried to kill him last night.

Bad as that was, he couldn't complain that it wasn't being taken seriously. Here he was, after all, in protective custody; ferried by Diana Taverner, no less; the Park's Second Desk (Ops), who hadn't said much on the ride over, so rattled she was at how close they'd come to losing him. He'd nearly patted her hand, in fact—just in simple reassurance that he was still among the living—but had recognised that a physical overture might be misconstrued: another time, another place, lady. Because there was Kim, his girlfriend, to consider, and seriously: Lady Di ought to be focusing on keeping him safe right now, instead of allowing herself to be distracted by middle-aged fantasies.

(Middle-aged was pure chivalry, mind. She had to be in her fifties.)

Anyway, here he was, in the bowels of the Park, having been escorted here by the Dogs, the Service's cop squad. Who hadn't been talkative, and had forgotten his request for an energy drink while he waited. Still, if he got thirsty, he could help himself from that tap. Nobody could say Roddy Ho wasn't prepared to rough it while the powers-that-be worked out the best way to protect him.

Dragging the chair to a corner, Roddy entertained himself by discovering how sharp an angle he could balance it at before toppling to the floor. This proved to be about half as sharp as his first attempt but, it turned out, he had plenty of time to improve.

J.K. Coe said, "I think we've got a problem."

Lamb said to Flyte, "He doesn't speak much. Perhaps he's making an effort on your account. Let's see." He turned to Coe and said, very slowly, "Why. Might we have. A problem?"

Then he looked at Flyte again, tapping a finger to his temple. "Bit simple," he mouthed.

Coe twisted his earbud cord round his fingers. "There's been another incident."

"Did you wet yourself again? Don't worry, we didn't notice."

Catherine said, "Let's hear him out, shall we?"

"A bomb on a train," Coe said.

"And that came to you via the music, did it?" said Lamb. "Might have to try listening to jazz myself. Except I'd rather rub sand in my eyes."

He put his bottle to his lips, and drank wine like it was water.

"He's not listening to jazz," Catherine said.

"Yeah, funny thing, I'd got that far myself."

"We're in lockdown," said Flyte. "No comms. And you've been listening to the radio?"

Shirley said, "Give him some slack. He carries a knife." She'd found a plastic glass somewhere, and poured herself some wine, and her mouth was red from that or the Haribo. She looked like she'd applied lippy while no one was looking.

"Where was the bomb?" said River. "How many hurt?"

"Nobody. The device was found and disabled."

"Where?"

"On an HST from Bristol. Heading into Paddington."

The others already had their phones out, checking the news websites.

Flyte said, "Do I have to say this again? Turn your devices off. We're in lockdown."

"It's because you're new," Lamb said. "They're testing the boundaries."

"When I need your input, I'll ask."

River, eyes on his phone, said, "Nobody's claimed responsibility yet."

"Yeah, well," Lamb said. "Taking the credit for fucking up, that would be your department." He looked at Coe. "And as for you. I make a big announcement about the Abbotsfield killers having a crack at Ho, and you trump it with a story about nobody being hurt somewhere else?" He shook his head. "We have to start playing cards for money round here."

"There's more, isn't there?" said Louisa.

Coe had put his hands on the desk in front of him, and his fingers seemed agile and twitchy. "Yes."

Lamb's sigh would have filled a sail. "A few fucking details wouldn't go amiss. Whenever you're ready."

Coe collected the agile fingers on his right hand and turned them into a fist. He unbent them one at a time, still staring at the desk in front of him. "One. Destroy the village."

River opened his mouth to speak, but changed his mind.

"Two. Poison the watering hole."

Lamb leaned back in his chair, looking grim.

"Three. Cripple the railway."

Coe folded his hand away again, and stuffed it into the pouch of his hoodie.

There was a short silence, broken by Shirley. "Am I missing something?"

"He's saying these aren't random acts of terrorism," said River, not taking his eyes off Coe. "It's a destabilisation strategy."

"A bunch of penguins get shredded?" said Shirley. "Who's that supposed to destabilise? David Attenborough?"

"It's not the penguins," said Catherine. "It's the name. Is that what you're saying?"

Coe nodded.

"The Watering Hole," said River. "Why is that significant?"

"Think about it," said Lamb.

They thought about it; all except Coe, who seemed to have withdrawn into his private universe again.

At length, Emma Flyte said, "Well, if it's a destabilisation plan, it's not working, is it? Because whatever grand plan they're working to, the effects still look random. Which is bad enough, but hardly world-shattering. I mean, Abbotsfield? It's a tragedy, but nobody had heard of the place last week."

"Congratulations," said Lamb. "You're now an honorary slow horse."

"Because I contributed?"

"No, because you missed the fucking point."

"But she's right," said Louisa. "If this goes on, people'll get nervy about public spaces, worried what might happen. But it's not like they'll think some supervillain has a strategy. I mean, if this was happening in a tiny state somewhere—"

She broke off.

"There you go," said Lamb. "Penny drops." He looked at Coe. "They're operating to a plan that might pacify a local population. Because it's all singular, isn't it? *The* village. *The* watering hole."

Coe nodded.

"It was never meant for a state the size of Britain."

"So why," River began, then stopped. Then said: "If the strategy's not going to achieve its original aim, why is it being deployed?"

"And as long as we're playing twenty questions," said Lamb, "anyone want to hazard a guess as to how come our mad monk here recognises it?"

"Oh, Christ," said River. "It's one of ours, isn't it?"

Coe nodded.

The others stared at each other in incomprehension. Only Lamb, who had closed his eyes, and Catherine, who was shaking her head, seemed to grasp the implications.

Lamb said, "Oh, for fuck's sake. He might be simple, but compared to you lot he's a walking Sudoku. The plan they're working to isn't a foreign plot to destabilise Britain, it's a British plot devised to destabilise some troublesome tin-pot nation. And no, murdering penguins and failing to blow up trains isn't going to bring the country to its knees, but when these jokers, whoever they are, reveal that they're operating to a strategy developed by British Intelligence to undermine developing nations, well. Anybody want to join the dots?"

"It'll be an omnifuckingshambles," offered Shirley.

"For once, you have a point."

River said, "Poison the watering hole? How old is this plan?"

"It doesn't matter," Catherine said. "It may not be state of the art, but it's still a black op. People have died."

"And penguins," Shirley added.

Louisa said, "It could have been a lot worse. How many wine bars are called The Watering Hole?"

"How sure are we any of this is true?" said Emma Flyte. "I mean, forgive my scepticism. But—it's Coe, isn't it? Mr. Coe here mumbles something about this being a British plot, and just like that you're all convinced. I'd need to hear more, personally. And you're not going to smoke," she added, as a cigarette appeared in Lamb's fist.

"Ordinarily I wouldn't dream of it," said Lamb. "But it's the only thing keeps my upset stomach in check."

Before Emma could reply, Catherine said, "Seriously. Don't call his bluff."

Lamb inhaled, blew smoke everywhere, then said to Coe: "Well, you going to tell us the origins of this plot? Or is that your party piece done?"

Coe glanced at Lamb, then looked down at the desk in front of him. "It's from a working paper the weasels produced post-war. A strategy for destabilising a developing region, should the need arise."

"Before he was a fuck-up," Lamb explained to Emma Flyte, "he used to be a dickhead. Unless I mean egghead. I get them mixed up."

"You worked across the river?" said Flyte.

Coe nodded.

"Psych Eval," Shirley said. "He knows about the history of black ops."

"Maybe so," said Flyte. "It still sounds like a reach to me."

"Except for the watering hole bit," said Catherine quietly. "Because Louisa's right. There are plenty of bars called The Watering Hole. But if they'd chosen one of them, nobody would have said hey, watering hole! They'd have said, they bombed a bar."

"And this paper, it was dug out of its drawer a while ago," Coe said. "Some bright spark suggested it had value as a template. You take the basic principles and apply them on a larger scale. Or replicate them across a wider region, so the same events happen in more than one location at the same time." He paused, then said, "It was one of those games that get played over there. Never likely to be put into operation. Except some of them are."

"But this one wasn't."

He shrugged. "Is now."

"I'm not convinced," said Flyte.

"Yeah, well, the thing is, fuck off," Lamb told her. "Because you're overlooking the clincher."

"Which is?"

"Which is where whoever's doing this got the Watering Hole paper from in the first place."

"Ho," said River, Louisa and Shirley in unison.

"Poor Roddy," Catherine murmured.

"And Kim—" Louisa began.

"—his girlfriend—" inserted River.

"—must be the point of contact between him and the bad actors."

"Which explains why someone tried to whack him."

"Twice."

"And why Ho's got a girlfriend," finished Shirley.

Flyte looked like someone had just clapped her round the head with a bedpan.

"Someone tried to kill our resident tech-head," explained Lamb. "His colleagues here are suggesting that that's because he was honeytrapped into handing over this destabilisation template. And whoever he handed it over to didn't want him spilling the beans before they were ready."

"So why didn't Ho say he'd done that?" Flyte objected. "Once he realised people were trying to kill him?"

"Well, there's a strong chance he hasn't yet noticed that that's what's going on," said Louisa.

"There's a reason you lot are all here, isn't there?" said Flyte after a while. "I keep forgetting that."

"Whereas your own brilliant career," Louisa reminded her, "hangs by a thread that's dangling from Claude Whelan's thumb."

Louisa quite liked Emma, but didn't see that she had to take any crap from her.

"Careful," Lamb said. "She bites. Meanwhile, there's a simple way we can find out whether Coe's talking through his arse. Anyone want to hazard a guess?"

There was a pause.

"We could torture him," Shirley suggested.

Coe flicked her a glance she could have sharpened her buzzcut with.

River said, "He's only counted to three."

"It's nearly a shame you're an idiot," Lamb said. "When with a bit of application, you might have amounted to a halfwit. Because yes, in this rare instance, you're right. Coe's only counted to three." He tipped the neck of his wine bottle in Coe's direction, and took a drag on his cigarette before saying, "Okay, Mr. PMT, or PTSD, or whatever it is you've got. Do enlighten us. What are the nasty mans going to do next?"

"Assassinate a populist leader," said Coe.

The maroon blazer gave him the edge, thought Dennis Gimball, admiring himself in the full-length mirror. Anyone could wear a suit. Anyone did, mostly. But it took style to carry a less conventional look, and in this business, style was at a premium. How many politicians were remembered for what they wore? Not counting Michael Foot, obviously. He shifted to a profile, slid his hand between buttons three and four and puffed his chest out. He'd look good on a five pound note, he decided. Hell, he'd look good on a *stamp*.

He hurriedly withdrew his hand when Dodie entered the room. Not hurriedly enough, though.

"Were you posing, dear?"

"Just . . . scratching."

"Well you'd better not do that in front of the cameras. Not either of those things."

"One is supposed to pose for cameras."

"There's posing and posing." She eyed him critically: not the man himself, but the figure he cast in the mirror. He was carrying a few too many pounds, which was okay for politics. But if it all bottomed out and they ended up on *Strictly*, he'd need supervision. "Did you listen to the news?" she asked. "There's been another bomb."

"Oh God."

"Nobody hurt."

"Oh God. Well, no. I mean, good. Where? When?"

"On a train," Dodie said. "I'll get the news desk to email the details. When you're asked about it, which you will be, sound like you know more than you're saying. As if high-level intel crosses your desk."

Because these were also rules: sound like you know more than you can say; act like you'll do more than you intend. And when campaigning, lie your head off—the referendum's other great legacy.

Dennis nodded and was about to reply when his phone rang. Unknown number. He frowned, prepared to get dusty if it was a cold caller.

It wasn't.

"Speaking . . . Oh. Oh. When, now? . . . I'm not sure I have time . . . Oh. Oh. Well, in that case, yes then. At the flat, yes. Yes."

He disconnected, slightly cross-eyed, which tended to happen when he was puzzled. Dodie had spoken to him about it, but it was difficult to train someone out of an unconscious physical reaction. Electric shocks might work.

"What?" she said.

"That was Claude Whelan," he said.

"Claude . . . Claude *Whelan*? MI5?"

He nodded.

"What did he want?"

"He wants to talk," her husband said.

There you go," said Lamb. "Soon as a people's pinup gets whacked, we'll know we were right." He leaned back further, and shuffled his feet on River's desktop. Items fell to the floor. "Wake me when that happens."

River said to Coe, "That's it? A populist leader?"

Coe shrugged. "There's always one."

"It'll be Zafar Jaffrey," Shirley said. "Has to be."

"Why?"

"He's the nearest thing to a popular politician in years."

"Popul*ist*," said Coe.

"Same difference."

"Yeah, no, it really isn't," Louisa told her.

Catherine said, "If everybody talks at once, we're not going to get anywhere."

"Are you their nursery nurse?" asked Flyte.

"No, why, are you their new stepmum?"

Lamb said, "Well, this *is* going well." He swung his feet to the floor, with an agility that surprised no one bar Emma Flyte. "But I'm overdue for a Donald. You lot squabble amongst yourselves."

He stole Catherine's newspaper on his way out.

". . . Donald?" Flyte looked disturbed, more at Lamb's expression than his sudden departure from her custody.

"Trump," Louisa explained.

"Thank God for that. I thought he meant Duck."

"Dennis Gimball," said Catherine.

"Are we still doing rhyming slang?"

She ignored that. "If I was looking for a populist leader in the current climate, he's who I'd choose."

"Sooner you than me," Louisa said. "I wouldn't vote for him with a bargepole."

"I wasn't suggesting I approve of him," said Catherine. "More that, if I was planning on assassinating somebody in that category, he'd be top of my list."

"I'd kill Peter Judd," said Shirley. "Or Piers Morgan."

"Morgan's not a populist leader."

"Whatever."

River said to Coe, "Exactly how many stages were there to this blueprint?"

Coe didn't look up. He spread his hand out on his desk again instead, and seemed to draw inspiration from the number of fingers he could see. "Five."

"Five," River repeated.

"I think."

"You *think*?"

Coe shrugged.

"Because it's kind of an important detail."

"Yes. But I didn't know that at the time."

"So this was just, what, some random memo that crossed your desk?"

"It was something that came up when I was researching something else. I wouldn't have remembered it at all if it hadn't been for the penguins."

River said, "Well, now you have remembered it, can you give us a clue as to what the fifth stage might be?"

"Hey! Spoilers," said Shirley.

Everyone stared at her.

"Well, we haven't had the assassination yet."

"The general idea is, we might try to stop that bit," Louisa explained.

"You're all crazy," Flyte said.

"We prefer the term alternatively sane."

"If any of this is even remotely likely," Flyte continued, "you need to inform the Park."

"Yeah, right," River said. "Excuse me, Park, but our team gave one of your secret documents to some bad guys, and they're busy running rampage with it up and down the country. Can you imagine how that'll go down? And let me emphasise, we're already not popular."

"It isn't about popularity."

"No, but it is about who's left standing. And trust me, Di Taverner will dismantle Slough House brick by brick first opportunity she gets. And this, if you're still unsure, would count as one of those."

"Taverner isn't in charge. Whelan is."

"You keep telling yourself that."

"You're starting to sound like your boss," Flyte said.

"He didn't say 'fuck' enough," Louisa pointed out.

"Who didn't?" And this was Lamb back, of course. He could always be trusted to enter a conversation at its most awkward point.

"Your mini-me here," Flyte told him. "He's picked up your habit of twisted thinking."

"Has he? Because I'm not sure I've ever put that habit down." Lamb did put himself down, though: heavily, on River's chair once more. "What do you suppose they're doing with Ho?"

"I imagine they're trying to discover what connects him to the Abbotsfield killers," Flyte said.

"Yeah, I didn't think they'd invited him round for tea and jaffa cakes. What I meant was, what's the current protocol for debriefing squashy bodies? Will they be plugging him into something, hitting him with something or injecting him with something?"

Catherine murmured words. Nobody heard what they were.

"None of those are standard practice," Flyte said after a moment.

Lamb said, "Yeah, right, nor is pissing in a lift. But it happens. So which one is it, and how long will it take? Bearing in mind that Ho hasn't been trained not to reveal things under pressure."

"And that he knows fuck-all about anything," River muttered.

Flyte said, "The first thing they'll do with him is nothing."

"And is that nothing the kind you plug him into, hit him with or inject?"

"I meant literally, they won't do anything with him. They'll lock him in a room and let him sweat. Probably for a few hours. By the time they get to asking him questions, he'll be an open book."

"I hope they've got their coloured pencils ready," Lamb said. "So chances are, they haven't started on him yet?"

"Why does that matter?"

Lamb bared his teeth in an unholy grin. "It gives us a little time."

". . . You're going to have to elaborate."

Catherine leaned forward and gave Emma her sweetest smile. "Oh, I think Mr. Lamb has a plan."

"What makes you so sure?"

"Because he claimed he was going to empty his bowels. And he never takes less than fifteen minutes to do that."

Lamb smiled proudly. "If a job's worth doing," he said.

"So where did you really go?" Flyte asked.

"To fetch this," said Lamb, and he unfolded the newspaper he was still holding and showed her Marcus's gun.

Claude Whelan wouldn't have been surprised if a butler had opened the door. It was a mews flat not a mansion, but still: a grammar school boy, he retained that sense of expecting the worst when dealing with privilege. In the event, though, it was Dodie Gimball—arch-columnist; keeper of the flame—who answered the bell. She wore a knee-length grey skirt and matching jacket over a white blouse, which looked to Whelan like battle gear. Her smile was as false as her nose. The latter had cost her upwards of twenty grand; the former, years of practice.

"Mr. Whelan. So *marvelous* of you to visit."

"Mrs. Gimball."

"Oh, do call me Dodie. I imagine you're familiar with so many details of my life, it seems artificial to have you stand on ceremony."

Given his awareness of what her nose job had cost, it would have been disingenuous to contest that. "Dodie, then."

"You're on your own? No armed guards or, what do you call them? Dogs?"

"I don't know how these stories get about," he said.

"Of course you don't. Can I take your coat?"

"Thank you."

The rain had passed over, and while the eaves were still dripping and the gutters puddled, the sun was peeping from behind tattered clouds, and Whelan's raincoat quite dry. As he handed it to her, as she hung it on a hook, Dennis Gimball emerged from the front room. Or parlour, Whelan supposed.

"Ha. George Smiley, no less."

"If only," Whelan replied. "Thank you for taking the time to see me."

"I was given the distinct impression I had little choice in the matter."

There was an aggressive edge there, a bluster, which surprised Whelan not at all. Gimball's public performances always contained this element; an aggrieved awareness that not everyone present held him in the esteem he deserved—as compared to, say, Peter Judd, who successfully conveyed the impression that he gave no fucks for anyone who didn't cheer his every syllable. But Judd was presently waiting out a hiccup in his career—long story—while Gimball apparently presented a threat to the PM's position. One of the unforeseen consequences of Brexit, reflected Whelan, was that it had elevated to positions of undue prominence any number of nasty little toerags. Ah well. The people had spoken.

And if Gimball wanted aggression, that's what he'd get.

"No," he said. "You didn't."

Dennis looked taken aback, but Dodie pursed her lips, as if having a presentiment confirmed.

"I'm not sure I'm going to offer you a drink," she said.

"I won't be staying long. Perhaps we could . . ." He gestured towards the open door.

"If we must," said Dennis, leading the way.

The room had been knocked through, so there were windows at both ends, allowing more daylight than the property's outside appearance suggested; allowing, too, a pair of overstuffed sofas, facing each other across the middle of the floor. Perhaps the Gimballs each had their own, and lay in parallel, purring across the divide. For the moment, though, neither sat, nor offered Whelan the opportunity to do so.

"It might be best if I spoke to your husband in private," he said to Dodie.

"Seriously?"

"It's always best to say that up-front," he said. "That way, nobody can pretend they weren't warned."

"Oh, if warnings are being passed around, here's one for you.

If you attempt to come the heavy with my husband, you'll understand the meaning of the power of the press."

She thought herself impregnable, Whelan knew. What she hadn't yet realised was that the leash her editor kept her on might be long, but remained a leash. She just hadn't felt its limit yet. But her editor imagined a knighthood in his future, and her paper's proprietor a seat in the Lords. There was little doubt whose interests would win if it came to bare knuckles.

He looked at Dennis. "I gather you have plans for this evening."

"That's no secret," Gimball said. "It's a public engagement, widely advertised. You're welcome to attend, in fact. Come along. You might learn something."

"And you're going to use the occasion to make wild accusations about Zafar Jaffrey."

"Wild accusations?"

"That's the information I have."

"I don't suppose there's any point my asking where it comes from? No, of course not. The establishment closing ranks, as usual."

Dennis Gimball, as all present well knew, was the public school-educated son of the owner of a High Street fashion chain. It was funny, if tiresome, how self-appointed rebels always believed themselves to have ploughed their own furrow.

Whelan said, "Be that as it may, with the national mood as it is, there's a feeling that it would not be useful to have you indulge in rabble rousing."

". . . 'Rabble rousing?'"

"Stirring people up."

"I'm aware of what the phrase means, Whelan, I'm questioning your application of it."

"There've already been public disturbances in several cities, mostly in areas with a high immigrant population. It's in nobody's interests that we see any more."

"I'm flattered that you think anything I say could have such a wide-ranging effect."

"You really shouldn't be."

"But what we're seeing is the natural revulsion felt by the law-abiding majority to the atrocity in Abbotsfield. And if you imagine I'm going to keep quiet when I have information which might lead to those responsible being apprehended, well. That's rather casting doubt on my patriotism, wouldn't you say?"

"Nobody doubts your patriotism for a moment. But if you have any such information, I'd suggest you convey it to the appropriate authorities rather than deliver it to a public gathering."

"The appropriate authorities being . . . ?"

"The police, obviously. Or, if you prefer, you could give it directly to me."

"Ah yes. To be suppressed or twisted, no doubt."

"That's not how we operate."

"Really? Because my impression was, the PM speaks and his poodle barks. That's really why you're here, isn't it? Nothing to do with Jaffrey. Everything to do with the effect that what I say will have on the PM's chances of remaining in office."

"I'm not interested in party politics, Mr. Gimball. I'm interested in national security."

"And a fine job you're making of it. What was today's triumph? A bomb on a train? How many people have to die before you admit you're unfit for office?"

"Nobody died today, Mr. Gimball."

"But twelve people died at Abbotsfield," Dodie Gimball said. Up until now, she'd been watching this like a ferret watching someone juggle eggs. "And that would be on your watch, would it not?"

He wanted to say: there's no system in the world can prevent a bunch of homicidal lunatics shooting up a village if they get the urge—no system, that is, that anyone sensible would want to see. It was a question of balance. You lived in a democracy, and accepted that certain freedoms came hand in hand with certain dangers, or you opted for full-scale oppression, which severely curtailed the opportunities for unofficial slaughter, but potentially maximised the official kind. But this was not a conversation to

have with Dennis Gimball. So instead he said, "I take full responsibility for all the failures of the Service. And have a duty to
prevent, as far as it's in my ability to do so, any further such failures. Which is why I have to ask you not to make the speech you're
intending to make tonight, Mr. Gimball. It might have serious
consequences."

Gimball had puffed himself up now. Someone, somewhere,
had once used the word Churchillian in his presence, and the
memory lingered on. "Serious consequences my arse." His eyes
flickered towards his wife, but she seemed onboard with the
vulgarity, so he continued. "All you're doing is shoring up your
own position. You might not be interested in party politics, but
you're still its creature, and as long as I'm a threat to the PM,
I'm a threat to you too."

He evidently rather liked the idea of being a threat. His eyes
had acquired a little light. The image that occurred to Whelan,
oddly, was marsh gas: flickering flames where gas was escaping.
He'd never seen the phenomenon; only read about it.

"And I can assure you—"

Enough, thought Whelan.

"Dancing Bear," he said.

Gimball stopped mid-sentence.

"Do you need me to say more?"

". . . I have no idea what you're talking about."

"We both know that's not the case."

Dodie Gimball's face had sharpened to a point, all but
her expensive nose, which retained its shape while the rest
of her features contracted. Whelan's reading was, the name was
strange to her, but its implications weren't. Which didn't matter
either way. She had never been the intended target of any necessary revelation.

He said to her, "I did warn you."

"Dennis and I have no secrets."

"Perhaps not from each other. But there are a lot of people out
there who might find your husband's . . . proclivities surprising."

"Dancing Bear doesn't even exist any more," Gimball said. "It closed down years ago. And what of it, anyway? It was a perfectly legal establishment."

"So I understand."

"Just a little bit of dressing up."

Whelan nodded. His face was blank of any obvious emotion: while he had no qualms about dropping a bomb in the Gimballs' parlour, he didn't want to give the impression he was enjoying it. That would lack class.

Dodie had gathered herself now. She said to her husband, "Darling, should I call Erica?" Then, to Whelan, "Our lawyer."

Before Whelan could answer, Gimball was shaking his head. "No. No. Let's just wait and . . ."

See, probably. The word escaped him. Or suggested another implication:

"I suppose you're going to tell me there are photographs."

"Good God, no."

". . . No?"

"No, I'm not going to tell you that. It would be a little retro, wouldn't it? A few polaroids in a manila envelope? We've moved on since those days."

"Spit it out," said Dodie.

"There's video. Do you really think a club like Dancing Bear would pass up the chance to film its members having fun? That was its main revenue stream. If we hadn't bought up its archive, you'd have heard from its proprietors by now. Given your rise to prominence since."

Dennis was shaking his head, though more as an indication that he was still in his denial phase than in actual disbelief.

"So here we are, then. Fair warning. If you go ahead with the speech you're planning, your career will be over before the shipping forecast's aired. I'm not suggesting the evening news, nor even tomorrow's papers. All due respect, Mrs. Gimball, but they're no more of the moment than a polaroid would be. No, we all know that Twitter, YouTube, reach parts of the planet where they're still puzzling out the wheelbarrow. And you'll be tomorrow's big star. I'd ask you both to consider that carefully."

There was nothing more to say on either side, so he left them there and made his own way to the front door. But Gimball caught him as he was retrieving his raincoat, and barred his way, looking as if he hoped there were something that might be said or done to render the last few minutes impotent. But hope was all it was. So it was almost with pity that Whelan said, "I lied, by the way. I do that sometimes, for effect," and reached into the pocket of his coat and took out an envelope. It was creamy white, the kind birthday cards arrive in, and wasn't sealed, and when he held it slantwise a single photograph slid out, face up. It showed Dennis Gimball in a happy mood. He was on a small stage, and appeared to be singing—karaoke, probably—dressed in what Claire, Whelan's wife, would almost certainly identify as a flapper dress. It brought to mind *The Great Gatsby*, anyway.

As Gimball studied it, the way one might an alien artifact, Dodie appeared at his shoulder. She glanced at the photo in his hand, no more, and then at her husband with what Whelan identified as sympathy.

At Whelan himself, she directed a gaze of pure hate.

Gimball spoke. "There's no crime in it."

"Nobody suggested there was."

"No one gets hurt by what I do."

"I doubt anybody will claim that. No, I think what most people are going to do is laugh, Dennis. I think they're going to laugh their fucking hearts out."

Afterwards, Whelan was ashamed of saying that—the whole sentence, not just the profanity—and knew that Claire would have been disappointed, but it came naturally in the moment. This probably had something to do with the way Gimball had attacked him in the House.

His raincoat over one arm, he walked through the mews to the road, where his car was waiting.

• • •

"'Alternatively sane?'"

"Top of my head."

"It showed."

"It was off the cuff, River. I didn't know I was going to be marked on it."

Louisa and River were fetching their cars, or in River's case, Ho's car. Well, Ho wasn't using it, and Lamb had known where he hid his spare keys: in an envelope secured to the underside of his desk. "The second most obvious place," Lamb called it, the first being if Ho had just Sellotaped them to his forehead. River didn't feel good about using Ho's car without permission. He felt fantastic.

The rain had eased off, and the breeze that was kicking up felt fresh and ready for anything.

Ho used a resident's parking permit he'd applied for in the name of a local shut-in, not far from where he'd nearly been run over the previous morning. Louisa was on a meter, which was nearly as expensive as, though without the obvious benefits of, a second home. They reached Ho's car first. Before Louisa could walk on, River said, "You really think there's something to this?"

"What Coe said?"

"That, yeah. Plus what happens next. Someone's going to try to whack Zafar Jaffrey? Or Dennis Gimball? Tonight?"

"Everything else has happened in a hurry. Abbotsfield. The penguins. The bomb on the train."

"Yeah, but."

"I know."

"We can't even be sure it's Jaffrey or Gimball. Let alone tonight."

"Well, we have to do something."

"On account of Lamb."

"On account of Lamb, yeah."

More specifically, on account of Lamb pulling a gun on the Head Dog.

"I didn't think he was going to do that."

"It would worry me if you had. Emma's already got you down as Lamb's mini-me."

". . . You agree with her?"

Louisa said, "Nah. You've a way to go yet."

"Thanks. I think."

What Lamb had done: he'd aimed Marcus's gun in Emma's direction.

Emma Flyte said, "You've got to be kidding."

"Well, you'd think so. But try seeing it from my point of view."

She stood up. "Seriously, you are out of your mind."

"It's been said before. But best sit down."

Flyte looked around the room. Everyone was staring at Lamb, except Catherine Standish, who was looking at Emma.

"I'd do as he says."

"He's not going to shoot me."

"Probably not." Catherine let that "probably" hang there a moment or two, then shrugged. "But it's your call."

Flyte said to Lamb, "You've lost your senses," but she sat down.

Lamb said, "Didn't we used to have a pair of handcuffs somewhere?"

". . . Why is everyone looking at me?" Shirley asked.

"We're not judging," said Catherine.

Grumbling under her breath, Shirley went to her room and came back with a pair of cuffs. River waited until she'd secured Emma Flyte to her chair before saying, "And this is a good idea because . . . ?"

Lamb said, "Okay, for those of you who weren't paying attention, or are just slow, or are called Cartwright, let me point out what you've missed. These last couple of days, the terrorist massacre, the dead penguins, the bomb on the train, yada yada yada, it can all be laid at our door."

"Ho's door," Louisa said.

"You think Di Taverner cares which door? Once she's got an opening, she'll use it. By which I mean, she'll drive a bulldozer through Slough House, and the best you lot can hope for is,

someone'll pull you from the rubble before burying you again."
He remembered his bottle of wine, and reached for it. "And before
you ask, no, that's not a metaphor either."

Louisa said, "You're not seriously saying the Park would black
ribbon us?"

Black ribbons were what were wrapped round closed files.

"I'm saying," Lamb said, "that if they don't want you around to
tell tales, then you won't be around to tell tales."

River said, "There was that protocol, a few years ago. Waterproof? But there was an inquiry. They don't use that any more."

"Oh, believe me," J.K. Coe said. "They do."

River stared, but Coe said nothing more.

"Waterproof?" asked Shirley.

"Black prisons. Eastern Europe."

"Fuck."

Emma Flyte said, "Will you lot listen to yourselves? The Park
does not bury its mistakes any more. Or ship them off to foreign
dungeons."

"They brought you in to run a clean department," said Lamb. "That
doesn't mean there aren't still dirty bits you don't get to hear about."

"You've been rotting away in this slag heap for too long. You've
all turned paranoid. If there's even any remote truth in this scenario you've conjured up, this is not the way to deal with it."

"Nobody's actually keeping minutes," Lamb said. "But if anyone
had been, rest assured, your objections would have been noted."

"I thought you had enough on Taverner to keep her onside,"
Louisa said. "Or at least to stop her going all medieval on us."

"If what happened at Abbotsfield turns out to be our fault,"
Catherine said softly, "that'll trump anything Diana Taverner's done."

"Yeah," said Lamb. "To be fair to her, her civilian casualties are
probably still in single figures." He surveyed his assembled crew.
"The good news is, if they're holding off on questioning Ho, we've
got a window."

"The last time you had a window," Flyte pointed out, "a body
went through it. That doesn't fill me with confidence."

"You're not helping. Shut up. Zafar Jaffrey and Dennis Gimball, any advance on those two? For the role of most-likely-to-be assassinated?"

"You're making decisions based on—"

"You want to let me get this done, or do I need to put a bag over your head?"

River said, "She has a point. There are any number of politicians. Why would the target be one of the first two we put a name to?"

"We're talking about a bunch of mindless bottom-feeders whose general ignorance of our way of life is tempered only by their indifference to human suffering, we're all agreed on that?"

"Is this the politicians or the killers?"

"Good point, but I meant the killers."

Shirley shrugged. "Then yeah. I guess."

"Good. So as one bunch of idiots second-guessing another, you make the perfect focus group. Besides, we don't have the horse-power to cope with more than two potential targets." Lamb paused. "Horsepower. See what I did there?"

Now, out by Ho's car, River said, "So Gimball's doing a public meeting back in his constituency, and Jaffrey's what? He's not a public servant, or not yet. He doesn't publish his itinerary. How do we work out where he is?"

"I thought we could phone his office," said Louisa.

"Oh."

"And ask what he's doing tonight."

"Oh. Okay. Yeah, that might work."

She said, "And River? We can't let that pair go together, you do realise that?"

"Shirley and Coe? Why not?"

"Because we're trying to prevent a disaster, not cause one." Louisa was fumbling a coin from her jeans pocket as she spoke. "Call."

"Heads."

She tossed. "It's tails."

"... Loser gets Shirley, right?"

"No, loser gets Coe."

"Maybe we should have established that before you tossed."

"Why, would that've made you win?"

Damn.

He said, "But I get to choose which target, right?"

"So long as you choose Gimball, yeah."

"Why does it feel like I'm playing a stacked deck?"

"Welcome to Slough House," Louisa said, and went to fetch her car.

Dennis Gimball felt like a victim.

There were lots of reasons for his feeling this way, and—as was his wont—he set them out as mental bullet points:

- the Prime Minister hated him, so
- he was being picked on by the Secret Service, which meant
- he wasn't going to be able to set his brilliant plan in action, because
- they'd make him a laughing stock.

No wonder he needed a cigarette.

Dodie was tight-lipped, a bad sign. Tight-lipped meant she was thinking things through, and when that happened Dennis often found himself in deep shit, or that general postcode. Not for the first time, he wondered how things could go tits up so suddenly. A couple of hours ago, he was walking a shining path; now he was looking at, what? A public climb down. Because as far as the political world was concerned, this was the perfect moment for him to bid for the leadership, and the thing about perfect moments was, they didn't hang around. Announcing his return to the party fold was one thing, but without follow-through, without revealing that the PM's go-to Muslim moderate was hand-in-glove with an illegal arms dealer, the evening could be spun through 180 degrees, and his announcement welcomed by

Downing Street as a declaration of support. Like hammering the ball straight over the bowler's head, only to be caught on the boundary. They didn't give you two lives. It was back to the pavilion, bat tucked under your arm.

The car wasn't due for an hour, so Dennis slipped into the handkerchief-sized garden, leaned against one of the huge pots Dodie was apparently growing a tree in, lit a cigarette and brooded. If his planned triumph mutated into public capitulation, what could he expect? Twenty minutes in the spotlight as a prodigal son, a few weeks of speculation in the run-up to the next reshuffle and some chuckling paragraphs in the broadsheets when a Cabinet post failed to materialise. He'd join the ranks of those who'd confidently expected to swat this weak-kneed PM aside, and were now seeking opportunities elsewhere. A pub quiz question a decade from now: one for wonks only.

Okay, he thought, feeling nicotine course through his veins. That's the downside. But let's adjust this picture, shall we? It was always possible that, instead of a victim, he was in fact a hero, who had single-handedly forced everyone else into a corner:

- the Prime Minister was scared of him, so
- he was being picked on by the Secret Service, which meant
- they thought his brilliant plan would work, so
- . . . they'd make him a laughing stock.

Fuck.

He reached into his breast pocket, where something with sharp corners was digging into him: the photograph from Dancing Bear. Ancient history, but he'd had happy times there—and was that a crime? Nobody could look at this photo, surely, and not see past the ill-applied blusher (okay, that had been unwise) to the joy behind. Yes, he was wearing a dress; yes, elbow-length gloves—but so what? Was he hurting anyone? The only damage being done was to his own future, and since he couldn't have known that at the time, even that was an innocent injury. He had known Dodie then, but they weren't married, and it wasn't until years later that he had confessed to her this aspect of his personality. So, all this photo showed was a single man, happy in the company of like-minded fellows. A little bit of dressing up—have we not come far enough, as a society, to accept that? He could feel himself slipping into speech mode. This, this: this was normal English manhood, letting off steam. Hadn't Mick Jagger once declared that no Englishman needed encouragement to dress up as a woman? And look at Eddie Izzard—he was popular; beloved, even. So why shouldn't Dennis Gimball receive the same treatment?

It's not like he was gay, for God's sake.

So he could be a pioneer. Could break the mould.

And—once it was known he was being persecuted for who he was—he could be the poster boy for a whole new politics. The sanctity of personal choices, that would be his banner. Identity, selfhood, fiscal responsibility, strong borders and a ground-up rethink of the benefits system. What's not to vote for?

A scorching sensation at his fingertips warned him he'd finished his cigarette. He ground it out on the terracotta pot and buried the stub in its soil. His speech would need a new shape: how the Secret Service had tried to prevent him telling the truth about Zafar Jaffrey with blackmail threats. How they had tried to destroy Dennis Gimball with their bullyboy tactics. And how he was not a man to allow any citizen, himself included, to be ground beneath the Establishment's boot . . .

He would be carried from the hall shoulder high, he decided. His people's cheers would echo through the nation; his name would ring between the very stars.

Taking one last look at the photograph, he tucked it carefully away in his pocket.

And wished he could see the look on Claude Whelan's face when the spook realised he'd been outmanoeuvred.

Most of the crew had departed Slough House: Cartwright with a reluctant Coe; Louisa Guy with an oddly subdued Shirley

Dander. Catherine worried about Shirley; would have worried less if she'd spent the months since Marcus's death kicking holes in walls and throwing desks through windows. It was when a bomb stopped ticking that you should be nervous.

J.K. Coe, too: Catherine couldn't read him at all. It wasn't that he was a bad person; more that bad things had happened to him, and there were bound to be consequences. Plus, of course, he might be a bad person. No point pretending otherwise.

Probably, though, who she ought to be worrying about was herself.

Lamb had disappeared into the toilet, having loudly announced that this time was for real, and he'd be taking no prisoners. "No offence," he'd added to Emma Flyte, still handcuffed to a chair. And this was the main reason Catherine should be worried: Lamb had kidnapped the Head Dog and sent the horses on a madcap errand which, if it turned out not madcap after all, demanded seventeen times the number of agents and a hell of a lot more resources if they weren't to make a bad situation worse. Which, as someone had once pointed out, was their specialist area. So why did it all have a just-another-day-at-the-office feel? She must have been here too long.

She said to Emma, "Tea?"

"You're kidding, right?"

"I wasn't, actually. I'm having some. But it's up to you."

"Do you have the key to these things?"

"There used to be one somewhere. I hope Shirley didn't lose it."

Catherine went and made tea, and when she came back Emma didn't appear to have moved at all; hadn't hopped around the room on the chair, battering it against the walls, hoping to break it in pieces. That wasn't a great sign. Situations like these, you were probably better off if your hostage wasn't calm, cool and calculating.

She had to hold the cup to Emma's lips so the woman could sip her tea. It was a potential Hannibal Lecter scenario, but passed without dental assault. When Emma had had enough, Catherine put her mug on the desk, sat down too and smiled gently. "When he's in a specially grim mood, Lamb likes us to come up with mission statements," she said. "I've always thought 'Apologies for the inconvenience' had a ring to it."

"How about 'Fucking up the parts other fuck-ups can't reach'?"

"I'll add it to the list."

"Are you really happy to see your career flatline because your lord and master had a rush of blood to the brain?"

Catherine said, "I really don't know where to start with that. Career, lord and master, or brain."

"Even if you're right, even if Coe's onto something, how can you stop it by yourselves? Those four—I mean, seriously? Louisa's got her head screwed on I'll grant you, but the other three are dangerous. And not in a good way."

"River's better than that. It's not his fault he was assigned here."

"That's what makes him dangerous. He's got too much to prove."

"Maybe we could just agree to differ."

"Let me go. We'll take your theories to the Park. The worst that could happen, you're proved wrong. And if you're proved right instead, well. It could turn all your careers round. But not if you go about it like this."

Catherine said, "This is Slough House. We could produce a signed affidavit from whoever's running Daesh today, outlining their plans for the next twelve months, and Di Taverner would screw it up and bin it before she'd act on it."

"People might die," Emma Flyte said.

"People already have," Catherine said. "And whatever you think of Jackson, take it from me. If he can stop another Abbotsfield happening, he will."

I'm very nearly positive about that, she thought.

Flyte opened her mouth to reply but before she could do so, he was back in the room: their supposed lord and master.

"I didn't hear a flush," Catherine said suspiciously.

"No," said Lamb. "The Guinness Book of Records people might want a look first. I feel about two stone lighter."

"And you thought being handcuffed was cruel and unusual," she said to Emma.

Lamb scooped up the bag of Haribo Shirley had abandoned and collapsed onto a chair: his usual challenge to the office furniture. Which sooner or later would surely rise up and smite him, but this didn't happen today. "So. Has she confessed yet?"

"...Confessed?"

"Sorry. Flashback. I meant, has she had a cup of tea? Don't want anyone thinking I don't know how to treat a guest."

Emma Flyte said, "We were just discussing how much shit you're in."

"You could hear it from here?"

"That's even without whatever happens once your crew start playing Mission Impossible. If either of those pols are actually at risk, they should be under Protection Orders. Not being surreptitiously babysat by the Teletubbies."

Lamb said, "I feel like I should warn you at this point, last guy we used those handcuffs on, it didn't end well."

"For you or for him?"

"I'm still here," Lamb pointed out.

"How long have you been getting away with this?"

"This?"

She jerked her head, a gesture meant to include everything. "This. Slough House. Your crew. The whole making-it-up-as-you-go-along schtick."

Lamb said, "I've been here since the start."

"That doesn't surprise me."

"It was my idea, in fact."

"What, you took a long hard look at your career and decided to franchise it?"

Catherine said, "He was a joe."

Emma turned her way. "What?"

"He worked undercover."

"I know what it means. I'm wondering why you're defending him."

"I'm not. I'm warning you not to underestimate him."

"If you're going to wrestle," said Lamb, "I may have to film it for later study." He looked at Catherine. "Do we have any jelly?"

"Let me go now. It's not too late to straighten this out."

"By informing the Park? That's not really going to help."

"Because the Park won't pay attention, I know."

"And because Coe was right." Lamb watched her reaction, multitasking by shovelling Haribo into his mouth and washing them down with a swallow from the bottle of red. "He opens his trap maybe once a month. When he actually says something, he's usually sure of his ground."

"He looks like a disaster victim."

"And you look like a catwalk model. Does that mean we shouldn't take you seriously?"

She said, "So let's say he's right. Even if the Park don't listen, tell them about it and you've covered your back."

"Yeah, not really. Because if these guys are laying waste to the country using a script the Service wrote, there are few lengths the Park won't go to to cover it up. And anyone who knows about it will be in the firing line. Which includes you, if you'd lost count. Don't make the mistake of thinking you'll be safe when they start playing London Rules. Because you're not a suit, Flyte. You're a joe. And joes are expendable."

"I'm a cop."

"There's less difference than you might think."

"If this is an attempt to get me onboard by appealing to our common heritage, we're in for a long evening."

Lamb shrugged. "I'm in no hurry to be elsewhere. But what I'm appealing to is your survival instincts. How far would you trust Diana Taverner?"

"Not much further than I trust you."

"So if you head back to the Park now, tell Lady Di that my crew, far from being locked down, are out on the streets with their

Batcapes on, how do you think she'll react? Pat on the back? Or kick up the arse?"

"I'd like to see her try," Flyte muttered.

"There's the cop talking." Whatever Lamb had just put in his mouth was the wrong flavour, and he paused to spit it back into the bag. "But I'm betting your job won't survive her discovering you've fucked up again."

"Again?"

"When David Cartwright went walkabout," he said. "You didn't exactly emerge from that one covered in glory."

Flyte said, "Look who's talking. But why would I take it to Lady Di? I already know she doesn't like me. I'd go straight to Whelan."

"Claude Whelan has a lot on his plate right now," Catherine said "If he can't trust you to do your job efficiently, what use are you to him?"

"However good you look in the attempt," Lamb said.

He tipped the bottle into his mouth again but it was empty, so he dropped it on the floor.

"We're gunna let you go now," he said. "But before you make your next move, consider your options. Either Coe's right and there's a gang of killers out there poised for a high-level hit. Or he's wrong, and your career's fucked anyway, because you let my crew loose when you were supposed to have 'em wrapped up. If you can't handle a simple job like that, you've been promoted beyond your abilities."

"Let's not forget that you're fucked too," said Flyte. "On account of Slough House being the source of the leak. If it happened."

Catherine produced the handcuff key from a pocket in her dress, and went round the back of Emma's chair to uncuff her. "Oh," she said, "that's just the usual story. If we weren't *fucked*, as you so graphically put it, we wouldn't be here in the first place."

Freed from the handcuffs, Emma rubbed her wrists. "And what do you expect me to do now? Just keep my fingers crossed everything works out okay?"

"See?" said Lamb. "We are on the same page after all."

• • •

River hadn't asked Coe if he wanted to drive, and Coe hadn't indicated a preference, but the way he was slumped in the passenger
seat, eyes closed, suggested he was happy being driven. Except you
couldn't really use "happy," River amended. Actually, a brief scroll
through his mental thesaurus, and the best he could come up with
for Coe was "alive." Even then he'd have to keep checking every
half hour. There was no question: he'd rather have been with
Louisa, who he knew he could trust, or even Shirley, who was at
least a known quantity; a lit firework, but not an unfamiliar one.
J.K. Coe, though—River couldn't even remember what the initials
stood for without putting work into it—had been sharing his
office for the best part of a year, and River couldn't have told you
where he ate lunch. Nine to five he occupied his desk, almost
constantly plugged into his iPod: quiet music, you had to give him
that—none of the tinny leakage that warned you Ho was near—
but you could tell he was using it as a barrier; a way of minimising
contact with his fellow humans. Plus, of course, he'd murdered
that guy not long ago: three bullets to the chest of an unarmed,
manacled man. That was always going to weigh in the balance
when you were alone in a car with him.

But for the time being, Coe was asleep, or as good as, and River
had something to occupy his mind, after weeks of staring at digital wallpaper. What had he been tasked with? Oh yeah:
cross-checking electoral rolls against properties on which Coun-
cil tax and utilities were regularly paid and up to date, to determine
whether apparently occupied properties were in fact standing
empty. This, Lamb had suggested—with the enthusiasm of one
to whom the idea had occurred after a lunchtime which had
started early, finished late and been mostly liquid—being a foolproof method of compiling a list of possible terrorist safe houses,
though River suspected that a more accurate approach might
involve wandering round the British Isles knocking on random
doors.

"You want me to do this for everywhere in the country?" he'd asked, a vision of hell yawning before him.

"Christ, no," said Lamb. "You think I'm some kind of monster?"

"Well . . ."

"You can skip Sunderland. And also Crewe. But yeah, do everywhere else."

So River had now been playing Spider Solitaire for a record-breaking three weeks straight. Every couple of days, a random cut-and-paste job produced a list of properties which, if they fulfilled Lamb's criteria, did so purely by chance: he passed these on to Catherine, who, he suspected, knew damn well he was flying kites. Probably Lamb did too, and was waiting for the right moment to dump on him. Well, okay, River thought. Roll the damn dice. There was only so much punishment he could take. Rooming with Coe might turn out the last straw.

Back when he'd first arrived in Slough House, he'd shared with Sid Baker: Sid for Sidonie, very definitely female, though River hadn't got to know her as well as he might have done, on account of her being shot in the head not long afterwards. Head wounds were tricky: lots of blood, and a general expectation that even if you pulled through you were going to be straw-fed thereafter, but bubbling alongside that was an awareness of all the many exceptions. River had read the same stories as everyone else about gunshot survivors living for decades with bullets lodged in their craniums. But whether Sid would have turned out one of these lucky ones, River didn't know. The Service had dropped a fire blanket over the incident, and whether that meant they'd cremated the body after slapping a Natural Causes sticker on it or had her nursed back to health in a lakeside sanatorium was anybody's guess. He tried not to think about her often. If she was dead, which she probably was, he hoped they'd spread her ashes somewhere nice.

But the past was his daily passenger at the moment: right there next to him wherever he went. And it wasn't what he thought it had been, either; not so much a passenger as a hitchhiker; one who gets weird a few miles down the road. River had met his father for the first time earlier that year. This was not a meeting he had ever expected to happen. His father, he'd always assumed, had been a drive-by from his mother's wayward youth, and this explained the scant information she'd ever released as to his identity. This had long ceased to matter to River, or at least, had become something he was prepared to bury under the psychological debris of the everyday: the actual father figure in his life was the O.B., under whose guidance he had grown to be the man he was. So his had been an unplanned birth: so what? The same could be said about a fair proportion of the world's population, not many of whom had enjoyed his safe upbringing. But now it turned out this picture was askew; that far from having been a vague figure who had emerged from a bar or nightclub to enjoy an overnight fling with Isobel Cartwright, his father had lived on Spook Street, same as his grandfather; that far from being unplanned, River's birth had been plotted, his very existence a counter in a bigger game. And now his father was out there in the world, and while this had been true before River had ever laid eyes on him, its continued truth now carried a different weight.

He thought he might kill his father next time their paths crossed.

And he also thought that Slough House was no longer enough for him; that the tenuous promise it offered of future redemption, a return to the shining fold of Regent's Park, could sustain him no longer. Weeks of playing computer games rather than fulfilling another of Lamb's Sisyphean tasks; wasn't that his psyche telling him he was ready to quit? At the very least, he was asking to be fired. And no coincidence that this was happening while he was waiting for the O.B. to die.

The thought blurred his vision momentarily, and he had to slow down. Because that would be a great way to go: checking out in a borrowed car with a surly companion, just as he was starting to make decisions about his future.

They were about half an hour from Slough; traffic a little sludgy, but not too bad—the fag-end of rush hour, not its evil heart—and the sky starting to think about changing for the evening. The car was nice to drive—it was an electric blue Ford Kia: its very name enough to generate outraged emails—but only in the sense that River wasn't worried about pranging it. Ho, presumably, had chosen this car because he felt it suited him. River could only agree.

He glanced across at Coe, and was surprised to find he had his eyes open.

"How sure are you this is gunna happen?" he asked.

Coe didn't react.

iPod. Of course.

River tapped him on the knee and made a take-your-fucking-earbuds-out gesture, which Coe reluctantly did.

"How sure are you this is gunna happen?" River repeated.

Coe stared ahead for a while, watching the road being swallowed up by the car's front wheels, then shrugged and started putting his buds back in.

"In the interests of a healthy working relationship," River said, "I should warn you that if you do that, I'm gunna pull onto the hard shoulder and beat the snot out of you."

Coe paused and then nodded. "You could try," he said, and carried on inserting the earbuds.

That went well, thought River.

But a minute later, Coe pulled them out again. He said, "On a scale of one to ten? Maybe three."

River nodded. That's about what he'd figured.

He said, "But you felt it worth raising."

There was another pause, then Coe said, "I'm right about the bigger picture. The template they're using. The chances of us guessing right which pol they'll try to hit, and it happening tonight, that's a stretch."

He didn't look at River while saying this, but stayed focused on the road ahead of them.

Just for fun, River said, "But supposing we guessed right, and they'll go for Gimball. Tonight. How'd you rate our chances of stopping it? On the same scale?"

J.K. Coe raised his earbuds again, but before slotting them into place he said, "Less than zero."

"Yellow car," said Shirley.

"Yeah, not really."

"Yes really."

"Not really," said Louisa. "On account of one, it's a van, not a car, and two, it's orange, not yellow. So orange van, not yellow car."

"Same difference."

Louisa suppressed a sigh. Until ten minutes ago, the rules of Yellow Car had seemed pretty straightforward: when you saw a yellow car, you said, "Yellow car." There wasn't much room for controversy. But that was before she'd introduced Shirley to the game.

Nor had the game stopped Shirley fidgeting. She'd already been rooting about in the glove compartment, and had found a pair of sunglasses she was now wearing, and also some gum. "Can I have this?"

"Jesus. It's like being trapped with a ten-year-old."

"I get bored on long car journeys."

Louisa said, "I can drop you at the next services. Just say the word."

Shirley admired herself in the mirror on the sunshield. "These shades are about six years out of fashion."

"That's why they're in the glove compartment," Louisa said. "And not, for instance, on my face."

"Are we nearly there yet?"

Not nearly enough, thought Louisa.

There was the east side of Birmingham: a phone call having determined that Zafar Jaffrey was in his home city that evening, delivering a talk in a library. The woman who'd given Louisa this information had added a gloss or two, emphasising Jaffrey's manifold qualities which, Louisa suspected, might have included walking on water if she'd prolonged the call long enough. Nice to know he had his supporters, though when a politician seemed too good to be true, that usually meant he was. Still, if you had to pick one you'd rather not see assassinated, Jaffrey had the edge on Dennis Gimball, which was why she'd left Gimball to River. Faced with the task of keeping Gimball alive, she couldn't put her hand on her heart and say she'd do her damnedest; there was a strong argument that knocking Gimball off his perch would be doing the nation a favour. Or at any rate, not doing it so much harm it would need therapy.

As for the voice of support, Louisa recalled that Jaffrey was famous for recruiting his staff from the ranks of ex-offenders, which meant, if this were a movie, that he'd turn out to be running a crime syndicate under cover of a political campaign. Then again, if this were a movie, Louisa's shades wouldn't be six years out of style.

Shirley said, "What are the chances Coe's right about this?"

"Not high."

"How not high?"

"Really not high." Louisa pulled out to overtake some middle-lane hog who was dawdling along at 75. "I mean, okay, the whole watering hole thing, maybe he's on to something. But if you mean, is a terror gang about to try and whack Zafar Jaffrey, I can't really see that happening, no."

"So why are we here?"

"Gets us out of the office."

Shirley turned to give a little wave to the overtaken driver, then blew a bubble with the gum and let it pop. "If he's as clever as everyone says he is, how come he's a fucking idiot?"

"Who, Coe? I don't think he is a fucking idiot."

"He barely ever says a word."

"Not a sign of idiocy," Louisa said pointedly, though that barb didn't land.

"Plus he's a psycho."

"Well, yeah. He is that."

"I bet his phone's smarter than he is."

"Everyone's phone is smarter than they are."

"I bet his has a more exciting sex life."

"Is he gay, do you reckon?"

"I don't want to think about Coe's dick."

"I'm not asking you to think about—"

"Yeah, you're asking me to speculate where he likes putting it. And I don't want to think about that."

Louisa said, "You're the one who brought it up." She raised a finger from the wheel and pointed it at the opposite lane of traffic. "Yellow car."

"I don't want to play that any more."

Like an eight-year-old, Louisa mentally amended. It was like being trapped with an eight-year-old.

Maybe she'd have been better off partnering with Coe—she'd certainly have had a quieter journey—but, yes, he was kind of psycho. This didn't mean his overall analysis of the situation was off. The whole destabilising project sounded barking enough to ring true to Louisa, and that was enough to make this journey worthwhile—she hadn't been kidding about getting out of the office. Because sooner or later, Ho was going to tell the boys and girls at Regent's Park that he'd handed over a Service document to some bad actors, who were using it as a blueprint to a murder spree, and then hellfire was going to rain down. Best to be elsewhere when that happened: let Lamb soak it up on his own.

And even if nothing happened in Birmingham, this didn't make the journey a waste of time. She'd screwed up last night. Ho could have been killed, and, whatever anyone felt about Ho, Slough House had seen enough death. Besides, if Ho had been whacked, what would that say about her own abilities? She'd been there to protect him. So today she was going the extra mile: call it penance. Also, she'd closed River down when he'd suggested Shirley was missing Marcus, and she felt bad about that too.

Maybe it was time to start probing. Maybe, instead of bouncing off each other like spinning tops, she and Shirley could do each other some good.

So she said, "You never talk about Marcus."

Shirley proved her point by not replying.

"I know what it's like to lose someone close."

"And when you talk about them, do they come back?"

It was Louisa's turn not to say anything.

Shirley said, "How long has this gum been in there anyway?"

"Longer than the sunglasses."

Shirley spat it into her hand. Then her face brightened. "Yellow car."

"I thought you didn't want to play any more."

"No," said Shirley. "I just didn't want to lose."

Are we nearly there yet? wondered Louisa.

A sign told her: fifteen miles.

See? We are on the same page after all.

When a police officer, Emma Flyte had never fallen into the trap of thinking cops and villains two sides of a coin, closer in outlook than a civilian could understand. She preferred to hold to a more fundamental verity: that villains were arseholes who needed locking up, and cops were the folk to do it.

Here on Spook Street, the option of arresting the bad guys wasn't open to her.

If it had been, Jackson Lamb would have been on her list. She didn't care that he used to be a joe—didn't buy into that whole romantic notion of the bruised survivor of an undercover war— and wasn't impressed by his apparent determination to bully or alienate everyone around him. She simply thought him a bastard, and the best way of dealing with bastards was to cut them off at the knees. And even Lamb himself, deluded ringmaster that he was, would have to agree that over the last hour or so, he'd provided her with a sharp enough axe to do just that.

Emma pulled back her hair, tied it with an elastic band.

Anything less utilitarian—even the most basic of scrunchies—
and she'd get sideways looks from male colleagues, who seemed
to think any hint of decoration meant she was playing the gender card. That these same men wore ear studs and sleeve tattoos
didn't figure in their calculations . . . She was in her car, though
hadn't yet turned the key. Hadn't yet figured out her next move.

She hoped it hadn't showed, back in Slough House, but rage
was sluicing through her body. Being cuffed like a prisoner; fed
tea from a cup in someone else's hands—what she really wanted
was to bang heads together; corral the slow horses and have each
of them hobbled. Boiled down into glue.

But . . .

But she didn't much care for the bigger picture either.

The Standish woman was right: Claude Whelan had his hands
full, and wouldn't appreciate the mess she'd made of locking down
Slough House. And Taverner would be less than no help: she'd
happily accept any ammunition that could be used against Lamb,
but she wasn't the type to waste ammo, and if she could bring
down Emma with the same round, she'd do precisely that. Emma
had *disappointed* Taverner by failing to nail her colours to Taverner's mast, and Diana had a robust approach to alliances, one which
refused to accept the notion of a neutral. If you weren't for her,
you were fair game.

Besides. There was always the possibility Lamb was right. And
whatever she'd said back there about Waterproof, about how the
old ways no longer applied in Regent's Park, she had the feeling
that if the Abbotsfield killings turned out part of a cataclysmic
self-inflicted wound, then anyone who knew about it would soon
wish they didn't.

She drummed her thumbs on the steering wheel. The day was
packing its bags and tidying up; would be drawing the curtains
before long. Whatever she was going to do, she'd better get on
with it.

There was a phrase she'd heard bandied about: London Rules.
Rule one was cover your arse . . .

What she really hated about reaching this conclusion was knowing Lamb would expect her to do just that.

Thank God she had at least one ally in this dog-eat-dog universe. Before starting the car, she reached for her phone, and called Devon.

Catherine said, "Happy now?"

"You know me. Like Pollyeffinganna on Christmas morning."

"I'm guessing Santa brought you mostly coal," she said.

They were in his office. Outside, the afternoon was dying; in here, it could have been any time from 1972 onwards. Lamb had poured himself a medium-huge glass of whisky; had poured one for Catherine, too, which he did sometimes. Perhaps he wanted her to drink from it. Perhaps he just wanted to watch her resisting. So much of his life seemed to consist of testing other people's limits. Presumably he'd grown bored testing his own.

"You do know," she said, "that Flyte's probably rounding up her Dogs even now. And that wherever they're keeping Roddy, there'll be a space next to him just for you."

He looked indignant. "What did I do?"

". . . You want a list?"

"She's not going to go crying all the way home," Lamb said. "She did that every time a nasty man handcuffed her, she'd never have any fun."

"You know, I'd think twice about offering that in mitigation."

Lamb waved her objection away, unless he was chasing off a fly. "She's a cop," he said. "She knows damn well that if there's even the slightest chance what Coe said is true, then it needs chasing down. And stopping to file a complaint about what happened here's just gunna clog the wheels." He paused to raise his glass to his mouth. He's already drained a bottle of wine, Catherine thought. She could almost taste it, if she tried hard enough. But that was a door she wasn't walking through: not today. He was talking again. "Besides, she's not gunna want everyone knowing what a crap job she made of it. Dander went out for sweeties, for Christ's sake. I'm pretty sure that's outside the lock-down guidelines."

"I don't think they were drawn up with you in mind."

He nodded seriously at that. Guidelines never were.

Catherine said, "You sent our crew out after a bunch of killers."

"I'd have gone with them, but—"

"But you couldn't be arsed, yes. That wasn't my point. Coe's carrying a knife if you believe Shirley, but other than that they're unarmed. Just supposing a pair of them do run into this gang. How's that likely to turn out?"

"Well, I'm an incurable optimist, as you know," he said. "But I expect it'll all go to shit, as usual."

"That's reassuring."

"Oh, grow a pair. Actually, on second thoughts, don't." He stared at his glass a moment, as if trying to work out what it was, and where it went, and then solved that puzzle in the usual way. When he'd done, he said, "These killers aren't up to much. Slaughtering a bunch of pedestrians is one thing. But they failed to whack Ho twice, and let's face it, he's a walking wicket. Nah, they're amateurs. I'd back Guy and Dander against them most days."

"What about River and Coe?"

"Okay, you've made your point. But at least we'll have a spare room."

"Jackson—"

"The targets, both of them'll have a police presence. Armed police, more than likely. If our crew spot anything, all they have to do is raise the alarm. It's not like I'm expecting them to lay their lives down."

"... All right."

"Of course," he said, "if they weren't fuck-ups, they wouldn't be here in the first place."

"You're wasted on us," she told him. "You should be writing greetings cards."

A shattered sneer pasted across his face, he reached for her glass.

• • •

There were five of them, and one was dead.

They'd wrapped him, tight as they could, in what came to hand, which was cling film. This lent a horror-film sheen to the corpse, and every time Danny looked at him—it—he had the feeling it was about to move; to extend its mummylike arms and shuffle to its feet. Just yesterday, he'd been among the living. Joon, he'd been called then. Now Joon was an it, and cling film-wrapped, as if sheets of skin-thin plastic could keep him fresh.

They all knew that wasn't going to happen.

"Bad fall," Shin had said.

Apparently, there were good ones. In Joon's case, this would have involved not landing neck first, after falling through a big window. And pretty clearly, even before his meeting with the pavement, Joon had not been having a successful evening: if he'd completed the task in hand, there'd have been no need to take such a dramatic shortcut. He could have padded down the stairs and let himself out through the door. No, the target was still upright, that was clear.

Which was Shin's fault, and while it was not Danny's place to offer criticism, it was becoming harder to hold his tongue. He had been in the country three years, and still the flabbiness of life in Britain startled him on a daily basis. There was no direction. No leadership. The newspapers—the media—delivered a chaotic medley of constant opinion: contradictory, mindless noise that was affecting them all. Since Abbotsfield, they had had more failures than successes; and of the latter, the watering hole bomb had been down to Danny alone: a simple, beautiful physical action, after which he had ghosted himself away, invisible to the shocked crowds around. But the target, Ho, had escaped unharmed twice, and the bomb on the train had been a humiliating debacle. There were two reasons for this that Danny could see. The first was Shin himself, who appeared to have no stomach for a leadership role.

The second was the absence of uniform. Having shed their uniforms, they had let the chaos in.

Shin was looking at his phone now, his back against the side of the van they'd been living in for the past week, scrolling through Twitter feeds, through news headlines, as if consulting an oracle. Danny felt contempt worming through him: if Shin were to lead he should *lead*, not look for answers in the rubble of the internet. His resolve was weakening by the hour. He thought the best way of getting results was letting them know the plan they were working to, whereas a true commander would expect obedience to be blind, and deal with infraction severely. He had not even punished An when An failed to run the target over the previous morning. Was even now unable to draw a line between these two events: because An had failed yesterday, Joon was dead today.

He closed his eyes and tried to find the calm space. Their mission had stumbled, but had not been compromised. As for Shin, Danny would report him once it was over. There could be no other way. His leadership was a mistake, a disgrace, and he would understand that for himself had his head not been turned by the chaos. As for the rest of them—who had been four and now were three—they would keep their cool and see the plan through. That was the phrase he was after: keep their cool. It wasn't, after all, the details that mattered; it was the simple fact of the plan's implementation. This was the oldest of all stratagems, the lesson you delivered to your enemies: that the stronger they built their citadels, the more securely they sealed the instruments of their own destruction within.

All that Danny and his comrades needed was to remain . . . cool.

That was the phrase.

Cool cats.

PART TWO

HOT DOGS

River parked in a metered space, and was fumbling for change when he remembered—duh—that it was Ho's car, so stopped. He looked around. Dusk was smudging distant outlines. Next to him, Coe was still plugged in. His eyes were open, but had an unfocused, glazed expression which in anyone else River would have taken to mean high.

Coe, he suspected, didn't get high. Just reaching a level would be a stretch.

He made the get-your-earbuds-out gesture again, a necessary piece of sign language when dealing with Coe, and said, "It's kind of funny, being in actual Slough."

Coe stared.

"I'll explain later. You okay with this?"

"No."

"Which part especially?"

Coe thought, then said, "All of it."

"Well, just so long as you don't shoot anyone this time."

"I don't have a gun."

"Yeah, I was hoping for commitment. Not just lack of means."

It wasn't that River thought it likely there'd be gunfire, violence, blood, but he figured at least one of them ought to raise the possibility, since they were, at least nominally, here to prevent a possible assassination. Or perhaps just interrupt one. But now the journey was over, that possibility had receded into the realms of the far-fetched. Nothing exciting ever happened to the slow horses. Well, okay, there'd been that gun battle a while back, and the psycho who shot up Slough House, but mostly it was just the daily grind. And that they were currently in the actual Slough only rubbed that in, somehow. The actual Slough wasn't somewhere he'd been before, and all he knew about it was that it had managed to crawl this near to London and then given up. No ambition. There was also a poem about bombs, but he wasn't reading too much into that.

"We should check the place out," he said. "See what's what."

"In case there's a group wearing Team Abbotsfield T-shirts?" River looked at him.

"Or sitting in McDonald's, enjoying a Happy Terrorist Meal?" Well, it was better than nothing. "Yeah, something like that."

"Where's the meeting?"

It was a couple of streets away, two minutes' walk. Coe kept his hands in his pockets, and had the look of an adolescent on a forced excursion, except—River noticed—his eyes never stayed still: he checked out everything, traffic and pedestrians alike. River had the feeling he expected the worst on a continuous basis. What he'd do when and if it showed up, River didn't know, but Shirley was always banging on about him carrying a knife. Handy that at least one of them was tooled up, but how a blade was going to help if a bunch of paramilitary maniacs made an appearance was a question best unasked. Not that that was going to happen, River reminded himself—even Coe had said as much, and it was his fault they were here in the first place.

The meeting hall looked like a primary school: redbrick, with green windows and pipework. It sat behind a low wall into which iron railings had been set, and with a gateway big enough for cars. This was manned by private security guards, their uniforms official-looking at a distance, but their belts weighed down by so much fussy nonsense—radios, torches, puncture repair kits—that you couldn't take them seriously. But maybe he was just jealous.

A fully-fledged member of the Security Services, River carried about as much weight as a supermarket trolley wrangler.

Coe said, "Looking at your future?"

"Shoot me now," said River, before remembering who he was talking to.

"Don't worry, you're not likely to finish up a car-park attendant. Current scenario, that would be a happy ending."

It was nice Coe was finding his voice, but River wished he'd shut the fuck up.

"Let's separate," he said. "Make sure Team Abbotsfield haven't got the building staked out."

As if, he thought.

On the other hand, stranger things had happened.

Miles away: a little later, another public meeting.

The library was on a side street, and from a distance could have been any municipal building: health centre, brothel, tax office. A flyer taped to the door announced the evening's event. *Zafar Jaffrey will be speaking on the important issues facing the community, and answering questions about his candidacy for mayor.* A thumbnail photo confirmed Louisa's impression that Jaffrey was a looker. There were rows of chairs at the back of the room, beyond sets of freestanding bookshelves; some occupied already, though the event wouldn't begin for thirty minutes. Returning to the car, she'd clocked the other vehicles lining the road. All were empty. There were vacant parking spaces too. Louisa thought about taking a photo, to show people in London.

Back in the car, Shirley sat with folded arms. Despite the sunglasses, she weirdly resembled a Buddha. "All I've eaten today is a bunch of Haribo," she said.

"Remind me whose fault that is?"

"We could have stopped at a service station."

"We could have gone for a candlelit supper," said Louisa. "Only I took an executive decision to get on with the job."

"Who put you in charge?"

My wheels, my rules, Louisa thought, but didn't say. There came a point when squabbling with Shirley reached a brick wall: you could either bang your head against it or walk round.

So she said, "Jaffrey's talk starts in half an hour. It's scheduled to last forty minutes, with a twenty-minute Q&A. One of us should go inside, the other stay out here and . . ."

"Secure the perimeter?"

"I was trying not to say that," she admitted.

"That's not really a one-woman job," Shirley said.

"Yeah, no, I didn't say it was an ideal plan. But it is a plan."

"Are you armed?"

"No. Are you?"

"I wish."

"There's a monkey wrench in the boot."

"Dibs."

Shirley with a monkey wrench, Louisa thought: yeah, that was someone you'd want on your side. She might look like a mini-Buddha, but she didn't share the same attitude to peace and oneness and all that. Though, in her defence, she'd given a few unsuspecting souls a nudge in the direction of reincarnation.

She took her phone out, Google-Earthed. "There doesn't seem to be a rear entrance. The building backs onto something else, an office block I think."

"What about the roof?"

"It looks like, you know, a roof. There's a skylight."

"They don't seem the subtle sort."

So descending through a skylight was Shirley's idea of subtle. Interesting. And what did they think they were doing, Louisa wondered; a question she'd successfully avoided until now. The crew who'd massacred Abbotsfield weren't taking prisoners; they were spraying bullets. Waving a monkey wrench wasn't going to put them off. And Shirley and Louisa only had one monkey wrench between them.

But it was the longest of shots that anything would happen, and besides, shying away from risk wasn't going to win anyone a

Get-out-of-Slough-House-free card. Sitting at a desk, compiling lists of library users, wasn't the reason she'd joined the Service. And if most ops involved heavy backup and protective clothing, there were always the off-the-cuff moments when you were expected to rely on your training, and the expertise hammered into you on the mats at the Service schools, or on the plains near Salisbury. Put your hands up, hide in a corner until the worst was over, and you might as well be a civilian. This way, when the score was taken at the end, she'd be able to say she'd been there, and ready. Wasted on a desk job, in other words.

Still, though. Just the one monkey wrench.

But nothing bad was going to happen.

"I've got a bad feeling," Shirley said.

. . . Great.

"Thanks for that. You're having an intuition?"

"No, I'm having a stomach cramp. I really need to eat."

"Shirley—"

"There's a takeaway back there. We passed it just before we turned."

There were people arriving; little groups of the civic-minded, come to take the political temperature. An elderly couple, walking with sticks; another pair who might be students, one carrying a stack of leaflets.

"There's no time. You'll survive."

"Easy for you to say."

"It's an op, Shirley. Not an away day."

"I'm pretty sure Lamb would say yes."

"Lamb's not here. Which means I get to say no."

"You don't give me orders."

"No, but I can let you walk home."

"There are trains," snarled Shirley.

Trains! You had to laugh.

"As of now," Louisa said, "we're live. One of us needs to be in there, to check out the audience. If anything's gunna happen, we stand a better chance of stopping it if we spot the bad guys before they make their move. So. Are you gunna keep grousing, or get with the programme?"

Shirley mumbled something. Louisa assumed it was assent.

"You want to be inside or out?"

"I want the monkey wrench," Shirley said.

"It's in the boot," Louisa told her, and left to join the crowd in the library.

"**I need** a cigarette," Gimball told his wife.

"No you don't."

"I'm not going to get through this without one."

She rolled her eyes. "You gave up. Publicly. Very publicly. If I'm seen with a cigarette between my lips again, don't vote for me. Your words."

"Well, yes, but I didn't *mean* them. It wasn't an electoral promise."

Actually, he reflected, he'd have been better off saying it *had* been an electoral promise. Only infants and idiots expected you to keep those.

"You've done this a thousand times. What are you so worried about?"

He could tell her, he thought. Explain that he was about to get up on stage and ask for acceptance for who he really was. That done, he could probably let slip he was still smoking too, and get away with it. It wasn't going to be what his audience focused on.

But if he came clean now, and she expressed doubt—which she would—he'd crumble like a cupcake in the rain. He needed her support, and to get that he'd have to present her with a fait accompli. Following which there'd be some bad moments to get through in private, but in public she'd back him to the hilt, having little choice. Unless—but no. He couldn't believe she'd abandon him. There'd be mileage in that—the deceived wife—but standing by her man would guarantee acres of coverage, with material for a year's worth of columns. And also she loved him. So this was the way to go.

"It's a crunch moment," he said. "For both of us."

No word of a lie.

"We're keeping our powder dry," she told him. "That's all. Doing as Whelan said isn't the end of anything, Dennis. It's an interruption."

He still needed a cigarette.

"If you get caught," she said, "you're never borrowing my Manolos again."

Which was her way of giving assent. He'd never fit in her Manolos in a million years.

He checked, with a tap of a finger, that fags and lighter were in his breast pocket, then retreated from their commandeered room to find one of the volunteers staggering past under a ziggurat of plastic chairs.

"Is there a back door? Need to gather my thoughts."

There was.

River walked the block, and the neighbouring one, to get his bearings. At one point he saw J.K. Coe crossing a junction up ahead, a mobile slouch, and shook his head. Even now, when he could halfway kid himself he was doing something that mattered—was on an op—the reality of life among the slow horses kept asserting itself. His colleagues were mostly useless, so bowed down by issues they might have been in art school rather than the Secret Service. Louisa excepted, maybe. And himself, of course. Always important to remember that: there was nothing wrong with River himself.

There was a TV van at the hall, and this would be a good disguise for a bunch of armed maniacs, but the more River looked the more like a real TV van it seemed. Most disguises would have maxed out with a logo on the sides and a few peaked caps and clipboards; here, two men were unreeling a marathon's length of cabling through a propped-open fire door, and there was still enough equipment in the van to shoot a Harry Potter movie. Of course, if you were going to carry out a successful assault on a political gathering, this might be the way to do it—rig out transport, stack it with authentic-looking kit, then park near the target and take your time. But River didn't think so. Unleashing gunfire on a village street, or leaving a homemade bomb on a train; lobbing a pipe bomb into a penguin enclosure—it all smacked of a bunch of fanatics slipping through the cracks. Any move they made, he thought, would be more a headlong dash for victory than a minutely planned assault. Passing themselves off as media professionals, with all the fake credentials required, was surely out of their league.

He watched a while longer, waiting for some sign that all was not as it appeared, then left them to it.

Not far off was a building wrapped in scaffolding: its upper half freshly painted, the lower grimy and road-splashed, years of urban living etched into its façade. Alongside it ran a narrow lane along which the scaffolding continued, making passage difficult, and which dead-ended in an area occupied by wheelie bins. The building was in use—lights shone in the upper storeys—but a sheet of tarpaulin flapping overhead gave it a forlorn, abandoned air. River walked to the end of the alley, found no human presence and returned to the main road.

When he looked back, the building reminded him of Slough House.

No special reason. Just that it was a little dismal, a little so-what?; the kind of place, if you worked there, you'd find yourself reaching for a drink the moment you got home. Difference was, somebody was going to the trouble and expense of having it repainted: if not a bright new future, at least a fresh coat to cover the past. And he felt a familiar internal slump. He wasn't sure how long he could keep this pretence up, where he was nominally one of the nation's protectors but actually an irrelevant drone. He could count on his fingers the number of times he'd been dispatched from Slough House on a mission. Not including fetching takeaways for Lamb. It wasn't what he'd wanted from life. Not what his grandfather had wanted for him, either.

So if something didn't happen soon, he'd quit. Anything was better than this. Standing by scaffolding as the evening descended, this was the decision River came to, but if he'd expected his heart to lighten with the moment, he was disappointed. It felt as if something had deflated instead.

Ach, he thought. And then: shit. And then he made his way round the metal poles obstructing the pavement and walked back to the hall, outside whose doors a queue had formed.

He wondered where Coe had got to.

Shirley waited until Louisa had been in the library for ten minutes before going to fetch some chips, and then waited another ten, because if she'd been Louisa, hoping to catch Shirley in the act, that was the timeframe she'd have adopted. If she'd been Louisa, she'd definitely have caught Shirley in the act. As it was, being Shirley, she'd be back with her chips before the gathering dispersed.

She was halfway to the takeaway before she remembered the wrap of coke in her pocket.

Sixty-three days she was on, and the sky was gloomy; the evening gathering pace. Not long now, and she'd have sixty-four. What then? Sitting back and watching the numbers grow held no pleasure for her, but still: there was a nagging concern at the back of her mind that there'd be a tint of . . . *failure* in setting the calendar to zero. As if she'd set out to do something, and given up before getting there. As if she were unable to carry it further.

But there was no reason why anyone would think that; no reason anyone would know. She was on her own. She could get off her tits on a nightly basis, and provided she rocked up to Slough House every morning, life would crawl on as usual. Because she wasn't an addict. A user, sure, but for recreation only. And it was nobody's business how recreational she got.

If she had a problem, how come she had sixty-three days straight?

A fresh batch of cod had just been put into the deep fryer, so Shirley ordered a hot dog while waiting, and ate it watching fat spit and sizzle. She remembered once sitting in an all-night laundrette, studying the tumblers as their loads rose and fell, rose and fell, like dolphins. It might have been hours she sat there, lost in fascination. That was the sort of thing that happened then, but didn't now. Now life was set to normal, was a long string of grey moments, as if the mood in Slough House were leaking through its walls, and infecting everything, everywhere.

It got to them all in the end, the curse of the slow horses. It sapped them of energy, and left them to wilt.

Her order arrived. Armed with a plastic fork, still chewing the last of her hot dog, she left the shop thinking about Marcus, and what he'd have made of her self-imposed clean stretch. He'd have said little. He'd have nodded, though, or something; made one of those macho gestures of his, to remind her that he might be behind a desk same as she was but he'd kicked down doors in his time, and she'd have felt good, seeing that nod; felt she was on the right track. But on the other hand: fuck off, Marcus; what's it to do with you? Not as if he'd waltzed through life unaccompanied by demons. Towards the end there, the back half of last year, he'd been pouring money into slot machines like he'd found the secret to eternal life.

The chips were good, though.

When she reached the car she was relieved, despite herself, to find that Louisa hadn't reappeared, and decided to eat standing up, using the car roof as a somewhat high table. Stink the inside out, she'd never hear the end of it. She attacked the cod with the two-inch fork—a weapon unsuited to the task—and managed to convey a reasonable chunk into her mouth before remembering she was supposed to be "securing the perimeter": yeah, right. Still chewing, she stepped round the car and into the quiet road, giving the parked vehicles a quick onceover. Everything as it had been.

Except, she thought, before stepping back to her al fresco dinner—except: that van, a hundred yards away. Had that been there five minutes ago?

It hadn't.

• • •

When Coe saw Cartwright heading for the hall, he stepped inside
a shop doorway and hid. He didn't feel needed. *I think we're in
trouble* he'd said, and meant it, but he didn't think trouble was
going to happen here. The odds were on a par with aliens landing
on that scaffolding, or America's comedy president forswearing
Twitter.

But as far as the bigger picture went, he knew he was right.

He slipped his iPod's earbuds in and listened to the headlines:
an update on the surviving penguins; a woman found dead in her
London home. Not long ago, he wouldn't have been able to do
this: the most he'd been able to bear was long stretches of unscored
piano music; improvised melody that had him drifting like a leaf
in a rowboat's wake. But that was fading; had begun to do so once
he'd fired three bullets into a killer's chest. Strange, the things that
eased tension. This one wasn't likely to crop up in self-help books,
but you couldn't argue with results.

And whatever else was going on, whatever static buzzed in his
background, his brain worked fine, so yes, he knew he was right.
He'd always had an ability to retrieve written information: to recall
the shape of words on a page, the arrangement of paragraphs, at
what depth of a book a sentence lay. "The watering hole" was a
Kiplingesque phrase that lingered. Whoever had tossed the bomb
into the penguin enclosure at Dobsey Park had been following
instructions that Coe had seen written down, and beneath that
plan a bigger one was shifting. The point of all this was to whip
the curtain away, and show the machinery behind. Expose the
plan as one the nation had written itself, or its secret sharers had.
And a nation's secret sharers were the keepers of its soul.

He left the doorway and headed down the street, then into
an alley between the worked-on building and the next. At the
alley's end wheelie bins jostled, but there was no through way,
and he was about to head back when he noticed the ladder fixed
to the scaffolding. Okay, he thought. From up high, he could

watch the street. Cartwright was bound to call and ask what he was doing; "maintaining surveillance" might shut him up. And he'd be out of harm's reach. He scaled the ladder, and then the next, which took him up to a walkway thirty feet above the street. The wooden boards had give in them, but not enough to feel unsafe. Just a slight swaying motion. Panic attacks, Lamb had accused him of having. Okay, but it was people who triggered them. He was fine with heights. Was fine with most things, provided they didn't come with people attached.

By the top of this second ladder was a sealed paint tin, which probably shouldn't have been left there. Coe stepped round it, leaned on a horizontal bar, and looked down on the street below.

"The watering hole." At Regent's Park he'd have had to back his assertions with hard evidence or statistical probability. In Slough House, all he'd had to do was convince Jackson Lamb. But then, Lamb had done his time behind the Wall, and could still read the writing on it. People talked about Spook Street—life in the covert world—but Lamb had served down the dismal end, where your instincts stayed sharp or you suffered, and he recognised the truth when he heard it. Which didn't mean he wasn't a fat bastard, just that he was a fat bastard you dismissed at your peril.

None of which indicated that Coe would be proved correct here and now, or that Guy and Dander would strike lucky in Birmingham. Zafar Jaffrey and Dennis Gimball were just examples of the kind of target the template advocated: there'd be others, the deaths of whom would cause a tremor through the body politic, and various levels of grief, stress and rejoicing. There'd be angry mobs on streets, and bottles uncorked in dining rooms. It would all go on for days, and the headlines would stoke up outrage, and when the time came for these clowns to reveal whose strategy they'd been applying, the house of cards would be ready to collapse.

It didn't matter who they were, he thought. Russians, Chinese, Cornish secessionists. Their identity barely mattered against the point they were making: that the target nation, always so eager to squat the moral high ground, had designed its own destruction.

And then he wondered what Dennis Gimball was doing down below; weaving round the scaffolding; scurrying along the alley to where the wheelie bins were gathered.

There was a decent number of people in attendance: fifty-two, more than she'd have expected. Then again, the last time Louisa had attended a public forum on local issues was never. Jaffrey was talking, outlining what might be challenges, might be opportunities—he was big on proclaiming that it all came down to attitude—and she had to admit he had something. Call it charisma, because people usually did. Whatever it was, it was striking that he could be bothered to turn it on in a local library, uncovered by media; and that he seemed to genuinely care about what he was saying, and so far hadn't dodged any questions, which ranged from residents' parking issues to the possible fate of the library itself, which was looking at closure. Louisa should feel worse about that, but she was already mentally ticking it off her spreadsheet: at least she'd be spared having to study the lending stats for its terrorism section.

As for the crowd, she wasn't expecting a killer to erupt from its midst. It would include a police officer: plainclothes, probably not armed—the country might have been in a heightened state of tension since Abbotsfield, but that had been indiscriminate violence, and there was nothing to suggest politicians were in greater danger than at any time in the recent past. But Jaffrey had a national profile, and he was a Muslim: there were always going to be those who saw either as inflammatory. A police force with one eye on its reputation would keep the other on its local heroes, so the crowd included a police officer, which she guessed was either the Asian woman in the front row—petite but handy-looking, if you knew the signs—or the bulky man doing his best not to look bored a few seats to her left. There was also a pair might be from Jaffrey's own team among the audience: young, male and female, very watchful, very engaged. At first sight, Louisa pegged them as the two most likely, and her heart had accelerated. But when the male half got up to help an elderly woman with her bag, she'd relaxed. Terrorists came in all shapes and sizes, but helping the aged wasn't the standard package.

Outside, she hoped, Shirley was keeping her eyes open, though more than likely she'd sloped off to find food by now. She'd half a mind to pop out and check, but it didn't seem worth the bother: Shirley would do what Shirley did, and was unlikely to appreciate commentary. So here Louisa was, and she had to pause to remember precisely why. Back in Slough House, this had felt like a plan worth pursuing; here and now, it seemed like it had been a good way of getting out of Slough House. Trouble was she was now in Birmingham, a two-hour drive home, with Shirley beside her, doubtless smelling of chips.

Never let anyone tell you it's not a glamour profession, she thought.

Jaffrey was growing animated—Brexit, and its effect on local manufacturing—and Louisa settled back, but kept an eye on the door. People would burst in soon with guns, and try to kill this man. It didn't seem likely. Nor was she clear on what she was supposed to do about it if they did.

But she supposed that would resolve itself, should the situation arise.

There was something delicious about sneaking off for a crafty cigarette, thought Gimball. It brought his school days back. Out of bounds and after lights—there'd been friendships based on such adventures.

The air felt fresh after the dusty interior of the meeting hall. It was darkening, and the people queueing at the entrance— always a gratifying sight—were grey, indistinguishable shapes, but he decided to slip round a corner anyway. Those grey shapes came armed with smartphones, whose standard apps included a bogus sense of journalistic responsibility: light up here and he'd be trending on Twitter two puffs in, the modern equivalent of being collared by a beak. Ten minutes, no more. Time to calm himself, compose his thought. Thoughts. Mentally rehearse his address to his people.

Yes, people, because he had those now. Friendships, not so much. He had alliances, but that was different. Even Dodie, without whom he'd not have got this far—and he was big enough to admit this; careful enough to mention it every so often, too—was his best friend inasmuch as there was little competition for the role. "Only friend" sounded equally valid. Which made what he was about to do, get up in front of the cameras and reveal who he really was, even more dangerous. Because Dodie would support him, but she'd be furious he hadn't cleared it with her first. She had her own agenda to maintain, and standing up for her husband's right to express himself might involve a little backtracking on previous public pronouncements, which would hardly be a novel experience for a columnist with forthright opinions, a six-figure contract and a pair of junior hacks to do the actual writing, but nevertheless required a certain amount of ground preparation. So yes, that was a storm he'd have to weather, and he wasn't looking forward to it. But needs must.

The alternative: he'd be Five's cat's-paw, now and forever. If he gave in to Claude Whelan's pressure just once, he could kiss any idea about political independence goodbye. So, again:

- this was what he needed to do, so
- he was going to do it, and
- damn the torpedoes.

Gimball felt better, now it was laid out clearly. Still needed a cigarette, though.

He found an alleyway and nipped down it, plugging a cigarette into his mouth before he reached the yard at the end. Catch me here, he thought—what would people make of it if they caught him here, skulking among wheelie bins like a feral cat? He breathed out, and smoke drifted up into scaffolding while a long-lost schoolboy memory retrieved itself and burned across his mind like a cave painting. Three of them behind the gym, passing a cigarette hand-to-hand. The image vanished, but he wondered: what had happened to those old companions, and what were their names, and what were their lives like? However they'd turned out, they'd be reading about him in the papers tomorrow, or on their screens later tonight. BREXIT HERO ADMITS PERVY LEANINGS. The headline refused to adjust itself, no matter how hard he tried. CROSS-DRESSER CROSSES FLOOR. He shook his head, but it was too late: the full horror of what he planned to do had landed, and there was no pretending it hadn't. Stand up and publicly announce his most private of peccadilloes—really? Spike Claude Whelan's guns by throwing himself in front of a cannon? It was madness. Because it wasn't Whelan he had to fear; it wasn't even the media, which would do what the media always did, and feed on whatever red meat was thrown its way. No, it was his own people who would turn on him if he dared reveal the truth about himself. What had he been *thinking*?

He could feel damp on his neck, and that loosening inside which comes with narrow escape. It had been a few small hours of angry bravado, that was all. The future that awaited him was too grand, too important, to jeopardise out of pique. So yes, fine, he'd do what Whelan wanted. It would make no difference, not in the long run. He couldn't announce, tonight, Zafar Jaffrey's dealings with an underworld enabler; couldn't undermine the PM by exposing his tame Muslim, but you couldn't stop the clock on history: the story would break, sooner or later, and if Dennis Gimball wouldn't be the one to announce it, he'd certainly be there to add colour and noise. In the end, that was what counted—that it was you who were there, at the end. Because politics was all about timing: hell, you could stick your dick in a dead pig's mouth and get away with it if your timing was right. And provided you were shame-free, but that was a given for Eton. He'd come close to forgetting that lesson, but had pulled himself short in time, thanks to the sacred habit of smoking: if he'd not slipped away to clear his head with a nicotine blast, he might still be in the grip of the delusion that exposing himself in public was the thing to do. Christ. And Dodie got on his case about it.

Well, he thought, given what else he kept quiet about, what did the odd cigarette matter? And just to prove that comforting thought true, he lit another from the stub in his hand, and drew deeply on it while gazing up at what could be seen of the sky through the trapezoids of scaffolding, and then down again, along the alley, at the threatening shape heading his way.

Shirley stood with the takeaway wrappings spread out on the car roof, thoughtfully eating, making sure nothing suggested she was on sentry duty. The van was parked so its rear faced her way, and nobody had emerged from it, though Shirley thought she'd detected a rocking motion, as if somebody—some somebodies—were shuffling about inside. But hard to tell. A latecomer hurried past, heels clacking on the pavement, and disappeared inside the library. When the door opened, a brief exhalation of laughter floated out. The local pol, amusing his masses.

The van was grey with lighter patches, as if recently sprayed and some bits missed, and its registration plate was below her sight line. She considered taking its photo, but decided she might as well raise a big red flag at the same time, and jump up and down with her arms in the air. Maintain a nonchalant awareness, she warned herself. Gaze around at things in general; don't stare at the van. You're eating fish and chips on an early summer evening. Things like this happen—they happen all the time.

Other things happened too. Last night, she'd been sprawled outside Ho's house, while somebody, maybe one of the somebodies in that van, fired a gun at her. She'd found brick dust in her hair this morning, proof that it had happened. At the same time, bruised cheek apart, it felt like a chapter from someone else's memoirs. Marcus had told her about this phenomenon—the way remembered excitement has a distancing effect, so you view action you were involved in as if through a TV screen. This was one of the reasons you kept going back for more. Like any other high, he'd said, an adrenalin rush couldn't be faked.

Marcus had known about stuff like that, and if he'd been standing here instead of Shirley, he'd be coming up with a plan.

Which would involve assuming the worst. There was no point treating the van as innocent, because being wrong could prove a disaster. So: would they recognise her, that was the first question. Were they watching her through a peephole, planning to whack her before heading into the library? Or had it been too dark last night, and Shirley just a moving target in the chaos? Their bullets had gone high—was that because they'd been aiming to miss, or were they lousy shots? She had a low centre of gravity, of course—in layman's terms, was "short"—and that might have thrown their aim off. Being a non-traditional shape had its advantages.

None of which would count for much if they emerged from the van, guns blazing.

She ate a chip, nodded as if in appreciation—every move she made now, she had an audience—and then, still nodding, moved round the car and opened the boot. Watching or not, they couldn't see through metal, so wouldn't have been able to observe as she rummaged about in Louisa's detritus—an old blanket, a wine cooler, walking boots—until she found, tucked under the blanket, the monkey wrench, and slid it up her right sleeve. Then, her arm ramrod straight, she closed the boot and returned to her meal, her right hand hooked into her jeans pocket, her left plucking chips and lumps of fish from the mound of paper and steering them mouthwards. *Watch me now, Marcus*, she thought, and imagined him saying *You go, girl*.

And she would.

She was just waiting for her moment.

He had no clue where Coe had got to, and when he tried calling got no response. This probably meant the dickhead wasn't answering, rather than—say—that the dickhead had cornered a hit squad and had his hands full, so River couldn't get too worked up about it, except for Coe being a dickhead: that never got old. The meeting hall was full now, an air of expectation hanging like fruit. Dennis Gimball, River gathered, was set to make some grand pronouncement: a declaration that he was about to rejoin the party he'd once defected from, a return trip across the Rubicon which many expected would end in his contesting the leadership. That would make as much difference to the ship of state as a koala taking over from a wombat, River thought, though he accepted he wasn't a political expert. If he were he'd be looking for honest work, like every expert since 2016 should have been.

Anyway: no Coe that he could see. And nothing else to alarm him, or no more than such gatherings always offer: the swivel-eyed fervents; the union-jack-bowler brigade. A man wearing the widest pinstripes River had seen outside a zoo; a woman carrying a pot plant. The one thing absent was Gimball himself. A group by the stage, chatting among themselves and checking their watches, were presumably local dignitaries, and the dangerous-looking woman in blue might be Mrs. Gimball, but there was no sign of her husband. Perhaps, like a rock star, he delayed his entrance until every seat in the hall was damp, though with this particular demographic that might prove a risky business.

He headed outside. There were people still waiting to get in, and the TV van was mildly buzzing: all powered up and ready to shoot. But not that kind of shooting, River reminded himself. He tried to recollect the odds Coe had quoted on anything going down here tonight, but couldn't. What he did remember was Coe's equal insistence that he was right; that machinery was whirring; had already chewed up Abbotsfield, and fourteen innocent penguins. Dennis Gimball wasn't necessarily next on the list, but that there was a list was beyond dispute. That was what the dickhead reckoned, anyway. And dickhead logic was as powerful as any other kind.

So where was Gimball, anyway? Maybe he had nerves before an event of this kind, and was bent double over a toilet.

And where was Coe?

Deciding to walk the block once more, River rounded the corner and approached the building clad in scaffolding, which flaunted a cemetery spookiness now, the metal poles lending it a rackety, haunted air. And he was just starting to reach for his phone, to call Coe again, when he reached the alleyway instead, and saw two figures at the far end: one large, broad, intimidating; the other Dennis Gimball.

"She's eating chips," Shin said.

"So?"

"So would she be eating chips if she was on surveillance?"

Danny shrugged. It might be a good disguise; somebody saw you eating chips, they figured you were hungry and that was all. But they saw you hanging around outside a building, they might think you were keeping an eye on it. So he thought it best to keep an open mind.

Shin, though, was keen to close it down. "We don't move until the streetlights have come on. I expect she will have gone by then."

Danny caught An's eye, but neither spoke.

This last twenty-four hours, every order from Shin's lips sounded like a suggestion.

An had drilled a peephole in the van's back door. Danny shuffled across to it, and Shin—weak-willed fool that he was—moved away to let him see through.

The woman was short, a little wide, would probably have been better off with a salad, and was clearly on her own. What kind of operation involved a woman on her own? She moved awkwardly too: stiff-armed. Not what you'd expect from a soldier.

Still, there had been a woman outside the target's house last night, at the exact moment Joon came tumbling from the sky like a stork had dropped him. She'd hit the ground when Danny shot at her, and maybe that was because she'd been well trained, and maybe it was the human instinct at work: when bullets were flying, you dropped to your knees. He couldn't recall anything specific about her: he had learned this at Abbotsfield, that when you held a gun in your hands, the people around you lost definition. They became wraiths, and anything they carried of personality dropped away, no longer of consequence. If you wished to retain your human stamp, stay away from the battlefield. This proposition remained true whichever end of a gun you were looking down.

Besides, they'd been out of there so quickly—Joon stuffed into the car like a bin bag—that he couldn't be sure the woman hadn't been shot: that might have been why she'd hit the deck. So maybe there was a dead woman in London, and this one was someone else, just eating chips.

It didn't matter to Danny either way.

He said, "If she's still there when we move, I will take her."

"I have given my instruction," said Shin, but he glanced at the others as he said it—at An; at Chris, who was up front, in the driving seat—as if enlisting their support.

When it was at last offered to him, Danny held Shin's gaze as if it were something grubby he couldn't put down, for fear of soiling the nearest surface.

It was his moment, he realised.

He said, "I wonder if your commitment is total."

"...Total?"

"At Abbotsfield, your aim was all over the place."

"What do you mean? What are you saying?"

"That your bullets flew wild and free, but didn't actually hit anything. Except a chicken coop. You killed a chicken coop."

"I fired straight and true."

"You shot up the sky."

"I killed two, maybe three."

"I don't think so."

"I fired straight and true," Shin repeated.

"Then it is surprising we did not kill more."

"I have command of this unit," Shin said. "Do you really think my daily report will not contain this conversation?"

"I make daily reports too," Danny lied.

Shin fell silent.

An, squatting against the side of the vehicle, looked down at his feet, then at the panels opposite, or anywhere that wasn't Danny, wasn't Shin.

Danny said, "I'm going to kill her first. Before we go in."

"I am in charge!" Shin said. "You don't do anything without my orders!"

"Then your orders should include this," said Danny. "That I'm going to kill her first. Before we go in."

He leaned back against the panel and closed his eyes.

From his vantage point J.K. Coe watched Dennis Gimball smoke a furious cigarette, then light a second from the trembling stub of his first. Something was going on in the politician's mind: you didn't have to be John Humphrys to work that out. Which was fine. The way Coe felt about pols in general, Gimball in particular, he'd have been happy watching the man's head explode.

Even so, he tensed when a new figure appeared in the alley; rumbling towards Gimball like a threat on legs. There was something wrong with his face, Coe thought, then decided he was wrong. It was the shadows cast by the scaffolding, making crazy the features they fell upon.

When the newcomer reached Gimball he raised his shoulders; made himself bigger.

He was big enough to start with: even with the foreshortening his perspective brought him, Coe could see that. He was black, in a big overcoat, and his hair was razored to straight lines across his brow and round his ears. And still there was that crazy shadowing, and it took another moment for the penny to drop. He wore tattoos. Across his face, his cheekbones, inky markings swirled.

Whatever he said was a low grumble, and Coe couldn't catch the words.

Gimball stepped back. He waved his cigarette, as if sketching in smoke, and said one word over and over: "Now now now . . ."

Coe walked back towards the ladder, so he was directly over where the pair stood. *Is this it?* The newcomer didn't appear to be armed, but didn't have to be: he looked like he could break Gimball in half if he felt like it. Which didn't mean he was going to, and didn't make him a terrorist: he could be a concerned constituent, an overenthusiastic pollster, or just one of the forty-eight per cent—that tiny minority, some of whom hadn't yet got over and moved on—making a valid political point. And since any or all of the above could feasibly involve dumping Dennis Gimball in a wheelie bin, interfering would be putting a spoke in the democratic process.

So Coe thought: I'll just watch for a moment.

Then River came down the alley too, and things got complicated.

Louisa stood, and the bored man along her row looked sharply round: you're the cop, she thought. Pretending not to notice, she retrieved her mobile from her pocket as she walked to the entrance, muttering into it as if in reply to a caller. Through the windows she could see Shirley by the car, eating chips from the roof. Busted. Everything else looked quiet, though there was a van which had arrived since she'd entered the building. No logo on the side, but a driver at the wheel. He was looking behind him, as if talking to someone in the back. Could be something, could be nothing. If this were a proper op, instead of the Slough House equivalent—more like a work-experience outing—the van would have been opened up by now, and its occupants made to sing the national anthem. But they were playing off the cuff, and the most they could do was keep both eyes open.

Unless Shirley did something ridiculous, of course.

River shouted "Hey!" and the man with the tattoo turned. He seemed expressionless, despite the nature of the moment, as if his ink-job was left to do all his features' work.

"Not your business," he said. "Back off."

River came to a halt two feet in front of the pair. "You okay, Mr. Gimball?"

Gimball said, "I have an important meeting to attend. Address. Get out of my way."

It wasn't clear which of the two he was talking to, but River ran with it anyway. "You heard the man. Let him by."

"I hadn't finished speaking to him."

"But he's finished speaking to you."

Gimball said, "This has gone on long enough. Shall I call the police? Is that what you want?"

"No need," River said. "This gentleman was just leaving."

But this gentleman had other ideas. When River reached out to grab his elbow he swatted it aside and squared up. He was bigger than River, broader, and it didn't look like this was the first time he'd raised his fists in an alley, but River had been taught to fight by professionals, and if he hadn't come top of his class, he'd never come bottom either. Which was a great comfort to him when the tattooed guy kicked him in the stomach.

All of this observed from above by J.K. Coe, who was coming to the conclusion that he'd better either intervene or climb into the building and disappear.

River bent double, and the man put a hand on his head and pushed him backwards. He fell over.

Gimball said, "That's it. I'm calling the police." He had his phone out: a visual aid. He waved it about. "I'm calling them now."

The man plucked the phone from his grasp and threw it at the wall, where it shattered.

"Now now now now now . . ."

"Now nothing. You listen to me."

"Now now now . . ."

The man grabbed Gimball by the lapel one-fisted, and pulled him close.

Oh Christ, thought J.K. Coe.

River scrambled to his feet.

"Now now now . . ."

"Shut the fuck up."

River seized the man by the shoulders, and the man released Gimball and turned, ready to plant a heavy fist in River's face, but River drove his elbow into the man's nose first. Blood flew, but the man blocked the follow-up punch with a forearm and lunged forward. The pair went crashing into a wheelie bin, then slid to the ground, the man on top. He raised his fist again, but River was already twisting free: he grabbed the man's wrist, aborting the punch, and at the same time headbutted him in his already damaged nose while Gimball watched in horror.

"Let me by!"

But he trembled on the spot like a man at a dogfight, worried that if he tried to pass, one or the other would turn on him.

River was on his feet now, and planted a kick which caught the man on the shoulder, though Coe assumed he'd been aiming for his head. This produced a grunt but no serious damage, and then the man was upright too, bobbing and weaving, muttering words: *come on then, come on.* He dodged River's next punch, and the one after, then threw one of his own, aiming for the throat: if it had connected, River would have been all messed up. But he'd pulled back and the jab kissed air: from where Coe was watching, it looked choreographed, deliberate. Gimball was wedged against one of the bins, and might possibly climb inside it soon, if assistance didn't show up; River and his opponent seemed to have forgotten he was there. It was all about the fight, now. It was all about being top dog. Coe checked his options again, and they hadn't changed: fight or flight. River didn't even know he was here, for God's sake. He could force a window, clamber through and make his way to the street. Go back and scrape River off the ground later. Except . . .

Except if it was him down there and River up here, River would come to his aid.

He thought about that for a moment, long enough to see the next two seconds of action, neither of which were much fun for River, who caught a blow on the side of the head which would have him hearing bells for a while. Helping River, it occurred to

Coe, would involve getting in the way of such moments: giving the man another target to bounce his fists off while River caught his breath. So okay, a window it was, and Coe turned to retrace his steps, but as he did so his foot caught that stray tin of paint, knocking it from its perch; sending it swirling, lid over base, thirty feet down to the alley below.

Oh shit, he thought.

Five minutes later, miles away, Shirley finished her chips and the streetlights flickered on, making the world subtly different. It was time, she thought. Whatever was going on with that van: it was time for her to make a move. Because if anything was going to happen, shadow-time was its cue.

She should fetch Louisa, really, but what good would that do? Two of them and just one weapon: if there were bad actors in the van, bringing Louisa would double their targets. She crumpled the fish-and-chip paper, wrapped it round the empty polystyrene carton, and left the resulting brick-shaped wedge on the car roof. She could feel the wrench up her right sleeve, its head digging into her palm. When she loosed her grip it would drop into her hand seamlessly, or that was the idea. In an ideal world, she'd have got to practise the move.

Marcus?, she thought.

You go, girl.

She went.

Shin was staring at his phone. "There is something," he began.

"She's coming."

"What?"

"The woman," An said. He had taken over the watcher's role; had his eye pressed to the peephole in the van's back door. "She is approaching."

"Then we move," Danny said.

He was holding a semiautomatic weapon, nursing it as if it were his newborn.

"We move," he repeated. "I'll take the woman, then we go in."

It would not be like Abbotsfield, Danny knew. There they were uniformed, and in the open air: blue skies above, and old stone buildings echoing to their presence. There had been water babbling nearby, and deeply rooted trees bearing witness. It was as though they had stepped through the centuries, bringing warfare to a world that thought itself free of bloodshed. Here, there were no hills to scream down from, and no birds to take flight. There would be walls and windows, that was all, and the dying would know themselves deep in the heart of their city: but they'd still die. It was the final, necessary lesson. That they'd die.

And first among them would be that woman with her stiff-armed walk; approaching them now, An said; walking towards them with intent.

Danny reached for the handle on the back door.

"No. Wait."

And this was Shin again, still caressing his phone, but looking at Danny, and speaking with more authority than of late.

Danny scowled, and gripped the handle. The gun hung over his shoulder, its webbed strap as familiar to him as the feel of his shirt, of the belt round his waist.

"I said wait!"

The door released, and air broke in, a sudden waft of summer evening pushing past the reek of male bodies.

Then An put one hand on Danny's sleeve, and with the other reached across him and pulled the door shut.

"What?" Danny said.

Shin, putting his phone away, said, "It's already done. We must leave."

"What do you mean, already done? How—"

"Go! Drive!"

This to Chris, who sat at the wheel.

"—can it be done?"

Chris started the van, which gave a sudden lurch.

"No! We have a mission!"

Shin leaned forward and struck Danny across the face. "Enough!"

Danny looked wide-eyed at An, but An refused to meet his gaze.

"This goes in my report," Shin hissed. Then, to Chris again, "Why are we still here?"

The van pulled away.

Louisa had come to the window again, ignoring the irritated glances from her fellow citizens, while Zafar Jaffrey explained how a modern city, a model community, found space for all within its embrace: there were no exclusions, no pariahs. Yeah, fine. Until a bunch of them turn up with guns and start their own exclusion process. But she was a little ashamed of that knee-jerk response: occupational hazard, she supposed. Which didn't mean other people shouldn't be setting their sights higher.

Outside, Shirley had left her car-roof picnic; was walking down the road in a purposeful way, her stiff right arm offering a clue to the monkey wrench's current whereabouts. She seemed to be heading for the van, whose back door popped open at that moment. Something happening, Louisa thought, and at the same moment became aware of a murmuring behind her; Jaffrey's audience, responding to an external event. Shirley flexed her arm, and Louisa saw the wrench drop cleanly into it, and then the van door closed again and the vehicle coughed into life. Shirley started to run. Behind her, Louisa could hear chairs scraping, and shocked noises, *oh my God*s and *bloody hell*s. Her phone buzzed. The van pulled away, and Shirley was going full pelt now, shouting something, Louisa couldn't hear what. Oh Jesus, she thought, and then Shirley was in the middle of the road and the wrench in full flight; it arced, graceful as a swallow, and hit the departing van's back door with the business end before clattering to the ground. Shirley came to a halt, put her hands on her knees, and stood panting and doubtless swearing, but her quarry was gone. The whole thing had taken maybe four, five seconds.

Louisa shook her head. If they were ordinary solid citizens in that van, we're going to be hearing about that, she thought.

It's tails, she'd told River. *You get Coe.*

She shouldn't have lied. Coe would have been less trouble.

Then she returned to the crowd behind her, to discover what the fuss was about.

Lamb said, "**Fuck me.** So that happened."

On the BBC website, video had been posted of a scaffolding-clad alleyway, where folk in white jumpsuits teamed about. Either ABBA had reformed in Slough, or a body had been discovered there.

Dennis Gimball, according to social media.

Catherine said, "There's been no official confirmation, but . . ."

"But everyone's favourite Europhobe just made a hard Brexit." Lamb magicked a cigarette from thin air, then thinned the air further by lighting it. "And here's me having gone to the bother of sending Flopsy, Mopsy, Cottontail and the other one to stop that happening." He shook his head wearily. "I sometimes wonder why I get out of bed in the morning."

"Probably just to spread sweetness and light." Catherine was texting; calling River and Louisa home. She didn't call it "home," obviously. When she'd finished she looked up to see Lamb glaring at her iPad: she'd put it on his desk to show him the breaking news. Aware of how brief Lamb's relationships with technology could be, she plucked it from his ambit. "So. Gimball's dead and the bad guys are winning. Not our finest hour."

Lamb sniffed. "On the other hand, this proves our theory's right. So, you know, swings and roundabouts."

"I'm sure that's a great comfort to the deceased."

"He sleeps with the silverfishes," said Lamb. "That'll have to be comfort enough."

Catherine left the room to boil the kettle. When she came back with two cups of tea, Lamb had his unshod feet on his desk. All five toes were showing through one sock; three through the other. It was as close as you could get to not wearing socks, she thought, without actually not doing so. She put a cup in front of him and resumed her seat. Lamb farted meditatively, then said, "So where does this leave us?"

"Well," Catherine said. "You had working knowledge of the possibility of an assassination attempt on Dennis Gimball, but all you did was send a couple of unarmed desk operatives to stand around while it happened. And failed to inform the Park because you were worried they'd issue some scorched earth protocol to cover up the fact that the potential assassins are following the Park's own join-the-dots destabilisation playbook. Did I miss anything?"

Lamb stared for a while, then said, "That was hurtful. Tact's just something that happens to carpets far as you drunks are concerned, isn't it?"

"I did miss something," Catherine said, unperturbed. "You had Emma Flyte locked to a chair while this happened." She sipped tea. "That's going to look good on the report."

"Nah, that plays in our favour. If she'd called it in soon as we loosed her, we'd be neck-deep in Dogshit by now. We're not, or no more than usual. Which means she kept it to herself, which means she took my point. Anyone who knows what's going on needs to keep their head down. This one's toxic."

"They're all toxic, Jackson."

He looked at her sharply, but she was staring into her tea, as if expecting to find leaves there, as if expecting them to offer answers.

Her phone buzzed, and she checked the incoming text. "Louisa and Shirley are heading back."

"A grateful nation sighs its relief."

"Claude Whelan's a sensible man, you know. Bypass Lady Di, take this straight to him. He's not going to have us all buried in some black prison somewhere just because we know more than we should." She sipped tea. "They don't really have troublesome agents taken care of any more. If they did, you'd not have lasted this long."

"Depends how much trouble they cause. But let's wait and see what the Fantastic Four have to report before making any decisions. I mean, I don't wipe my arse before taking a dump, do I?"

"I'd rather not speculate."

Lamb sneered, then, having brought his arse to mind, scratched it vigorously. "Could be worse, I suppose," he said. "I mean, it's not as if one of our lot actually killed the bastard, is it?" And then he stopped scratching. "What was that?"

Someone had just entered Slough House.

Roderick Ho was enmeshed in a dream in which Kim—his girlfriend—was explaining that the various credit card refunds she'd asked him to arrange had been a ploy, to allow her to amass enough cash to buy him a present. This went some way towards explaining her phenomenally poor luck in her online dealings, whereby one retailer or another was forever deducting funds from her card without the promised goods showing up. It was the act of a gentleman to put such matters right, particularly if the gentleman in question (the Rodster) had the ability to wander untramelled behind the world's digital mirror, moving numbers from one place to another as the mood took him. Even so, he felt a very specific kind of pleasure wash over him at the news. Indeed, if the watch she then presented him with hadn't been a small octopus, he might have remained in the dream longer. As it was, it wrapped tiny boneless tentacles around his wrist and emitted a strange *kerthunk* noise, which, as Ho opened his eyes, coincided exactly with the opening of the door.

The new arrival was kind of a babe.

After wiping his drool-plastered lips with the back of his hand, then wiping the back of his hand on his T-shirt, Ho gave her his second-best smile, the one involving an ever-so-slightly raised eyebrow. No point unleashing full gamma force at Moment One. You have to earn that shit. And it looked like she was going to play the hard-to-get game, because she remained stony-faced as she folded her arms and leaned against the wall. She was blonde and taller than Roddy, but only by the usual four inches or so, and he recognised her now, because she'd been caught up in that mess earlier in the year, when Roddy had heroically climbed out of a window to avoid being shot. It was Emma Flyte, Head Dog. Hot dog, come to that. He'd Google-imaged her once or twice, on the off chance, but all he'd found were a few newspaper shots from her time in the force. She'd probably purged her online biography. That was cool: he liked them mysterious.

She said, "This Kim. Your girlfriend."

Roddy nodded apologetically. It was as well she knew upfront he was unavailable.

"Let's start with her," said Flyte.

River Cartwright was taut as a tennis racquet.

"Christ on a bike," he said.

"I've often wondered about that," said J.K. Coe. "What kind of bike," he added.

"Are you insane?"

Coe looked out of the window. They were heading back to London, River driving as if Ho's car were made of glass: every limit observed, every rule of the road adhered to. Not the time to be a bat out of hell, not when half the country's law enforcement and most of its media would be focusing on local activity.

Before getting into the car Coe had called a news site: anonymously, from his pay-as-you-go. An alley in Slough; a man dead. Then he'd dismantled the set, tossing battery, phone and mangled sim card onto the hard shoulder once they were under way.

"That was a serious question," River said. "Are you insane?"

"They used the word 'troubled.' And 'distressed.' Nobody ever said 'insane.'" Coe pursed his lips at the memory. "And these were experts," he said.

"Because you not only act like a fucking psycho, you're starting to rack up a score. What do we do now?"

"I think we stay on the motorway."

". . . Are you finding this funny?"

"No," said Coe, though his tone suggested: Well, maybe a bit.

A police car flashed past in the opposite direction; then another, and another. River had the feeling he was driving into the heart of a storm, from which these vehicles were being hurled at great speed. The thought of what awaited them at journey's end made him want to slam the brakes on. On the other hand, what lay behind needed intervening distance, fast.

It might be wise, he thought, to concentrate on driving for the time being.

"See your phone?" said Coe.

"Why?"

"News."

River fished it from his pocket and tossed it at Coe, hoping it might take his eye out or something.

"PIN?"

River told him.

Coe went online and looked at Twitter. "There you go."

There were already seven tweets hazarding, announcing, speculating about what had happened in Slough. An eighth appeared. Then more. It seemed a self-propelled process, like watching facts being established through sheer weight of numbers.

"And how does that help?"

"I think the more confusion the better, don't you?"

As a guiding principle, thought River, not necessarily. Though under the circumstances, maybe it was for the best.

Coe had more colour in his cheeks than River remembered seeing before; the hood of his hoodie was pooled around his shoulders and his earbuds were loose round his neck. Once before he'd killed someone: had the same thing happened then? River had the horrible feeling it might have.

He said, "We talked about this. Didn't we? You said you weren't going to kill anyone."

"I said I wasn't going to shoot them."

"This isn't the time to split hairs."

Coe said, "I didn't do it on purpose."

"You dropped a tin of paint—"

"Knocked."

"—must weigh God knows how much—"

"It shouldn't have been left on the scaffolding."

"—from a height of like forty feet—"

"I'd say thirty."

"—onto a man's head."

"In my defence," said Coe, "if I'd been aiming for him, I'd have missed."

"That's not really a defence, though, is it? More an admission of guilt."

"Well, it's not like he's a huge loss," said Coe.

"Again, not helping." River realised he was starting to accelerate, and forced himself to ease up on the pedal. "Cast your mind back. The whole point was to foil the bad guys. Not do their job for them."

"Well, mission creep—"

"Don't," said River. "Just don't."

If he wasn't driving he'd sink back in his seat and close his eyes, but if he closed his eyes he'd see it again: that tin of paint hurtling out of nowhere and damn near taking Gimball's head off. One moment he was stuttering a single word over and over, *now now now*, and the next he was bouncing off a wheelie bin like a discarded puppet. The tin meanwhile hit the ground, leaped into the air and struck the black guy River was wrestling: he'd yelped—a high-pitched note; strangely feminine for some-one who seemed, just River's opinion, to be made of rubberised concrete—then taken off when he'd seen Gimball's body. And still the tin's lid remained tightly in place: they could have used that in their advertising, thought River irrelevantly. The paint manufacturers. Although it wasn't necessarily a point in its favour, as presumably there'd be moments when you'd want the lid to come off without hassle. When you were painting a wall, for instance, rather than killing a politician. So probably not the hook for an advertising campaign. Anyway: not an important issue.

What was important was, they'd left the scene.

He'd got to his feet. His assailant was gone; River was left staring in fear and astonishment, and J.K. Coe had appeared. *We'd better go,* he'd said, and then he was hustling River out of the alley, leaving a scene of quiet destruction behind them: one dead Gimball, one tin of paint. All those wheelie bins, clustered round like mourners.

"We shouldn't have left," he said now.

"Yes we should," said Coe.

"You said it was an accident. So—"

"It was."

"—so why did we leave? It only makes us look—"

"We had to."

"—like we're guilty of something, like it was a hit."

"We had to," Coe repeated. He glanced across at River, then back at the road unfurling in front of them, all its marginal twinklings, its brief reflections, amped up to maximum. "Think about it. We were there unofficially—"

"Lamb sent us."

"—because we're Slough House, not Regent's Park, and Slough House doesn't get sent anywhere, doesn't matter what Lamb says."

"We left the scene of a crime."

"An accident. One in which the Security Service's loudest and most public critic was . . . glossed over. Sorry."

"Oh, for Christ's sake—"

"So any suggestion of service involvement in his death, including our presence, will be blanketed. You understand? The Park will cover it up. Whatever the cost. And you and me—we're not expensive, if you see what I mean."

"This is a fucking nightmare."

"It is what it is," said Coe. "On the upside, we do have a ready-made scapegoat."

"You're gunna put this on the black guy?"

"Let's not play the race card. I don't care what colour he is, he was there to kill Gimball. The fact that he didn't—"

"That you did."

"—by accident, yeah, the fact that he didn't's neither here nor there . . . Its lid stayed on, did you notice?"

"The paint?"

"Yeah. Would have been a real mess if it hadn't."

"It's a real mess anyway," River pointed out. "Was he one of them?"

"One of the Abbotsfield crew? How should I know?"

"Because he didn't have a gun, did he?"

"I imagine he'd have used it if he did. Are you going to drive this slowly all the way?"

"I thought it best not to attract attention," said River, through gritted teeth. "In the circumstances."

"Not sure five miles under the speed limit is the best way to do that."

That this was a good point didn't improve River's frame of mind. He sped up though, nudging, then jostling, the limit. Coe meanwhile—at last—closed his eyes; assumed what had until recently been his default setting, though without inserting his earbuds. He had one final comment to offer.

"Probably a tricycle," he said.

River didn't ask.

She wanted to know about his work, Ho said.

"And why was that?"

". . . Because she was interested."

"You told her you worked for the intelligence service?"

No. She thought he worked for a bank, but she'd quickly cottoned on that he was no mere desk jockey.

"Imagine me just shuffling papers?" Ho shook his head. "No, she could tell I did the digital dance, you know?" He trilled a little riff on the tabletop in front of him. "The keyboard solo."

"And how did she work that out?"

". . . I told her."

"And once she knew you were a computer ace, Roddy, what did she ask you for?"

Just to help her out occasionally, that was all. So that's what he did. Because she was Kim—his girlfriend.

Emma Flyte was trying hard not to shake her head, or sigh deeply, or even just burst into tears. "Help her out with what?"

Little stuff.

Sorting her credit card troubles, for example: she was always having trouble with her credit card. Or being defrauded in restaurants. So occasionally he'd step into the breach and, well, yeah, make sure everything got sorted.

Flyte didn't have a word for the expression that accompanied this. It seemed intended to be a conspiratorial smile, but looked like a wasp-victim's smirk.

"And you didn't have a problem with that?"

Well, you know, he explained. Chicks. Right?

"So when did it stop being about the money?"

Well, it wasn't the money as such, more the principle—

"When did it stop being about the money?"

And so it was that Emma Flyte learned that a few months previously Ho had woken up one morning and, well, it must have been the tequila's fault, because he had no memory of the previous evening and Kim, his girlfriend, was acting all moonstruck, telling him how much it turned her on, all the secrets he'd told her. But that was okay, because she was basically family, right? She was his girlfriend.

Sweet God in heaven, thought Flyte.

"Your girlfriend. But apart from her name, and a false address, and the fact that she's Chinese, you know damn all about her, right?"

For the first time, Ho looked puzzled. "Chinese?"

"Well she is, isn't she?"

"No," said Ho. "She's Korean."

"I don't get it," Danny said. "How come Gimball's dead?"

Shin said, "Somebody killed him."

"But who? And why does that mean we let Jaffrey live?"

An said, "Because the plan calls for a populist leader to die. And a populist leader died."

"But we didn't kill him!"

"It doesn't matter."

They had left the scene at speed, the van still ringing from the wrench hurled by the madwoman.

An said, "Gimball's dead, and nobody will believe it's a coincidence. They will believe it was part of the plan, and that in itself will mean the plan works. Don't you see?"

Danny stared, as did Shin, though Shin was trying to pretend that he too had been going to say that very same thing.

"So for now, we should lie low."

Lying low meant parking near the university, where the natural camouflage was greatest. Still bewildered at the sudden alteration in the evening—still angry he felt two steps behind the others—Danny found himself thinking about the girl, Kim, a low-rent con artist who'd been working the target. She had family back in North Korea; distant, but not so distant she was happy to let them become the object of official attention. Or perhaps she was just savvy enough to realise that some offers, you didn't say no to. However distant those family members might be, her own face, her eyes, her teeth, were within reach, and easy collateral.

Her name had been given to them by the SSD, which had recruited Danny and his companions when they were children and had provided all their needs since. Their task was to bend her to the SSD's will, which was, in turn, the will of The Supreme

Leader, whose destiny was to bring low His enemies, and see them scuttle in terror. Like his four—now three—companions, Danny was an instrument of that destiny. Like them, he had come to this country as a student, under the flag of a different nation, his studies a mask for a mission years in the planning. The van they now lived in, the jeep they had long since torched, the weapons they had collected from a lock-up garage on the outskirts of Preston—all had been provided by the SSD. On the other side of the world, The Supreme Leader feasted in His palaces, and Shin made nightly reports, and nightly received instructions. Through His vessels, The Supreme Leader spoke to them, directing them in their mission. And all around the world, other groups like theirs would be activated too, and tearing down the houses of His enemies. The mad American had woken the tiger, and now he and all his allies would pay the price. The world would learn that there were many different ways of being locked and loaded.

The Supreme Leader's glory was a global fact. Kim understood the serious folly of refusing Him. So she had accepted the orders they gave her, along with the pills she had slipped in the target's alcohol, ensuring a night of oblivion. In the morning, she had convinced him this had been spent sharing secrets. If the target thought he had already let slip the true nature of his employment, he would find it easier to release subsequent, apparently trivial proofs.

A week later, the document was in their hands. And so it began.

Later still, once the wheels were in motion, they had been instructed to cover their tracks; to get rid of the girl and Ho too, before the significance of the stolen document became apparent. As with any conjuring trick, it would not do for the magic to be revealed before the final flourish. So Shin had finished the girl in her own home; but as for Ho, twice they had attempted to deal with him, and twice he had eluded their efforts. Despite himself, Danny felt respect. Ho was evidently a highly skilled agent, adept at evading danger. A worthy enemy in this milksop nation.

But he worried. They had been told that the plan was

unalterable, and yet here they were, altering it. For the moment, he would go along. But if there were further derailments, further rearrangements, he would have to take action.

The Supreme Leader would expect no less.

"**I don't** get it," Shirley said. "How come Gimball's dead?"

Louisa was tailgating some idiot crawling at eighty. "Because the bad guys got him."

"Yeah, but they were in Brum. In that van. Coming for Jaffrey."

"Until you scared them off," said Louisa.

"Yeah."

"With a monkey wrench."

Shirley nodded seriously.

"You actually saw them?"

"They were in the back of the van."

"So you actually saw them."

"It was a van, not a shop window."

"So you didn't actually see them."

Shirley shrugged. "They were opening up. That's when I went for them."

Running down the road, brandishing a chunk of metal: you could see why the folk in the van had decided to be elsewhere.

Especially if they were, say, a bunch of locals, rather than a tooled-up gang of murdering psychopaths.

Shirley said, "Did you see my throw? It actually stuck in the door. Hung there for a second."

"So I noticed."

"No wonder they scarpered."

"Shirley, do you really think that van was full of terrorists?"

"Yep."

"Really? Armed terrorists?"

"No match for Superwoman." Shirley mimed throwing the wrench, though there wasn't room in the car to do it full justice. It looked more like she was chucking an imaginary ball for a non-existent dog.

"You don't think they might have been, say, ordinary citizens? Who you terrified?"

"Nope," said Shirley.

"So what happened in Slough? If the terrorists were in that van, coming for Jaffrey—"

"Before I frightened them off."

"—before you chased them with a metal stick, what happened in Slough? Are there two gangs out there, or what?"

"Maybe they split in two."

Maybe they had, conceded Louisa. It was difficult arguing a point when you had no reliable information or accurate knowledge. Unless you were online, obviously. "Does it say how Gimball was killed?"

"Nope." Shirley scrolled through Twitter again, where precise intelligence was being posted by informed witnesses. "But I expect he was shot. Or stabbed."

"Or poisoned or suffocated," agreed Louisa. "You're probably right."

She was thinking about the sequence of events back there; the precise moment when news of Gimball's death had wafted through the public consciousness like wind through long grass. She said, slowly, "The van left as soon as the news broke. There were people in the library finding out about it on Twitter while I was standing by the window, watching."

"So?"

"So maybe that's why they left. They hear that the other group has succeeded, so there's no need for them to do anything. They only need to hit one pol, and that's job done."

"So you do believe me," Shirley said.

"I don't know. I don't know what's happening."

"I think I do," said Shirley.

"Oh, please. Do tell."

"I think shit's hitting the fan," said Shirley. Then she brightened. "Yellow car."

It was more gold than yellow, but Louisa let it ride.

• • •

Some years back, it seemed, a ship-in-the-night Minister had determined that what the Service really needed was a lot more record keeping. Despite an in-house suspicion that this was precisely what a covert organisation could get by happily without, transparency and openness had been in vogue in Westminster at the time, largely because of the widespread hope that if there were concrete examples of these virtues available for the pointing at, it might foster a belief that they were operating across the board, and nullify the need for further enquiry. Thus was born the Service Archive, a "tool for correlating current events with historical precedents," which would be of incalculable strategic use assuming it was ever actually operational. Currently, though, its status was not dissimilar to that of countless other Civil Service projects, in that its existence had been ordained, the process for bringing it into being had been set in motion, and it would thus continue gestating until it was officially put a stop to, despite it having long been forgotten about by everyone concerned in its conception. In this particular instance, its obscurity was exacerbated by the Service having accepted its brief in the same spirit in which it was delivered, and assigned the task of "archive maintenance and augmentation" to Slough House. In other words, to Roderick Ho.

This, it should be said, was Flyte's interpretation of events, not Roddy's verbatim account.

"And you gave access to your ongoing work product to this . . . Kim?"

"My girlfriend," Ho supplied.

"You gave your girlfriend state secrets?"

He leaned back in his chair. "I did what now?"

The man who appeared at the top of the stairs was black, thickset and snappily dressed by Slough House standards, though there were, Catherine Standish admitted, days when any male arriving with his flies done up could claim that. It was a moment before she recognised him, because his hair was shorter than on their previous encounter, but this was Welles, one of the Dogs. He had a strange first name. Devon, that was it.

Lamb said, "Chimneys all been swept, thanks. Maybe next year."

"You're Lamb," said Devon Welles. "I've heard about you."

Lamb scowled at Catherine. "You been on Facebook again?"

Welles came in, gave the room a quick once-over, then returned his gaze to Lamb. "I gather there's been a little trouble."

"Your ladyboss dropped the ball," said Lamb. "I assume you're looking for it."

"Mostly just making sure you've not kicked it through a window," Welles said. "You'd be Catherine Standish," he told Catherine. It wasn't a question.

"There are more chairs next door," she said. "And there's always tea."

She made it sound a philosophical apophthegm, though whether of consolation or dread, it was hard to tell.

Welles said, "I've only seen the stairs and this office. But I'm not inclined to drink anything brewed on the premises, thanks all the same."

Lamb raised an eyebrow. "I'm militantly antiracist, as you know," he reminded Catherine. "But sometimes uppity's the only word that fits."

"Is he like this all the time?"

"I expect so," said Catherine. "I don't work weekends."

Welles found a chair that was hidden under what might have been an old coat, might have been the shed skin of a previous inhabitant. Pulling it nearer the desk, he accepted Catherine's wordless gift of a tissue and wiped it down before sitting. "So," he said. "Slough House. I have to say, it lives up to its billing."

"If you're hoping to be voted least popular visitor," Lamb said, "I should warn you the competition's stiff. But keep talking."

Welles looked at Lamb's feet, still propped on the desk, but masked any emotion they prompted, and addressed his next words to their owner. "Ms. Flyte explained what happened here. In detail."

"And yet you've come alone, unaccompanied by the pack. So you're, what? Her special friend?" Lamb waggled his eyebrows. "Anything you'd like to share?"

Ignoring this, the newcomer said, "You're supposed to be in lockdown."

"There was some talk of that."

"And you had a gun. Where is it now?"

"I think it's in the lost property box," said Lamb. "Which I appear to have mislaid. What are the odds, eh?"

Without taking his eyes off Lamb, Welles said, "Ms. Standish?"

"It'll be in his desk drawer."

"How unpleasant do you want this to be, Mr. Lamb?"

"The last person who asked me that charged eighty quid."

"Are we going to have a problem?"

"You tell me." Lamb produced a cigarette, which was somehow already lit. "Your boss left some while ago, and you're here alone. If you're going to pretend this visit's logged at the Park, I'm going to laugh so hard it'll wet all our pants." He inhaled. "No, you're here covering your boss's back. So, you know, brownie points for you. No offence." He exhaled. "But I can't see how I'm involved."

"You pulled a gun on the head of the internal security division, and you don't think you've got a problem," Welles said slowly.

"Well, if I did, it's been overshadowed by events," said Lamb. "Because a couple of hours ago, I let the head of the internal security division know about a real and credible threat to a member of her majesty's parliament, who's currently decorating an alleyway somewhere in Slough. I rather think that comes under the heading total fuck-up, don't you?"

There was a noise from downstairs.

"Speaking of which," he added.

River and Coe entered a moment or two later.

"Ah, the conquering heroes," said Lamb. "Well, that was a good job well done. Which part of 'prevent an assassination' gave you trouble?"

"There were two of us," River told him. "And we weren't armed."

"Versus?"

River and Coe exchanged a glance.

"No conferring," said Lamb.

Coe said, "We only saw one."

Catherine narrowed her eyes.

Lamb said, "Okay, so you were outnumbered." He looked at Welles. "I always round them down and the opposition up. Gives a more accurate reading of the likely outcome. Oh, I didn't introduce you." He turned back to his slow horses, jerking his thumb in Welles' direction. "This is someone or other from the Park. And these dicks belong here. I can't remember their names."

"River Cartwright," said Welles. "And Jason Kevin Coe."

"I prefer J.K."

"I totally understand." He turned back to Lamb. "Dennis Gimball's been killed?"

"Hard to know whether to laugh or laugh, isn't it?"

"Where's, ah," River began.

"We felt we'd detained her long enough," Catherine said.

"So we uncuffed her," Lamb added, then said to Welles, "Damn it, you're good. See what you made me give away?"

Welles asked Catherine, "When are the other two due back?"

"They have further to come," she told him. "But Louisa's a fast driver."

"Whatever unravelled earlier," Welles said, "we need to put it back together again. That way, maybe we can all get through the day in one piece."

Lamb rolled his eyes in shock. "Are you suggesting some sort of cover up? That we pretend we didn't know what we knew?"

"I'm suggesting that it's not in the best interests of the Service for there to be public doubt about its ability to protect its citizens. Not with this . . . series of events under way."

"Well, the Service's most vocal critic won't be expressing his disappointment, will he? On account of being dead. Of course, that in itself might cast doubt on the Service's ability to blah blah blah." He looked at River. "I'm used to hamster-boy's sullen silences. But you're suspiciously quiet."

River shrugged. "A man died."

"I wasn't expecting you to burst into song. But you were there, weren't you? Contributions welcome. Who was this 'one' you saw?"

J.K. Coe said, "Black guy. Face tattoo."

"And he killed Gimball?"

"Looked that way."

"I hope you're not making assumptions based on his colour." Lamb turned to Welles and shook his head sadly. "I can only apologise."

Welles said, "You saw him with Gimball?"

"He followed him down an alleyway," River said. "And Gimball didn't come out."

"So where's the suspect? In your boot?"

"We thought it best to leave the scene. Gimball's known to be a thorn in Five's side. Us being around might have . . . muddied the waters."

"So instead you let him get away."

"A face tattoo?" said Catherine.

"You're about two conversations behind," said Lamb, and for Welles' benefit mimed someone tilting a glass.

"Something?" Welles asked.

Catherine said, "I did some research earlier. On both potential targets."

"The other being Zafar Jaffrey," said Lamb.

"Who has an aide, or a PA or whatever. He appears in several photos."

"And has a face tattoo," said Welles. "Okay, that's interesting."

Lamb said, "You were a cop too, weren't you?"

"You have a problem with that?"

"No, I quite like cops. You know where you stand with them." He gestured to Catherine. "Got a fiver? We could buy him off."

"This infinite patience of mine," Welles said. "It's only an act. You do realise that?"

"I'm gunna hypothesise," said Lamb. "So pay attention at the back. You served with Flyte, didn't you? Or at any rate, came into the Service on her coattails. She's Whelan's blue-eyed girl, or was until this afternoon. Because let's face it, if she'd done her job right, my little bunch of never-weres would have spent the day sitting on their hands, and Five would have had Dennis Gimball wrapped in cotton wool. As it is, an MP's been whacked and the Park has egg all over its Oxbridge chops, so Emma Flyte's brilliant career looks set to hit the buffers any moment. Which means you'll be out too. That's why you want to hush up what happened here this afternoon. You're covering your arse."

Welles looked at the others, one by one, then returned his gaze to Lamb. "And you're now going to give me a lecture on ethical behaviour?"

"Nah," said Lamb, tapping ash into his own lap. "Ethical behaviour's like a vajazzle on a nun. Pretty to picture, but who really benefits?"

"Mr. Lamb's colourful imagery aside," said Catherine, "cover-ups are never a good idea. Look at Watergate."

"People always say that," Lamb told her, "but they never ask what was really being covered up at Watergate. That shit got out, you'd see fireworks."

"It's safest to assume he's kidding," Catherine told Welles, "and move straight on."

"That was my plan." Welles turned to Lamb. "From what Flyte told me, you had a whole lot of speculation this afternoon, and not an ounce of evidence. If she failed to report back on that, it's hardly an error of protocol. She might as well report on gossip in the supermarket."

"Sadly," Lamb said, "it's possible Flyte didn't paint you in on the whole picture. By which I mean how we knew what we know. Are you still in the room?"

This last to J.K. Coe, who nodded.

"Just checking. Tell the nice man about the pretty piece of paper."

But before Coe could speak, Welles said, "I know about the document. Like I told you, Flyte gave me all the details."

Lamb narrowed his eyes. "She really does trust you, doesn't she?"

"Get over it. If that paper even exists, it doesn't prove anything. I could write down a list of targets—"

There was more noise, more commotion. Louisa and Shirley returning; the latter entering the room first.

"Did you eat all the Haribo?"

Lamb threw something at her, which she caught gratefully, but turned out to be the wrappings from a takeaway. He then nodded at Louisa. "Congratulations. Your guy's still alive."

"Thanks."

"Of course, there's the teeniest possibility he had Gimball whacked," Lamb went on. "Which complicates matters, as you might imagine."

"Shirley and I still win," she said. "Who's this?"

"Devon Welles. And you're Louisa Guy."

Louisa straightened her hair. "Yeah."

River looked at her, then at Welles, and rolled his eyes.

"Which makes you Shirley Dander," Welles continued. "So the gang's all here."

"Apart from Roddy," Catherine said.

"Round about now we usually have a singsong," Lamb said. "But in the circumstances, let's press on, shall we? You could write down a list of targets. The village. The watering hole. And so on."

"And claim it came from Service files, yeah. So what? It's fake news."

"Unless they've got something else up their sleeves," River said.

Louisa said, "What do you mean, he might have had Gimball whacked?"

"Well," said Lamb, "that depends on how much we trust the Chuckle Brothers here. Coe's little eyes are all sparkly, you notice, and that's never a good sign. So either he and Cartwright slipped in a knee trembler somewhere between here and Slough or something else lit his candle. But,"—and here he turned to Welles once more—"I digress. I'm almost certain you weren't finished."

Welles said, "So all we need do is agree that you all spent the afternoon safely in lockdown. And everything's tidy."

"Yeah, not really," said Lamb. "Because you wouldn't need to be here for that to happen, would you? Flyte could have said all that herself. But she's somewhere else, which I'm guessing means she's tracking down that piece of paper it would be so easy to fake."

"The Watering Hole Paper," Coe said.

"Thank you, boy wonder. And if she's doing that, it's probably because she's wondering exactly the same thing I am."

"How come they knew about it," said Louisa.

"We know how they knew about it," said River. "They honey-trapped Ho. Remember?"

"Funnily enough, yeah," said Louisa. "But not really what I was getting at."

"But thanks for the mansplanation, Cartwright," Lamb said. He looked at Louisa. "Mansplaining is when a man tells a woman something she already knows in a patronising, condescending manner," he said, slowly and clearly.

"Thanks."

"Do you need me to repeat that?"

"No, I'm good."

"Excellent." He turned to Welles. "We can pretend all we like that we know nothing about what's happening, but once the Dogs have finished with Ho, that's not gunna wash. Meanwhile, the big question is, how come these clowns knew the Watering Hole Paper existed in the first place?"

"Oh, right, yeah," River muttered.

"So we can stick our heads up our arses and pretend it's not happening, like you suggest," Lamb continued, "or we can walk back the cat and see who we're really up against. Ideally before they move on to the next stage in their schedule."

Welles looked round the room. Everyone was staring at him, except Coe and Shirley Dander, the former of whom was focused on his shoes and the latter peering hard into the gloomier corners of the room, possibly trying to locate the missing Haribo.

He sighed and said, "So just what is the next stage?"

Everyone turned to J.K. Coe.

Who said, without looking up, "Seize control of the media."

Shirley made a scoffing noise. "Yeah, like *that*'s gunna happen."

"They're right on schedule so far," Louisa said.

"So what, they're gunna hijack the BBC?"

"Well, it worked for Graham Norton."

"If you've finished amusing yourselves," Welles said, "do you have an actual suggestion to make?"

Lamb shifted his weight from one buttock to another, and everyone in the room bar Welles flinched. But when he spoke it was without intestinal accompaniment. "Yeah, I suggest you put your thinking cap on. You need to come up with a story."

"For what?"

"For getting me into the Park," Lamb said. "For some reason, they don't much like me over there."

Darkness had fallen over Regent's Park when news of Dennis Gimball's death broke: the darkness would roll away in time, but news once broken remains forever unfixed. Claude Whelan was heading out the door: a fresh shirt, dinner with Claire; neither seemed a lot to ask. But all he had time for was a brief dalliance on the steps; a few deep breaths holding the summery tang of leaves from the park opposite. Heading back in, summoned by his beeper, he encountered, inevitably, Diana Taverner, also on her way to the hub. Despite the hour and the punishing past few days she looked alert and fresh. There were rumours she had a room on one of the upper floors where she enjoyed blood transfusions, or perhaps sacrificed virgins, always supposing any made it past security. Her chestnut brown hair, naturally curly, was worn short of late. Whelan wondered whether the colour used help. Lady Di would see grey hairs as a sign of impending weakness.

"It's Gimball," were her opening words.

Whelan groaned. "Don't tell me—he's making his speech."

"No, but that would be headline news," Lady Di conceded. "Given his current state. He's dead, Claude."

"He's *what?*"

"Dead. In an alley in Slough. Someone damn near took his head off."

"They took his—oh, Jesus! What with, a machete?"

"A tin of paint. Don't look at me like that, reports are confused.

But it's definitely him, he's definitely dead, and there are no current sightings of any hostiles. Which is . . . strange."

"Someone murdered Dennis Gimball with a can of paint," Whelan said faintly, "and there's something you're finding strange?"

"It's not the usual pattern. Terror bots don't hit their target and fade away, they score as many victims as possible and go out in a blaze of glory. All we've got is an anonymous sighting of a black male with a face tattoo, and given the general level of eyewitness reliability, this'll probably turn out to be a teenage girl with a birthmark. If it's not a smokescreen to start with."

"Let's move out of the hall, shall we?" They headed for the stairs, and on the first landing down, Whelan stopped her and said, "I spoke to him this afternoon."

"To Gimball?"

"Before he set off for Slough."

"I see. To warn him off flaming Zafar Jaffrey in public, I presume."

He said, "It would have upset a few applecarts."

"The PM," said Lady Di.

"For these purposes, yes, he's an applecart. It's an open secret Gimball was announcing his return to the fold this evening, and the odds are good he was also going to break whatever story his wife had up her sleeve. I was . . . advising him against such a course."

"You were doing the PM's dirty work."

"In the national interest."

"Are we sure about that?"

"I don't much care for your tone, and this isn't the time for a strategy review. What's done is done. We now need to make sure that whoever's responsible for this appalling act is identified as swiftly as possible."

"Before anybody speculates that it might have been us, you mean."

"That would be a ridiculous assumption."

"Of course it would, but that doesn't mean it won't be made,"

Taverner said. "Gimball was your, I mean our, fiercest critic. If you were coming the heavy with him the afternoon he was killed, well. It's not going to look pretty." She reached out and removed a speck of lint from his lapel. "To be blunt, Claude, it's going to look like we had something to do with it."

A horrible possibility was forming, like a cloud taking shape, in Whelan's mind. "And did we?"

"Now you've lost me."

"You're Ops, Di. Did we have anything to do with this?"

She said, "The small print's a pain to trawl through, but if you look at the T&Cs carefully, you'll notice I'm not allowed to have serving MPs whacked. With or without your knowledge."

"That's a comfort."

"But I'll not forget you felt the need to ask. A little trust wouldn't go amiss." She led the way down the next flight and into the lift lobby, and while they waited said, "What if it's connected?"

Whelan was still processing the new information. "To . . . ?"

"To all the rest of it. Abbotsfield. The zoo bombing."

"What connection could there be? They were random attacks, this is a targeted assassination."

"Maybe so. But there's a guerrilla cadre operating within the UK, so they're automatically top of the suspect list when it comes to the death of a serving politician. Regardless of whether or not you had a meeting with that politician hours before he died. You're the head of the Security Service, for God's sake. For all anyone knows, you were there to warn him of impending danger."

"Well, yes, but . . ."

"Ah." The lift arrived. Diana Taverner stepped into it, then said, "So someone else was present."

"His wife. Dodie."

"The journalist," she said flatly.

"That's right. The journalist."

"You do have a way of complicating matters, Claude. Couldn't you have done it over the phone?"

"Well, I didn't think GCHQ needed to know."

They stepped out onto the hub, and made their way to Lady Di's office. Behind her closed door, she said, "Flyte didn't have precise details of the dirt Gimball has on Jaffrey. Have you run that down yet?"

"She's been running smear stories on him for months. The details barely matter, it's the timing that's the problem."

"Well it might be an idea to find out," said Taverner. "If it's real, it could be just what we need to keep the public occupied while we track down the Abbotsfield crew."

"I don't think the PM's going to be in favour of Jaffrey being exposed to bad publicity. That's precisely what we were trying to avoid."

"Yes, but the PM's going to have to lump it. If it comes to a choice between feeding the media our own head or lobbing it Zafar Jaffrey's, I'm not going to think long and hard, are you? Especially not when Gimball's own wife can do the job for us. We need to steer her in the right direction. Whatever she thinks about you, us, she's got to hate Jaffrey more."

Whelan stared out at the hub. All the boys and girls—they were always boys and girls; it didn't matter that some were fathers and mothers themselves—were intent on work, mostly centred on the weapons used at Abbotsfield. The pipe bomb lobbed into the penguin compound had been homemade; the device on the train was based on an internet recipe. Any reasonably competent psychopath could have devised either, given a WiFi connection and a full set of digits. But automatic weapons implied serious backing.

Taverner said, "Claude?"

"I'm listening."

"You're going to have to decide which flag you're flying. The Service doesn't exist to further the interests of the party in power. In fact, the party in power is arguably our natural enemy. Given that it's holding the purse strings."

"We serve the nation, Diana," Whelan said. "And the party in power is democratically elected to lead that nation." He turned back to the glass wall, and the worker ants beyond, but continued talking. "I tried to get hold of Flyte earlier, but she's not around. I was told you had her on something."

"She's at Slough House. It's in lockdown. And can stay that way until we've determined what connects Jackson Lamb's pet nerd with Abbotsfield. Has he talked yet?"

Whelan said, "I was leaving him to soften up. A crew was sent to his house, they've collected his IT. Quite a lot of it, apparently. Have we got anyone in Slough?"

"We'll wait on the police reports. It's not like our forensics'll be better than theirs. We're using the same contractors half the time."

"Keep me posted. I'll talk to Dodie Gimball."

"No, let me," said Taverner.

"Diana—"

"If she thinks you had her husband killed, how happy is she going to be to see you?"

He paused. "Maybe so. All right, then." He turned to go, then turned back. "Are we really calling them 'terror bots' now?"

"They always turn out devoid of personality. It seems to fit."

"If we end up throwing Jaffrey to the wolves," he said, "I'll need to be sure he deserves it."

Taverner waited until Whelan had gone before she replied. "He's not one of us, Claude. That usually suffices," she said. Then she turned the dial on her desk which frosted the glass wall, hiding her from view.

Apart from that, how was the show, Mrs. Lincoln?

An old gag, which he'd have to make sure didn't slip out at an inappropriate moment. Which, for a budding pol, was any moment, ever.

So otherwise, you enjoyed the motorcade, Mrs. Kennedy?

Zafar Jaffrey ran a hand through his already enjoyably tousled hair and shook his head, though there was nobody with him.

Apart from the whole thing about Dennis Gimball being murdered, and the news breaking on Twitter midway through, the evening at the library had gone passably well. The answer he'd given on the likely impact of Brexit on the local hospitality industry would, under other circumstances, have caused chatter; as it was, his talk had been eclipsed, and all attention drawn like iron filings to Twitter's magnet. Utter confusion. As usual with social media, rumour had the inside lane, and by the time official confirmation came through—death; cause still unknown—it had been definitively stated by observers as far away as Texas that Gimball had been attacked by burka-clad suicide bombers. But facts could wait. The immediate aftermath was a deliciously stunned sense of news happening; of the dark heart of political conspiracy being exposed once more.

What Jaffrey needed to know was where Tyson was; what his bagman had done.

He'd escaped as soon as possible—easy to claim he was needed elsewhere—but waited until he'd reached home before calling.

"Were you there?"

"I'm in the car, boss."

"I appreciate that you're in the car, Tyson." He could hear the usual ambient noise: the humming of the engine; the swishing of traffic. "That's not what I asked you. Were you there?"

". . . Was I where, boss?"

There was something he'd noticed about youngsters who'd lived on the criminal margins; who'd dipped a toe— both feet, sometimes —in a lifestyle which prided itself on disregarding the civilised norms, and it was this: they were incredibly fucking childish. They thought widening their eyes proof of innocence.

"Come to the house, Tyson. When you're back."

"I thought maybe in the morning, boss?"

"No, Tyson. Tonight."

So he'd waited in the dark; a gradually strengthening sequence of gin and tonics for sustenance. Gins and tonics? Gins and tonic, he settled on. The gin element was well past plural; the tonic still coming from the same half-bottle. He was a bad Muslim, he knew, but there were limits to how strong one could be, how good.

Earlier, he had spoken to his mother. She had wanted to know

what she always wanted to know: how many had been in attendance, what questions had been asked, whether anyone mentioned
Karim. Always that last question, and still Zafar didn't know why,
precisely. Was she worried his younger brother, the Syrian "martyr," had forever scuttled Zafar's political career? Or did she just
want to know he wasn't forgotten? Sometimes Zafar wanted to
tell her that his own public life, far from being hampered by his
brother, had been made by him; his own awakening germinated by
the news of Karim's death. It was true that there were those for
whom his sibling connection would ever bar him from political
credibility, and sections of the media which would fan those flames
every chance they got. But the deeper truth was, if not for Karim's
wasted life, Zafar would never have entered the public arena. As it
was, he felt the need to eradicate the stain left by his brother's
unwise choices—and prove, too, that being Muslim did not mean
being an enemy in his own country. It was shameful that there was
need to prove such things, but that was how the world span.

But he hadn't known how long-lasting the tremors of one
Hellfire missile could be; how they would continue to churn the
ground beneath his feet so many miles and years away from their
detonation point.

Tyson arrived at last; late enough that it was clear he'd been
dragging his wheels. Razar poured him a coke and sat him on the
sofa. An interviewing arrangement, not dissimilar from the one
he'd used when he'd first met Tyson Bowman, and seen in him a
young man worth saving. There were many who wouldn't have
looked past the tattoo.

"Did you speak to Mr. Gimball?"

". . . Kind of."

"Kind of yes? Or kind of no?"

Tyson was frightened. That was something else it was important to remember about the young: they were often frightened,
because there was always the chance they'd be sucked down into
an abyss they'd only gradually become aware of. And they always
tried to hide this fear, but it never went away.

"It's all right, Tyson," he said. "Whatever happened, we can fix it." This was a lie. "But I need to know what it is I have to fix."

He'd become the shining light in these youngsters' lives: the only one to show faith, offer support, without demanding their souls in return. But this meant a lot of them thought him capable of any manner of impossibles, including fixing things that couldn't be mended.

"I wanted you there to observe," he reminded Tyson now, hating himself for doing so; hating that he was making sure his own essential innocence was part of Tyson's story. But he'd started, so he'd finish. "To talk to him if the opportunity arose, but not to force the issue."

"Didn't force the issue, boss."

"I just wanted to know what he planned to say."

Because if Ed Timms had been right, and Gimball had been preparing to throw shit at the walls, Zafar would have needed as much warning as possible. To wrap up the Dancer Blaine business, and then cover his tracks.

"So what happened?"

"I was gunna explain to him," Tyson said. "Tell him not to dis you, like. Keep his mouth shut."

Zafar's heart was all the way deflated now, a useless piece of rubber curled up and drying in his chest. He could see it happening as clearly as if it were projected onto his sitting room wall: Tyson catching Gimball unprotected; overconfident swagger on one side, panicky reaction on the other. Fists clutching lapels. A struggle, a blow.

"And did you—?"

Did he what? Zafar didn't even know what question to ask. There'd be no consoling answers.

"It was just a bit of argy. I didn't touch him."

"You didn't touch him?"

"Not hardly." Tyson rolled his shoulders. "Just messing a bit. He wouldn't stay still."

It was like talking to a child who'd stoned a cat. *I didn't mean to hurt it. It was the cat's fault.*

He thought, Tyson has to disappear. And I'll have to finish what he started. Like most of his decisions, it was no sooner made than he was formulating the strategy: he'd need to cancel tomorrow's meetings; fake a head cold, whatever. All of that was doable. He was good at details.

But still he could feel the ground trembling beneath his feet; those shockwaves ploughing up the earth.

Catherine said, "I think it's about time you explained what happened, don't you?"

Lamb had left, with Welles on his heels like a man who'd been rabbit-punched then put on a leash: there really was cause, she sometimes thought, to hang a warning notice on Lamb's door. She'd have gone home herself, if not for the gauntlet of pubs, bars and off-licences she'd have to run. As it was, the role of den mother had once more dropped onto her shoulders.

Shirley had found what was left of the Haribo, and had tucked in before Catherine could warn her about Lamb's rejection policy. Louisa was leaning against the radiator—they were in River's room—and frowning about something, or possibly everything. J.K. Coe was at his desk, hood up. River was also seated, but visibly arriving at the conclusion that Catherine was mostly talking to him, and unlikely to take silence for an answer.

"We've told you," he said at last. "A man followed Gimball up the alley, and Gimball didn't come out again."

Catherine pursed her lips. After a moment, River looked at Coe. "That's what happened, right?"

Still hooded, Coe said, "That's what happened."

Shirley said, "The bad guys were in Birmingham."

"But Jaffrey wasn't attacked," said River. "Was he?"

"They were in a van. I chased them off."

"Be that as it may," Catherine said. She returned her gaze to the two men. "'We only saw one,'" she said. "I'm quoting here."

"Quoting who?" River asked.

"Mr. Coe. That's what he said when you got here."

"Well, he counted right."

"It's not his arithmetic that bothers me. It's more that he was so keen to volunteer information. It usually requires strong persuasion before he opens his mouth in company. Doesn't it, Mr. Coe?"

Coe shrugged.

"And like Lamb said, he appeared a little more bushy-tailed than usual. And I think we all remember the last time that happened."

"You don't seriously think," River began, then stopped.

"We don't seriously think what?" Catherine asked.

For half a moment, maybe less, the only sound in the room was a fly banging against the dust-tracked windowpane; just one more futile attempt to escape from Slough House.

And then a penny dropped.

"Oh Christ," said Louisa. "You didn't!"

"It was an accident."

Louisa, mouth wide, looked at Catherine, who was staring into whatever abyss had just opened inside her own mind. Shirley had frozen mid-chew, and her face had the blurred rubbery look that comes from being caught between two expressions. The men exchanged a glance, then resumed their defensive postures. And the fly hurled itself at the glass once more, and vomited invisibly on contact.

It was Catherine who spoke first. "You killed him?"

It was Coe she was talking to, and Coe didn't answer.

"Mr. Coe? Pull your hood down and answer the question."

Unexpectedly, Coe did as he was told. "... Not exactly."

"But imprecisely, right? In some vague, nonspecific, possibly even daydreamy fashion, you killed him? Please say you didn't."

"He was hit by a tin of paint."

"How?"

"... It got knocked off some scaffolding."

"By who?"

"Whom."

"Don't even—"

"It was an accident," said Coe.

"Yeah, I think we've established that," Louisa put in. "But whose fucking accident was it?"

"His," said River.

Everyone in the room turned to River.

"Well it was! I was fighting the tattooed guy!"

"So you didn't invent him?"

"Christ no," said River. "He attacked Gimball."

Catherine said, "I feel faint. You know? I actually, seriously feel faint."

"I told you they were in the van," said Shirley.

"What?"

"The actual bad guys," said Shirley. "Whatever happened in Slough, that was just a cosmic fuck-up. The actual bad guys were in Brum. And I chased them away."

"Yes, great, thanks for that," said Louisa. "Meanwhile, what do we do about having accidentally assassinated someone who might have been our next PM? And when I say 'we,' incidentally, I mean Coe. I had nothing to do with it."

"Nor me," said Shirley.

"That's right," said Catherine. "You were busy assaulting somebody else somewhere else."

"Gimball's dead because the guy with the tattoo attacked him," River said. "And we've already established he's Zafar Jaffrey's man. That's what's going on here. In addition to, you know. The country being under attack and all."

"So the fact that it was you and our resident psycho here—"

"Louisa . . ."

"—who whacked him, that's just a detail, is it?"

Something hit her in the chest, and she caught it reflexively. A phone.

Coe said, "You want to call the police?"

Louisa looked at the phone, then at Coe.

Who repeated himself: "That's what you want to do? Go right ahead. You weren't there. Uninvolved, like you said. You've all made that very clear."

After a moment, Catherine said, "Protocol would say we report to the Park, not the police."

"And it's pretty clear that's not happening, isn't it? Unless you think that's what Lamb's doing."

"Lamb doesn't know about this yet."

"Yeah, 'cause he's notoriously slow on the uptake, isn't he?"

Catherine seemed about to reply, but changed her mind.

Louisa said, "If we don't report this, we could all end up in deep shit."

"It was an op," said Coe. "Authorised by our team leader. We report back to him and him alone. Anything else and we're in breach of the Secrets Act. Which is equally deep shit."

Shirley said, addressing the others, "He got away with it last time."

They stared.

"Just saying."

"Let's wait until Lamb gets back before deciding our next move, shall we?" said Catherine at last. "And it might be an idea to keep an eye on the news."

"Might also be an idea to pretend this conversation never took place," said Louisa, and tossed Coe's phone back at him.

Welles checked in via the car park, showing his pass to the guard on duty but signing Lamb in using the standard visitor soubriquet "Lindsay Lohan," a hangover from a few years back, when Lohan was turning up everywhere unannounced. The guard didn't bat an eye. Jackson Lamb's own name might cause ripples even among the young and unblooded, but his public appearances were as rare—and as welcome—as a fin on a Bank Holiday beach, so his physical presence rang no bells. The guard probably had him down as a local joe, working undercover in a food bank queue.

This side of the Park was for trade and passing talent: little chance of bumping into your Diana Taverners, your Claude Whelans. Waiting for the lift to take them down into the bowels, Welles said to Lamb, "Remind me why I'm doing this."

"If we want to know what this killing crew plan next, we need to know who's pulling their strings. They knew exactly what they were after when they trapped Ho in their honeypot. Which means they had inside knowledge, if not an actual insider."

"You think there's a mole?"

"It's happened before. But no, honest answer, I think somebody fucked up. That's usually what turns out to have happened."

"We should kick it upstairs," Welles said. "We should *definitely* kick it upstairs."

"Yeah, but before committing Hare Krishna, let's see if we've got wiggle room when it comes to assigning blame."

"*Hara-kiri.*"

"You're welcome."

When the lift doors opened, they were on Molly Doran's floor.

She was already rolling out to meet them because, as she later explained to Lamb, she had a sixth sense for impending unpleasantness. "When you're in the area, it's like everything grows darker." He would simply blink at this assertion, as if the obvious had been stated once too often for his liking. Meanwhile, in the here and now, Molly was a short woman, and would be shorter were she standing, as both her legs were missing below the knee. This lack contributed to the impression of spherity she radiated, as did—somehow—her overabundance of makeup, a quantity which would have drawn comment had anyone else indulged in it, but with Molly Doran seemed to be a challenge. Her cheeks were white; her lips scarlet. Her wheelchair cherry red, with thick velvet armrests.

When she saw Lamb and Welles her expression didn't change, but the light in her eyes shifted a pantone, from dark red to darker. There'd always been stories about Molly Doran—how she guarded her fiefdom like a lioness its kill—and she had always encouraged them, because there's nothing Spook Street enjoys more than a legend, unless it's a myth. The distance between the two was paper thin; the exact space between one's last breath and the next thing. Welles had met her in passing only; had once asked—quite late at night—if she needed help getting into a lift. The look he received in response was one they could have usefully taught down the road, where new recruits were drilled in unarmed combat.

"Jackson Lamb," she said. "I hardly need to ask, do I? You're after something."

"Would I be here otherwise?"

"Pay the troll."

He bent and kissed one overpowdered cheek. For Welles, it felt like a moment that should have been preserved somehow, though not on a camera, not on a phone. It needed Goya, with a lump of charcoal.

Molly said to Welles, "He doesn't do social calls. Only time he shifts his fat arse off a chair is when something promises to relieve his boredom."

"I'd visit more often," Lamb said, "but you cripples make us normal people uncomfortable."

"Jesus, man," said Welles.

But Molly Doran laughed. "He likes to give the impression he's sparing us the bullshit," she told Welles. "Truth is, he's just peddling a different line of bullshit altogether. How've you been, Jackson?"

"My knees have been giving me gyp," he said. "But I don't expect sympathy."

"See?" she said to Welles. Then: "I don't allow Dogs on my floor."

"I'm not sure you have a choice in the matter," he replied.

"That's because you've never tested the proposition," she said, and smiled sweetly.

A flake of powder floated loose, as if it hadn't been expecting that particular muscle to throb.

Welles opened his mouth to reply, but Lamb leaned towards

him. "Probably best do what she says. She's run over bigger boys than you in that thing."

"And it takes forever to scrape the treads clean."

"You're pushing your luck," Welles told Lamb, unpeeling the other man's fingers from his elbow.

"You're a dear boy, I'm sure," Molly Doran said. "But on this floor, I make the rules. And while not much brings me pleasure these days, fighting my corner does get the juices flowing."

"And trust me," said Lamb. "You don't want to see her juices flowing."

Welles looked from one to the other. "I'll give you ten minutes," he said. "But ten minutes only. Once that's done, I'm coming in there." He nodded towards Molly's doorway.

Molly considered for a moment, then beamed. "I quite like this one," she told Lamb. "He's less damaged than your lot."

"Give it time."

"This once only, you may remain right here," Molly said to Welles. "But no whistling. I can't abide whistling."

She spun on the spot, and headed into her room.

"If we're not finished, there'll be a sock on the doorknob," leered Lamb. "One of mine, obviously," he added, following Molly into her lair.

Which was a long room lined with upright cabinets, set on tracks allowing them to be pushed together when not in use; like library stacks, and imbued with a similar sense that knowledge, information, *words*, never really died, but simply burrowed down out of the daylight and waited for curiosity to dig them up again. Here were Regent's Park's older secrets. Those that were freshly minted were stored in more instantly accessible form, of course, and many had consequently enjoyed fifteen minutes of fame on social media since.

Molly reversed into a cubbyhole just wide enough for her chair, and braked. Jackson Lamb eyed a nearby stool with distaste, but perched a buttock on it regardless. If this had happened in Slough House, the team would be praying, hard.

"I hear David Cartwright's entered the twilight," Molly said. "Best place for him."

"Young River must find that difficult."

"Young River finds dressing himself difficult," said Lamb. "I don't want to speculate on his emotional trials."

"Oh, he's bright enough. He just has the disadvantage of having you as his team leader. That would make anyone question their own competence."

"I don't encourage them to think of me as team leader," Lamb said. "I prefer 'pagan deity.'" He looked at the wall above her head. "There was a picture there. Why'd you take it down?"

"Because I fancied a change?"

"You like change the way I like milk." He glanced round the room, searching out more clues, then turned his gaze back to her. "You're moving?"

She said, "I'm being let go."

Lamb nodded, and gestured towards her wheels. "Just so long as they don't do it on a slope."

"I don't expect sympathy, Jackson. But spare me attempts at humour. I've been here decades. They built this room around me. It's what I know, it's where I'm comfortable. But apparently I'm . . . surplus to requirements."

He nodded again. The room was mostly dark, only this particular nook of it illuminated, and this satisfied whatever inside him thrived on gloom and unacknowledged corners. The rows of files were secret histories, and some would be his own; reports made by and of him; lists of the survivors, and an accounting of the dead. Molly Doran lived among past lives he'd discarded, and those of joes he'd known in Cold War days. She belonged here as much as any of those black-ribboned folders. She'd steered her wheelchair into this cubbyhole without hesitation, as easily and unthinkingly as anyone else might step through a doorway.

"What will you do?" he asked, and had any of the slow horses been present—except Catherine—they'd have wondered where the words were coming from, where the tone had arisen.

"Well I don't see myself settling into civilian life, do you? Even if I found another job, I'd be there to tick boxes. Age, disability, gender. Jump right in as soon as you think of something offensive."

"I don't know why you're always expecting me to be the comedian," he said. "You'd be quite the stand-up yourself, if not for the obvious."

Whatever softness had blurred his edges was gone.

"I've lived a useful life," she said. "I've made a difference. Now they want to replace me with an intern, Lord help us all. What will I do? What would you expect me to do, Jackson?"

He sniffed. "This one of Lady Di's plans?"

"She's signed off on it."

"There you go, then," said Lamb. "Taverner's the word of God round here. I mean, Whelan rattles the cup. But she's the one grinding his organ." He fished a cigarette out of nowhere, and rolled his eyes before Molly could speak. "I'm not going to. It helps me think, that's all. How do you intend to do it?"

"'It?'"

He drew a finger across his throat. "Turn the lights out. Once you've been given the push. I assume that's what you're getting at."

"Oh. Pills, I expect. That's the favoured option, isn't it?"

He shrugged. "Seems to me it's one area you have a wider choice than most. Nice coastal path. Big steep drop. You might set a new record for unassisted flight." He sucked his teeth. "Or at the very least, a personal best."

"You're always a comfort, aren't you? But then, you're not here to listen to my woes."

"Christ, you got that right," he said. "Do I look like a fucking social worker?"

"Our ten minutes is ticking away. And I don't think our friend is likely to offer much leeway."

"Someone came for Roderick Ho the other night," Lamb said. He tucked his cigarette behind an ear. "He's the one does my internet and stuff. And when I say 'came for,' I mean, with guns."

"I presume they didn't actually succeed."

"He was lucky enough to have the right pagan deity onside."

"Fortunate for him," said Molly. "But from what I've heard of your Mr. Ho, you don't require a shortlist of suspects as much as the electoral roll."

"There is that," said Lamb. "But as it happens, we know who it was. The same homicidal cretins who shot up that Derbyshire village."

"Oh dear," said Molly. "Stepped into something nasty, did he?"

"And been treading it round on his shoe ever since. Course, he's the last to notice."

"Where is he now?"

Lamb pointed floorwards.

"But you don't want to wait until they've finished wringing him out."

"He gave someone something. We know that much. The Watering Hole Paper, Coe's calling it."

"Mr. Coe? I remember him. Pleasant young man."

"Yeah, he's had a personality transplant since. Anyway, it's a post-war planning document, some nonsense about destabilising a third-world state, or developing nation, or whatever we call them now. Tin-pot hellholes?"

"I'm not sure that's the PC term, but I think I know what you're getting at. Where's this paper come from?"

"This is Ho we're talking about. He snatched it out of the ether."

"Well, there you go. If it's been digitised, it won't be here. The point of putting records on the Beast is so they're not taking up space elsewhere. The original will have long since been shredded."

The Beast was Molly's collective name for the assortment of databases the Service operated. She barely hid the hope that one day the whole vast edifice would crumble into spiralised landfill, leaving her realm the Service's sole bank of reliable memory.

"That's what I thought," said Lamb. "Except." He scratched an ear, found a cigarette there, stared at it for a moment, then put it back. "Except I think there's more than one version. The original was ancient, like I said. But at some point or other it was picked up and dusted off, which is how come it ended up on a database. Might not have been put into play, but it was certainly on an agenda at least once in recent decades."

"So you're thinking the original might still exist, because the one your boy snatched from the Beast was an updated version." She grimaced, and her nose twitched. "Could be," she said at last. "Especially if whoever updated it didn't want it known they'd copied someone else's homework."

"Excellent," said Lamb. "Couldn't find it for me, could you?"

"Well, of course. I mean, I've nothing better to do."

"That crew who shot up Abbotsfield? They're using this thing as a blueprint."

"Oh dear," Molly said.

"So, you know. A bit of legwork'd be appreciated."

She sucked in breath, but after a moment in which detonation seemed possible she exhaled again, blinked slowly and shook her head. "You just can't help yourself, can you, Jackson?"

"Well, be fair," he said. "You're a sitting target."

Someone appeared in the doorway, and they both turned, expecting Welles.

But it was Emma Flyte.

"You are seriously starting to piss me off," she told Lamb.

Nobody was going anywhere, but that didn't mean they had to stay where they were. Louisa, Shirley and Catherine departed to their own offices while awaiting Lamb's return, each contemplating the possible blowback that might be—would be—was definitely heading Slough House's way. For Shirley this meant taking the twist of coke from her pocket, picturing the rush she'd get were she to take it and trying to find a compelling reason for not doing so. The only one she could summon was that if she took it now she couldn't take it later, when she might have greater need. As for Louisa, she'd gone online; at first dipping into various dodgy forums, looking for Abbotsfield chatter, but ultimately giving this up and shopping for boots instead. She found a promising pair, maybe a little pointy-toed—she'd heard it said boots can't be too pointy, but never by anyone she completely trusted—but hovered over the Buy Now button so long it started to feel like she'd contracted retail paralysis, a condition she'd always thought gender-specific. Christ, it was only money. She clicked, and enjoyed a brief endorphin release. Upstairs, Catherine was tidying places that were already tidy. Her office was like a chamber of her own mind: everything was where it ought to be, but keeping it so required constant vigilance. Across the landing was Lamb's room, its door lazily ajar; in Lamb's desk drawer was a bottle of whisky, and with no conscious effort—as if it were marked with a pencil—Catherine could recall exactly the level at which its contents stood. It was as if she were perpetually geared up for departure, and always knew where her nearest exit was. In case of emergency, grab glass. Or no, forget the glass; go straight for the bottle.

Still in their own room, River and Coe were picking at the evening's scab.

"I thought you dumped your phone out the car window."

Coe said, "You only have one phone? Seriously?"

"You keep the spare for dramatic gestures, right?"

River was remembering Coe tossing the phone at Louisa: *You want to call the police? Go right ahead.* Remembering the gesture, perhaps, because it was preferable to dwelling on the consequences had Louisa done precisely that.

He said, "The entire country is focused on an alleyway in Slough. Do you really think they're not going to work out what happened there? Someone will have seen us. Even if there's no CCTV, someone will have seen us. Ho's car'll be on camera entering and leaving town."

"Along with hundreds of others," said Coe. "Besides, there was a genuine bad guy there, remember? We were trying to protect Gimball."

"And a damn fine job we did."

"Stop bitching. He'll be on camera too, and he won't have the advantage of being a member of the Service. We were there to protect Gimball. He was there to hurt him."

"He might have his own story to tell though, mightn't he?"

"Yeah, well," said Coe. "That depends on whether he gets to tell it."

". . . Are you serious?"

"He looked like a player. Let's face it, he was giving you trouble. So when a SWAT team comes through his door, what are the odds he'll put up a fight?" Coe made a facial shrug, mostly using his eyebrows. It was as much expression as River had ever seen him wearing, and meant, in this instance, Game Over.

"There'll be an investigation," he said. "Even if they arrest tattoo guy's corpse, they won't just leave it at that. They'll piece things together."

"How long have you been doing this? There'll be an official version of events. That's what happens. And what really went down, if it's inconvenient, will be buried."

"Yeah, but we're not inconvenient," said River. "We're Slough House. We're pretty much made to measure, if they're looking to hang someone. Not to mention," he added, "that you really did kill him. You know? So it's not even a fit-up."

"We're Service," said Coe. "Slough House or not. This gets public, it'll go global in a heartbeat. Half the world will believe we were following orders. The other half'll know it for a fact."

"You keep saying 'we,'" said River.

"There's a reason for that."

River remembered again, second time in as many days, sharing this room with Sid Baker: that was the last time the office had heard this much conversation. Well, argument. He said, "We sit here much longer, I'm going to start throwing things through the window." Beginning with you, he didn't say. "If you're so keen on constructing a more favourable narrative, what's your game plan?"

"'Constructing a more favourable narrative?'"

"I read the *Guardian*," said River. "Well, sometimes. Well, the cartoons."

Coe said, "What happened today's part of the Abbotsfield sequence. That's the *narrative*. Tattoo guy, Zafar Jaffrey's man—he's mixed up in that bigger picture. We were trying to foil him."

River realised Shirley was in the doorway, her left hand curled into a fist—gripping something—and her right leaning against the doorframe.

"Come up with a plan yet?" she asked.

"I was thinking, prayer," he said.

"That's your best option," she agreed. "But you're still fucked."

"Yeah. But thanks for the pep talk."

"Want a Haribo?"

"Is this your idea of constructive help? Because I have to tell you—"

"You need to find Kim," she said.

"Ho's girlfriend?"

Shirley said, "She's the one he passed the Watering Hole Paper to. She's the one with the connection to the Abbotsfield crew. Find her, you find them. Probably."

Coe said, "Ho's been at the Park all afternoon. Anything he can tell them about Kim he'll have told them, in which case they'll already have her or they can't find her. Probably because she's already dead."

Shirley said, "It's true, isn't it?"

"What is?"

"You get a lot perkier after killing someone." She tucked whatever she was holding into her jeans pocket. "Lamb'll probably adopt it as office policy."

Coe ignored her. To River, he said, "They tried to kill Ho. Stands to reason they'll have cut the other loose thread by now."

"That's what you would have done, is it?" said Shirley.

"What's what who would have done?" Louisa stepped past Shirley and came into the room.

River said, "Oh, we're just discussing the office rota. You know, whose turn it is to wash up. Who Coe's going to kill next. That sort of thing."

"We watched Kim the other night. She's pretty fly," said Shirley.

"I don't speak disco."

"I mean, they tried to kill Ho, and couldn't even manage that. And he can barely tie his laces. So I think they'd have had trouble whacking Kim. She seemed pretty . . . smart."

Coe was looking something up: woman found dead in her London home. He read the headline out. Then said, "Black?"

"Not Kim then," said Shirley.

Louisa said, "You're thinking if we can find her we can trace the Abbotsfield crew."

"Or at least get some idea of what they might try next," said River.

"Seize the media," said Shirley. "That could be anything. You're basically seizing the media if you buy a newspaper these days."

And now Catherine was with them. "Have you tried checking his phone?"

"I assume it's at the Park," said River. "With Ho."

"I think he's got two."

Coe gave River a told-you-so look.

Shirley said, "Yeah, but one of them might be a bit broken."

"If it's still got its sim card, we can use it," said Louisa.

But Ho's broken phone—the one Shirley had sent flying the previous day, "saving his life," as she reminded them—provided no clues, even once they tracked it down to his desk drawer: Kim's number, listed as "Kim (Girlfriend)," yielded only that empty, echoless silence signalling unequivocal departure.

"Told you she was fly," said Shirley.

"Or dead," added Coe.

"Either way," said Louisa, "our chances of finding her are like a one-legged man's in an arse-kicking contest."

"Who organises those events, that's what I want to know," Shirley complained. "And when are they gunna tighten up the entry criteria?"

Catherine said, "Any other bright ideas?" and said it with the air of a primary school teacher scraping the barrel, but keeping a brave face regardless.

"They're in a hurry," said River at last. "It's all kicked off very quickly."

"Because they have no backup," Louisa said.

They looked at her, but Coe was nodding.

She went on, "They're racing the clock so they get to the end before they're caught. Because if they don't finish the plan, nobody's going to finish it for them."

Catherine said, "That explains why they've taken shortcuts. The bomb on the train, that fizzled out. Ticking things off the list matters more than doing them right."

"So whatever media strike they're planning, they're going to implement it as soon as they possibly can "

"Which means it's already been scheduled," said J.K. Coe.

"Hardly narrows things down," River said.

But Shirley had brightened again. "We found them once," she said. "We can do it again."

"Remind me where we found them?"

"They were in a van," she said stubbornly. "In Birmingham."

"Are you sure you were in Birmingham? You got back very fast."

"Louisa was driving."

Louisa shrugged modestly.

Catherine said, "So let's work on the assumption Kim's still alive. She's discovered she's expendable, and she's gone to ground. But she is, as Shirley claims, pretty smart. So where would she hide?"

"The last place they'd look," said Louisa.

"And where might that be?"

River said, "Ho's place."

There were still glass splinters in the gutter, their brief brilliance catching the eye when the angle was right, but the house itself was in darkness. The curtains were undrawn, though the big broken window had been cardboarded over, the resulting black eye adding to the air of vacancy. Crime scene tape sealed the door. It looked like a property about to succumb to dereliction: give it a week, River thought, it would be festooned with graffiti, and occupied by crusties, dogs and mice.

They'd arrived in the same two cars, Louisa's and Ho's. Same pairings, too. "Why split up a winning combination?" Louisa had asked. River had spent the journey working on a comeback; now they were here, his attention was focused on the fact that the spare keys taped beneath Ho's desk hadn't included one for his front door. Shirley, though, was already forging ahead. River expected her to kick the door in, or headbutt it into submission. Instead, having ripped away the tape, she produced a set of keys and tried each in turn. The third worked.

"... You've got keys to Ho's house?"

"They were Marcus's."

"... Marcus had keys to Ho's house?"

"Duh." Shirley waggled the key ring. "Universals?"

Marcus hadn't always kicked doors down. Sometimes he'd gone the quiet way.

They trooped into the house, and fell to whispering.

"The Dogs have been," River said. This was obvious: there were traces of official, inquisitive presence—drawers hanging open; spaces where electrical equipment had sat. It was an article of faith that anything you could plug in could transmit data: even toasters weren't above suspicion. Roderick Ho had had a lot of kit, and now he had a lot of empty shelves.

Louisa said, "Well, I damn well hope so. That's their job."

"So if Kim was hiding here they'll have her."

"Unless she waited until they'd been and gone."

She's a kid, River wanted to say, a club hustler, scamming idiots like Ho: what would she know about tradecraft? But he could feel his chest constricting again. His organs felt like they'd been wrenched a notch tighter. But he managed to say, "I'll do upstairs."

Louisa said, "Yeah, me too. Shirley, you clear down here. Coe—watch the door."

It was halfway through River's mind to ask how come Louisa was giving instructions, but his wiser angels hushed him. There were recent, compelling reasons why neither River nor Coe should be allowed unsupervised charge of a tin opener, and the idea of Shirley taking command: well. His wiser angels had better things to do than finish that sentence.

Louisa led the way, and they parted company on the landing; Louisa taking the door into Ho's bedroom—which accounted for the appalled look she was wearing—and River heading into the sitting room with the big, now broken, window.

Someone had entered the room, so she made herself stiller than ever. She was a coat on a hanger, a folded-up sweatshirt; something you'd expect in a wardrobe: one glance, you'd turn away and close the door. And then she'd be alone in the dark, and before long could start to breathe once more.

The trick was to occupy a space just slightly smaller than yourself, and then to keep doing that, over and over. Once you were done you'd vanished, and nobody would find you ever again.

The floorboard creaked. Something opened and closed. There

were only so many places a hider could hide; so many a searcher could search. The time left to her was measured in seconds, and she could feel them dropping away, slipping through the gap beneath the door. They were noisy seconds, and made fluttering noises; they would give her away.

It had been an unwise choice, Roddy Ho's house. She'd have been better off risking the streets.

Kim clenched her fist, around which she'd wrapped a wire coat hanger, and waited.

In Ho's kitchen, Shirley was thinking: this doesn't get used much.

By the back door was a tower made of pizza boxes; next to it, an overflowing bag of plastic bottles: energy drinks, coke, some brand names she didn't recognise. The fridge was huge but underused, though its freezer section contained more pizzas and two bags of oven chips, putting Shirley in mind of a corner shop on a Sunday evening. Mind you, her own fridge was nothing to boast about; its only hint of green was bottled beer. But it was a relief Ho lived down to her expectations. If he'd turned out a secret gourmet, with a stash of white truffle oil and unrecognisable vegetables, she'd have had trouble with it.

She'd already checked the people-sized hiding places, the cupboards and under-table areas. No sign of Kim. It was a long shot anyway. Sooner or later she'd be found in a bin bag, just as misshapen as the one full of bottles, but squashier, and starting to stink.

Shirley hoped not, but hoping was one thing and brutal truth another. You didn't have to be a slow horse to pick that much up.

She opened a cupboard, expecting mugs or plates, spices or flour. It contained a lot of tins of beans. A lot.

In her pocket, Marcus's keyring felt heavy. It was the first time she'd used his universal key set, a trophy she'd snatched from his desk drawer. She'd been hoping for his gun, but Lamb didn't hang around when it came to snaffling dead men's trifles. She'd thought at first that he'd left the keys because he hadn't realised they were a housebreaking kit, had assumed they were Marcus's spares, but it hadn't been long before a more credible explanation occurred: Lamb hadn't taken Marcus's keys because he already had a set of his own. Fine by her. She still wished she'd been first to the gun, though.

As Marcus himself would have pointed out, there were times when a gun came in handy.

Bad as things were—her heart pumping so hard, the wardrobe was probably pulsing in time—they could have been worse. The wardrobe could have been a coffin. When she'd stood by the window in her own house, too late to launch herself through it, there had been no sensation like this, of time leaking away; instead, every thing had come to a stop. It was Shin who came through the door, holding a gun. Kim's bladder had given, a little, and in that moment she learned that a getaway bag was not enough. What she needed was a second life, in which none of this had happened . . . She was not a good person, but she blamed this on circumstances: she was surrounded by victims, and whose fault was that? There were two kinds of men, she had long ago determined; the kind you could use as money-pumps, and they'd chalk it off to experience; and those who spat blood and came looking. One or two had found her. She'd not survive many encounters like that.

But Shin and his crew had been different. They'd known who she was, what she did, and it was clear their information came from some higher agency. There'd always been rumours about girls being recruited by the intelligence services: honeytraps were a popular device, and girls like Kim were honey. But she'd put it down to urban myth, generated by the girls themselves, to whom it lent mystery: they weren't just mattress ornaments but players in a high-stakes game. The last thing she'd expected was to discover that she'd crossed paths with an actual spook. Even more gobsmacking was that this was Roddy Ho, whom she'd been fleecing for months without breaking a sweat. It might even have been funny, if Shin's group hadn't made clear the consequences of rejecting their advances. There was family in North Korea; aunts and uncles she'd never seen. A cousin with two infants—they'd shown her photos. These people could have been anyone, and blood relations, well—Kim's life had not been made happier by the blood relations she knew. She thought she could live with the discomforts suffered by strangers.

Then they had shown her a mirror; her own face, its many small perfections.

If it had been easy persuading Ho to steal from credit card companies, it was a cakewalk having him plunder secrets. By the time she'd given him the code number of the file she wanted, he was convinced that poaching it was his own idea.

She had known, of course, that delivering the file to Shin would not be the end of the story; that once honeytraps were sprung, someone came to wipe away the honey. So her timing was off, getting caught at the window; she should have disappeared already, and be lying low elsewhere. But she was a London girl. Any other city, and she'd be game rather than huntress. And besides, there were only two kinds of men, and Kim never played one end when she could be playing both.

She had stood by the window, her getaway bag a lump on the lawn below, and made her mouth the right shape to greet Shin, who had come through the door holding a gun.

"Thank God it's you!" she had said, and reached for him.

A car moved down the street at average speed, and though Coe took a tighter grip on the blade in his pouch, he gave no outward reaction. The driver studied him anyway, by the glow of the nearest streetlight. The neighbourhood would have been well aware that something had been going on in Ho's house. Last night a body hurled through a window, and shots fired; today, black vans removing most of Ho's possessions. But anyone curious enough to have approached the Dogs would have had their fingers nipped. That kind of word got round fast.

And even if it hadn't, thought Coe, I am a bad man. Approach at your peril.

Oh shit had been his reaction when he saw the paint can hit Gimball. It hadn't been pretty. But what he mostly thought now was how swiftly he'd got his act together; nearly as quickly as tattoo guy, who'd been away faster than a cat could blink. Even having to climb down two ladders, Coe hadn't been far behind; collecting Cartwright, who was cartoon-stunned; propelling them both to the car. He was pretty sure nobody had seen them emerge from the alley. Which didn't mean they were in the clear, but at least he'd won some breathing space.

And Cartwright thought they were on borrowed time, but Coe knew that one thing the Service liked tightly wrapped was a fuck-up. London Rules meant build your walls high, and the order in which you chucked your people over them was in inverse proportion to their usefulness. So as long as he was more useful than Cartwright, he'd not be first in line to be pitched over the wall. Coe didn't feel great about thinking this way, but he did feel alive, and that was the first priority. You were all in this together until you weren't. That was also London Rules.

And another thing he wondered about was *bright-eyed and bushy-tailed*: was that how he'd come off this evening? When he'd joined the Service he'd been in Psych Eval, which had involved evaluating operational strategies for psychological impact—on targets as well as agents—but had also meant carrying out individual assessments; who was stressed, who'd benefit from change of routine and who was a psychopath. Every organisation had a few, usually at management level, and it was handy to know who they were in case there was an emergency, or an office party. J.K. Coe had become adept at recognising the signs, but perhaps he should have been taking a hard look at himself, especially since his own trauma. Maybe that had opened a door into his dark, one never since closed. And that was why he reached for his knife every time he was startled; why taking a life left him feeling buoyed, and in control. If he'd been writing

a report for his own Psych Eval folder, half of it would have been
in green ink.

But J.K. Coe thought that was probably okay. Everyone needed
an edge. This was his.

The car had gone; the street was dark and quiet. His blade was
where it ought to be.

Behind him, in Ho's house, something clattered and someone
shrieked.

A floorboard creaked again, and Kim readied for flight.

On her first approach to Ho's house, there'd been activity; a
black van, and serious-looking men loading Roddy's computer
equipment into the back of it. There was broken glass on the
pavement, and a couple of chunks carved out of the brickwork.
From the back of last night's cab she'd called Shin and said *He's
home alone* and *Make it quick? He's harmless.* Had she really thought
it would be painless? The important thing was that it hadn't been
happening to her. Those were the rules of the game: number one
came first and foremost.

And just for insurance, she'd tended Shin from the outset.

You're in charge, aren't you?

The others have to do what you say.

You're not like them . . .

None of them were ever like anybody else. That was what men
liked to hear about: the many ways in which they were unique.

Kim had walked straight past the black van; found a café to
nest in for the afternoon, and had returned to find the house in
darkness. She'd let herself in with the key Roddy had given her,
then lain on the bed, planning her next move.

He was probably dead. They'd probably killed him. Would have
killed her, too, if she hadn't played Shin. *You're in charge, you're not
like them.* This had been necessary, not least because she was
frightened of Danny, who had a dangerous look. And it had paid
off, because Shin had let her leave; had watched her drop through
the bedroom window, visibly swelling with the promises she'd

made him. They'd be together, once this was all over. She would wait for him. They would fuck happily ever after.

But for every trick that paid off, there was another left you in the dust. So here she was, crouching in a wardrobe, and there was somebody out there—any number of somebodies. If it were Shin and co., the same ploy wouldn't work twice. Shin on his own, she could shape like putty. Shin with the others watching would be a different story.

But she didn't think that was who was in Ho's house now.

Waiting, ready, she tightened her fingers round the wire hanger; reshaped and wrapped around her fist, its hook straightened to a jabbing point.

If someone else's eye was the cost of her freedom, that was fine by her.

There was a draught, because the cardboard that had been wedged over the broken pane didn't fit properly. River peeled it aside, and let dark air waft across his face. If he'd had the sense to have parents like Ho's, perhaps they'd have kitted him out with a property too, with a front door of his own, and neighbours who were occasionally visible during daylight hours. But the thought of his mother gifting him a deposit on an ordinary house in an ordinary street almost made him smile. No, his family support came in the shape of the O.B., support that was rotting away now, had rotted away, would give any moment, and then just be a memory of timber: something that was strong and upright and always there, until it wasn't. Well, at least he'd be spared knowing about the god almighty fuck-up River had been part of today. That was when you knew things were bad; when your grandfather's mental slippage was a silver lining.

He came away from the window. There wasn't much here, now Roddy's toys had been carted away. A brisk, efficient job the Dogs had made of it; nice to know, given they'd soon be doing the same for him. Well, good luck with that. You could pile most of what he owned into a skip without anyone deeming it a waste. No, the real waste was his career, which had turned out to have a damp fuse attached; so much so that the thoughts he'd had earlier, about walking away, themselves seemed a pipe dream now. Once the Park had taken stock of the day's events, he'd either be offered up as a sacrifice or swept under a carpet. And again it gripped him, behind his ribs: cold panic. He didn't dare check his phone to see what the news was saying; at the same time, he wanted to hear somebody's voice, someone on his side. His mother? Hardly. His grandfather? He'd need a stronger signal than his phone was capable of. So who else—his father? But Frank was a renegade with blood on his hands, and River might kill him if the opportunity arose.

So there was only the here and the now; there was only this moment. Until it all fell apart, and the Dogs came and dragged him away, he'd keep on with the matter in hand, searching for someone who might be dead, which felt like the story of his life. He dropped to one knee and checked under the sofa, which was far too low to be a hiding place, but allowed him to feel he was doing something. And then rose at a crash from across the landing, and a startled shout: Louisa.

Ho's room was heavy with an acrid, non-specific odour which, caught and bottled, would probably kill rodents, or old people. Louisa was breathing carefully. On any list of rooms she was never likely to find herself in, this one was right behind Benedict Cumberbatch's, though for diametrically opposite reasons. Still, at least Ho wasn't here. Just the evidence of his being: the anime posters on the walls; the clutch of dirty mugs on the floor, rimmed with chocolatey sludge.

She didn't want to think about the used tissues blossoming between them, like failed, discarded attempts at origami.

The bed was wide; its sheets dark blue, its duvet cover brown. Seriously, thought Louisa. She dropped to her knees, checked under the bed. More discarded Kleenex roses; enough dust bunnies to dehydrate Watership Down. There'd been a bedside lamp, but it was gone—you'd think the Dogs were running a boot sale on the sly—but there were drawers in the table it had sat upon, and Louisa looked through these. Okay, so Kim wasn't likely to be hiding in one, but how often did chances like this crop up? Not that Ho would conceal anything interesting by putting it in a drawer: his life would be parcelled into bite-sized data chunks, and distributed among the laptops and drives that were now visible only by the marks they'd left behind; the dusty outlines of removed hardware. It would all be back at the Park now; like Ho, in the process of being dismantled. Chances were, it would never be put back together again. Whether this went for Ho too was a thought Louisa didn't dwell on, though she was conscious of a rare flash of empathy for her colleague, who had been useful on occasions, if likable on fewer. But who was she to talk? She'd not gone out of her way to make Slough House a happier place. She'd made efforts with River, true, but Jesus: after today, the one-time Most Likely To Succeed was well and truly holed below the waterline. What they were doing here, a pointless search for a probably dead witness, was basically marking time: River and Coe were fucked, and it would take a miracle for the rest of them to survive the morning-after recriminations.

So thinking, she opened the wardrobe drawer, and a demon burst out, its right fist a thin metal spike it jabbed straight at Louisa's face.

The last thing she'd ever see from her left eye was a screaming witch with a pointy fist: that so nearly came true, it haunted Louisa's sleep for weeks. But she jerked her head aside in time and stepped backwards, her left foot coming down on one of Ho's discarded mugs, which broke beneath her heel and sent her pitching to the floor. She shouted as she fell, and saw from a crazy angle, like a fragment of jigsaw puzzle, River appear in the bedroom doorway.

There was no time for strategy, only for action. The woman who'd opened the wardrobe door was out of the game; the following second, a man had joined her. Kim had hit him full tilt: her head, his stomach. He was lean enough—it wasn't like butting a pillow—but her head was harder, and full of bad thoughts. He staggered back and Kim whipped under his outstretched arm and took the stairs four at a time; more of a controlled fall than a mannered descent, but even so another figure materialised before she'd reached the bottom and grabbed her collar so her feet left the floor. The pair collapsed in a heap, and Kim slashed wildly behind with her makeshift weapon, catching flesh and hearing an outraged squawk from the barrel-shaped creature who'd caught her. The grip loosened. Kim was on her feet immediately, opening the front door. From overhead there was noise, numbers one and two getting upright and coming after her, but she was outside now, on the street, and here was another one: a man in a hoodie, a dangerous odour coming off him. He was reaching into his pouch and Kim couldn't have that, she knew what men like this reached for, and she slashed again, the wire hanger a diagonal flash in the night air. He jerked back but she caught his chin: a few drops of blood kissed her face. No time to worry about that, because he'd recovered already, had grabbed her arm, and for a moment it was over; the three in the house were regrouping now, and this one had her in his grip, but it required no thought for Kim to do what she did next, which was knee him in the balls: a traditional move but it still had legs, and he folded immediately. Free from his grasp, she headed down the street at speed.

Go to ground. Find a corner, occupy it. Lose the coat hanger, which makes you look crim.

Without slowing she wriggled her hand from the hanger, which fell to the pavement like a discarded Easter crown. She crossed the road, ran past a line of parked vehicles to the junction and was about make a sharp left when a car door swung open in front of her. Kim smacked into it, bounced back and hit the ground so hard that all the bones in her body lit up like fairy lights.

Something heavy emerged and stood over her; an awful beast about to shatter its prey.

"I'm strictly antichauvinist, as you know," it said. "But I do like to open a door for a lady."

But Kim had stopped listening by then.

Whelan made some phone calls, and while he spoke, while he listened, watched the boys and girls on the hub. One young woman in particular he kept an eye on; purely paternal—she resembled a young Claire—but his gaze tightened if she leaned across her desk to address a colleague, or bent to a drawer. There was a blank space in Claude Whelan's memory. He kept it that way. If someone had taxed him with the details of that long-ago night, the conversation with the girl on the corner, the appearance of the plainclothes officer, the hours in custody before it was all made to go away, he'd have been genuinely puzzled for a moment, unable to remember whether it had happened to him or been something he'd read about, so hard had he tamped the episode down. A blip, he'd have said, if pressed. A regrettable lapse, long behind him. He was content with Claire, with their perfect marriage, and if her interest in the physical side had waned from not-very to nothing, that was a small price to pay for her constant support.

Jackson Lamb, of course, had ferreted out the details; had dangled them in front of Claude like a dog with a kill, its mouth full of feathers, but all he appeared to want was that Claude leave him and his alone.

For the time being, that would have to do.

Whelan spoke to the editor of Dodie Gimball's paper; then to that paper's lawyer; then to a Service lawyer, and then to the paper's editor again. That second conversation was fairly short. When he had all the details he needed he rang the number the editor had at last given him, and spoke to a man named Barrett, whose rich voice it was a pleasure to listen to. Barrett, a former cop, carried out investigative work for the paper, a necessary gap in the news-gathering process now that most journalists rarely ventured beyond Twitter and the nearest Nespresso machine.

Barrett relayed the details of his job for Dodie Gimball without hesitation, repetition or deviation. When he'd finished Whelan thanked him and disconnected. Then resumed staring through his glass wall.

The PM was not going to be happy.

Night keeps its head down during daylight hours, but it's always there, always waiting, and some open their doors to it early; allow it to sidle in and bed down in a corner. Molly Doran was among this number. She had become a creature of the dark, the brightest hour she felt comfortable in the violet one, and had long ago washed up in this windowless kingdom some floors below where Claude Whelan sat. Home was a ground-floor apartment in a new build, a twenty-minute taxi ride away, but that was simply a box she hid in when custom deemed it necessary. Here was where she felt alive, especially now, on the late shift, when night was out of its basket, and prowling behind her as she propelled herself along the aisles.

There were rows and rows of files in her archive, each containing lives; there were operations minutely recounted, whose details would never be open to the public, and she was fine with that. It was called the Secret Service for a reason. Transparency and openness were for pressure groups to bleat about, but Molly Doran knew that much of what keeps us safe should be kept hidden. The appetites that keep democracy alive can be unseemly. There were stories here to make liberals combust, and while Molly occasionally felt she could have done with the warmth, such a bonfire might easily get out of control.

Sometimes she spoke to her files.

"So, my dears," she said aloud. "What are we looking for tonight?"

They didn't answer, of course. She wasn't insane. But she spoke to the world gathered round her the way shut-ins might speak to their walls; it was another way of talking to herself, of underlining her presence.

"The watering hole," she said. "Such a quaint turn of phrase."

Quaint, in this case, meaning old; post-war, but old.

Her chair made little noise. She often wondered, were she to get down on hands and useless knees, whether she'd detect grooves in the floor from her years of ceaseless trundling. Didn't matter any more. They'd be ejecting her soon—another six weeks; *no need to work your notice; why not take a little holiday?*—fuck them. What did they think, she'd go surfing? The idea had occurred that she could simply refuse to go, and lock herself in, but there was a lack of dignity in that; she'd become the wrong sort of legend. Better to exit on her own terms.

"Let's start here, shall we?"

Here being the late fifties, and some never-implemented contingency plans, strategies, adventures, from the fag-end of empire.

Hardly worth saying that the hunt she was on was a sacking offence. Jackson Lamb was so much persona non grata that Regent's Park practically amounted to a no-Jacksons club, and even if he hadn't been there were protocols, none of which involved having someone just turn up and beg a favour. So the whole six-weeks'-notice-and-why-not-have-a-skiing-break? could turn out to be moot: one slipup now and being dumped on the pavement without fanfare would be the upside, inasmuch as prison would also be possible. Molly Doran didn't fancy prison much.

But nor did she like being handed her cards by Diana Taverner. Not that Lady Di had made an appearance herself, but her fingerprints were all over this: Taverner mistrusted the eccentric, her definition of which covered anyone whose vision didn't coincide with her own. Though if she'd ever spent time here among the records, she'd know it was the eccentrics and fantasists, the borderline cases, who'd always flown the Service's flag highest.

Besides: Jackson Lamb. The temptation to hand him whatever rope he was looking for was not one to shrug off easily. Sooner or later he'd wind up swinging from it—nobody could be Jackson Lamb forever without paying the price—but the certain knowledge that aiding him would give Lady Di the screaming abdabs was good enough for Molly Doran. She had a sudden image of Lamb's carcass, dangling from a gibbet. The reek of it would empty buildings. But he wouldn't have it any other way, she knew. After half a lifetime battling the forces of oppression, he'd spent the second half revenging himself on a world that had fucked up anyway. If things had gone otherwise, he might have been something to behold. As it was, he was a spectacle anyway; just not the kind to draw admiring glances.

Easy to spiral away into such thoughts. Her days and weeks, her years, down here; so many of them had been lost to flights of fancy, her earthbound wheels notwithstanding. It was as if the files were slowly leaking; gracing the air with secret histories, with private visions.

"It's Regent's Park," she reminded herself now. "Not bloody Hogwarts."

So saying, she reached out and plucked from the shelf the first of the night's treasures.

She was alone in the car, and this was what grief meant. Grief meant being alone in the car.

Would she remember that, or should she make a note for future reference?

Technically, Dodie Gimball supposed, she wasn't alone, because of the driver, but such were the details art skimmed over. Her husband was dead, and she was alone in the car, and evermore would be. Her life-mate had been destroyed—here one moment, gone the next. What was she to do now?

There were lights behind her, lights ahead; the police escort was running without sirens, but both cars were flashing their blues, and the BMW's interior pancaked in and out of colour. Every so often, too, it blurred, as tears filled Dodie's eyes, but the outpour never came. It was as if a valve had stuck, refusing to allow the free passage of water.

Dennis was gone. They had killed him. They would pay.

Nobody had been able to tell her what had happened. It was

"under investigation." It was "too soon to tell." The area had been cordoned off, and there'd been a roadblock in place when her motorcade exited Slough, but all of that was not for her ears, not for her eyes. Under any other circumstances she'd have blown a dozen different holes through the careers of everyone in earshot, but tonight she felt powerless. This was grief; grief was being alone in the car. But it was something else too, something she hadn't got to the bottom of yet.

Her last words to Dennis had been *If you get caught, you're never borrowing my Manolos again.* And that was that.

This, too, would benefit from a rewrite. As I embraced him, I had a strange presentiment, of a kind I've only ever once had before, when my beloved grandmother—no, grandfather—grand-mother—sod it, the interns can handle the details. "I love you, my darling." I'll always be glad those were the last words I—

The blue light in front slowed, drew to a halt.

Her own car followed suit.

They were on the Western Avenue. Up ahead, lights picked out the Hoover Building, under reconstruction. On the road, red fireflies streamed into Central London; here, blue lights looped slowly fore and aft of her, and she was stationary in a lay-by, and the driver was saying something: it included the word *ma'am.*

"... What?"

"I've been asked to pull over."

"... What?"

"You have a visitor."

And then the driver was leaving, and she truly was alone in the car.

"How did you know where to find us?"

Lamb sighed. "Give me credit. You were clearly going to be looking for the girl, and where else would she be hiding?"

"Also, I told him," said Catherine.

"Well, if you want to get technical."

Kim—Roddy Ho's girlfriend—was flat on her back on the

office floor with everyone gathered round her, the spectrum of concern to indifference running from Catherine Standish at one end to Jackson Lamb so far off the other, he was barely visible. "Timing," he'd said more than once. "Now *that* was timing."

"There might have been gentler ways of accosting her."

"Yeah, right." He surveyed the assembled: J.K. Coe with a slashed chin; Shirley Dander with a torn earlobe; Louisa and River both moving gingerly. "Because you lot handled her with such fucking panache."

The conversation with Catherine had taken place over the phone in Welles's car, after they'd left the park; Flyte and Welles up front, Lamb sprawled in the back.

"We need to find the girl," Flyte had said.

"I know."

"If they haven't killed her yet."

Traffic was light. London wore its evening gown: glittering sequins and overstuffed purse. Some nights it looked like an empress in rags. Tonight it was a bag lady in designer clothes.

Lamb had said, "I'd have killed her. But these numbnuts had two goes at Ho and barely bruised his ego. Given that a five-year-old could take him down with a walnut whip, I don't have much faith in their abilities." Before she could reply he shifted his bulk, and the seating squeaked indignantly. "I can't help noticing you're in the car."

"As are you," said Flyte, pinching the tip of her nose briefly.

"Well, I'm hardly walking home, am I? But what's your excuse?"

"You think I should be jogging?"

"I think you should be in your office, making your report. Yet here you are." He scratched his ear, and when he'd finished, he was holding a cigarette. "Because you're in this up to your neck now, and so's Cornwall here."

"Devon."

"Whatever. You fucked up, and he had your back at the wrong moment." Lamb glanced towards Welles. "Bet you're wishing you never answered your phone."

Welles ignored him.

Flyte said, "Gimball's dead."

"Boo hoo. Shall we buy a teddy bear, tie it to a lamp post?"

"You said he was in danger. If I hadn't ignored that, it might have turned out differently."

Lamb eased back. "When they reassign you, I'm gunna put you in with Cartwright," he said. "You've bumped heads before, I seem to recall."

"I'll shoot myself first."

"I've a gun you can borrow."

That was when his phone had buzzed: Catherine Standish, with the latest from Slough House.

While Lamb was talking, Flyte said to Welles, "When I asked you to cover for me, I didn't know things were going to hell. I'm sorry. You're still off duty. You can walk away now."

Welles said, "I signed Lindsay Lohan here into the Park. There'll be questions about that."

Flyte thought for a while, then settled on a one-size-fits-all response. "Shit."

"It's not so bad over my gaff," Lamb said, ending his call. "We have a new kettle."

"You're enjoying this."

"It's called a positive attitude," said Lamb. "Watch and learn. Oh, and Hampshire? Change of plan. My team think the girl's at Ho's house."

"Alive?"

"Too early to say. Their last search and rescue didn't work out so well. Worth a trip, though."

Welles pulled into a lay-by. "We should head back to the Park," he said. "Lay it all out for Whelan or whoever."

"Yeah, not a great idea," said Lamb. "Remember?"

Flyte rolled her eyes. "What now?"

But it was Welles who answered. "When they came for the blueprint, they knew what they were looking for. They had inside info."

"Shit," she said again.

"Which means someone's been a bad apple," said Lamb. "Be nice to know who before we go waltzing in like Little Red Riding Crop."

"Hood."

"Different movie." He looked at Welles. "You gunna sit there all night?"

"Depends on what my boss says."

"Did you train him with a stick? Or send him to school?"

Flyte said, "If they had inside info, how come they needed Ho?"

"Just one of the many things we're not gunna find out sitting here."

"I screwed up," she said. "That happens around you a lot, doesn't it? Like gravitational pull. And I'll take the rap. But I don't plan to spend the rest of tonight in a room next to Roddy Ho. Not if there's a chance we might track these bastards down."

So they'd headed to Ho's house instead, arriving there, as Lamb hadn't yet tired of saying, with impeccable timing.

Now, in Slough House, Catherine knelt to hand another paper tissue to Kim, who snatched it and pressed it to her nose. The nine that Shirley, Louisa and River had granted her the previous evening was looking more like a three-and-a-half now she'd been slam dunked by a car door; maybe a four, Shirley conceded, if you were into that kind of thing, "that kind of thing" being bruised and swelling features. Mental note: don't land on your face, she thought. Not from any kind of height. Height was about the only physical thing Shirley had in common with Kim. Well, that and, presumably, a yearning for medication, though in Kim's case that would be a current predicament rather than an ongoing condition.

"Has she said much yet?" Lamb asked.

"You've been standing right there," Catherine reminded him.

"Yeah, I might have drifted off," he said. "On account of I can see up her skirt."

Catherine straightened Kim's clothing.

Emma Flyte said, "Don't get me wrong, it's purely academic

interest. But do you plan to pull a gun on her and cuff her to a chair?"

"Twice in one day? Not without medical supervision."

Kim, still prone, swore at him. She'd been doing this at intervals since coming round in the car on the way to Slough House.

"We should take her to hospital," said River again, his tone indicating that he didn't hold out much hope of being listened to.

"Yeah, we could do that," said Lamb. "Or you could shut up."

Louisa said, "It's gone midnight."

"If I wanted the speaking clock, I'd have dialled your number."

"I was just pointing out, it's a new day. And it seems we're set on making it even worse than the old one."

"You were a Gimball fan?"

"I'm a fan of not worrying that we're all about to be arrested."

"I'm starting to sense a guilty conscience." Lamb looked at River, then Coe, on whom his gaze lingered. "Wonder whose it could be?"

Welles said, "If she's got a line to the crew that shot up Abbotsfield, we should be asking her questions. Not watching her bleed out."

"I might have misjudged you, Dorset," Lamb told him. "Though as spectator sports go, I've heard worse ideas." He dropped to his knees. "Let's be clear about this," he said to Kim, and though he spoke softly, nobody had any trouble hearing every word. "We know what you've done, and we know what happened as a result. You'll tell us everything we want to know, or your life as a free woman is over as of tonight. That clear enough?"

"Fuck you," she told him through gritted teeth.

"That was gunna be your second option."

"Jackson . . ." Catherine warned.

"Yeah, all right. Jesus. When did making a joke get to be a criminal offence?" He got back on his feet and turned to Emma Flyte. "There you go. I've warmed her up for you."

"You're going to let me do this?"

"You're supposed to be the expert."

She knew better than to congratulate him on his attack of common sense. "In that case," she said, "the rest of you can clear out."

Which, once they'd looked to Lamb for confirmation, they all did.

As she approached the Gimball woman's car, Di Taverner's mobile rang and she paused on the edge of the lay-by to take it. Traffic was light, but moving fast, and she had to speak, to listen, against a background of engine noise.

"We've confirmation of a known face at Slough."

"Tell me."

"Picked up on CCTV in the town centre, minutes after the news of the death came in."

"Quick work."

"He rang bells on the face-recognition software, on account of being highly decorated."

For a moment, Taverner's mind swam with images of valour. "He's a soldier?"

"An ex-con. With facial tattoos."

The speed limit, and possibly a local record, was just then broken by a passing hothead.

Taverner waited until it had echoed into the distance before saying, "Let's leave the imagery aside, shall we, and stick to the facts?"

The Queens of the Database, as the Park's comms and surveillance tribe were known, were prone to sporting verbal fascinators; one of the consolations, they claimed, for not getting out much.

"Sorry, ma'am."

"Who is he?"

"Name of Tyson Bowman. He's an aide to Zafar Jaffrey, who's—"

"I know who Jaffrey is. Any idea why he was in Slough tonight?"

"Not yet. The police have barely started trawling their captures. We got this sooner because Jaffrey's flagged, and any associates light up the circuits."

The CCTV feeds had been supplied to the Park, the theory being that any hits would be shared immediately. Everyone knew this rarely happened, though the reason wasn't usually policy driven; was more often due to information snagging on the red tape that dangled on jurisdictional borders like flypaper.

She said, "Okay. Was Jaffrey in Slough too?"

"No. He was addressing a meeting in Birmingham."

"Okay," she said again. "Let's see if we can organise a pickup without the locals getting into a tizzy. It's probably a coincidence. But."

"I'll see who's within range. Shame he didn't flag earlier. We had a pair on the ground."

Taverner, who'd been about to disconnect, held her thumb. ". . . What?"

"A pair of agents in Slough. They flagged too."

"I see," she said slowly. "Yes, that is a shame. Remind me who they were?"

Up close, the girl didn't resemble the younger Claire as much as he'd thought; was narrower of feature, with skin ever so slightly pitted where adolescence had left its cruel marks. But even if you stripped away all other reference points, the facts remained that she was young, she was female, and that was enough to provoke certain memories. And there was this, too: he'd summoned her and she'd come. Sometimes, that was all it took.

"Sir?"

"Josie."

She waited. ". . . Was there something you needed?"

Whelan blinked and recovered himself. "A man called Blaine, goes by Dancer. He runs a stationer's somewhere near St Paul's, but it's a cover for various . . . activities, I'm told. Is he on our books?"

"I can find out."

"Good girl. I mean, thank you."

He watched through the wall as she returned to her desk at

a trot and began harvesting information: a digital rake, a digital scythe. He noticed how her blouse protested when she stretched; how she bit her bottom lip in concentration, and his throat clicked.

There was someone in his doorway.

". . . Yes?"

"This for you, sir."

This was a transcript of the interrogation of Roderick Ho.

Whelan frowned when he saw the name at the top: Emma Flyte? Wasn't she supposed to be at Slough House? It was on the tip of his tongue to ask, but he was alone again, the transcript's bearer having slipped back into anonymity.

He scanned the pages. Ho was a slow horse—all branches of the Service went by one unofficial name or another; Whelan himself was a weasel; but the slow horses were different, their name tinged with contempt—and like the others of his type, his brief bio was a study in decline. From Regent's Park to Slough House; a distance that could be walked in a brisk thirty minutes, though the return journey was unclockable, because nobody had ever made it. Oddly, though, there appeared to be no defining blot on his copybook. Exile was usually preceded by some catastrophic performance failure; Ho was simply assigned there, as if he'd been misaddressed in the first place, and his redelivery a simple correction of error.

Which wasn't the point. Whatever had sent Ho to Slough House, he clearly belonged there, because the honeytrap he'd fallen into was ludicrously familiar. If the Park ever got round to producing a training manual in comic-book form, here was its template: a bar girl latching onto a keyboard warrior whose sex life probably depended on a WiFi connection. And having got what they wanted, the girl's controllers evidently decided to eliminate him, which was where Ho bucked the odds by getting lucky. But what the hell had they been after, anyway?

Josie was back, panting a little, but Whelan barely noticed. He'd focused on two pieces of information on the typescript in front of him, the first of which concerned the girl. A UK citizen, but of North Korean descent.

The second was the nature of the document Ho had passed her way.

"... Sir?"

It took him a moment to swim back to the here and now.

"You wanted to know about Dancer Blaine," Josie said.

"... Did I?"

"Are you all right, sir?"

"Do you know," Whelan said, "I'm not entirely sure."

"Your name's Kim Park. You're Roderick Ho's girlfriend, or passing as. And he supplied you with documents you subsequently dealt to some very bad actors. You've been aiding and abetting terrorism, Kim. You know what the penalty for that is?"

"Fuck you."

While her nose was a mess, and her eyes black and swollen, the girl's mouth was intact and functioned fine. Underneath the hostility, though, Emma Flyte could hear fear. Hard case or not, she was young and she was damaged. And Flyte didn't feel good about pressing down on a fracture; on the other hand, this kid had greased the wheels on a series of events that had the entire country reeling. Having a car door slammed in her face was about as gentle a reception as she could currently expect.

"This isn't going to last long, because if I don't get answers within five minutes, I'm washing my hands. The next crew who come for you—and it will be a crew—they'll be rougher than me. They see a young girl like you withholding information and they light up like football players at a roast. I think you know what I'm saying. There are different ways of doing this, but all of them end with you spilling everything you know. Your choice."

"This is England," the girl said. "They can't do that. So fuck you."

"This is England, and a few days ago a village got shot up by the bastards you've been playing show and tell with. Maybe you had reasons for going along with them. Maybe they threatened you, threatened your family. But you might as well hear this now because you'll certainly hear it later. It makes no difference to anyone what forces were brought to bear. Not to anyone. As far as the rest of us are concerned, you might as well have been there yourself, Kim. You might as well have been pulling a trigger."

"I was nowhere near."

"Doesn't matter. Never did, in legal terms, and less than ever in the current climate. All you can do now is cooperate, in the hope it gets less nasty down the road. Tell me you understand that. And don't say—"

"Fuck you."

"Four minutes. The clock's running, Kim."

"Fuck you."

But the fear was getting louder.

She was alone in the car, but only for moments. When the door opened, a woman climbed in and joined her on the back seat. She was about Dodie's age, and wearing it without obvious surgical assistance. Her shoulder-length hair was chestnut brown, and her suit Chanel, dark blue or black; her blouse crimson. She nodded at Dodie and said something. Dodie had to ask her to say it again.

She said, "I'm sorry for your loss."

"Who are you? What are you doing in my car?"

"My name's Diana Taverner." She paused, as if anticipating recognition. "And I'm sorry to interrupt your journey, but it's important that we speak."

"Are you with the police?" But even as she was asking the question, Dodie was answering herself: shaking her head; an angry denial. "No. No, you're not, are you? You're MI5."

"I can't confirm my precise role, but yes, I'm with the Security Services." She flashed a card which might have been a John Lewis gift token for all Dodie took in. "And we need to talk about what just happened."

"My husband was murdered."

"Your husband died, yes, and I'm very sorry about that. But the cause of death has yet to be established. And it won't benefit anyone, least of all yourself, if rumours start to circulate."

"They're already circulating!"

Dodie Gimball hadn't meant to shout, but it seemed she had as little control of her volume as she did of her tear ducts.

"Here!"

She showed her phone to this woman, this Taverner woman. A Twitter feed, a trending hashtag. An orchestra of outraged lament, screaming blue murder.

"See?"

"I know." Diana Taverner leaned back in the seat, but kept her eyes on Dodie. She said, "I'd as soon seek information from a wasps' nest. What happened could have been an accident. It could have been natural causes. Nobody can be sure yet. All we know for certain is that it's now open season on your husband's life and career, and if you want to honour his memory, and your own career to prosper, you've got to be very careful about which donkey you start pinning tails on."

"My Dennis was a great man! His life will be *celebrated*—"

"And accompanied by photos which will be less than flattering, Dodie. You know the kind I mean."

Beside them, on the road into London, traffic hissed its displeasure.

"So here we are," said Dodie. "My husband dead a few hours, and already you're back with your nasty threats. Do you know how many people share the same . . . tastes as Dennis? Do you really think it matters?"

"I don't, as it happens. Not one bit. But the people who read your column do, Dodie. Even those who read it wearing their wives' underwear. You'll have heard all this from Claude Whelan already. It doesn't matter how innocent it is, it doesn't matter that nobody gets hurt, or that it's nobody else's business. There's only one slant a newspaper like yours is going to take on it, and that's to splash it as a sordid little secret. You know the difference between a dead pervert and a live one? A dead one can't sue."

"My husband was *not*—"

"So here's what you're going to do. You're going to publish the story you were planning on Zafar Jaffrey. You can even let it be known that Dennis was intending to reveal that same story in his speech tonight. What you will omit from that narrative is any mention of Secret Service involvement. Are you clear on that?"

She wasn't.

The blue lights were still looping, ahead and behind. Their wash turned her visitor's face different colours: indigo, then purple, then sudden, ghostly white. It occurred to Dodie that, ten minutes ago, she'd thought the police cars there to protect her. Now, it seemed, their purpose had always been to deliver her to another tormentor, whose own mission it was to confuse. She was already nostalgic for simple grief; for the time spent alone in the car.

She said, "But the whole point of Whelan's visit was to warn us off Zafar Jaffrey," and even to her own ears, her voice sounded lifeless.

"Things change," Taverner told her. "Alliances shift. And you'd be advised to bear that in mind, Dodie. For some reason, you seem to think we're the enemy. That couldn't be further from the truth. We're not perfect, sure. Sometimes, things get past us. But the rest of the time—all the rest of the times—we're there, doing our job."

She turned and observed the passing traffic for a while, as if conscious that this too was under her protection. Then turned back to Dodie.

"Nothing can bring your husband back, Mrs. Gimball. But if you want him to be remembered as a hero, we can help that happen. In due course. And his little embarrassments don't ever have to see the light of day."

She opened the car door.

"I'm going now. Again, I'm sorry for your loss. But if you want your husband's legacy to be one he'd have been proud of, you'll remember what I said and omit any mention of Service involvement. I'm sure we understand each other."

She left. Alone again, Dodie focused once more on the string of red tail lights on the road ahead, breezing into the city. She barely noticed when the driver got back in, and the little procession recommenced its journey.

Dawn had come once more, and slipped in unnoticed. In Slough House she was met with the unfamiliar spectacle of living, waking humans; most of whom, true, might have been mistaken for some other kind. River Cartwright and J.K. Coe both had their eyes shut, though in Coe's case this reflected an effort at memory: he was trying to recall the exact shape of an emotion, the precise geometry of a particular moment, when he had fired three bullets into the chest of a manacled man. River, meanwhile, was screening horrors on his eyelids: the neverending tumble of a lethal can of paint; its repeated collision with a human head. Both men were seated, both on the floor; in fact, of all those present, only Louisa Guy was upright, her back ramrod straight against the wall, her right leg raised level. She held this position for a full thirty seconds, then lowered that leg and raised the other. Through crocodile eyes Jackson Lamb watched her, his mind busy with other things.

Shirley Dander was also on the floor, curled into a ball, but she wasn't sleeping either; she was adding another day to her tally, and wondering where this numerical sequence would end. An hour earlier Catherine Standish had laid a coat across her, which had given her a tremor. Being tucked in didn't really figure in her lifestyle. Catherine, mother-henning done, had settled in an office chair, on the opposite side of the desk from where Lamb was sprawled; a configuration replicated from Lamb's own office, as if they remained engaged in the same dance, regardless of location. She seemed alert and unruffled, her hair tied back in its usual manner; her dress as uncreased as if she'd put it on an hour ago. Lamb had fetched his bottle from upstairs, and it stood, a nearly empty sentry, on the desk in front of him. But there was only one glass there—his—and Catherine's eyes never lingered on it or the bottle itself.

They were in Roderick Ho's office, though Ho himself, of course, was elsewhere. Of those in the room, only two gave any thought to this, and one of those was Catherine.

From across the hall she could hear a low murmur, which had started as a singular flow, Emma Flyte's voice, with the occasional interjection. Now there was a mumbled counterpoint, hesitant at first, a drip from a faulty tap, which had since become more regular; a steady trickle which would, in time, fill any vessel provided. This was what happened when you opened up: there was no stopping what you'd started. It was one of the reasons Catherine was wary of AA meetings.

Now she thought of that poor girl's face, her nose a mess, her eyes black and swollen; and then of the TV footage from Abbotsfield, the Derbyshire fastness which guns had undone, in part because of that girl's actions. It was odd she could feel sympathy for the one in spite of the other. Or that even now she worried about Roddy Ho, when really they should have banded together ages back, and dangled him from a window. Made him realise there were hard facts beyond the bubble of his own ego; among them, the nearest pavement.

Lamb stirred. "Isn't this cosy?"

"I'd have made her talk by now," said Shirley, her voice muffled by her own arm.

"You'd have made her scream. There's a difference."

Louisa said, "What if she doesn't know anything?"

"Well if she's that fucking ignorant she can join the team," said Lamb.

Catherine turned on her iPad, and flicked through news

channels. All were burning up the same story: the death of Dennis Gimball in an alleyway in Slough. Speculation ranged from assassination by Remainers—as unlikely a theory as it was inevitable—to a conspiracy hatched in Downing Street. The latter, admittedly, wasn't getting coverage on the mainstream sites, but was popular with idiots on social media. Then again, idiots on social media had dictated world events of late, and clearly felt they were on a roll.

Elsewhere, there were follow-ups on Abbotsfield; a Home Office spokesperson saying that investigations were continuing, arrests would be made. The lack of concrete detail was explained by the need not to compromise ongoing operations; a need that most readers understood would be jettisoned as soon as concrete details became available. Meanwhile, a service for civilian casualties of war, rededicated as a memorial for Abbotsfield would be held that afternoon at Westminster Abbey, attended by the younger princes, the PM and everyone with a desire to have their tears recorded for posterity. A less star-spangled, somewhat hijacked service would take place in Abbotsfield itself. She found a shaky little video from the village: its church; a weathered cemetery; the multicoloured dullness of stained glass viewed from the wrong side. The lych-gate was draped with wreaths, and the small offerings the living consecrate to the dead, toys and ribbons, flowers, photographs. Catherine wasn't sure how she felt about this. On the other hand, it wasn't her grief.

"Seize control of the media," said Lamb. He seemed to be pouting, his lower jaw thrust forward. Could mean anything from deep thought to imminent flatulence.

Shirley sat up. The left shoulder of her sweatshirt was spattered with blood from her torn ear, a spattering which her attempts at rinsing the top without first removing it had made substantially worse. The ear wasn't pretty either. There had been no sticking plasters of the appropriate size in the first aid box, and by the time Catherine had trimmed an overlarge one down to size, Shirley had self-medicated with a length of Sellotape. This had clogged the bleeding right enough, but gave Shirley the appearance of a mended doll.

She said, "TV. That's their next target. Shepherd's Bush or wherever. Where's Sky?"

For a brief confused moment, Catherine thought Shirley had just asked where the sky was. More worryingly, she'd found it a reasonable question.

"They're not going to attempt to take control of a television company," said Louisa. "I mean, seriously?"

"Why not?" River asked.

"Because they couldn't even plant a bomb on a train successfully. Which, let's face it, isn't much more difficult than forgetting an umbrella."

"Somebody wandered into Dobsey Park and blew up a lot of penguins," River reminded her.

"Yeah, penguins. Hard target or what?"

"Okay, but they got in, they got out, they weren't caught."

"It's not a maximum security prison, it's a zoo. You buy a ticket. TV studios have checkpoints, they have guards, you need passes. You need to know what you're doing. This bunch have tripped over their own dicks twice."

"Three times," said Shirley.

"Whatever, they're hardly the A-Team. Shooting up a village full of pensioners, that's one thing. But what they're best at is falling through windows."

"Well, okay, maybe not TV," River said.

"Newspaper? Same story," Louisa said. "You don't just waltz into a newspaper office unchallenged. In fact, you *especially* don't waltz into—"

"Radio?" said River.

"They could hang a few DJs," Shirley suggested.

"—a newspaper office."

Devon Welles said, "Is this brainstorming? I've often wondered what it looked like."

"Seize. The. Media," said Lamb again, and they all looked at him. "Where does that mention a building?"

J.K. Coe said, "The original plan—"

"The Watering Hole Paper," River offered.

"—was predicated on a developing nation state." He spoke slowly, as if reading from notes. "Pre-satellite. Pre-internet. One where there'd only be a single TV channel. A single radio station. So seizing control of the media would be a straightforward business."

"You could do it with a couple of machine guns," said Shirley.

"That was more or less my point."

"But it's not so simple in Big London, right? Different rules."

Coe rubbed his chin, and opened the scratch Kim had given him.

Welles, despite himself, was drawn in. "Remind me how they attempted to bring down the transport infrastructure?"

"With a dud bomb," said Shirley.

"On a train," said Welles. "That's the key point. They put a bomb on a train."

Louisa said, "Ri—ight."

"A dud bomb," Shirley repeated. "We've established they're screwups. How is the small print helping?"

"Doesn't matter that it was a dud," Louisa said. "It matters that it was a train."

"Because blowing up a train, even with a bomb that works, is just blowing up a train," said Welles. "It's not bringing down infrastructure. Get it?"

"They're ticking boxes," said Louisa. "Good thinking."

"Oh God, she's in heat," said Lamb.

"So they're gunna blow up a TV set?" said Shirley. "Set fire to a newspaper?"

River said, "Not the media. A media *event*."

The door opened, and Emma Flyte came in.

"Did she talk?" Welles asked.

"She talked," said Emma.

• • •

Claude Whelan tugged a loose thread on his shirt collar, then wished he hadn't. Sometimes, when you pulled at things, all you did was make them worse.

Oh God, he thought. Way too early in the day for symbolism.

In a different world, he'd done what he'd intended yesterday evening: had left work, gone home, suppered with Claire. Some nights they shared the same bed, but not often, and always chastely. Was it any wonder—but no point going down that road. He loved his wife. Had phoned her at midnight, to tell her he wouldn't be home; that things were moving, that he was on top of them. He'd had an image of young Josie while saying that: an image of being on top of her while she was moving. Was that his fault? He supposed it depended who you asked.

She had returned to him with her rundown on Dancer Blaine:

"A small-time fixer, sir. Fake IDs, sometimes safe houses, the occasional used firearm. But mostly it's IDs."

"And he reports back to us?"

"Not on everything, or we'd have hauled him from the river by now. But he's been helpful."

She had a sheaf of printouts: a rough tally suggested Blaine had helped put away a dozen bad actors, none of them marquee names, and through it all had been allowed to continue his dreary little enterprise hard by St Paul's. A little fish, Whelan had thought, leafing through the pages. One we throw back. Surely there's an argument for feeding him into a waste disposal unit instead? Because let's face it, the big fish are still out there. Sparing the little ones never changes that.

But it was late and things were sour, and you couldn't change the rules once the game was underway. He was pretty sure that was one of Lady Di's dictates.

"Sir?"

He must have been staring at the pages too long.

"Was there anything else you want?"

God, no, she hadn't said that. Hadn't said anything like it.

She returned to the hub. Everyone was working late; the perspective had altered now they knew they were no longer looking at Islamist extremism. The net they'd thrown had too wide a mesh. ISIS had claimed responsibility, true, but stop all the clocks: a death-worshipping bunch of medieval fascists had taken time off from beheading hostages to tell porkies. And if he said that out loud, he'd be the one in trouble: "porkies" was a no-no . . . No wonder he was exhausted. Watching the world go mad was a tiring business.

Di Taverner had come into his office, and was staring. "Are you feeling all right?"

"Sorry." He had run a hand through his hair, thinking, even as he did so, that it was a dramatic gesture more than a grooming need. "Things have happened."

"They never stop."

This was true. Was it yesterday he'd been charged with ensuring Zafar Jaffrey was squeaky-clean? And he'd fulfilled that mission by determining the exact opposite, which meant the PM wouldn't be happy. On the other hand, the PM's days were numbered, Jaffrey's lack of squeaky-cleanliness being one more nail in what was starting to appear an over-engineered coffin.

"Your presence at the Gimballs' yesterday officially didn't occur," Lady Di told him. She'd removed her raincoat and hung it over the back of his visitor's chair. She didn't sit, but didn't pace either, preferring to remain upright with one hand lightly on the chairback, as if posing for a magazine shoot.

"Thank you," he said.

"We stand together," she said, which he took to mean, for as long as it suited her. Now was not the time to see her boss sink beneath the waves, not with them both on the same liner. She wanted him around until a lifeboat moved into view. "Now. What things?"

He rose, went and closed the door and returned to his seat. Then frosted the office wall, blurring Josie and all the other girls and boys to dim shapes huddled over monitors. "These attacks. It's not ISIS. It's North Korea."

Taverner nodded. Her refusal to be surprised was one of her more irritating traits. "Okay. I think we've all been expecting that shoe to drop. Does Number Ten know?"

"Not yet. There's more."

Of course there is, her silence said.

He told her about the document Ho had passed on.

Outside, the dim shapes kept up their blurry movements. Inside, the only movement was that of time passing, while Taverner caught up with the implications.

"They're using our playbook," she said at last.

"Well, it's not exactly a—"

"They're using our playbook."

He nodded.

"That," she said, "is not going to go down well."

"Your input's always welcome. But I'd got that far myself."

"A North Korean black op. Here. Jesus." At least she had the grace to swear, even if her expression remained unperturbed. He wondered if she Botoxed; thought about finding out. Shelved the thought as not important right now. She said, "So what's the order of play?"

"The what?"

"They're following a list. What's next?"

"I haven't checked."

"You don't think that would be useful?" she said, after a pause.

"I don't think it would help to have a paper trail," he said. "Not if we're going to achieve deniability."

Taverner nodded. "Like I said the other day, you're learning. What are the boys and girls doing?"

"Whereabouts of Korean nationals, and ethnically similar. Not exactly the time for PC niceties."

"Of course not. But this is good. We're nearer catching them. Now we know what they aren't, I mean."

"And we also know they're not simply trying to slaughter their way through the countryside. They're using our own imperial past as kerosene. It's the propaganda coup to end them all."

"Only if they complete their mission," Lady Di said. "The penguin thing, that was them too?"

"And the bomb on the train, I think. And the Gimball death's a mess, but it could easily be part of the pattern."

"Yes, and could easily be the flotsam and jetsam of everyday reality. Welcome to 2017." She went to the frosted wall. Up close, it was like seeing the world through a film of gauze. As if there were ghosts on the other side; or reality on the other side, and ghosts on this. "The whole thing has the look of a masterplan cooked up by a fantasist in his mum's box room. So we find them before they reveal what they're doing, and that bursts their bubble." She was saying all this to the wall, or to herself. "The Supreme Leader can spout all he likes about how this crew were acting on a British blueprint, and we can say, sure they were. And you lot firing warheads into the Sea of Japan, that's right there in Nostradamus."

"They'll produce the document."

"And we'll deny it's genuine. Come on, Claude. We're playing a propaganda war here. The winner's the one with the pokerest face."

"'Pokerest?'"

"It's two in the morning. What do you want, Will Self?"

"And if the killing crew show up, saying look what we did?"

"Yes, well, that part can't happen." She turned to face him at last. "They have to die, Claude. I would have thought that was obvious."

"It can't look like an execution."

"It doesn't matter what it looks like. You think their deaths will play poorly? Maybe a year from now, when one of the Sundays does an in-depth. But three days after Abbotsfield, and there'll be a street party in The Mall, with crowds queuing up to see their corpses. And any lefties screaming judicial murder had better be wearing hard hats."

"It's the sort of decision we don't make without Home Office input."

"Fuck that," said Lady Di. "They started it. They want to play London Rules, they should have known to write their wills first." She shook her head. "We end this. And then we take a long look at the SS fucking D. Starting with chopping their balls off."

When she left he'd tried to take a nap, which turned into a feverish ten-minute wrestling match: he'd come to with an erection frighteningly close to a victory cheer. Its memory still an ache in his groin, he'd splashed water on his face and patrolled the hub, hovering by Josie's desk, trying to feel paternal. He asked whether she ever went home; she laughed and said she could say the same thing. There was something in the air, the ozone that crackles during an emergency.

Around five, two names popped up at almost the same time. Students, on Chinese passports, both of whom had dropped out of sight the previous weekend.

"Let's find out where they are," he said, as if saying the words made a difference. All around him, the boys and girls were already focused on this very task.

Those loose threads, he thought again. Let's start tugging.

"Dancer Blaine," he said to Josie.

"Sir?"

"Call him," Whelan told her. "It's time I had a word."

"They're kids."

"Kids?"

"Students. Nineteen, twenty, like that. Planted here years ago. Could I get a cup of tea?"

Catherine made to move, but Devon Welles was faster; was out of the door, heading kettlewards, before she was on her feet.

Emma Flyte lowered herself into the chair he'd vacated. Exhausted as she was, she still possessed a radiance. From the overhead bulbs a high-watt light left everyone else—Welles and

Shirley excepted—colourless. Falling on Flyte, it found hidden golds and greys.

River said, "Middle East?"

"North Korea."

Louisa whistled softly. "That's big."

"But nothing new," said Lamb. He poured the last of his bottle into his glass. "The Fat Controller's sponsored so many terrorist acts, it's a wonder he hasn't had T-shirts printed. Have you locked her in?"

"Trust me," Flyte said. "She's not going anywhere."

Welles returned with a mug of tea, and she took it gratefully. "Thanks. They recruited her a couple of months ago. Picked her up in a club. She has relatives, she said. They showed her pictures."

"They're probably already dead," said Coe. When looks turned his way, he shrugged. "That's how they do things. The State Security Department."

"The SSD," said River.

"Thanks. If I have trouble with any other sets of initials, jump right in."

"She was already involved with Ho," Flyte continued. "Scamming him, pure and simple."

"Told you," said Shirley.

"And they reeled her in, on the SSD's instructions. They wanted the blueprint. The whatyoucallit—"

"The Watering Hole Paper."

"Which they already knew about," said Lamb, almost to himself. "That's interesting."

"So glad I've got your attention," said Flyte.

"How come they didn't kill her?" Louisa asked.

"She did what she does. She wrapped one of them round her little finger."

"I doubt it was her finger."

"Yeah, this is the parental control version. Shin, his name is. That's how she got away. The others think he killed her, after they came for Ho."

"Clearing house," Welles said. Chairless now, he'd planted himself against the wall next to Louisa, who'd ceased her exercises.

"Uh huh. Because they're nearly done."

"And when he wasn't rolling around for her to scratch his tummy," said Lamb, "did this Shin mention what their final act would be at all?"

Unconscious of doing so, they all leaned in as Flyte answered.

"Not as such," she said. "What he did tell her was, the whole world would be watching. And then he said something about the snake eating its own tail."

Everyone fell quiet for a moment.

Then: "Oh for fuck's sake," said Louisa.

"Sorry. But it's what she said."

"Where's it from? Sun Tzu?"

"More like *Kung Fu Panda*," said River.

But Lamb said, "I keep forgetting you lot are idiots."

St Paul's was bathed in heavenly light, or that's what it was hard to avoid thinking. In his heart, Zafar Jaffrey knew it wasn't so, and would have felt the same had it been a mosque. Which it actually looked like, a bit. A thought best kept to himself.

On the commuter train, surrounded by businessmen, voters, he'd tried to disappear; to cloak himself in the early-morning misery colouring the carriage. All he'd wanted was anonymity, just another upright stiff on the daily pilgrimage: whisked through the half-light, dumped on a platform, spat underground. They'd barely left Birmingham before a man leaned over and touched his elbow. "First class travel, eh?" Chuckling. "Not quite the man of the people after all."

"Go fuck yourself," Zafar had told him.

A vote lost, but a moment won.

Last night, he'd given Tyson all the cash he had to hand; instructed him to go as far as possible as soon as possible. Short-term advice, but that was the only kind Tyson was likely to hear, the long term always having been a puzzling perspective where that young man was concerned. What could be more important than the here and now? For Tyson's own good, what Zafar should have done was call a lawyer. All he'd done, really, was buy breathing space.

He had the address memorised.

"A stationer's?"

"Office supplies an' stuff, yeah."

For some reason, this was the detail Jaffrey's imagination snagged on; that a criminal enterprise was being run from a stationer's. Pick up a few roller-ball pens, a notebook, some Post-its. Want some fake passports to go with that? A driving licence? A gun?

"He needs the rest of the money, yeah? Funny looking geezer."

Said the man with the face tattoo, thought Jaffrey.

Tyson left, his pocket full of cash. How far would he get, Jaffrey wondered. Soon, if not already, people would be hunting Tyson Bowman, who wasn't an unnoticeable man; had gone out of his way to be someone you gave a second look. He was a moving violation of the law of common sense: someone who'd spent his adolescence in criminal activity, and just to simplify things for everyone, had had himself branded to that effect. Which made Zafar Jaffrey wonder whether that was why he'd recruited Tyson in the first place. Not to offer redemption, but on the off chance he'd need a partner in crime one day. It was Tyson who'd known how to solve Jaffrey's problem, Tyson who'd shown him the way to Dancer Blaine's door. It was the way the world turned. You dipped a toe in the criminal waters, you could always get dry again. But once you'd inked your face, nobody would ever truly believe it.

Jaffrey located the stationer's easily enough, but it wasn't open yet, so he circled the nearby streets, glad to put the moment off. How did one approach this, exactly? *My name is*—hell, no. *I believe you have something for me?* One of the speeches he habitually delivered, addressing young people at risk, was to explain that the criminal life was the easy option, that they had to believe themselves capable of the tougher choice, but he wondered now whether that was true. There were difficulties in criminal enterprise that had never occurred to him before. A whole new set of rules.

London was stirring; coming to life. It had been full enough already, but that was with people hurrying to work. Now came the new wave, of those who weren't in a rush. Those with time to look in shop windows, or to pause at corners and check their phones.

When he reached the shop again, it was open, and he went in.

A youngish man was the only creature visible: behind the counter, reading his phone. A mug of something steamed on a shelf beside him, not quite aromatic enough to mask the sweet-sick smell of marijuana coming off his clothes. He took no notice of Jaffrey's arrival. Barely looked up when Jaffrey spoke.

"I'm looking for Mr. Blaine."

"Never heard of him."

Okay, Jaffrey thought. So what now? Buy a ream of A4 and wander back to Euston? He reached into his pocket, brought out the envelope he'd been carrying for days, scared to leave it anywhere in case it disappeared. A frightening chunk of his savings account. The remaining half of what Blaine was owed. He slapped it on the counter, hard; the unmistakeable sound of money.

The young man looked up.

"Heard of him now?" said Jaffrey.

The body was starting to smell.

Truth is, it wasn't clear it was the body on the turn; the body was wrapped in clingfilm, which should be keeping it fresh, and there were other possible sources: Shin, for a start, and An, and Chris. The back of the van was a mobile oven, and it was days since any of them had showered. So it might be that Joon was blameless, the only one not contributing to the rancid atmosphere, but he was also the only one currently dead, so there was little chance he could evade blame.

As well as body odour, tension muddied the air.

Shin said, "There will be armed police."

"We do not know that," said An.

"And helicopters."

Again: "We do not know that."

Danny nodded, to show An his agreement. Noticing this, Shin scowled.

But Shin had diminished overnight, and his presence carried no more weight than Joon's. They no longer believed in him. Shin had yet to threaten to raise this in his precious daily report, but only, Danny thought, because he knew how weak it would make him appear. When Shin's face crumpled in frustration or rage, he pretended it was the tightness of his collar enraging him, or the looseness of his belt, and he would fumble briefly at the supposed cause of offence. But in truth, it was Danny and An who were angering him; their having seen through his weakness and failure.

They had left Birmingham an hour ago, Chris at the wheel once more. Of all of them, Chris alone seemed unchanged by events; seemed happy to drive, to wait, to follow orders.

Shin said, "They know what we are capable of."

An was down on his haunches, a position Danny found impossible to believe was comfortable in a moving vehicle, and was holding one of the assault rifles across his lap. One palm was laid flat across its trigger guard, and the barrel was pointing at the back door.

"And they will be expecting us to make a move."

An said, "But they cannot know where."

He stroked the gun.

Shin tried again. "They will know the document we are following. Ho will have told them. We are no longer working in darkness."

An said, "But Ho knows nothing of our actual plans. There is nothing he would be able to tell them."

"But maybe the girl," said Shin, and stopped.

The van went over a pothole: always potholes on the roads.

The whole country was sliding into a pit, one small chunk at a time.

Danny said, "What did you say?"

"Nothing. I said nothing."

"You said something about the girl."

"The girl knew nothing either. That is all I was going to say."

Danny said, "The girl is dead."

"Yes," said Shin.

"So why do you say she knew nothing?"

Shin said, "Because even if she were alive, it would not help them. That is all I meant."

"You said you killed her."

"I did."

"When you came out of her house, you told us she was dead, that you had ended her."

"Yes."

"But nobody else saw her body."

"I saw her body," said Shin.

Danny looked at An, waiting for him to reach the obvious conclusion: that Shin was lying. That Shin had betrayed them.

But An said nothing.

Shin said, "Why are you asking me these questions? Have you forgotten who is in charge?"

Nobody had forgotten who was in charge.

The heat in the van increased as sunlight took hold. In here for hours now, for days, and their old lives as lost as a snake's sloughed skin. It was true, though, that they were no longer working in darkness; somewhere there would be doors being knocked upon, computer records shuffled, names and descriptions gathered in. But they only had one more thing to do, and all that mattered was that they do it.

Because they were soldiers. As a student in this strange world, Danny had been amazed at the words and antics of those who imagined their lives their own to do with what they would, never realising that everything they thought they desired had been imposed on them by forces greater than themselves. It was only in accepting those forces that true freedom could be found. Example: when he learned that The Supreme Leader had had his own uncle executed with an antiaircraft gun, Danny understood that such a thing had been necessary to punish dissent. When he further learned that this story had been concocted by the Western media, Danny understood that The Supreme Leader was a gentle soul, vilified by his enemies. In neither of those different worlds was his faith in The Supreme Leader shaken.

As if he were reading Danny's mind, An spoke. "It does not matter," he said. "They are expecting us, they are not. It makes no difference. We will fulfil this destiny."

Then he reached up for the transistor radio that hung by a strap from a hook; a small, cheap, apparently indestructible device, that didn't mind being slapped against the panel every time they took a corner or hit a bump. When he turned the knob, a news broadcast chirruped into life. The subject under discussion was the service that afternoon at Westminster Abbey, where there would be princes and politicians, the PM among them and all of it taking place under the eyes of the world's cameras.

Shin said, "I am not afraid. I am simply saying we should be careful. That is all."

Danny said nothing. Shin had let the girl go free. Shin had endangered all of them. He was a traitor and a coward, and this should not go unpunished. And he tried to communicate all this to An, but An's eyes were closed, and the look Danny gave passed harmlessly by him.

And on they drove through the lengthening day.

To step out into morning air—to leave the dentist's surgery, or a job interview—to find one's feet on firm pavement again, with the day stretching out bared and steady as a racetrack—is to know oneself alive, thought Zafar Jaffrey. He emerged from the warren of alleyways to catch a glimpse of St Paul's, a moment of purity he felt to his toes. In his jacket pocket nestled the package he'd just collected. Everything might still be worth it. Even the mess Tyson had stepped into, the death of Dennis Gimball—there was no law that said things couldn't work out right.

Dancer Blaine, as Tyson had said, was a funny-looking fellow, with grey-streaked hair folded into a rope, and squirrelly brown eyes behind thick round glasses. Even during their short conversation, he'd allowed Jaffrey to understand that his nickname was honestly earned; that he was nimble as a flea. Jaffrey had nodded politely. Oddly, he had no trouble picturing this creature floating an inch or two above a dance floor; no difficulty imagining him executing balletic movements. What he couldn't see was the woman who would partner him. Beneath his dirty rope of hair, his pocked and greasy skin, lurked an odour of rot. Blaine smelled the way Jaffrey's toenails did, if left too long between clippings.

But this didn't matter. Dancer Blaine was a crook, an underworld fixer, and he had done what fixers do and fixed Jaffrey's problem. So despite the pitch he'd had to breathe—*because* of the pitch—Jaffrey was now light and free, and believed in possibility again. He was tethered to the earth by habit, nothing more. He was suddenly ravenous. He was deeply relieved.

There was a coffee shop with tables outside, despite the narrow pavement. He sat and ordered coffee and two croissants, and stretched his legs as far as they would go. The weight in his pocket was that of his own heart. He rang his mother and spoke to her of nothing much; listened to her talking until the coffee arrived, and then told her he had to go, that he had a meeting. He was starving; he was empty. He didn't so much eat as inhale the first of his pastries, and ordered a refill of coffee before he'd finished the cup.

He closed his eyes. Dancer Blaine saying, *A pleasure doing business with you.* He hadn't been able to reply. The pleasure lay in it being over.

A shadow fell.

Zafar Jaffrey did not open his eyes. Until he did so it could be ignored, this new reality. It was the waitress, to refill his cup; it was the manager, eager to know all was satisfactory. As long as he kept his eyes shut, this could easily be the truth: everything was satisfactory, everything shone.

"Mr. Jaffrey?"

This happened too. He was recognised; his was a known face. Even here, in large London, where different rules applied.

"Mr. Zafar Jaffrey?"

"I'm resting," he said.

"My name's Claude Whelan," the shadow said, and Zafar knew that soon he'd have to pretend to wake up.

"Emma Flyte."

"Ma'am."

"You look rough. Bad night?"

"I've had better."

She'd have worse.

The pair had met in the lift lobby: Flyte having just arrived back at the Park; Diana Taverner taking a break from the hub.

Flyte did seem tired, it was true. Taverner herself had been awake for more hours than she could remember, and could have given Flyte a decade and still come out ahead. But there was something within her that thrived on emergency, and she was glowing at the core. That said, she wasn't deluded enough to think she outshone Flyte, for whom looking rough was on a par with Trump looking presidential: all the wishful thinking in the world wasn't going to make it happen. But Taverner was Second Desk, and outranked any mirror in the building. And Flyte wasn't likely to take it to HR.

"Well, you've certainly been busy."

"I'm sure we all have."

"Though in your case, it's kept you from following instructions. You were supposed to be at Slough House."

"Yes."

"Which was supposed to be in lockdown. Any special reason that didn't happen?"

"Things got out of hand," said Flyte.

"That happens when Jackson Lamb's involved," Taverner conceded. "Which is why I put you on it. Aren't you the expert on crowd control?"

"He's not so much a crowd, though, is he? More a road traffic accident."

"Nice. Doesn't explain why you came back here and interrogated Roderick Ho, though."

"It seemed important to find out what he knows."

"What he knows is, he passed a classified document to his girlfriend. He's going down for a long time."

"Is he?"

"I beg your pardon?"

Flyte said, "He claims the document wasn't classified."

"That's his defence? Good luck with that in court. He downloaded it from the Service database, Flyte. That's not like nicking Post-its. You're aware what use the document's been put to?"

"I am."

"You see, that worries me too. That knowledge puts you way out of your depth. And interrogating Ho without authorisation, that's outside your jurisdiction too. Mind telling me what you're up to?"

"With respect, ma'am, I'm authorised to interview Service members at my discretion."

Taverner paused. It was true: as Head Dog, Flyte had authority to question any Service member, herself included, though if it ever came to that there'd better be seconds involved, and an ambulance on standby. "But you abandoned a lockdown I instigated. Where's your authorisation to do that?"

"As a division head, I can delegate as I see fit. I had Devon sub me."

"Devon?"

"Devon Welles, ma'am. You can't miss him. He's the Dogs' diversity appointment."

Taverner said, "You might not have escaped Lamb swiftly enough. You seem to be infected." She consulted her phone, aware that Flyte was all but ticking in front of her: she was carrying news; it was ready to break.

"Ma'am—"

"One moment." She finished checking the duty calendar, and flashed it at Flyte. "According to this, Welles was off roster. He should be halfway through a forty-eight hour furlough."

"Yes, he should. But like I said, I asked him to sub me."

"And he's still there now?"

"Yes."

"So you can categorically state that Lamb's team have been locked down for the past twenty four hours?"

Flyte took a deep breath. "There might have been a slight interruption."

"Which would make this a disciplinary—"

"It would. But can that wait? I need to see Mr. Whelan."

"He's not in the building. You're seeing me."

"Then you might not want to hear this."

"Anything I might not want to hear, I definitely want to hear," Taverner said. She stared at Flyte hard. "Let's go to my office."

The boys and girls on the hub didn't look up. They were too busy bouncing off each other like pinballs in a machine: there came a point when it stopped mattering that they were individuals. They swarmed. There was a day when all the butterflies arrived, Flyte remembered reading once: a town on the Black Sea, she thought it was. On one single day, marking summer's arrival, the town became alive with butterflies. That thought came to mind, seeing the hub bright with activity. It wasn't just the work being done. It was the knowledge that results were taking shape. The boys and girls were becoming butterflies.

It was possible Diana Taverner didn't feel the same way, because she frosted the wall once they were in her room.

"This had better be good," she said.

"The final item on the Watering Hole list," Flyte said.

"The what?"

"That's what they're calling it. The Watering Hole List."

"I'm making a list myself," Taverner said. "And it's getting longer by the minute. What's the final item?"

"Seize control of the media," said Flyte. "But it doesn't mean exactly what it says."

"You seem to know a lot about this."

"It was actually Lamb who saw it. This final thing, the media thing, what they're going to do is some kind of attack on camera. Somewhere there's a lot of press, a lot of media. Somewhere public. Somewhere soon."

"The Abbey," said Taverner.

"Yes, the Abbey," Flyte said. "Today. The Abbotsfield memorial service."

They brought him some pizza. A meat feast, he'd ordered; the jokers arrived with a plain cheese-and-tomato onto which extra anchovies had been added: you guys, he thought, shaking his head, scraping the offending morsels to the edge with his finger. You guys.

Then they left him alone.

It had gone on all night. After his session with Emma, after he'd finished putting her straight on a few things, the guys had come in and he'd had to go through it all over again. *You don't talk to each other?* he'd wanted to ask. But Roddy Ho knew how it went, because Kim—his girlfriend—was just the same: whenever they were together for more than ten minutes, she found it too intense and needed to be somewhere else for a while, somewhere quiet, on her own. That was gender politics for you—chicks need their downtime. Was he right, or was he right?

That aside, the fact that they were keeping him here suggested a high-level threat remained in place. It made sense, cotton-wooling him—God knows, you wouldn't want to hand the bad actors a propaganda coup like rubbing out the Rodman—but you'd have thought all concerned would have copped on by now: that if there was any rubbing out going on, it would be Roddy Ho doing it.

Because there was a word for the kind of cool he had, and it was this: feline. Cats, you only had to look at them to know they never put a paw wrong, or if they did, it was a temporary disarrangement. They landed on their feet, cats. And that was the kind of cool Roddy Ho enjoyed, where there might be the occasional excitement—a bit of a tussle, like the other night—but you always knew who was going to come out on top.

At the same time, he could hotdog it with the best of them. Your typical maverick. Best of both worlds.

Like he'd told the guys: "So sure, they sent someone to take me out. And look where it got them. Next time, they'll know to send two."

And the guys had exchanged a look.

So now he finished his pizza, except the anchovies, and as he sat licking his fingers it occurred to him that nobody had yet told him what had happened to Kim, his girlfriend. Now he'd explained that the document he'd shown her wasn't even classified—seriously: the Dyno-Rod, passing on secrets? *C'mon*—she was surely cleared of everything except curiosity, and since when was that a crime? But they were leaving him in the dark.

Or maybe . . .

But there was a corner of his mind Roderick Ho preferred not to visit, and he backed away from it now. It was a corner where different decisions had been made, and different destinations reached; one which, if he'd spent more time there, might have meant he'd be a little more slow horse, a little less The Rodster. It would have meant he'd asked more questions when Kim came into his life, and had more people around to help answer them . . . But there was no going back. This was who he was now, and Kim was his girlfriend, right? Kim was his girlfriend. And if he was partly in the dark right now, well, that was the thing about the secret world. A lot of it was just too . . . secret.

Roddy shook his head. It would all come out in the wash, he guessed. Meanwhile, he supposed he'd have to stay here so nobody got too worried about him. He smiled to himself. *Who is this guy?* is what they're wondering, he thought. Some kind of Bond/Q combo? Scouts the Dark Web by day, and come nightfall goes clubbing with an uber-foxy chick, tossing villains through windows?

Who *is* this guy?

That's what they're wondering.

In the room next door, the two guys were sharing a meat feast. They didn't speak much, but at length one of them paused to say, "Who *is* this guy?"

And they both shook their heads, and carried on eating.

Claude Whelan was back in Downing Street, in one of the cubbyhole incubators. The PM had kept him waiting—not a great sign—but the time had been swallowed by a call from Di Taverner, with an update from the hub. When a funeral-suited PM arrived at last, his face was red with exertion. "I'm in Cabinet all morning, no time to change later. This is awfully formfitting. It doesn't make me look fat?"

"I really don't . . ." Whelan made himself stop; start again. Nothing would happen until this bridge had been crossed. "Black is slimming."

"It's supposed to be, but when I stand sideways . . . 'Tubby' is a cruel word, isn't it? But you hear whispers."

"You look . . . Prime Ministerial."

He looked like a side of ham at a wedding, but nobody wanted to hear that.

"I should get more exercise," the PM brooded. "But all the chaps I played tennis with . . . Well." His face assumed a Shakespearian cast. "It's the ones who make dodgy line calls turn out to be snakes in the grass. That's telling, don't you think?"

"I think we've more important things to discuss."

The PM sighed theatrically. "You think I don't know that?" He undid the lowest button on his jacket and released a breath. "Zafar Jaffrey's in custody. It's still a rumour, but a true one, yes?"

"I'm afraid so."

"I wanted to know he was a safe pair of hands, and it turns out he's involved with some underworld fixer. Really, Claude?" It sounded like he held Whelan responsible. "It's like a bad Michael Caine movie."

Technically, the PM was too young to remember any other kind, but now wasn't the time.

"Perhaps. But the Gimball news is going to eclipse everything else for today at least. As things stand, you're ahead of the curve. Make a statement now, and it'll be the first anyone knows about it."

"A statement? I don't even know what he was up to yet. He's what? A secret ISIS supporter? I don't *believe* it, Claude, the man follows Warwickshire—"

"It's his brother."

"So his brother gets killed in Syria, which was his own stupid fault by the way, and that means Zaff, what, converts to the cause?"

"His brother didn't die."

"Oh."

"His brother was the reason he needed a false passport."

"Oh." The PM drew a breath in, and rebuttoned his jacket. "We all thought he died."

"His own family thought he did. Hellfire missile, drone-fired, August 2016. Young Karim wasn't the target, but he was known to be near the impact, and there was a body unaccounted for." Whelan shook his head. "There's a ninety-five per cent accuracy reading on these strikes. Karim fell into the five. It happens."

"So he what, just walked away?"

"We don't have the details. What we do know is, he got in touch with his older brother four months ago. In France at this point, living rough. He played the prodigal card. All he wants is his old life back, because now he's seen what it's like, it turns out jihad isn't a bed of roses."

"Yes, well, I could have told him that. *Anybody* could have told him that."

"And Zafar agreed to help him."

"Call me a pedant, but I was under the impression ISIS don't much like it when you change your mind. Like swapping Celtic for Rangers."

"No. That's why the whole underworld fixer business."

"Ah. Of course. So Jaffrey was sorting out a new identity for his brother so he could get back to Blighty undetected and, what, just pick up where he left off? Except pretending to be someone else, so his sins would go unpunished?"

"Something like that," said Whelan.

"Why didn't Zafar come to me?"

"Probably because you'd have seen to it young Karim stood trial, following which he'd have gone to prison. Where he'd probably have been killed."

"No, that's true."

"Avoiding which was rather the point."

"Families are a nuisance, aren't they? I forget, do you have siblings?" The PM didn't wait for an answer. "Well, anyway. I suppose it's as well I know all this before I issue denials. Lying to the house never looks good. By the fourth or fifth time, there's a distinct air of disapproval."

"There's more."

"There always is." The PM produced a tin of breath mints from his trouser pocket. "Care for . . . ?"

"Thank you." Lodging it inside one cheek, Whelan continued. "There may be an attack on the Abbey this afternoon."

"At the service."

"At the service. It's not intelligence, as such. More an informed guess."

"And where's this guess coming from?"

"Diana Taverner."

"Ah. The fair Lady Di." The PM fiddled with the knot of his tie. "Except not fair, obviously. Still. Fine looking filly. Wouldn't mind taking that round the paddock. Though if it ever gets back to her I said that, I'll have you killed."

"Yes, well, as she's the one you'd have to speak to, that might be a self-defeating exercise," Whelan said. "Meanwhile, she thinks it's a credible threat. She got wind of a phrase, the snake eating its own tail. In other words, the campaign comes full circle, finishing up at a memorial service for the very first attack. It's a self-fulfilling victim list. They'd know who'd be there. The princes, you, the Opposition Leader—"

"Oh, God. Her."

"—half the front bench, and the Mayor, and so on. There'll be maximum security, obviously, but plenty of potential for serious damage. It's the old story. They only have to get lucky once."

The PM's many critics took delight in highlighting his political cowardice, but occasionally, unobserved, he shone. "Well, we're not cancelling, and we're not entering the Abbey in tortoise formation. But let's make sure the crowds are kept further back than usual, eh? In case of, whatever. Shrapnel."

"Of course."

"There's no time for COBRA, but I'll speak to the Chiefs about upping the military presence. Not that there'll be room for much more. At least three thousand on the streets, and shooters— they call them shooters, don't they? Not snipers?"

"I believe so."

"Shooters on every rooftop. Good God, man. What have we come to? London used to be somewhere you felt safe. There were *rules*."

"We're not immune to the world's problems. We never will be." Whelan shifted his mint from one cheek to the other. "The Palace needs to be warned, obviously."

The PM snorted. "I'd like to be a fly on the wall for that. No, it will go ahead as planned. All public events are targets, these days. But what are we supposed to do? Hide in our basements?"

"Of course not."

"I don't want any more lives endangered than we can avoid. That said, I want these bastards taken alive, Claude. I want prisoners in a dock. I want to see them applying for legal aid, and pleading not guilty, and appealing to the Supreme Court, and standing on all the rights we afford them. I want the world to see them begging for clemency from a system they despise. And then I want them banged up to rot for the rest of their miserable fucking lives. What I don't want is martyrs. We've had too many bloody so-called *martyrs*."

Whelan bit down on the mint, and felt it crack between his teeth. For a moment, sinking heart, he thought it was the tooth that had cracked, and had to gather the pieces with his tongue, grade them bit by bit, to be sure. He almost was. It was probably just the mint. The PM was still talking:

"This might be my last big day, you know. The wolves are gathering at the gate, if that's even a bloody phrase. Gimball would have led the charge, but you know what? With him gone, others will come out of the woodwork. Nobody was going to make a move when he'd secured the popular vote. But now it's anybody's game. All anyone knows for sure is, who's got the *un*popular vote. And that would be me."

"You can't know for certain," said Whelan, who was pretty sure that in this instance you could.

"No, my days are numbered. But you know what? You catch these murdering swine on my watch, and that'll do me, as swan songs go. Then I think I'll buy a shed. Write my memoirs." He checked his frontage again; seemed to accept there was no way he was losing three pounds in the next thirty minutes, and nodded. "Interesting times, Claude. Good meeting." Then he left.

Whelan swallowed fragments of mint, and checked his teeth with his tongue. Not been my finest few days, he thought. Jaffrey, by now, would be lawyered up, but he'd know his career was over, his election lost. And that wasn't much of a result, not for the folk of the West Midlands. He'd have been a good mayor, and what had got in his way hadn't been greed or hatred or any of the myriad temptations of public office, but his love for a brother who'd have been better off incinerated by that missile. Or maybe not love: maybe loyalty. You didn't have to love somebody to remain true to them. Who knew if the reverse also held?

As for Dennis Gimball, whatever his failings, what Whelan himself had done was unconscionable: used a harmless activity to bring pressure on the man. God knows, thought Claude: I'm one to talk. But there it was. He had a brief, and he was doing what he could to fulfil it. There'd be casualties, because there always were, but there was also a higher agenda, and it was his duty to pursue it. If he expected forgiveness from those he'd wronged, he'd not have lasted this long.

He had other problems too, of course. Sometimes, you had to make sure your own back was covered: what Diana Taverner would call London Rules.

Which meant the show trial the PM wanted wasn't going to happen, for a start.

Whelan left the building, reaching for his phone. There'd be more armed soldiers in London's streets this afternoon than at any time since the last war, and his job right now was to make sure they all had the same instructions. But first, he wanted a swift word with his wife. Her voice always fell on his ears like a kind of forgiveness. And he had a lot to be forgiven for right now.

They parked some miles short of their destination, and ate what food they had left: some congealing noodles from an icebox whose catch didn't work. Danny felt a lurking foulness on his tongue, and at the same time savoured this experience: a working mouth; a body receiving nourishment. There would not be many more meals, perhaps.

Shin did not appear to feel the same way. The first mouthful, he spat into a handkerchief; the rest he left.

There were different ways of being a warrior, Danny knew. But Shin knew none of them. Shin was a coward, and deep in his belly, recognised this. It was why he could not eat now. It was why he had let the girl live.

That in itself, Danny could forgive. It was an error and a betrayal, but it was a forgivable weakness to feel pity for a woman, and if this had been Shin's only fault, Danny would have taken no pleasure in seeing him die for it. But in letting her go free Shin had put the mission at risk, and in lying about it afterwards had shown contempt for Danny and An and Chris. So when Shin died, Danny would look him straight in the eye and make sure he knew that Danny would piss on his corpse, and burn it in a ditch.

And if they survived this final assault, he would go looking for Kim, and put an end to her too. Because this had been part of their mission, and no part could be left unfinished.

An looked at his watch. "Four hours," he said. Like Danny, he had put on the same scrappy uniform he had worn at Abbotsfield; like Danny, he now carried a revolver in a holster at his waist. There would be no mingling within crowds when the hour came. They would arrive like furies, in a storm of war.

"It sounds quiet," Shin said hopefully.

"Quiet or not. We go in four hours."

"We should send someone out first. To make sure our approach is clear."

"You are tying yourself in knots," Danny told him. "You are like a dog leashed to a kennel. You bark when there are noises. You bark when there are none."

"If we are to succeed, we must proceed cautiously," Shin said. "And we go at my command, not yours," he added, looking at An.

Danny said, "You are scared."

"No more than you."

"I am not frightened," Danny said.

It was true. He was something, he wasn't sure what—elevated, perhaps; in expectation of glory—but he wasn't frightened. What came next, even if it included his death, would be a heroism not offered to many. He would be fulfilling The Supreme Leader's vision, and his name would burn like an everlasting candle. Few futures had been offered to him, but this one he would seize.

Shin, though, would cower from any future more dangerous than a putrefying noodle.

"You let the girl go," Danny said now.

"I killed her."

"You lie."

Shin said to An, "He is a fool," but his voice shook.

"Did you hear that?" Danny asked. "He knows I know. We all know. He let the girl go."

"That is enough," said An.

Chris said, "You let her go? You should not have done that."

"He endangered the whole mission," Danny said.

"I did not endanger the mission!" Shin shouted.

His words rang round the van's interior, as if a stone had been thrown.

Danny said, "Before you let her go. Before you disobeyed your orders. Did you tell her what we planned next?"

"I told her nothing."

"But you let her go."

"I disobeyed no orders. I am in charge!"

"You are not worthy of command."

"Who are you to say—"

"At Abbotsfield, you fired wild. You shot up the sky. You killed a chicken coop."

"At Abbotsfield, I did my duty," said Shin, his voice trembling with fury.

"And what about today? Can we trust you today?"

"Can we trust *you*?" Shin demanded. "I am in charge here. When I speak, I speak for The Supreme Leader!"

Chris said, "I am worried that you let the girl go."

"Enough," said An.

Danny said, "When we set out, when we go to complete our mission. What will you do this time? Will you hide behind a dustbin? Will you throw your hands up and surrender?"

"This will all be in my report!" said Shin. "It is you who's the traitor!"

Danny looked at An. "He endangers us all."

"I am in charge!"

"Who is to say what he told the girl? Already they might be coming for us."

"You are a traitor," Shin told him. "You break ranks. You spit on The Supreme Leader himself."

"Enough," An said again.

"Yes, enough," said Danny. He looked at Chris, then at An. "He is not to be trusted. If we are to complete our mission, we must do it without him. He will betray us all."

"Liar!" screamed Shin.

An took his gun from its holster and shot Danny in the face.

Once the echo died away, he said to Shin, "The Supreme Leader put you in charge. To question that is to question Him."

Shin nodded dumbly.

"We go in four hours," An said, and put the gun down, and resumed eating noodles.

Noon comes with bells on, because this is London, and London is a city of bells. From its heart to its ragged edges, they bisect the day in a jangle of sound: peals and tinkles and deep bass knells. They ring from steeples and clocktowers, from churches and town halls, in an overlapping celebration of the everyday fact that time passes. In the heat, it might almost be possible to see their sound travel, carried on the haze that shimmers in the middle distance. And in time with the bells, other devices strike up: clocks on corners and hanging over jewellers' premises strike the hour in their staggered fashion, all a little behind or a little ahead of the sun, but always—always—there's one single moment when all chime together. Or that's what it would be nice to pretend; that twice a day, around midnight and noon, the city speaks as one. But even if it were true, it would be over in a moment, and the normal cacophony reestablish itself; voices arguing, chiding, consoling and cracking jokes; begging for ice cream, for lovers to return; offering change and seeking endorsement; stumbling over each other in a constant chorus of joy and complaint, bliss and treachery; of big griefs, small sorrows and unexpected delight. Every day is like this one: both familiar and unique. Today, like tomorrow, is always different, and always the same.

And today, London has slipped onto a war footing. Armed police on the streets are an unhappy outcome, but it seems there are prices to be paid for the common liberties London enjoys: the freedom of its citizens to walk its streets, to show their faces uncovered, to hold hands in public. Months go by without a civilian seeing a gun. But recent lessons have been harsh, and the capital's dead, and the dead of its sister cities, are a familiar presence wherever crowds gather, so armed police are on the streets today. In the Abbey's environs the pavements have been trammelled by metal barriers, and behind them Londoners, visitors too, are gathering to pay their respects to the Abbotsfield dead, because Abbotsfield could have been anywhere, and London is anywhere too. This is what London and its sister cities have learned: that hate crime pollutes the soul, but only the souls of those who commit it. When those who mourn stand together, their separate chimes sounding in unison if only for a moment, they remain unstained. So the people gather and wait, and the armed police officers study new arrivals, and twelve o'clock comes and goes in a welter of bells, and afternoon begins.

It was hours since anyone had put their head down. Claude Whelan was back at Regent's Park; relieved to be at his desk, where he could at least feign some semblance of control; Di Taverner, likewise, was *in situ*, though roaming the hub now, looking over the shoulders of the boys and girls. She lingered longer than usual at one particular desk; a young woman—Josie— whose Breton-hooped T-shirt accentuated her breasts, and who had a way of blinking shyly when spoken to. The casual observer would have found it impossible to guess what Taverner was thinking, but a seasoned Lady Di-watcher would have known a mental note was being taken, information stored.

"Sit-rep," she said.

Josie blinked, then read from her screen. "The Royals are due at the Abbey in fifty minutes. PM in forty. There's been a disturbance on Great Smith Street, but it's already over. A few drunks getting out of hand."

Taverner said, "We don't call them the Royals, and we don't call him the PM. Let's maintain coding protocols, shall we?"

"Sorry, ma'am."

"What's our street-level status?"

"Kestrel-one's on Westminster Bridge, two's on Millbank. Neither reporting anything suspicious. Three through five are strung out along Whitehall. The crowd's mostly subdued, they say, with a few angry outbreaks. Chanting about Dennis Gimball. Probably orchestrated by one right-wing group or another."

That lines of connection were being drawn between the Abbotsfield massacre and the death of Dennis Gimball didn't much surprise Taverner. Conspiracy theories bloomed at the rate of one hundred and forty characters a second.

She said, "Any arrests?"

"A handful, ma'am. That we know of."

Taverner placed her hand on the shoulder rest of Josie's chair. It felt warm. "Are you keeping Mr. Whelan up to speed?"

"Yes, ma'am."

"Email, or . . . ?"

"He prefers me to step into his office."

Taverner nodded, as if her mind was on something else entirely. "Tread carefully," she said, and returned to her room.

Kim Park, Roderick Ho's girlfriend, was downstairs now, delivered by Flyte and Welles. On first time of asking, she'd had little to say she hadn't already told Flyte, though her interrogation would continue for some while yet. Kim had been well aware of her rights; of how long she could be detained without charge. What she was now in the process of learning was that this only counted when she was under arrest, which she wasn't. Legally, she'd been abducted. And the best of luck to her making an issue out of that, thought Taverner. She had at least provided identikit drawings of the terror suspects, though like every such picture Taverner had seen, the resulting images resembled automatons: batteries not included. She suspected their real-life counterparts would look a little different. Terror bots, she'd called them earlier. Those prepared to murder for their beliefs were inevitably absent empathy, the human light in their eyes dimmed to nothing. She

occasionally felt a little detached herself. But she'd never waged
war on children.

Josie looked like she might be fair game, though. And if she
was sitting on Claude's lap while delivering her memos, she'd
better be prepared to learn the meaning of collateral damage.

For a moment Taverner dimmed her own eyes. Emergencies
tested the systems, her own not excluded. When this was over,
she'd need to sleep for forty-eight hours. But not yet.

She turned the TV on, found a news channel. Aerial images
of London filled the screen. Just ten years ago, it had looked so
different: no Heron Tower, no Needle. Fold back twenty years,
and you lost the Gherkin, the Eye, half the skyline. And twenty
years from now, who knew; there might be monorails stretched
between hundred-storey towers. But it would still be London,
because that was the rule. Under the glitter and glad rags, the same
heart beat.

Meanwhile, at ground level, the Met's Chief Commissioner
currently ruled the streets. But Di Taverner had agents out there
too; Kestrels one to five, watching, taking the city's pulse. If an
attack came, the terrorists were unlikely to be taken alive. Having agents on the scene pushed the odds a little further in that
direction.

And it would soon be over either way, following which, there
were other tasks in hand. Emma Flyte needed dealing with; her
bagman, Devon Welles, too. The pair were confined to the Park
for the duration. Taverner suspected conspiracy about seventy per
cent of the time; whatever Flyte had been up to possibly fell into
the cock-up category, but that was enough to come down on her
hard. Slough House, too, was on her agenda. It was long since
time Jackson Lamb got the message: among the bells heard toll-
ing today were some that tolled for him.

Protecting the Service was her top priority, now and always.
Chopping away the dead limbs that threatened to choke its
healthy trunk: that was good husbandry.

Up on the screen, footage of the gathering crowds was on both

channels. Londoners were taking to the streets in a show of solidarity with the distant dead. It was a predictable, admirable
response, and one the killers were relying on. Di Taverner hoped
that, come tomorrow, there would be no more victims to remember. But it was true of every crowd that if you broke it down into
its constituent parts, there would always be victims among them.

River Cartwright was in the crowd, threading through knots of people, most of them sombre, serious, aware of the day's burden and
conscious of making a statement. *We are not afraid.* The talk was of
Abbotsfield, Dennis Gimball's death figuring highly too, and connections were being drawn. Every time he checked the BBC
website, he expected to find his own face staring at him, alongside
Coe's. *The police are seeking these men.* But so far, nothing.

Twice he'd had to show his Service card to be allowed through
a barrier: he didn't remember London ever being tied this tight.
But it made sense. An attack at the Abbotsfield memorial service
would be more than a propaganda coup; it would be a dagger in
the heart of the establishment, even if the shooters got nowhere
near the Abbey itself. Which they wouldn't. Any armed hostile in
Central London right now would last seconds, no longer. Which
didn't mean he couldn't take dozens of bystanders with him,
writing headlines that would scorch their way around the world.

The snake eating its own tail. . .

He was exhausted, but couldn't imagine what sleep might feel
like. Every nerve inside him jangled like a landline.

He called Louisa. "Where are you?"

"Storey's Gate. You?"

"Not far. Stay there?"

"You asking or telling?"

"Asking."

"Yeah, okay then."

He disconnected, and headed up the street; a two-minute walk
under normal circumstances, which now would take nearer ten.

Some hours before, they'd all been at Slough House. Flyte and

Welles had departed, taking Kim; the slow horses were in Ho's office, because that had become their common room, now that its regular occupant was absent. They should get rid of the furniture, River had thought; get a pinball machine. A jukebox. Not that he would have long to enjoy the amenities. That rumbling noise he could hear in the distance; that wasn't traffic surging up London Wall. It was fate bearing down.

Catherine, who'd been reading her iPad, had said, "They're expecting thousands of people. Tens of thousands. That's what happens when there's a tragedy. People want to show solidarity."

"Yeah, well, they'd be better off parking their arses at home," said Lamb. "Not like the dead are paying attention."

"It matters," she said sharply. "When bad things happen to the innocent, the rest of us should stand together. Otherwise we might as well live behind barricades."

"You know why bad things happen to good people?" Lamb asked. "It's because of all the dickheads."

"Well, that's theology's big issue wrapped up. Thanks for that." She looked around the assembled crew. "Everybody's exhausted. There's nothing we can do. Why don't you all go home?"

"We should get out there," Shirley said. "To the Abbey."

"And do what?" asked Lamb. "Chuck staplers at the bad guys?"

"A stapler can do a lot of damage," she muttered.

River said, "Flyte's reported to the Park, the Park'll have brought the Met up to speed. There'll be police, there'll be army, and Five'll have eyes on the ground. I think they'll struggle by without us."

"I imagine it had already occurred to them today's service was at risk," Catherine said. "It's not like they'd let the princes attend without serious security in place."

"A suspicion corroborated becomes a working theory," Coe said.

"Thank you, Confucius," said Lamb. He turned to River. "Once bitten, twice chewed, huh?"

"I don't even know what that means," River said.

"That last night's little adventure's left you gun-shy. What's the matter, don't want to be nearby in case more . . . *accidents* happen?"

"I just want some sleep," he said.

"We all do," said Catherine. "We should all go home," she repeated. "Whatever happens today, it's not our watch."

As if she hadn't spoken, Lamb said, "I don't know what happened in Slough, but the pair of you clearly pissed upstream. What are the odds we're all going to be drinking from that soon?"

Louisa stretched theatrically. "Well, Catherine's got a point. If we're gunna be drinking piss tomorrow, we might as well bag some sleep."

"I'm not sure that was precisely what I said."

Coe was looking out of the window.

Lamb said, "So, I mention Slough, and everybody wants to go home. A suspicious mind might find that curious."

"They went to Slough," Louisa pointed out. "I drove to Birmingham. And back. And haven't slept."

"So you don't plan to make a nuisance of yourself round the Abbey then."

"State I'm in? I'd be about as effective as Donald Trump Junior."

"There's a Donald Trump Junior? Christ. Just when I thought things couldn't get worse."

A phone buzzed, but nobody reached for a pocket.

"Will someone shut that bloody thing up?" Lamb said.

"It's yours," Catherine pointed out.

"In that case, will everyone fuck off elsewhere?"

They trooped from the office and reconvened in Shirley's room.

"Now would be a good time," Catherine said. "Just go. All of you."

"He knows, doesn't he?" River said.

"You're probably better off if he does," she told him. "If what happened gets out, then Slough House is in trouble. Which means he'll be on your side, for as long as it takes to sort things out."

Unless Lamb had the power to restore life, River didn't think things were about to get sorted out too quickly.

Shirley had disappeared. Coe was inserting his earbuds again, though whether he was listening to a news channel or his interminable jazz soundtrack was anyone's guess.

River said, "Okay, I'm done," and left the building.

On Aldersgate Street he'd waited for Louisa to catch up. "You heading home?"

"That seems to be our instruction."

"So are you?"

"Hell no."

"Me neither."

"Didn't think so. What was with the, 'I think they'll struggle by without us' bit?"

"Last thing I want right now," River told her, "is pairing up with Coe again. Or Shirley."

"You think they'll head that way too?"

"I'm not making any predictions about Coe. Except that whatever he does, I hope he does it far away. But Shirley, yeah."

"You're probably right. We tubing it?"

He'd left Ho's car keys on his desk; besides, Central London's traffic would be jammed to a standstill. "Yep."

They'd separated on arrival, patrolling streets that were slowly, then quickly, transformed by the public. It was a pointless exercise, but it was hardwired into them all the same. It was the job they'd trained for, before they'd soiled their copybooks. It was that tiny spark of hope, not quite dead, that, carefully nurtured, might light their way back to their careers. Two hours in they'd rendezvoused for a Coke, then headed back into the throng. Now, ninety minutes later, the memorial service was gearing up to start, one o'clock ready to strike its ragged antiphony. River saw Louisa up ahead, by a streetlight; holding two cups of coffee one-handed while she checked her phone.

"Anything?" he asked, relieving her of a cup.

"Nada. You?"

"Same."

Cars went past, a little way distant. The only traffic carried VIPs to the Abbey. That would be the princes arriving, he thought, or the PM. It was starting.

"Seen Shirley?"

"Nope. Coe neither."

"I expect they've gone to bed."

Louisa spat coffee.

"Christ, no. I meant—"

"I know what you meant. I just—"

"Yeah."

"I mean, can you *imagine*?" She slipped her phone back into her pocket. "You think it's gunna work out?"

"The service?"

"Everything." She glanced around, to check nobody was listening, but dropped her voice anyway. "Coe. The Gimball thing. Shit, River, it's fucking huge."

"I don't know what's going to happen," he said, keeping his own voice level. They began to walk, past a row of parked cars.

"Have you thought about taking it upstairs?"

"Yes."

"And?"

"I don't know what good it'll do. I was there, same as Coe. We both know what that'll mean, if it comes to handing down verdicts. There are reasons why the Park might want to cover it up, but probably plenty more why they won't. Not least being, we're not their favourite people." His coffee was too hot. A hot drink on a hot day. Better than nothing, though. "You want to know something funny?"

"Please."

"I was planning on quitting. Before it all kicked off. I'd decided I'd had enough, and was gunna jack it in. Start a new life." He laughed: not a real laugh. "Good times."

Louisa put her hand on his shoulder. "You're all over the place right now, though. With your grandfather and all."

"Yeah. Still."

"So I wouldn't make any big decisions. Not until—yellow car."

"What?"

"Nothing. Not until it all shakes down a bit. We catch these guys, we get to be heroes. That'll alter the picture. Besides, you know. Lamb. He has a way of sorting things out."

River said, "There are limits. Anyway, catching these guys, that's not gunna happen, is it? Realistically. Even if they do turn up here. In which case, frankly, we're more likely to get shot than be heroes."

Louisa dropped her cup into a bin. "Now, that's just defeatist." She fished her phone out again. "I still think it's strange we've not seen Shirley."

"It's a big crowd. She's a small person."

"But with ways of making her presence felt. I'm gunna call her."

"You'll probably wake her up."

Louisa said, "Yeah, that'll be fun too," and made the call.

Fixed to the wall were two TVs, currently mute, each showing footage from Westminster Abbey. The PM was just disappearing inside, shadows swallowing him as surely as history would, any moment now. Then again, people had been saying that for a while. The other screen showed crowds lining the roads. It might have been a celebration, but there were few flags flying. Close-ups showed serious expressions, occasional tears.

Emma Flyte said, "Have you ever seen so many blues on the street?"

"Royal Wedding?"

"Even then. And khaki, too. There must be two full regiments out there. You could basically stage a war in Central London."

Welles said, "You're worried something's going to happen? Or that it's not?"

They were in the Dogs' quarters—"the kennel," naturally—having been told by Taverner to remain there for the foreseeable, which as far as Flyte was concerned, might turn out not that long. Yesterday she'd sat in Slough House, handcuffed to a chair, and listened to those idiots discussing which of Gimball or Jaffrey might end up dead. If she'd brought that straight to the Park, maybe Gimball would have made it through the night. As it was, her career probably wouldn't survive him by much.

But here she was, and she'd dragged Devon along behind her. She'd yet to hear him complain about it.

She said, "The Abbotsfield crew, they're what, five strong? And probably one down now, given someone went through a window."

"Two words," said Welles. "Suicide squad."

"Okay. But even then, how close to the Abbey could they get? There's no traffic within quarter of a mile. And on foot, they won't get that close. Not with every pair of eyes on the lookout for dodgy actors."

"They don't need to get close," Welles said. "These aren't combat rules, remember? To be a target, you just have to turn up. This crew, if they mow down a crowd at a zebra crossing, they'll call it a result. Any crowd, any street. They just have to open fire."

"Sure," she said. "But that's not exactly seizing the media, is it?"

"No shortage of news crews out there."

"I don't like it."

"Nobody likes it." Welles hoisted himself out of his chair. There was a table in the corner on which an ancient coffee machine muttered to itself. "You want some?"

"I'm caffeinated beyond belief," Flyte told him. "Any more, you'll have to peel me from the ceiling."

"Wouldn't be the first time." He filled a cardboard cup from the jug. "I'm not even supposed to be here," he reminded her. "I'm off duty."

"Yeah, boo hoo."

"I feel a discrimination lawsuit coming on."

"You make such a thing out of being black," she said. "Try being blonde. Then you'd know what harassment feels like."

He laughed.

On one of the screens the picture changed, and Flyte tensed. A disturbance, people pressing forward so a barrier fell.

"Dev?"

He'd already abandoned his coffee, the cup dropping to the tabletop, rolling onto the floor.

And then there were policemen on the screen; helping people to their feet, moving the barrier so nobody else tripped.

Welles exhaled heavily.

Flyte said, half to herself, "So many people there. It's like a coronation."

"We are not afraid," Welles quoted. "They want to be there, show the bastards they're not winning. That they'll never win."

"But some of us will lose, all the same." The screen showed someone who'd borne the brunt of the collapse; a young woman, her face contorted in pain. Broken leg? Broken something. Two officers were crouching beside her, one laying a hand on her forehead.

Welles said, "Would you prefer it if the streets were deserted? If they had a memorial service and nobody came?"

She said, "They've picked soft targets until now. They're in for a shock."

"Not sure there'll be many of us feeling sorry for them."

"No. But it makes me wonder why they got so ambitious. They're not going to get anywhere near the Abbey."

"A snake eating its tail. This wouldn't be happening if they hadn't shot up Abbotsfield. They've ordered their own victim turnout. What's the matter?"

Emma had gone white.

Lamb was not far from Regent's Park, waiting at a junction where a tree overhung the pavement. There were no crowds; outside of the Abbey's environs, London was muted, as if the arching blue sky were an upturned bowl, clamping down on everything. He had contrived to be late, but not late enough, and it was a full minute before Molly Doran approached, her cherry-red wheel-chair buzzing, as if pursued by mosquitoes. He lit a cigarette, then ran a finger round his collar. It came away damp.

"What speed can you manage on that thing?" he asked, when she'd come within range.

"Faster than you'd think."

Lamb grunted. "Might get one myself. Walking's hell in this weather. Makes my feet swell up."

"Is there not a small part of you that gets tired of this?"

He leered. "I have no small parts. Remember?"

"Must be fun working under you, Jackson." She steered her chair into the shade. "Tell me about Catherine Standish."

For a moment, the near-impossible happened, and Jackson Lamb looked thrown. But he was looming above Molly Doran's eye level, and it was possible she didn't notice. "She's a drunk. She makes my tea. Does the typing. So what?"

"Nobody types any more."

"Yeah, I don't micromanage. Typing or whatever. What's it to you?"

"Seems only fair I get some information in return."

"In return for what? You've told me nothing yet."

"You seriously think I'd show you mine without seeing yours first? Come on, Jackson. Even when I did have legs, I didn't spread them that easily. She was Charles Partner's Girl Friday, wasn't she?"

"You never met her?"

"She was on the Exec level. I didn't get upstairs that often."

"You could have left that to me," he said. "There's a punchline in there somewhere."

"She crops up now and again, in the records. In Partner's files. Just another of those stories I'll never hear the end of now."

"She's a slow horse," said Lamb. "Like all the others."

"Except she was the first of them, wasn't she? She was the one you took with you, from the Park. Why'd you choose her? That's my price."

He said, "I needed someone to make my tea. And do the typing."

"Fuck off, Jackson."

He removed the cigarette from his mouth and examined the glowing tip. Veins of bright orange under a film of ash. He blew on it, and the ash disappeared. Within moments, it was back.

"She's a joe," he said at last.

Molly Doran laughed: half sneer, half cackle. Out here, she looked like she didn't belong to the daylight world. "She rode a desk her entire career. When she wasn't riding half the available males in her postcode. Reading between the lines, you understand."

"Partner used her as a cutout."

And now she inhaled deeply, satisfaction painted across her face like an extra layer of makeup. "So the rumours about Partner are true."

"Yeah, I wouldn't broadcast that. It remains pretty sensitive."

"So his suicide—"

"Enough," he said, with absolute finality.

She paused, and said, "But he used her. And that makes her a joe in your eyes."

"In Slough House, my eyes are the only ones that count. Have you finished playing now?"

"I'm going to miss all this."

"If I pretend to give a fuck, will you get a move on?"

"Jackson, Jackson, Jackson." She shook her head, as if releasing a few bad thoughts. Then said, "The document your boy Ho stole."

"You found the original'

"Uh-huh."

"And there's a papertrail?"

"Oh, you'd better believe it," said Molly Doran.

Flyte said, "We've got it wrong. Everybody's got it wrong."

"What do you mean?"

"It's the memorial service all right. That's where they'll attack. But not at Westminster. They're back at Abbotsfield."

"You think—"

But Flyte was already on the move; out of the door, heading up to the hub.

An said, "It is time you gave the order."

They'd hoisted Danny's body on top of Joon's, so the two lay like logs; the lower sheened in cling film; the upper growing waxier by the minute. Danny's last thoughts had been spray-painted across the van's side panel, but were drying now, and remained forever private.

Shin tried to speak, couldn't, and reached for his bottle of water. After a draught, he tried again. "We go now," he said.

"Louder."

"We go now."

Up front, Chris started the van. It pulled away from the edge of the unkempt road, leaving the weeds and long grass it had been parked upon to commence the struggle of becoming upright once more.

Down the hill, Abbotsfield awaited their second coming.

Shirley answered on the third ring. "Yeah. What?"

"Where are you?"

"Why, where are you?"

"I'm at the Abbey, Shirl. With River. Are you not here too? We haven't seen you."

"Well, yeah, that's because I'm not there," she said. "Simples."

Louisa stifled an exasperated sigh. "So where are you, then?"

"I'm at Abbotsfield," said Shirley.

Once Lamb had left Slough House, Shirley had crept up to his office. Crept might be the wrong word, just as hiding might not be what she'd been doing immediately before he left. But it was true she didn't want to be caught searching his desk, which was why she nearly hit the ceiling when J.K. Coe addressed her from the doorway:

"Looking for Lamb's gun?"

"It's Marcus's gun," she managed at last.

Coe shrugged.

She'd heard the back door open and close several times, and had thought everyone had gone. If asked to place a bet, she'd have put money on Coe leaving first.

"Not your business, anyway."

"No."

The bottom drawer on the left hand side was locked. Shirley fumbled in her pocket; found Marcus's universals.

Coe said, "You'll probably tell me anyway. If I stand here long enough."

"They shot at me," said Shirley. "Outside Ho's house. If they shoot at me again, I want to shoot back."

"At the Abbey?"

"Yeah."

"Anyone waves a gun near the Abbey today, they'll be cat food twenty seconds later."

Shirley said nothing.

The smallest key fit. She opened the drawer, and found a shoebox.

Coe said, "Thing is, I don't think they're going to the Abbey."

"The others?"

"The Abbotsfield crew."

"Why not?"

"Because basically, they're village cricket. And the Abbey's a test match."

She removed the box's lid. Nestled inside, head to toe, were a pair of guns. A Heckler & Koch she guessed was Lamb's, and the Glock that had been Marcus's.

"And I don't think these kids'll go up against the best London can offer. I think they prefer a soft target."

"So why didn't you say?"

"No one's listening to me right now."

"That'll be because you killed Dennis Gimball."

The Glock was loaded, which was nice. She didn't check the other. Stealing Lamb's gun, she thought, was worse than swiping his lunch, and nobody ever swiped Lamb's lunch.

She removed the Glock, then replaced the lid on the shoebox and tucked it back in its drawer, which she locked.

"If it makes you feel better," she said, "they should probably erect a statue to you."

"Thanks."

"But they're not going to. They're gunna put you in prison. Sorry."

"Got what you wanted?"

"Uh-huh."

"So now you're off to the Abbey."

It was where Louisa and River would be headed, without waiting for her, the bastards. And Coe was probably right about waving a gun around today, but she wasn't going to be waving it, was she? It was a just-in-case. Next time somebody shot at her, she wouldn't just drop behind a car.

"I thought you'd have gone home by now," she said, getting to her feet.

"Do you think I'm a psychopath?"

"Hadn't really thought about it," she lied. "Yeah, maybe. Why?"

"Just wondered."

"I'm not, you know, a professional. That's just my opinion."

"I know."

"You're the one from Pysch Eval, come to think of it. What do you reckon?"

"Not sure. I might be."

"You're certainly a lot more talkative lately."

"That's not necessarily an indicator."

"Suppose not." She felt a bit awkward holding a gun during this conversation. He might think she felt the need to defend herself.

It fit unhappily into her jacket pocket. She was going to need a bag or something.

"You haven't asked where I think they'll show up."

"Where do you think they'll show up?"

"Abbotsfield," Coe said.

". . . Seriously?"

"There's a memorial service there today. Same time as the Abbey. There'll be a security presence, I expect, but nothing like London's. And there'll be media."

"Hit it *twice*?"

He said, "I'm not sure anyone's done that before."

"Christ on a bike!"

"Probably a tri—"

"You need to tell someone!"

"Nobody's listening to me." He rubbed his nose, then said, "On account of what happened in Slough."

"Yeah, but—"

"And I might be wrong."

"Yeah, but—"

"So what I thought I'd do is head that way myself."

"... Seriously?"

"It's about three hours by car. Bit more than."

He tossed keys in the air and caught them. Ho's, she guessed.

"And what if you're right? What if they're up there?"

"You've got a gun now, haven't you?"

She should stick to Plan A, she thought. Everyone else was doing Plan A. She didn't want to be doing Plan B if everyone else was having fun.

"Or you could head for the Abbey. Join the crowds." He tossed the keys again. "Your choice."

"Why do you want me with you?"

"Sidekick?"

He didn't need a sidekick, she thought. He needed a dick whisperer. But same difference.

What would Marcus do? Abbey or Abbotsfield? Everyone was at the Abbey. Which meant, if there was glory going round, the shares would be measly, and no one would notice.

"You coming, then?"

Marcus, she thought, would make sure all exits were covered.

"... Yeah, all right."

And now they were there.

They'd spent three and a half hours in the car. Not a lot of conversation involved. They'd swapped at the two-hour mark, and Shirley had driven the second leg, SatNav chirping occasionally. The gun was still an awkward bulge in her pocket. In another pocket was the wrap of coke. It occurred to her that if they were stopped and searched, that combination wouldn't make for much of a character reference. So it would be best, she decided, if they weren't stopped and searched. Some problems were more easily solved than others.

The blood on Coe's chin had dried, but he hadn't wiped it away. Her ear felt unpleasantly warm, but the Sellotape ensured no dripping.

Every hour on the hour, they checked the news: nothing much. Dennis Gimball was still making headlines, his last-gasp bid for attention. And reports filtered in from round Westminster Abbey, where the streets were thronged with mourners.

"This better not be a waste of time, dipshit," Shirley said, but not out loud. Not because Coe might be a psychopath, but in case he wasn't. If he did have feelings, his future looked grim enough without Shirley hurting them.

In Derbyshire, they'd entered a different world. Hills rose all around, and trees shaded the roads. Hedgerows sprung up, sometimes giving way to ditches, and there were sheep and cows in all directions.

Last time she'd been in the country, she'd seen a peacock. It was one of the few living things she encountered there that probably hadn't been a Russian spy.

Where the road took a dip, a signpost appeared: ABBOTSFIELD. "You have reached your destination," the SatNav chipped in. Nice to have a consensus.

"Hey," she said. She didn't know what to call him: Coe? J.K.? You'd think that would have been settled one way or the other during the previous year. Whichever he preferred, he was asleep right now, or as good as. Shirley punched his shoulder: lightly, but not so lightly he could pretend to sleep through it, and he opened his eyes. "We're here."

Coe removed his earbuds and looked around.

There were police officers, quite a few of them; not armed, it didn't appear, but flagging down traffic. Coe flashed his Service card, which earned him a pair of raised eyebrows. Cars were parked along one side of the main street, and on the other side two news crews were shooting to-camera pieces. More cars were parked along the three side streets, each of which puttered into nothingness after a hundred yards or so. The main street, meanwhile, looped around the church, squeezing between what Shirley wanted to call its back garden, though was full of headstones, and a high wall which probably guarded a manor house or something. The country had its own rules, and she wasn't sure she understood them. But whatever they were, they originated behind that wall, or one like it.

There was a police van outside the church, near a porch-type arrangement which was garlanded with flowers and toys, and multicoloured scraps of paper, cut into shapes. Hearts and more flowers. Another van belonged to a third news crew, currently occupying the path leading into the church, which Shirley thought intrusive. On the other hand, she was turning up with a gun in her pocket. That too might seem a little uncalled for.

Now that she was here, she hoped it was.

She followed the loop round the church, found a space almost big enough for Ho's car and wedged it in. Engine off, she patted her pocket automatically—gun still there: where else would it be?—then studied the area. Beyond the church was a row of cottages, splashes of colour dripping from windowboxes; elsewhere, bunches of flowers were tied to lamp posts, and there was something chalked on the road too, a child's drawing it looked like: more colour. More flowers, in fact, Shirley realised, and then: *that was where one of the bodies fell.* There'd be a war memorial: most villages had one. And now Abbotsfield had one everywhere you looked.

"Why are you really doing this?" she asked Coe.

Coe stared straight ahead for a while. "If they come for me, over Gimball?" he said at last.

"Which they will."

"It might be a good idea to have something my side of the ledger."

So I killed an MP, she thought, *but I drove all the way to Derbyshire on the offchance of catching some bad actors.*

She really didn't think the one would cancel the other out.

"What now?"

He said, "The front street's pretty well covered."

"With unarmed policemen."

"At least three of them have guns." He pointed. "Two round that corner. One further down the road. We passed him first, just after the village sign."

She'd thought he'd been asleep. "Rifles?"

"One. Two machine guns."

"You're good at this."

He said, "Bit paranoid. It helps."

She wondered if that were a joke, then decided it didn't matter. "So what do you suggest?"

He shrugged. "Getting here's used up all my ideas."

"I might go in the church."

"You might not want to carry that thing in your pocket."

She'd jam it down the back of her jeans. The jacket would cover it.

That's what she did once they were out of the car. Coe nodded, presumably agreeing she was now less noticeably tooled up, then gestured down the road.

"I'm gunna take a look down there."

And once he'd done that, she thought, he could take a look the other way, and then they'd be more or less done.

She crossed the road alone. There'd been bells ringing when they drove into the village, but they'd stopped now. The TV crew were moving their equipment from the church path onto the pavement. They regarded her for a moment, but evidently decided her unnewsworthy.

"Full house?" she asked, meaning the church.

One of them, thirtyish, in a T-shirt that read *On Your Case*, checked her out briefly, then said, "Yep."

"Much TV here?"

He considered. "Four crews?"

Seize the media, thought Shirley.

"And a couple from the radio doing vox pops by the shop," someone chipped in. She said "radio" like she meant "measles"; one of those things you'd have thought had been cured by now.

They left her there, on a crazy-paved path through the grave-yard that led to the church porch. More flowers had been piled here: an untended mass of bouquets that made Shirley wonder what the point was; fifteen or twenty quid on a gesture nobody would notice, except as part of a large, undifferentiated orgy of sentiment. The only person left feeling better was the florist. But the scent met her as she passed: hit her like a swinging door. At that same moment, her phone rang.

Like an idiot, her first reaction was to reach for the gun.

Luckily, there was nobody to notice. From inside the church came a communal mutter of ritualised response, and then a shuffling that could have been anything, but was, in fact, a large congregation reaching for its hymn books. Shirley got to her phone on the third ring. "Yeah. What?"

"Where are you?" Louisa asked.

"Why, where are you?"

"I'm at the Abbey, Shirl. With River. Are you not here too? We haven't seen you."

"Well, yeah, that's because I'm not there," she said. "Simples."

Louisa stifled an exasperated sigh. "So where are you, then?"

"I'm at Abbotsfield."

"You're *what?*"

"Me and Coe."

"What the hell are you doing there?"

Same as what Louisa and River were doing at the Abbey, Shirley thought. Being in the wrong place at the wrong time.

Singing began. Something sacred, obviously, and freighted with sorrow. Shirley recognised the tune, but couldn't think what it was.

"Nothing much," she said. "What's happening there?"

She waited, but Louisa didn't reply. She'd lost the signal, she realised. Hick place like this, the wonder was her phone had rung in the first place.

Putting it away, she opened the door and slipped inside. The church was full, and everyone was standing, singing; the air was thick and warm; the light patterned with colour. A few people turned when she entered, but not many, and she closed the door behind her softly as she could. There were spaces on the back benches, but she wasn't sure she wanted to stay, now she was here, though didn't want to bow out immediately. It would be disrespectful. So she stood at the door and cast her eyes around. How

long since she'd stepped inside a church? And did she have anything to say to God right now? She supposed she wanted to ask
Him what made it all right to let those murderers intrude on this
quiet place. But He'd been overseeing village massacres since time
immemorial. Either He'd have a foolproof answer by now, or He
didn't give a damn either way.

The hymn swelled to a chorus, and the church filled with
sound.

It was a good few minutes before anyone noticed the shooting.

When Chris saw the sign reading ABBOTSFIELD, which also suggested that visitors drive carefully, he increased speed to thirty,
thirty-five.

"Drive normally!" Shin hissed behind him.

But An said, "No. This is good."

There was blood on Shin's shirt, not his own. It had sprayed
from Danny when he died. There were other bits too, that looked
like scrambled egg, and when he stepped into sunlight, he would
look a fright.

But he would look a fright anyway, on Abbotsfield's streets again.

"There will be cameras," An said. "Our victory will be seen
around the world."

And then what, Shin had wondered. The Supreme Leader
himself would see their victory, it was true. But then what?

"We take the church," An said, as if answering Shin's question.
"That is where they are gathered now. They will be praying, but
they will not get what they pray for."

Thirty-five, forty.

"We will seize their attention for all time."

The van bumped and swayed on the imperfect road.

Up ahead, a police officer stepped out, and waved for them to
stop.

When J.K. Coe saw the van approaching, he thought: *This is not
good.*

Vehicles were weapons now. Everything was a weapon.

He had reached the far end of the village, the scene of the attack, before turning back towards the church. Outside the sole shop, on a forecourt boasting a row of newspapers in a plastic display unit, a pair of journalists had approached, one wielding a microphone, but he fended them off with an open palm. A little further on a police officer had stopped him and he'd shown ID once more, but offered no explanation for his presence. *I'm here because if I go home, I'll just be waiting for a knock on the door.* The officer had examined his card as if it were the first time she'd seen one, which it probably was, then continued her slow patrol down the road. Half a minute later, having skirted the two TV crews, something made Coe look back. A van was approaching, moving fast.

This is not good.

The police officer stepped into the road to flag it down.

She was not armed. It would have made little difference if she had been: when the van clipped her she was thrown against the wall of the nearest cottage, where she hung for a fraction of a second before dropping to the ground. The van swerved in the aftermath of impact, sideswiped a parked car with a tortured screech, then righted itself and continued up the road towards Coe.

Who also dropped, taking shelter behind a car.

There was shouting, and sounds of running; someone yelling into a clipped-on radio. The journalists were running too, towards the fallen officer, but as the van passed them its back door swung open and Coe heard the *pop pop pop* of automatic gunfire. One of the journalists was hurled sideways and bounced off the bonnet of a car.

Somebody screamed.

As the van hurtled past, a police officer appeared from a side-street, took aim and fired three times, each shot hitting the rear door, which had bounced on its hinges and swung shut again. And then reopened as the van kangaroo-hopped: from where he crouched, Coe caught a brief glimpse of a khaki-clad figure, upright, armed. He smelled fear and metal and joy, and saw the policeman attempt a pirouette, and give up halfway through. His rifle hit the ground a second after his body. Up ahead, the van skewed to a halt.

Behind him somebody shouted *Are you getting this?*

The driver clambered from the van, raised a gun and died as two armed officers opened fire simultaneously.

Amid movement and confusion Coe got to his feet. His body appeared to be making its own decisions, he was interested to learn. Was operating slowly, but efficiently. At least two figures had jumped from the back of the van, and one of the police officers had run through the lych-gate into the church grounds and was firing from the shelter of the wall. The other had taken cover behind the abandoned van, and had dropped into firing stance, but wasn't shooting; was shouting instructions at someone. Himself?

Coe crossed the road and bent by the fallen policeman. Would have checked for a pulse, but there seemed little point, as the officer's throat was mostly missing. Coe wondered how he felt about this, and decided he didn't feel anything yet. Except, perhaps, that he would rather not be here. All the same, he discovered he was picking up the fallen rifle.

"Put that down! Put that weapon down!"

This time the instruction was pretty clearly aimed at himself so he did just that, put the rifle down, when more gunfire cut the repeated instruction in half, *Put that wea—*

It was no longer clear to him where the gunmen were. He couldn't see either, always supposing there were two, were *only* two. He could, though, see the police officer who'd been shouting at him a moment earlier: he was a heap on the road. So the gunmen were out of Coe's field of vision; must be along the side of the church, on the road that looped round it, where Dander had parked. Their driver was still by the van, which was similarly riddled with bullets. Bonnie and Clyde, thought Coe.

And a news crew was out in the open, filming proceedings.

Something ought to be done about that, he thought, without in any way volunteering for the role. Instead, he picked the rifle up again, and tested its heft, as if he knew what he was doing. Some hundred yards behind him, someone was wailing: only word for it. It was strange to note that the weather was still fine; the sky above still blue. Rifle in his hands, Coe walked towards the van.

This was wrong, he thought. He should be crouching, hiding, taking cover. But whoever was shooting was round the corner. Bullets, thought Coe, didn't handle angles well. As long as he stayed on the main road, he was safe.

He reached the corner, and paused. Was this psychopathic behaviour? It certainly wasn't sensible. He wondered where Shirley Dander had got to, and whether she was about to appear, gun blazing, or whether she was dead. He had spent a lot of time, these past years, hoping nothing would happen, or that if it did, he was nowhere near. So what was he doing now? He wasn't built for this. Last time he'd killed someone—fair play: last time he'd killed someone *deliberately*—they'd been unarmed and handcuffed to a radiator. It had been low risk. And even then, the recoil had sprained his thumb.

The nearest news crew was filming him now. They didn't have guns; perhaps he should just shoot them.

Instead, he stepped around the corner.

Across the road, the policeman behind the low church wall stood and loosed two quick bursts of ammunition, which stitched a neat line of holes into a row of parked cars, one of them Roderick Ho's. And it was behind Ho's car that a gunman was sheltering: on the pavement, legs outstretched, his back against the driver's door. He was fitting a new magazine into his weapon, an action he completed even as Coe watched. And then he half-rolled onto his knees, levelled the gun on the car's bonnet and issued a volley in the vague direction of the police officer. The stained glass windows along the side of the church shattered. Why wasn't this man looking his way, Coe wondered.

Coe had a perfect sighting on him, but it was like the man hadn't even seen him. Maybe fifty yards away. A tin duck in a gallery. Better safe than sorry, though. The gunman's weapon was semi-automatic; he could loose off a lot more bullets than Coe in a hurry. If Coe fired and missed now, he'd get more than a sprained thumb for his pains.

So he moved nearer, slowly but steadily, sighting down the barrel as he walked.

The singing had started to falter before glass began to rain.

Shirley saw it as a series of explosions: the church's side windows disintegrating into coloured hailstones that blew halfway across the vaulted spaces before scattering onto the congregation. It sounded like wind chimes, sounded like ice. And then the harmonies, too, disintegrated and scattered, and the hymn gave way to hysteria. The organ stopped, and screaming began. People ducked and covered, sheltering themselves and their loved ones from the kaleidoscopic downpour, and those at the end of the benches broke ranks and ran for the door, in front of which Shirley stood.

They can't go out, she thought. That's where the guns are.

There was a large, old fashioned key in the lock; she turned it, removed it, then stood facing the crowd with arms flung wide. *No!* she shouted, or thought she did; everything had broken down so abruptly, she couldn't be sure her voice still worked. The glass had stopped falling, but the alteration in the light, the swift exchange of harsh daylight for colour, was like a punch in the face. How quickly the congregation became a mob; how quickly screaming swallowed the air. A young man tripped while clambering from a bench, and the man behind trampled him in his fury to escape. She shouted *No!* again, but the crowd was upon her now; she was being pressed against the door, and the breath squeezed out of her. Prayer had become panic, another unifying force, but one with no thought, no time, for its components. Someone's foot came down on hers, and she jerked free, but it was like fighting a herd. Those caught at the front, like Shirley, were jammed fast, while those behind, still programmed for flight, pushed and shoved as if this would make a difference. She thought she heard more gunfire outside. But that was a distant problem, for on this side of the door, in this dense press of bodies, her vision clouded, and fear swallowed rationality. If this kept up, people would die. She'd be one of them. Someone was on her foot again, someone's elbow jammed in her face. Someone's head struck her nose, and then there was blood.

A man at the back of the crowd was tearing at the people in front of him. He hooked an arm around a woman's throat, and threw her to the floor.

Shirley closed her eyes, and felt the door groan. If it gave way now, she'd be crushed beneath this zombie onslaught.

She should have let them take their chances with the gunmen.

The screaming grew louder; the panic soared. Something pressed into her stomach, part of someone else's body, and she couldn't tell what it was, but it would be among her final sensations. The slow unlearning of how to breathe. This was what buried alive was like. Buried alive by people. She swallowed blood: her final meal. If she could reach her gun she would shoot herself. In the moment of arriving at this decision, it felt like a prayer, or as much of one as she'd made in adulthood. Let me reach my gun. I won't hurt anybody else.

Then there was a bell.

People were still screaming, still pushing; Shirley was still fighting for breath, but there was a bell behind the noise now: behind it, below it, alongside it; at last above it; the ringing of a bell. It was clear and musical, and the more insistent it became, the more the screaming subsided. The elbow was removed from Shirley's face, and whatever had been pressed against her stomach relaxed, and she breathed again: bad air, full of sweat and fear and the stink of interrupted death, but air. She realised she was clutching something—an arm—and let it go. The press of people pulled back, some still lying on the floor, and there was crying and whimpering and other scared noises, but the screaming had stopped, and the bell was still ringing.

Shirley could see now, all the way to the altar, where the vicar stood swinging a handbell high and low. Even as she watched, he slowed and stopped. Behind him, the rose window remained intact. But along the right-hand wall the tall narrow windows had been shattered, and whatever stories they had told lay in fragments on the floor and the benches, and caught in people's hair. Outside the church, another story had ended too: the gunfire had ceased. In its place came static and chatter, and bellowed oaths, and distant sirens.

And now, at the far end of the aisle, appeared a young man holding a short-barrelled machine gun.

The press of people fell away from Shirley, and she stepped over those who remained on the floor. Gradually, everyone was becoming aware of the gunman, but instead of renewed panic a desperate calm fell. Those still on the benches bowed their heads, as if a refusal to watch what he planned to do would negate its effect, and those who had scrambled towards the door scuttled for what cover they could find.

Some remained standing, however, staring him down.

How did he get there? Shirley wondered.

And then: back door. There was always a back door.

Almost without realising she'd done so, she had drawn her own weapon, Marcus's gun, and held it in front of her in a two-handed grip.

Half a dozen paces, and she was in the aisle herself.

"Put the gun down," she called.

The man stared at her. Glanced down at his weapon, then stared at her again.

She should shoot him without warning. He was armed, he was dangerous. He had been here before. There were dozens of people all around, every one of them an innocent target, and he could cut them to ribbons within seconds. Even dying, his finger could shred their lives. She should shoot him now: put a bullet in his head. She was a good shot. She could kill him from here.

He was, by the look of him, seventeen. Maybe eighteen. Hard to tell.

"Put that down," she said. "Or I'll kill you."

He didn't put it down.

She kept walking towards him. A good shot already, and he was getting easier by the moment.

Someone was hammering on the church door, from outside.

"Put it down," she repeated.

Off to her left, a child hiccuped in fear.

Again the hammering, which now became a dull thump, as if a battering ram were in use.

Behind the gunman, up on the altar, the priest had closed his eyes; was mumbling in prayer.

The gunman's mouth trembled.

"Now," she said.

One shot. She could put a bullet through either eye: it was up to him. Or he could lose his weapon, but he would have to do it now.

If she took another step, the muzzle of her gun would meet his forehead.

He looked down at his weapon once again. Shook his head as if denying its reality, or this moment, or his presence.

She should kill him now. Before he remembered himself. Before he taught Abbotsfield how to die again.

Her gun met his skin.

"I shot up the sky," he told her.

Shirley reached for his weapon, and he released it to her grasp.

Behind her the door splintered and gave, and the church filled with noise once more.

It might have been the following day; might have been the day after. Late afternoon had claimed Slough House, wrapping it in curdled heat. In her office, Louisa Guy was scraping paint from the window frame, in the hope of being able to open it and set a breeze loose through the building. River Cartwright was reaching for his ringing phone; J.K. Coe studying traffic. A smell of damp patrolled the staircase; lurking on landings, peeling paper from walls. Shirley Dander, flat on her back, was listening to the feverish ticking of a clock, wondering whether time was moving faster or she herself slowing down. Behind a closed door Catherine Standish was brushing her hair, nine ten eleven times; when she reached thirty, she'd stop. Roderick Ho was nowhere. And Lady Di Taverner was ascending the stairs, trying not to touch anything, even the stairs.

"Fuck off," Lamb growled from his room, as she raised her hand to knock.

"I'm not even going to ignore that," she told him, entering, closing the door behind her and crossing to the room's single window.

Lamb had his feet on his desk, one cigarette smouldering in the empty packet seeing service as an ashtray, another clenched in his mouth. Grey hairs poked through the missing button on his shirt, and he scratched them absentmindedly while watching her fiddle with the blind, her evident intent being to open the window it shielded. "I'd tell you you're wasting your time," he said, "except I'm finding it quite entertaining."

She gave up. "There's no air in here. Would you put that damn thing out?"

"Sure." He stubbed it out, then lit another. "That all you wanted?"

"You wish." She eyed the visitor chair with distaste, and dragged it further away from Lamb's desk. Then stood with her hands on the backrest. "We need to discuss your staff."

Lamb leered.

"This is me, not some intern," she said. "Dick jokes aren't going to cut it."

"Everyone's a critic."

"J.K. Coe. Thoughts?"

"Recent reports claim he's a hero." Lamb yawned. "Familiarity, on the other hand, suggests he's a dick. I expect the truth is somewhere in the middle. As usual."

"Thanks for the insight. The officer on the scene says Coe walked right up to the gunman, who was firing a semiautomatic at the time, and shot him in the head, point-blank range. With a rifle."

"Yeah, I saw the photos. They look like Jackson Pollock threw up on a pizza."

"Coe was asked why the gunman didn't see him coming. You know what he said? He said he approached him very, very quietly."

"I'm gunna start locking my door," said Lamb. "It's creepy enough when he just sits staring at his fingers."

"Shirley Dander, meanwhile, is endangering a churchful of people by waving an unauthorised gun around. Her target also had a semiautomatic weapon. The potential casualties don't bear thinking about. She should have taken him down the very first moment."

"She did an anger management course. It obviously backfired. But look on the bright side, you got one of them alive. Isn't that a treat for your knuckletwisters? Except, no, hang on—did I hear a rumour?"

"He was wounded in an exchange of gunfire before entering the church," said Lady Di. "He was DOA at the nearest hospital."

"Funny, Dander didn't mention him being wounded." He waited, but Taverner remained expressionless. "Huh. Well, I hope for his sake it was an authorised gun did the damage. We finished?"

"Not even nearly. You sent two of your crew to Abbotsfield. Are you out of your mind?"

"Opinions differ."

"Trust me, not at the Park they don't. And then there's Slough. Coe—him again. Cartwright and Coe were in Slough the night Gimball was killed."

"Cartwright and Coe," said Lamb. "Sounds like a solicitors firm, doesn't it?"

"You were supposed to be in lockdown. But unless they've got a pair of identical twins, we've CCTV coverage of them lurking around where it happened."

"Do you suppose they found any clues?"

"I'm sure the Met'll let us know. We're handing the coverage to them. I imagine your pair'll be invited in for questioning, ooh, twenty seconds later."

Lamb took the cigarette from his mouth and studied it, his face a blank. "You'd hand over two joes to the Met?"

"They're not joes, Lamb. Slough House doesn't do joes. You've been allowed to run this place on sufferance, because of what you did for the Service—"

"Yeah, I remember it well."

"—but there are lines and there are limits, and you're way over both."

"Nobody gave me a game plan. I was handed the keys. I still have them."

"Yes, well, you'll be asked for them back before long. This has got too messy. Your rejects are supposed to be shackled to their desks, not hotdogging it all over the map. And we haven't even started on Roderick Ho. A traitor? Here? You haven't the budget to replace the coat hooks, but you're glamorous enough to have your own full-fledged traitor?"

Lamb slotted his cigarette back into place, and his lip curled as he inhaled. Unless he was smiling. It was hard to tell.

Di Taverner said, "So you won't be getting him back, either. No, it looks like happy hour's over, Jackson."

"Unless," said Lamb.

"Unless what?"

"Unless I can make all your dreams come true."

She made to speak, then stopped.

There was a clock ticking somewhere, but she couldn't see it.

She said, "Is this going to turn into another one-liner about your staff?"

"You might get lucky. But first off, it's about our so-called traitor. Thing is, that classified document that's caused all this trouble? The one you really don't want to become public knowledge?" He breathed out smoke. "It wasn't classified."

Taverner laughed. "This again? It was on the database. Everything on there's classified."

"But not this." Lamb opened his drawer, pulled out a sheet of paper, handed it across. "That one's a copy. But check the coding."

She did, with narrowing eyes. "Is this a joke?"

"Oh, now you want me to bring on the funny? No, it's not a joke." From the still-open drawer, he produced a bottle and two glasses. He put them on the desk, paused, and put one of the glasses away again. Into the other, he poured an absurd measure of scotch. "Want to hear a story?"

"I'm pretty sure you're about to tell one."

"Yeah, but sit down." She didn't move. "I'm serious. You're gunna hear this. But you'll sit down for it."

"Your gaff, your rules, eh?" But she sat on the chair at last, still holding the sheet of paper.

Lamb nodded in its direction. "Nineteen years ago, that was declassified, just like the coding shows. Signed off on by Charles Partner, because he was First Desk then. And nobody can declassify except First Desk."

"Tell me something I don't know."

"But it wasn't his idea. It was part of an operation called Shopping List. Because there was a traitor in the Service at the time. Oh, not a great big one like Partner himself—we already know about him. But a low-level one whose name doesn't matter, a man who had heavy debts, and thought one way of settling them would be to sell some secrets."

He raised his glass to his lips, swallowed.

"Unfortunately for Mr. Nobody, he'd barely got as far as hanging his shingle out before he was rumbled. No payday for him. But some bright spark decided this might be just the hook to hang his brolly on. And so was born Operation Shopping List. You see, Mr. Nobody had already dipped his toe in murky waters, and there were a few interested parties who knew he was for sale. And what they wanted to know was, what were his goodies like?"

"So we provided him with a shopping list," Lady Di said.

"Oh, yes. He was given a load of worn-out secrets, all jazzed up to look shiny and new. Nothing like feeding the opposition a bowl of dogshit dressed up as caviar. But before said dogshit could be offered as bait, it had to be declassified, else Operation Shopping List itself would have been an act of treason. You can't go offering classified material for sale, even as part of a sting. Even when that material's of no strategic value."

"Like the Watering Hole Paper," she said.

"Yep. A worthless little strategy dreamed up by some ex-colonial, back when topis were the rage. Sounded good in summary, though. How to destabilise a nation state. Leave out the bit about it being fifty years behind the times, and you'd have a lot of Dr. Evils salivating over that one."

"So what happened?"

"Mr. Nobody topped himself, that's what happened. Overcome by shame or, I dunno, tied the knot too tight for his Friday night jerk-off. So Operation Shopping List never got past the initial stage. Which was to distribute the list of goodies around the interested parties."

"Which is how come the SSD knew of its existence."

"Oh yes. It was out there. It was just withdrawn from the shelf before the shop opened. But lo and behold, two decades later, the SSD decides it might be just the thing to get their grubby hands on, on account of the huge embarrassment it would cause us if they wound it up and set it loose right here in the green and pleasant. What looked like a random series of attacks suddenly has the Service's fingerprints all over it, from a document now dated to look less than two decades old. And here we are."

"Here we are," she agreed. "But I'm still waiting to find out how this makes my dreams come true."

"Well," he said. "That would be the identity of the bright spark who set the whole thing in motion."

Di Taverner closed her eyes briefly. When she opened them again, they were full of murky light. "Claude Whelan," she said.

"The one and only."

She nodded at the glass in his hand. "Spare me one of those?"

"I'm a generous-hearted soul, as you know," he said. "But buy your own fucking drinks."

". . . Who else knows about this?"

"So far? You, me and Molly Doran. I imagine you'd like to be the one to tell Claude."

"What, that his cunning little plan of two decades ago just bit us all on the arse? Yes, I think I'll enjoy that conversation."

"Oh, good. We're all gunna be happy, then."

"And here comes the bill. What do you want, Jackson?"

"What I always want, Diana. I want to be left alone."

"Suits me."

"Me and mine. So you can slap Ho's wrists hard as you like, but send him home when you're done. I've not finished with him. As for the other two—"

"There's a strong chance they were involved in Gimball's death."

"Yeah, boo hoo. No, I think what'll turn out to have happened is, Gimball went for a smoke and leaned against some scaffolding on which some muppet left a tin of paint." He made a spiralling motion with his free hand. "Gravity strikes again."

". . . Are you serious?"

Lamb shrugged. "Everyone keeps telling me smoking's bad for your health. They can't all be wrong. And if they are, well, Zafar Jaffrey's bagman was also on the scene. And if you can't fit up a black ex-con for Gimball's death, what's the country coming to?" He adopted a pious expression. "It's what he would have wanted."

"Maybe we'll go with the accident," said Taverner. "And that's it? You want your crew back in place?"

"Molly Doran too. She tells me you're turfing her out." He shook his head. "Not gunna happen."

Taverner recrossed her legs. "A suspicious mind might wonder why you want Molly kept on a leash. Don't want anyone else crawling round her little kingdom, eh? Who knows what they might unearth down there. Not like you're short of secrets."

"With what I've just given you, First Desk is yours for the taking. Claude'll never survive being known as the architect of Abbotsfield. Not to mention all those penguins. And unlike other recent fuck-ups this can be pinned on him alone, rather than systemic failure, leaving your path free and clear." He stubbed his cigarette out as nastily as possible. "So you'll do as I say and smile while doing it. Just like any other professional."

"What about Flyte?"

"What about her? She's not one of mine."

"You have a code all your own, don't you, Jackson?" She stood. "Okay, then. You get what you want. And here and now, I'll even smile. But I don't like being dictated to. Never have. You might want to bear that in mind."

"Where you're concerned, I bear everything in mind."

Lamb reached for another cigarette as she turned to go, but the action triggered something inside him, and his face purpled. He slumped back in his chair as the coughing took hold, one arm folded across his chest, while with the other he grabbed the desk, knocking his drink to the floor. His eyes watered in pain or alarm, and the effort it cost him to pull in air would have felled a good-sized tree. He looked, thought Diana Taverner, like a semiaquatic mammal, struggling to give birth. Sounded like one, too. Watching him, true to her word, she smiled. Then left his office, closing the door behind her.

Across the landing, she knocked once on Catherine Standish's door, and let herself in without waiting for a response. Catherine, at her desk, hair neatly brushed, had a stack of papers in her hand; she was tapping them on the desk's surface, aligning their edges. When she saw Taverner she stopped.

"Is he okay?"

"Don't get me started." Taverner leaned against the office door. "Tell me, Catherine," she said. "Something I've always wondered. Did Lamb ever tell you how Charles Partner really died?"

When dusk at last comes it comes from the corners, where it's been waiting all day, and seeps through Slough House the way ink seeps through water; first casting tendrils, then becoming smoky black cloud, and at last being everywhere, the way it always wants to be. Its older brother night has broader footfall, louder voice, but dusk is the family sneak, a hoarder of secrets. In each of the offices it prowls by the walls, licking the skirting boards, testing the pipes, and out on the landings it fondles doorknobs, slips through keyholes, and is content. It leans hard against the front door—which never opens, never closes—and pushes softly on the back, which jams in all weathers; it presses down on every stair at once, making none of them creak, and peers through both sides of each window. In locked drawers it hunts for its infant siblings, and with every one it finds it grows a little darker. Dusk is a temporary creature, and always has been. The faster it feeds, the sooner it yields to the night.

But for now it's here in Slough House, and as it moves, as it swells, it gathers up all traces of the day and cradles them in its smoky fingers, squeezing them for the secrets they contain. It listens to the conversations that took place within these walls, all faded to whispers now, inaudible to human ears, and gorges on them. From behind a radiator in Shirley Dander's office it collects the memory of her unfolding a wrap of paper and snorting its contents through a five pound note. "Back to zero," Shirley said aloud once she was done, and though dusk has no understanding of the words—has no vocabulary at all—it takes her tone of defiant regret and adds it to its purse. In Roderick Ho's empty room it finds nothing, but on the next floor there are moments of interest, items to ponder. Louisa Guy has left a trace of scent behind: dusk has no sense of smell, but there's a familiarity of intent here, a lingering sense of purpose it recognises. Dusk has seen a lot of action in its time. It appreciates the efforts that go into such occasions.

And in the companion office it dawdles longer, savouring the remnants of the day. It can still hear River Cartwright's recent phone call, a call consisting of one word only, *River?*, before the connection disappeared, leaving River grasping at a vacant space. *Sid?* he might have said; a word is only a noise, and easily lost amid other sensations: for example, River's understanding that any protection Lamb might offer will last only while he's a slow horse. For Lamb will go to any lengths to protect a joe, but would watch in mild amusement if the rest of the world hanged itself. This may not be true—there are corners in Lamb's life River has no knowledge of—but for the moment, at least, it seems that resignation is no longer an option; a conclusion that tarries in the room after River has taken leave. J.K. Coe, too, has long departed, but before doing so stood a while, seeming to smile as dusk peered out from a hole in the carpet. Dusk, unused to such greetings, wonders whether Coe has mistaken it for its older brother night. Perhaps an introduction is in order. But Coe has gone before that can happen, which is maybe just as well, for those who meet the night on equal terms are rarely left unbruised by the encounter.

There are more stairs, and dusk has already climbed them. In Catherine Standish's room, it now remembers, it lay beneath a filing cabinet while Diana Taverner described Catherine's former boss's final moments; how Jackson Lamb murdered Charles Partner in his bathtub; a sanctioned murder, but a murder all the same; one which precipitated Lamb's exile, and gifted him Slough House. The life Catherine now leads is built on the proceeds of Jackson Lamb's crime. Diana Taverner just thought she should know that. And once Taverner had left, dusk waited for Catherine to weep, or shout, or rage, but it heard nothing; and when time came for it to creep from its hiding places, it found the room empty, and Catherine Standish gone.

So at last dusk comes to Jackson Lamb's office, where, of course, it's already waiting. And finds there is nothing to find there, for Jackson Lamb carries his own darkness with him, and is careful not to leave any lying in unregarded corners. All that remains of his recent presence, spillage of whisky and ash aside, is a soiled and rotten handkerchief hanging off the lip of a bin. Dusk considers this, and adds it to its knowledge of the day; knowledge it will abandon soon, for this is the rule, in London and elsewhere: everything that happens—good and bad—dusk clocks, absorbs, then mostly forgets. For if dusk remembered everything the weight would nail it in place, keeping it from its eternal search for its twin, the dawn, which it has never met. Always, it's halfway behind, or halfway ahead. It's never known which.

Meanwhile, dusk's older brother night, which has hovered overhead this past hour, is beginning to lose its balance, beginning to fall. Soon everything will be different again, the same as it always is. Dusk has a last look round, but its vision is failing, its hearing dim. It has been everywhere, seen everything. It is time to go. It has already left. In its wake, in the dark, Slough House slumbers, Slough House snores.

But mostly, Slough House waits.

ACKNOWLEDGMENTS

Huge thanks, as ever, to my friends at John Murray in London, and at Soho Press in New York, especially Mark Richards, Yassine Belkacemi, Emma Petfield and Becky Walsh over here, and Bronwen Hruska, Juliet Grames and Paul Oliver over there. And to Juliet Burton, of course, for keeping everything on track.

Some while ago, I was lucky enough to be present while Helen Giltrow and Steph Broadribb discussed Mr. Tom Hiddleston. I hope I haven't misrepresented their views. And questions asked by Mark Billingham, Sarah Hilary and Will Smith suggested some avenues I'm gratefully pursuing in this novel and the next. My thanks to all.

I'm grateful, too, to various readers for their enthusiasm, support and gentle correction of error. Aakash Chakrabarty and David Craggs have been especially helpful, but all the many emailers, however brief their messages, lighten the days. And I'm indebted to the staff at Summertown Library in Oxford for tolerating my near-daily presence as I mooch around their shelves, shuffle through their DVDs, read their newspapers and use their computers. It'll surprise them to learn that I do occasionally get some work done.

The rules of "Yellow Car," as cited by Louisa, were laid down by Mr. John Finnemore in his delightful BBC Radio 4 series *Cabin Pressure*. But American readers should note that this is a British game devised for British conditions. Attempts to play it in—say—New York City will result in madness and death.

MH
Oxford
September 2017